USA TODAY bestselling author **Jules Bennett** has published over sixty books and never tires of writing happy endings. Writing strong heroines and alpha heroes is Jules's favourite way to spend her workdays. Jules hosts weekly contests on her Facebook fan page and loves chatting with readers on Twitter, Facebook and via email through her website. Stay up-to-date by signing up for her newsletter at julesbennett.com

Joss Wood loves books and travelling—especially to the wild places of southern Africa and, well, anywhere. She's a wife, a mum to two teenagers and slave to two cats. After a career in local economic development, she now writes full-time. Joss is a member of Romance Writers of America and Romance Writers of South Africa.

Discover more at millsandboon.co.uk

SCANDALOUS ENGAGEMENT

JULES BENNETT

BACK IN HIS EX'S BED

JOSS WOOD

MILLS & BOON

® and ™ are trademarks owned and used by the trademark owner and/or its licensee. Trademarks marked with ® are registered with the United Kingdom Patent Office and/or the Office for Harmonisation in the Internal Market and in other countries.

First Published in Great Britain 2020
by Mills & Boon, an imprint of HarperCollinsPublishers,
1 London Bridge Street, London, SE1 9GF

Scandalous Engagement © 2020 Jules Bennett
Back in His Ex's Bed © 2020 Joss Wood

ISBN: 978-0-263-27927-6

MIX
Paper from
responsible sources
FSC™ C007454

This book is produced from independently certified FSC™ paper to ensure responsible forest management.

For more information visit: www.harpercollins.co.uk/green

Printed and bound in Spain
by CPI, Barcelona

SCANDALOUS ENGAGEMENT

JULES BENNETT

To my very best friend, Michael. Thank you for giving me the best happily-ever-after.

One

Josie Coleman flung open the front door of her beach-front home and rolled her eyes.

"I've told you for years to just come on in," she exclaimed as she stepped back. "Why do you insist on knocking?"

Her best friend, Reese Conrad, shrugged like he always did when he refused to just walk into her home, where he was always welcome. She always just walked right into *his* house when she stopped by. They didn't live far from each other on this stretch of beach in Sandpiper Cove, North Carolina. It was one of the things she treasured about the place.

"Respect," he replied in that low, gravelly tone of his.

She always asked the same question and he always gave the same one-word response. She'd also offered him a key, but he always said he didn't need one because he only stopped by when she was home.

Typically, they were either at his place, out on his yacht or traveling together when their schedules permitted.

"I thought you were out of town on a work trip." Josie walked through the spacious open layout of her living room and headed back toward the wall of open glass doors leading to her patio. "I'm having coffee if you want to join me."

"It's five o'clock in the evening."

She stopped and threw a glance over her shoulder. "What does that have to do with the love of coffee?"

He laughed and shook his head. Like he didn't know her mad love of coffee?

"I'm good," he replied as he followed her out onto the outdoor living area. "And I cut my trip short because I had seen all I needed to see."

Something crossed through his eyes, something almost…sad. Reese was usually the happiest guy she knew. He had everything—a successful career in the restaurant industry, parents who doted on him and loved him unconditionally, her as a best friend. What more could he need?

Yet something was off.

"Everything all right?" Josie asked as she settled into her lounger and curled her hands around her favorite coffee mug, the one Reese had given her last Christmas.

Reese shoved his hands in his pockets and glanced out at the horizon. It was impossible to be in a bad mood with this view, but she couldn't get a bead on what was going through his head. That was a first. They always knew each other's thoughts. They could be at a party or in a crowded room and one look at each other and they'd smile or nod, knowing exactly what the other had on their mind.

There was something to be said for the unique bond between lifelong besties.

"Honestly—"

Her shrill ringtone cut off anything he was about to admit. Josie sat her mug back on the glass table and picked up her cell, then muttered a string of curses.

"What now?" she answered, totally not in the mood for her ex-husband.

Out of the corner of her eye, she caught Reese staring at her. Reese knew the mess she'd gotten into by marrying the wrong guy on a whim. The marriage had been a mistake and she was still trying to figure out how she'd temporarily lost her mind and agreed to marry a man she didn't love.

Oh, Chris was a nice guy; he just wasn't for her, and lately he'd been trying to win her back. There was no going back.

"Listen, I'm not trying to be rude," she said now into the phone, "but it's not going to happen. We're divorced for a reason." She sat up and swung her legs to the side. "You're a great guy, but we're just not good together, Chris."

Yet he'd been calling and texting more and more. Josie could see where Chris would be confused. They'd only dated for three months before they'd up and eloped. Never in her life had she made rash choices—she prided herself on being just as regimented and predictable as her military father—yet she'd been spontaneous with one of the most important decisions of her life.

For someone normally so methodical about her life, that rush to the courthouse had been completely out of character. But Reese had just gotten engaged and that act had made her wonder if *she* should be entering the next chapter in her life as well.

Obviously, the answer had been no.

Now here they were: she was divorced and Reese had a broken engagement. Maybe they just needed to stay as they were, as they had been for years. They were happy hanging out and traveling together. Having significant others enter the mix would only mess up their perfect best-friend vibe.

But she had yet to get Chris to understand her point of view. Unfortunately, no matter how much she told him she wasn't getting back together with him, he didn't get it. Maybe if he believed there was someone else he would realize there was absolutely no room for him in her life.

"I've moved on," she blurted into the phone as she came to her feet. Josie darted her gaze to Reese, who merely raised his brows in surprise. "That's right. He's here right now, so I have to go."

Josie disconnected the call and tossed her cell onto the lounger she'd just vacated. Reese continued to stare at her, but she just sighed and shrugged.

"He's getting relentless," she defended. "I had to say something."

"So I'm your rebound guy?"

Josie smiled, feeling a tiny bit guilty for using Reese. "He doesn't know who's here, and it was the first thing that came into my head. He has to think I've moved on with someone else or he'll keep wasting his time trying to win me back. He has to let it go."

She crossed the patio and placed her hand on his arm. "I'm sorry I used you as the scapegoat. Let's forget about Chris. What were you getting ready to say before?" she asked.

"I went to Green Valley, Tennessee," he told her. "It wasn't just about business."

Josie dropped her arm and wiggled her brows. "Something personal? A woman?"

He hadn't dated since he'd ended things with his fiancée nearly a year ago. He'd been too busy taking over his family's posh restaurant empire, with establishments up and down the East Coast. Recently his father had suffered a heart attack, which led to open-heart surgery. Reese's parents were now at some tropical resort to celebrate his life and their new retirement.

So what had Reese been doing in Tennessee if the trip didn't pertain to his business?

Before he could explain further, the doorbell chimed and echoed through the house and out the patio doors. Why did she have to keep getting interrupted when she was just trying to get the scoop on her friend, who obviously had something serious going on?

"Sorry about that," she told him as she came to her feet. "I'm not expecting anyone, so just give me one second."

Josie crossed the living area to the foyer and glanced through the sidelight. Seriously? What would it take for Chris to get the hint?

On a frustrated sigh, Josie opened the door. Her ex

stood before her. The man was tall and strong, and always took pride in his athletic build. He wasn't unattractive. He just wasn't the right guy for her. If she could keep him in the friend zone, that would be fine, but he didn't want to accept that.

"Chris," Josie groaned. "We just hung up."

"I know, I know, but I had just pulled up to your house when I called and I only want a few minutes of your time."

Chris stared at Josie with his heart in his eyes and she wanted to tell him to go out with some dignity, for pity's sake.

"I only wanted five minutes in person," Chris explained. "That's all. Just five minutes."

"Chris, we're not doing this again. We're not meant for each other."

"But what if we are?"

Before she could respond, Reese's arm slid around her waist and he pulled her against his side.

"Everything all right, babe?"

Babe? What the hell was he doing?

She glanced from Reese to Chris and remembered what she'd said earlier. Well, damn. Looked like she'd caused a minor mess here.

Chris's eyes went from Josie, to Reese, and back again.

"Can we talk alone?" he implored.

"Say what you want," Reese stated with a smile. "My fiancée doesn't keep secrets from me. Right, lover?"

Was he out of his ever-loving mind? She didn't need his help, and he was making this uncomfortable situation an impossible one.

Engaged? That was taking things a bit far. She'd only mentioned that she'd moved on, not that she'd moved on and was ready to walk down the aisle again.

"You're marrying this guy?" Chris asked. "I always knew there was something more than friends going on with you two. Were you seeing him the entire time we were together?"

"What? No, of course not," she said defensively, wondering how she could circle around and restart this conversation with less chaos and confusion.

"As you can see, Josie is not available," Reese added with another squeeze of her hip. "We're getting ready to go out for the evening."

His hand dipped down over the curve of her hip and too many thoughts and emotions hit her at once. First, why was he being so handsy? Second, was she *enjoying* this?

She shouldn't have a rush of tingles from her best friend's touch. It wasn't like they'd never touched before.

But they'd never touched like this. Not in a faux intimate way.

And it was like something shifted between them.

He was so firm, so strong, and he smelled too damn good.

No.

She shouldn't be thinking of Reese's muscle tone and his cologne. That would only lead to trouble, right?

Yes, trouble with a big fat capital *T*.

The last time she'd let herself step outside her comfort zone, she'd found herself married to the wrong man.

Reese was her *friend*.

Her best friend.

And she needed to keep him in that zone. She liked her life nice and tidy. She liked having everything, and everyone, in their own place.

But that excellent muscle tone...

To save her sanity, Josie extracted herself from Reese and offered Chris a sympathetic smile.

"I do hope you can move on," she told him. "There's a woman out there for you. She's just not me."

Chris's expression went from disbelief, to anger, to... hell, she wasn't sure, but the man wasn't happy.

His eyes scrutinized her. "Are you sure this is what you want? I mean, you're not even wearing a ring. You deserve better. You know I treated you like a queen."

Before Josie could reply, Reese stepped forward.

"What she deserves and doesn't deserve is none of your concern anymore. You've had more than that five minutes you asked for."

Without another word, Reese stepped aside and slammed the door in Chris's face. Josie stared at the space that had just been open and couldn't believe Reese had the audacity to...to...

"Are you serious?" she exclaimed.

Reese turned and started back toward her patio as if he hadn't just acted like a complete jerk. She marched right after him. This was her house, her ex, and Reese wasn't just going to do whatever he wanted and manipulate the situation to his liking!

"Are you going to explain yourself?" she demanded as she stepped outside.

Reese shrugged and took a seat on the sofa. "Explain what? He called and you told him you were in a relationship, so when he showed up, obviously I'm the one who had to play the role."

Josie tucked her hair behind her ears and crossed her arms over her chest. In the last twenty minutes, her ex-husband had said he truly believed they could get back together and her best friend had claimed to be her fiancé. Even stalling for a few seconds trying to gather her thoughts didn't calm her mood or give her any more clarity…especially over the fact that she'd liked Reese's touch more than she should.

"Engaged seems a little over-the-top, don't you think?" she asked.

"Not really. The guy is persistent. You have to push back with people like that. Subtlety isn't something they understand."

"Oh, an engagement and slamming the door in his face were far from subtle hints."

He offered her a wink and a grin. "You're welcome."

Josie growled and clenched her fists. Reese might be her very best friend, but he could be quite infuriating at times…in an adorable kind of way. He meant well, but sometimes that alpha quality took over and common sense vanished.

"Better drink your coffee before it gets cold," he added, pointing to her forgotten mug.

Josie reached for the drink and crossed to where he sat with that smug smirk on his face.

"I really want to throw this in your face," she grumbled.

"Aw, darling. Is that anyway to treat your new fiancé? Be nice or I won't get you that ring you need."

"You know he's going to tell people what just happened," she informed him. "We're both in the public eye. How will we dodge this?"

If she had a job where people didn't recognize her or didn't know her name, Reese's engagement claim wouldn't be a big deal. But considering Reese was a billionaire mogul splashed all over the internet right now for taking over his family's empire, and she was an influencer and columnist for the country's top-selling magazine, there was no way an engagement between them would go unnoticed.

"I'm not too worried about the public." Reese shrugged. Again with that damn shrug, like this was no big deal. "Just wait and see how it plays out. He may surprise you by keeping quiet, or we may need to play it up. What kind of stone would you like in your ring?"

Josie narrowed her eyes. "I'm going to need to switch to wine for this conversation."

Ignoring his chuckle, she stepped back into her house and moved into the kitchen. From her vantage point at the wine fridge, Josie stared out at Reese, who didn't seem to mind that he'd just upended both of their lives. He simply sat in one of the sturdy wicker chairs and stared out at the horizon.

When he'd first arrived today, he'd said he needed to talk. All she'd managed to learn was that he'd been away on personal business. If it hadn't concerned a woman, then what else would it be? He didn't have much of a social life. If he went out to dinners, they were all work-related, and the majority of the time, those dinners were in his own restaurant.

The man worked like a maniac, and that was say-ing something coming from *Cocktails & Classy*'s most celebrated columnist. Josie never took a day off either, but at least she could work from home and only travel to the headquarters in Atlanta when she absolutely had to. Reese traveled all over, constantly on the lookout for new ways to keep his restaurants fresh and upscale.

She poured a glass of pinot and swirled the contents before heading back out. She never got tired of the ocean breeze, and she always slid open the wall of glass doors when she was home. The added outdoor living space was what had sold her on this house right after her divorce.

Now that she'd calmed down a little, Josie stepped around the coffee table and took a seat on the sofa across from Reese.

"Want to tell me why you got so territorial?" she asked.

He propped his feet on the coffee table and laced his fingers behind his head as he stared at her, since she now blocked his line of sight to the ocean.

"Besides the fact that he was the wrong man for you to marry in the first place? I was trying to help you out."

Josie took a sip and set her glass on the table before leaning forward and keeping her gaze locked on his. "I can fight my own battles."

"You shouldn't have to," he retorted.

While she appreciated the way he was always ready to protect her, she didn't need him to. His failed engagement and her failed marriage had really opened her eyes to the fact that there was no rush to move on to what was expected. Who said she had to get married right now? There was no magical age when she had to be married, and who said she had to be married at all?

But she knew Reese might want a family and a married life of his own.

The day would come when he would find the woman he wanted to spend his life with.

The thought unsettled her. Or maybe it was that Josie could still feel his fingertips along her waist and her hip. She shouldn't still be tingling in those spots, but she was—which was both confusing and frustrating.

Josie's cell buzzed on the table and she glanced to the screen at the same time Reese muttered a curse. Chris's name popped up with an unread message.

"He's still not taking the hint?" Reese asked. "I slammed the door in his face."

She didn't bother opening the text; she would deal with it later…or not.

"Maybe I should've just talked to him for a bit," she stated.

"No. Every time you talk to him, that gives him hope. You just need to cut all ties."

Reese was right, but she really hated being rude. She'd told Chris as nicely as possible that they were really over, and they'd been divorced for six months already. Wasn't that enough of a sign that she was moving on? One would think divorce would be enough "cutting ties," but Chris hadn't wanted the divorce begin with.

"Don't worry," Reese added. "He'll get the hint once he sees us together and notices my car out front when he drives by."

Josie laughed. "It's not like you'll be here twenty-four hours a day, Reese."

His eyes flashed to hers. "Sure I will. I can work from here. It will be tricky, and I have to do some traveling still, but you're the top priority in my life right now. So which bedroom do you want me to take?"

"Bedroom?" she asked. "You mean—"

A naughty grin spread across his face that sent a curl of unwanted arousal through her.

This was her best friend…what was going on?

"I'm moving in, honey."

Two

Well, this wasn't what he'd planned when he'd arrived at Josie's house yesterday. But damn if he hadn't gotten completely sidetracked by feeling her against his side, having that curvy hip beneath his hand.

He'd always known his best friend was sexy as hell, but she'd always been his friend. Now she was his fake fiancée…how the hell was he supposed to play this out?

What had he gotten them into?

Yesterday he'd needed her advice; he'd needed her guidance and her shoulder to lean on. Not that he did that often, but his life had imploded and he had nowhere else to go.

He was still trying to process everything himself. From receiving a cryptic letter at his office while his father was recovering from heart surgery, to finding out his father wasn't his father at all…if the letter from a deceased woman was actually true.

Reese sank down on the edge of the bed in the guest bedroom of Josie's home and clutched the letter in his hands. When he'd left for Tennessee several days ago, he'd told Josie he'd be gone a week. He'd come back after two days.

Traveling from Green Valley, Tennessee, back to Sandpiper Cove, North Carolina, had only been an hour's flight. Those were the perks of owning your own plane and being your own pilot. He'd taken the time going both ways to think about all that had happened… he still didn't have a clear picture or any answers.

He'd gone to Hawkins Distillery a few days ago and met with Sam Hawkins and Nick Campbell, the two men who were supposedly Reese's half brothers. Nick's late mother had apparently wanted to leave behind a deathbed confession by distributing letters for the three men about their true paternity. She was the one who had mailed the letter to Reese.

They all shared the same father—Rusty Lockwood, billionaire mogul of Lockwood Lightning. Everyone knew the world-renowned moonshine company, but not many knew the man behind it…including Reese.

A week ago, he'd hired an investigator to dig up everything that wasn't easily accessible to the public, and Reese had also been doing his own online research. On paper, or the internet as the case may be, Rusty appeared to be a saint. The man owned the largest moonshine distillery in the world and donated thousands of dollars each year to Milestones, a charity for children with disabilities.

Unfortunately, last week, Rusty had been arrested for skimming from that same charity, and according to Sam and Nick, Rusty was the devil himself. Both guys had dealt with Rusty for years and neither one had a kind thing to say. They weren't happy with the knowledge that Rusty was their biological father.

Reese didn't know what to believe, because all of this had blown up in his face so fast and come without warning. He didn't like being blindsided by anything, especially not a revelation that meant he might have been betrayed and lied to his entire life.

The letter had arrived while his father was in the hospital, but once he was released, he and Reese's mom had gone on a relaxing vacation with the doctor's blessing and Reese didn't want to mess up their time away.

There had just been so much all at once… His father's health, the shifting responsibilities of the business, the letter claiming Reese wasn't his parents' child…

But by the time his parents got back home, Reese hoped he would have a solid plan and some much-needed answers.

Should Reese confront them? Or did he just let this knowledge go and ignore the past? What was the actual truth in all of this? There were so many questions and part of him wished he'd never learned the truth, but the other part of him wanted to know the history… *his* history.

Reese refolded the letter and sat it on the nightstand before coming to his feet. He hadn't gotten much sleep last night, mostly because this wasn't his home and he wasn't used to that cushy bed with all the pillows.

Josie might be very strict and straitlaced when it came to her fashion sense and her career, but she did love a cozy-feeling home. Granted, everything in her house was either white or gray. She really did lack color in her life, but he wouldn't change her for anything.

Especially those damn curves.

Who had known how well she'd fit intimately against his side? Just that simple gesture had conjured up a night of fantasies he shouldn't have allowed himself when it came to his best friend. Didn't he have enough going on in his life without adding an unwanted sexual attraction to Josie?

Reese rubbed a hand over his bare chest and padded from the room and down the hallway toward the kitchen. He needed coffee, because this was the time of day when it was actually acceptable to have a cup. It was too damn early, but he might as well get his day started.

He'd visited here so many times over the years, but he'd never made coffee, so he searched through her cabinets, trying to be quiet because he was positive she was still asleep. He hadn't heard a word from her this morning, and he also knew she wasn't an early riser.

He, on the other hand, had too much to do, including following up with his assistant about the RSVP to the new restaurant opening in Manhattan in two weeks.

Conrad's was moving up the East Coast and opening a big new space in New York. Reese couldn't wait to get into his favorite city. Manhattan had always been a goal of his.

He'd grown up here in Sandpiper Cove and he absolutely loved the beach. Loved it so much, he'd purchased his own private beach with his home, which was not far from Josie. His yacht was docked at the end of his own pier and he didn't want to lay his head down anywhere else.

But this new restaurant in Manhattan would be all his. He'd inherited his father's string of upscale restaurants from Miami up to Boston, but this was his first venture on his own and he had a few changes in place that he was excited to test.

"Good heavens."

Reese turned from the coffeepot to find Josie standing in the doorway, her hand over her chest, her eyes fixed on his. But his eyes immediately locked on the tiny shorts and tank she wore. The outfit left little to the imagination…and last night he'd done plenty of imagining.

"Could you put some clothes on?" she grumbled as she shuffled in.

Reese couldn't help but grin as she made her way to the cabinet and pulled down a mug. Her hair was all in disarray, like she'd had a fight with her pillow all night, and those pj's, black of course, weren't covering much, either. The simple tank dipped too low and the shorts literally covered the essentials and nothing more.

His body stirred in response.

There were some things he could control, like not telling her he'd like to strip her down and pleasure her beyond anything she'd ever known. But there were other things, like his arousal, that weren't quite so easy to hide.

Damn it. He had to get a grip. This was Josie. He couldn't risk a quick romp just because suddenly his hormones had woken up and realized she was sexier than he'd known.

They were friends…nothing more.

"You've seen me in swim trunks. This is hardly any different," he replied, taking the mug from her hands. "Go sit. I'll get this for you."

She shoved the hair from her face and went to the bench at her kitchen table. "Trunks are one thing, but boxer briefs are another. If you're staying here, put some damn pants on."

Reese poured two cups of coffee, leaving hers black to match her wardrobe and her bleak mood.

"I don't recall you being this grouchy in the mornings," he told her as he sat across from her. "I know you're more of a night owl, but this is a new side."

She curled her hands around her mug. "This is my only side before caffeine. Be quiet so I can enjoy it."

Reese sipped his hot coffee and waited on Little Miss Sunshine to perk up. Clearly, she'd had a restless night, too. He didn't even try to hide the fact that he was staring at her. She looked like a hot mess, which irritated the hell out of him because his boxer briefs were becoming more and more snug. There was going to be no hiding anything in a few minutes.

"Shouldn't you be lifting weights or jogging or going to some meeting where you fire people?" she asked around her mug.

Reese laughed. "Glad to know what you think of a day in the life of Reese Conrad."

She merely shrugged, causing one slinky shoulder strap to slip down her arm. Reese's eyes landed on that black string and he barely resisted reaching out to adjust it.

Hands to yourself.

A physical relationship would certainly change things between them, but the main question was—would they be better or worse?

Wait. What?

Why was he even letting his mind travel to that space? He needed to get control over his wayward thoughts and keep himself in check.

"You don't have to stay here, you know."

His focus shifted back to her face. She stared at him over the rim of her mug. Those dark eyes never let on to what she was truly thinking…just another way they were so alike. Both held their emotions close to their chest.

"How many times did Chris text you last night?" he asked.

Josie's eyes darted away as she mumbled something under her breath. He thought he heard a staggering number, but even one was one too many at this point. Beyond the fact that they were divorced, she'd blatantly told Chris no and Reese had mentioned they were engaged. A lie, sure, but Chris didn't know that. The man should back off.

"All the more reason for me to stay for a while," Reese replied.

Maybe his presence would keep Chris away, maybe it wouldn't. Reese really had no idea. He did know that he obviously enjoyed a round of torture before breakfast because he was in no hurry to move away from his newly appealing best friend and get going on his busy day.

Did she always sleep in something so damn…sexy?

Maybe they did need to set some clothing boundaries now that they were temporarily living together.

Their friendship was solid; it was perfect. They completed each other and there was nobody else he would trust with every aspect of his life. But he wasn't quite ready to open up about that letter. He still wasn't sure what to do with the truths it had revealed, and the strange things he was feeling since announcing their fake engagement weren't helping him figure it out.

Only a week ago, his main worry had been about his Manhattan opening and now…well, that opening was the least of his worries. He and his selected launch team had a good handle on the upcoming momentous day and Reese truly believed the opening would be nothing short of a smashing success.

"How's your father?" she asked as she set her mug down. "Still doing good?"

His father. Those two words sounded so odd now, so foreign. He had no idea how he felt about the changes in his family, except maybe a little deceived that the people he'd loved his entire life had lied to him from the beginning.

"Reese?"

He blinked and focused on Josie. "He's fine," Reese replied. "His doctor has checked on him every day since they've been gone."

"That's great. Your mom and dad have worked so hard and then for him to have heart surgery right after retiring—he deserves some downtime."

Which was one of the reasons Reese had been holding on to this letter, this secret. When the letter came, it had been with a stack of mail that Reese hadn't gotten to immediately. He'd been so swamped with taking over the Conrad restaurants, plus working on the launch of the new one, that if something didn't seem pressing or like an emergency, he'd put it on the back burner.

Josie sighed and came to her feet, bringing his attention back to her.

"I have to finish my article before my noon deadline," she told him. "I'm just going to grab a quick shower first. Feel free to use the guest bath or head on home and get ready there. We can meet up for dinner later if you're free."

She sashayed out of the room…and that was the best way he could describe those swaying hips beneath that flimsy material. It was driving him out of his mind.

He was going to need a shower, too. A very, very cold shower to get control of this new reaction to his best friend, one he should ignore.

Reese cleaned up the few dishes in the kitchen and headed to the spare room to throw on his clothes from yesterday and head to his house for a few things.

As he moved toward his room, he heard a thump from one of the other guest bedrooms. Then a string of muttered curses followed and Reese let his curiosity get the best of him. He circled back to the nearly closed door and tapped his knuckles on the frame.

"You okay?" he called.

The door flung open and Josie seemed even more frazzled than earlier. A strand of inky black hair fell across her face and she blew it away.

"What are you doing?" he asked, trying to peek over her shoulder.

"Nothing."

Because she tried to slip out the door, Reese took it upon himself to put a hand on the wood and ease it back open.

"You know you're a terrible liar."

He stepped around her and into the room. Simple furnishings with whites and neutrals, a white rug on the hardwood, a sturdy white chair in the corner with a black-and-white-striped pillow.

"Is this where you keep all your journalism secrets?" he joked. "Cocktail recipes or dinner party themes? Am I close?"

"Funny," she mocked, crossing her arms over her chest. "I don't have secrets and even if I did, you would already know them."

The closet door was open just enough for Reese to see a slash of red. Interesting, considering he never saw her in an actual color, let alone something so vibrant.

He moved to the closet and revealed a walk-in space full of the widest variety of colorful clothes he'd ever seen. There were two rows of hanging clothes…all with tags dangling from the sleeves. Boxes of shoes lined the perimeter of the floor and the most insane number of designer handbags in all colors and patterns topped off the high shelves.

Reese glanced over his shoulder, turning his attention to Josie, who glared back at him.

"Opening a department store, Jo?"

She tipped her chin in that defiant way of hers. "No."

"What's with all the brand-new clothes?" he asked, glancing back to the closet that clearly held thousands of dollars' worth of merchandise. "And all this color? Are you giving yourself a makeover?"

Josie's eyes darted to the open room, then down for just a second, but enough for him to see her vulnerability.

"Want to talk about this?" he asked.

She shook her head. "Nothing to talk about. I come in here every morning before I get ready."

"Trying to find something to wear?"

Why was she not just saying whatever she was thinking? For someone who wore black like it was her job, she certainly had a hell of a lot of funds tied up in a brand-new, not-black wardrobe.

"I can't be her," she murmured.

What? What did that even mean? Who couldn't she be?

Forgetting the lame joke he'd been going for when he first saw this shocking surprise, Reese took a step toward her, wondering what she'd been hiding and why she seemed so sad, so…almost helpless.

She'd just told him she didn't keep any secrets, but that had clearly been a lie because all of this was obviously something she wanted to keep to herself. How long had this closet full of color been here? And who couldn't she be like?

"Jo—"

An alarm went off from somewhere in the house. Josie immediately turned from the room. Confused as to what had just happened and what the annoying noise was, Reese followed her. He was tempted to grab something from the newly discovered closet to throw over her excuse for pajamas to conceal that dark skin of hers.

Granted, he wasn't covered much, either, but she was a temptation he was having a difficult time resisting.

There was only so much a man could take, but the risk of taking what he suddenly wanted was too much. Their friendship was too special, too perfect the way it was. He couldn't afford for his life to get any messier.

Reese found Josie back in the kitchen tapping away on her phone and thankfully killing that annoying alarm.

"Sorry," she stated with a smile. "That was my reminder to check my planner."

Reese stared at her as she continued to scroll. "You need a reminder to check your schedule? Isn't that just a given?"

Her eyes darted to his and for the briefest of seconds, that heavy-lidded gaze dipped to his chest. Well, well, well. Even with the caffeine and a somewhat better mood, she wasn't immune to his nakedness.

So now what? There was a sudden sexual pull that confused him, intrigued him…challenged him.

"I have an alarm to remind me about nearly everything," she informed him, setting her cell back on the table and turning to face him fully. "A reminder to drink all my water, feed my plants, check in with my new assistant because she seems a little overwhelmed at times, and—"

Reese held up a hand. "I get it. I knew you were structured, but I had no idea it was to this extent."

Josie smiled. "I can set up your phone so you are more organized with various reminders if you want."

"I've got it all up here," he said, tapping his head. "And my assistant is on everything before I can even think, so I'm good. I wouldn't know what to do with that annoying alarm going off all the time."

"Oh, I have different alarms for different reminders," she countered with a scoff. "I can't have one alarm, Reese. That wouldn't make any sense."

"Of course," he mumbled, then shrugged. "What was I thinking? I guess it's true that you never really know someone until you live with them."

Josie shook her head as she rolled her eyes. "We're not living together. You can go to your place at any time."

"You coming with me?" he asked.

"I'm good here, and Chris is going to be a nonissue," she stated with more confidence than she should have.

Why would Chris give up? Reese sure as hell wouldn't. Josie's ex had had the best woman in the world and he'd let her slip away.

"I'm really going to get a shower now," she told him. "I'm already behind on my morning routine."

As Josie started to pass, Reese took a step to block her. Her hands flew up and flattened on his chest, those dark eyes flashing up to his.

"What's with the closet, Jo?" he asked, really needing to understand what she was hiding, because he'd seen that flash of vulnerability and hurt and he hated knowing she experienced both.

Though it was damn difficult to concentrate with their clothes nearly nonexistent and her hands on his bare skin. Reese had to respect her, respect their friendship and remain in control.

Crossing that invisible barrier into something more intimate would be a mistake. Where had this damn attraction come from? Sexy was one thing, but the ache, the *need* was frustrating.

"Don't worry about the closet," she murmured with a flashing smile. "Why don't you worry about your upcoming restaurant opening instead of me?"

Reese smoothed her hair back from her shoulder, once again torturing himself with the touch of her satiny skin.

"Oh, Conrad's Manhattan is in the forefront of my worries, but what kind of fiancé would I be if I didn't add you to the list?" he joked.

Josie laughed, just as he thought she would, but her eyes dropped to his lips a fraction of a second before she took a step back and sighed.

"You're not my fiancé, Reese. We're just friends."

She licked her lips and blinked as if those last two words were painful to say.

"Just friends," she reiterated beneath her breath as she walked away.

Reese didn't turn to watch her disappear down the hallway. He needed a minute because this morning had been so bizarre. Did Josie have stronger feelings for him than she was letting on? Would she be interested in exploring more with him? And what the hell was up with all of those colorful clothes hanging in the closet with tags?

One thing was certain: now that they were temporarily living together, Reese had to evaluate his feelings and try to figure out what the hell was truly going on between him and his best friend.

Three

Rain pelted down in sheets, right onto Reese. He seriously missed his garage for this very reason. He ran from his SUV to the porch of Josie's beachside home. The second he stepped beneath the shelter, he raked the water from his face. He was absolutely drenched and his overnight bag with dry clothes was in the car because he hadn't wanted to get that soaked as well. He'd just have to dry off and wait out the storm.

He rang the doorbell and glanced in through the sidelight. He didn't see any movement, but surely she was home. He really should've taken that key she'd offered him a long time ago, but why would he have ever had a reason to be here without her?

He rang the bell again and waited. Finally, the lock clicked and the door flew open. Josie stood before him in a black tank and a pair of black shorts, but her hair dripped water droplets onto her shoulders and face and she swiped moisture from her cheeks.

"What the hell happened to you?" he asked.

"There's a leak above my closet," she growled as she turned to race back toward the guest room. "This damn storm."

He closed the door and slid out of his wet shoes so he didn't slide on the tile leading down the hallway. Reese followed her and realized the closet in question was the one with the hoard of colorful clothes. The contents were strewn across the room. Boxes of shoes lay haphazardly along the floor; dresses were in heaps over the chair in the corner and all over the bed. Handbags littered the space around the shoes.

Good grief, there was even more than he'd first realized. How had all of this fit in that space? Granted it was a walk-in closet, but still. Josie really could open a boutique with all of this variety.

Her muttered curse filtered out from inside the closet. Reese stepped in to find her strategically moving buckets beneath the drips.

"Every time I think I have it, another area presents itself," she told him. "I do not have time for this."

"Do you have more buckets?"

She shook her head. "I have vases. There are several on the kitchen island. Just dump the flowers in the trash."

Reese raced from the room and headed to the kitchen where he came to an abrupt stop. The most obnoxious display of flowers covered her entire island. A wide variety of colors and blooms…all fresh and nothing Josie would ever purchase for herself.

No surprise to find cheesy notes attached. Reese made quick work of getting rid of the flowers, then he took armfuls of vases back to the closet.

"Want to discuss this?" Reese asked, holding a vase up and wiggling it.

"Nope."

"You have thousands of dollars' worth of flowers spread across your island."

"Not my money," she said, taking one vase at a time and looking at the ceiling for where to usefully place it. "And before you say anything else, I definitely realize Chris is an issue now."

Well, at least that was something. Chris wasn't going to just slink away. Reese truly believed the man thought he stood a chance at getting Josie back, but that wasn't happening.

"Why did you marry him to begin with?" Reese asked, his thoughts coming out before he could stop himself.

Josie reached for another vase, her dark eyes locking on his for the briefest of moments. "That's a conversation for another time."

And definitely one he would circle back to, because he'd wondered this since the moment she'd dropped the bomb that she'd eloped at the courthouse. The courthouse, for crying out loud.

Josie deserved more than a quickie wedding. He remembered her always talking about wanting a ceremony on the beach, small and intimate. Her love of the beach was just another thing they had in common…granted, he wasn't looking for marriage.

That engagement of his had been a mistake and one he'd likely have to answer for when they circled back to the topic later. Josie deserved an explanation, too.

Reese took the last two vases and looked around, but didn't see any more leaks. He sat them aside and pulled out his cell. Getting his contractor out here as soon as this storm passed was imperative, before any more damage was done.

Minutes later, he disconnected the call and focused back on Josie.

"My guy will be here as soon as he can."

Josie glanced from bucket to bucket to vase. "This place is a mess."

"Have you seen any other leaks?"

Josie's eyes widened and she pushed passed him to exit the closet. In her hurried, frantic state, he assumed that was a no. Whatever room she went into, he looked in another. It didn't take long to find that there were two other small leaks, both in Josie's bedroom.

"This is an absolute nightmare," she sighed once the other vases were in place and they'd gone back into the kitchen.

"It can all be fixed," he assured her. "My guy is the best and once this storm passes, we'll get it taken care of."

Josie pushed her hair from her face and stared at the mess of blooms and greenery. "I do feel bad putting them all in the trash."

"Then don't." Reese reached for one stem and picked it up, examining it before glancing back to Josie. "We can make smaller arrangements and take them to the cardiac unit where Dad was. We could give some to the nursing staff and some to the patients."

Josie granted him the widest, sweetest smile. "I would have never thought of that. You're sweet sometimes, you know."

Reese shrugged, not really needing compliments for just trying to find a solution to this mess.

"He had excellent care there, so maybe these would brighten their day. And I know they always have patients with no family."

"Always thinking of others." Josie reached up and rested her hand on the side of his face. "One day you're going to find the right woman. She's going to be damn lucky."

"You're the only woman who puts up with me," he joked.

She dropped her hand and glanced to the flowers. "Well, you keep up with those sweet gestures and you'll be taken in no time."

Taken. The only place he wanted to be taken was to a bed with Josie. Or here in the kitchen would work.

But Josie had everything and everyone in a particular slot, and he was in the friend zone, which hadn't been an issue…until now. The structure in her life stemmed from her retired military father. Her mother had passed away when Josie was a toddler, so she didn't remember her and Reese had never met the woman.

"I'm not looking for marriage," he stated honestly. "Being engaged was enough of a scare to make me realize I prefer being married to work. That's a relationship I can feed into and grow, not to mention control."

"Ah, yes. Control. Well, that is why you'll always be alone. Women don't want to be controlled," she scolded. "Don't you want to have someone to come home to? Someone to share everything with? Someone to grocery shop with?"

Reese laughed. "First of all, I don't grocery shop. Second, I tell you everything. And when I come home, I have a glass of bourbon. All my bases are covered."

Josie rolled her eyes. "That sounds so lonely."

"And in my defense, I'd never want to control a woman," he told her. "I know not to fight a losing battle."

"You really are a great guy," she stated again.

"Are you vying for a new position?" he asked. "We are engaged, after all."

"We're not engaged," she laughed. "Though I might need to convince Chris you were telling the truth because clearly he didn't believe us or he just doesn't care."

"Or he's an idiot, which is my vote," Reese added. "Pack a bag and come to my place."

Josie's eyes widened. "What? I'm not just coming to your place. My house is falling in, if you haven't noticed."

"Your house isn't falling in. My guy will be here to fix everything and you don't want to be here during that construction anyway." Reese reached for her and raked his thumb over her ring finger. "We need to get a ring."

Josie pulled her hand away and laughed. "Can you focus for two minutes?"

"Oh, I'm focused."

She rolled her eyes and turned her attention back to

the flowers. "Let me find some tissue paper and ribbon. I'm out of vases."

"Just gather them all up and we'll find vases at my house," he told her. "Grab a bag of whatever you need to stay the night."

"This is silly, you know." Josie started gathering the flowers. "I can stay here."

"You can, but why?" he countered, helping her gather everything. "We'll do a movie night like we used to."

She stilled and gave him a side-eye. "I get to choose the movie?" she asked.

Reese cringed. "Don't tell me."

Josie squealed and a wide grin spread across her face. "Oh, you know it."

Yeah, he did. Her all-time favorite movie was *An Affair to Remember*. She'd first introduced it to him when they were in high school and he'd absolutely hated it. Since then, any time she chose the movie, that's the one she went with. He didn't hate it now—hell, he could say the thing word for word. If she enjoyed it, that's all that mattered.

"Go pack your stuff and I'll take the flowers," he told her. "I'll meet you at my house."

"Deal."

She practically skipped from the room and Reese couldn't help but feel a niggle of worry deep in his gut. Spending more time alone with Josie had never been an issue before, but his hormones had never entered the picture before, either. At least, not like this. Now she was coming to his house for the night and Reese couldn't help but wonder how much more he could take before he snapped and crossed the line they couldn't come back from.

He was a jumble of nerves—between the mysterious closet she hadn't explained, the letter he'd received and the fact that he wanted Josie more than anything he'd ever wanted.

One night. He just needed to take this fake engagement one night at a time. Surely he could control himself for one night…right?

Josie pulled through Reese's gate and wondered how she'd let him talk her into this. Granted, she hadn't put up much of a fight. She'd been tired, worried about her roof, and she really didn't want to be present when workers started banging around and making more of a mess.

Still. Was he going to parade around in those little black boxer briefs again? True, she'd seen him in swim trunks, but that was before something had shifted in her mind with the words *my fiancé*.

That was before he'd pulled her into his side and caressed her hip like only a lover would do. There was something so possessive, so damn sexy about the way he'd taken charge. Her entire life she'd prided herself on being independent. Yet the way Reese had claimed her had done something to that friend switch and she wasn't sure she could flip it back to the way it used to be…the way it was *supposed* to be.

Ugh. This entire situation had gotten out of control so fast, she was both confused and frustrated. For someone who always had every damn thing in order and under control, her mental state was a complete mess.

Josie pulled around the circular drive and stopped right in front of the steps leading up to Reese's insanely large beach house. The man never did anything in small proportions. His house was easily four times the size of hers and he lived alone. His chef and maid came and went—they were hardly ever seen, yet the house remained immaculate and there were always fresh dishes in the refrigerator.

Reese treated his employees like family and they remained so loyal and went above and beyond to please him. He might be a billionaire mogul, but he was literally the only person she knew with a selfless heart of gold.

Josie's cell chimed just as she put her car into Park. If this was another text from Chris…

She'd totally downplayed how much he'd texted and called because she didn't want Reese to go complete Neanderthal on her…though proclaiming upcoming nuptials had been pretty caveman of him.

She opened the text, relieved to see it was from her editor, Melissa, but that relief quickly turned to dread.

Congrats on the big engagement! We just posted a blog teaser, but I want a Q&A with you and Reese ASAP! This is so exciting!

With her breath caught in her throat, Josie reread Melissa's text. Josie had confided in her assistant, Carrie, earlier that morning, more joking than anything, that Reese had claimed they were engaged and her world had been flipped upside down, but she was still getting that column in on time.

Josie had thought they were just having random chatter and now this? A teaser blog post had already gone up on the site…the site that had hundreds of thousands of hits per day. There was no pulling back from such a dramatic announcement without tarnishing the stellar reputation of not only *Cocktails & Classy*, but of her own image as well.

Josie stared at the message, unsure how to respond. She did, however, know who was responsible for this leak. As if following up with her somewhat new assistant constantly to make sure things were done properly wasn't annoying enough, now she couldn't trust her.

And here they'd thought getting rid of Chris would be the biggest issue.

Obviously, Josie's assistant would have to be dealt with first thing in the morning. Right now, though, she had one other matter to handle.

She had to actually fake an engagement to her best friend. This had gone beyond just lying to her ex. Now the public was aware of her personal life, too.

Josie hit Reply and chose her words carefully. Thankfully, she wasn't responding in person and dealing with Melissa seeing her shocked face.

Thanks. I had no idea you would find out this way. We're still processing the news, so the Q&A might have to wait.

Josie knew her fans would want the scoop, especially since she was coming off a divorce only six months ago. The outpouring of love and kindness had overwhelmed her and left her feeling a little guilty, considering she hadn't loved Chris. He'd been a nice guy who'd come along at the wrong time. Why wouldn't he just let her set him free?

She prided herself on being available to her readers and really interacting with them, so it was quite understandable that Melissa would want to share the happy news with the world. Unfortunately, the last thing Josie wanted was another public relationship…another *failed* public relationship. Because this fake engagement certainly wasn't going to last.

Josie didn't wait for a reply. She grabbed her purse and suitcase and headed up the steps to the front door. She was going to have to tell Reese about all of this and then she'd have to see how he felt about a real, fake engagement.

Good heavens, he'd probably do something stupid like really go buy her a ring. And knowing Reese, the thing wouldn't be subtle or cheap.

If only she'd kept her mouth shut earlier on the phone. But in her defense, Josie hadn't had any reason not to trust her assistant. And maybe Carrie was just chattering and not thinking when she told Melissa. Still, the lie was out there and Josie was going to have to deal with the consequences.

The front door flew open and Reese reached for her suitcase. Josie jumped back at his abrupt greeting.

"Why didn't you use the elevator?" he scolded. "I would've gotten this for you so you didn't have to lug it up the stairs."

"It wasn't a big deal," she replied as she stepped into the open foyer. "I'm quite capable of carrying my own luggage."

He muttered something about her being stubborn, but she let that roll off. She was well aware of her stubborn side and she wasn't apologetic for it.

"You ready for that movie?" he asked. "We can set up in the theater room or we can go out onto the patio."

The outdoor patio with a viewing screen was quite impressive, but she couldn't focus on the niceties of his house right now. All she could think about was how fast this fire was spreading and who else knew she and Reese were engaged.

"What's wrong?" he asked, reaching for her hand. "Chris—"

"No."

Well, he had texted, but that wasn't the problem.

"Then what is it?" Reese insisted.

Josie smiled and pulled in a deep breath. "How do you feel about picking out that engagement ring?"

Four

Well, that wasn't at all what he'd thought she'd say. She'd been upset earlier when he'd joked about a ring.

"Engagement ring?" he repeated.

Josie pulled her hand from his and sat her purse on the accent table inside the front door. Tucking her hair behind her ears, she turned to face him once again.

"It's a silly story, really," she began with a nervous laugh. "There was some harmless talk, or what I thought was harmless, on the phone with my assistant about Chris and everything that had happened and then the way you got him to leave. You know…by saying we were engaged."

Reese listened, actually rather amused at her jittery state. Something really had her ruffled.

"We talked about work and moved on," Josie added, fidgeting with her hands. "When I pulled in just now,

I got a text from my editor congratulating me on the engagement and telling me that she's got a teaser announcement on the blog site and she needs a Q&A from us. All I can figure is my assistant thought I was serious. I mean, I don't know who else would've told my editor and I guess maybe I forgot to mention this info was confidential. I'm sorry this is all just a big mess now."

Reese continued to watch as she twisted her fingers, smoothed her black dress, toyed with her hair again. The woman was a bundle of nerves ready to explode. This faux engagement was quickly getting to both of them. Likely she was stressed because her life wasn't so neat and tidy right now, the way she liked it. And for him... well, he wanted to strip his best friend and feel those curves beneath his touch and he wasn't sure what to do about those feelings. So, yeah, they had one hell of a problem he didn't have time to solve.

"Then we'll get a ring and answer some questions," he told her, shoving aside his lustful thoughts. "Is that all?"

Her eyes widened. "Is that all? That's your response? We're not getting married, Reese. I can't do this again so publicly. I'm freshly divorced from a marriage that never should've happened in the first place and you and I are both public figures. I mean, we're no royal couple, but the media will be interested in this story."

Reese wrapped his arm around her waist and guided her on into the house. As they stepped down into the sunken living area, he tried to figure out how to assure her that everything would be fine.

"Listen," he started, then stopped and turned to face

her, placing his hands on her shoulders. "We play the role. Surely we can pretend to like each other."

She glared up at him and met his crooked grin.

"Would you be serious?" she demanded.

He leaned in just a bit more. Her eyes dropped to his lips, but she pulled her gaze back up to his and held steady.

"Oh, I am serious, Jo. We can answer the questions for your editor and make an appearance at my grand opening in two weeks as a couple. We can push through all of that and then figure out what to do after." He smoothed her hair back and framed her face with his hands. "We can always say we split because we realized we were better at being friends. That's very believable because people have already seen us together as friends—they know we already have a relationship."

"But I don't want to fail at something else," she stated. "Not even fake failing."

That's what she was afraid of? Failing? Nothing about faking being in love with him. Interesting.

"You've never failed at anything," he reminded her. "Not even that marriage you ended once you realized it wasn't working. And I sure as hell am not going to let you start now. We've got this. Together."

She closed her eyes and pulled in a breath, her slender shoulders tensed beneath his hands. Reese gave her a reassuring squeeze, needing her to realize he'd never let her get hurt. He was right here by her side.

"Trust me?"

Her lids lifted as she focused on him. Those deep brown eyes staring at him were usually so good at hiding emotions, but not now. He saw the fear, the vulnerability, the concern. He had all of those, too, but he also had faith enough in their relationship that they would make it through anything…even stepping over that invisible line.

The one he'd promised himself not to cross.

Josie ultimately nodded and a wave of relief washed over him. He would care for and protect her at all costs. He could juggle his family, old and new, plus the Manhattan opening, and still make sure Josie came out of all of this unharmed.

With her eyes still locked onto his, physical need consumed Reese. He leaned in closer, never taking his focus from her. Little by little, he closed the distance until his lips were a whisper from hers.

"Wh-what are you doing?"

Barely hanging on by a thread.

"Practicing," he murmured. "We need to be believable in public."

She licked her lips, but since he'd leaned within a breath of her, her tongue brushed across his bottom lip and Reese knew she certainly hadn't meant to.

But whether she'd meant to or not didn't matter. Just that briefest touch of her tongue snapped something in him.

Reese covered her mouth, gently to give her an opportunity to back up and stop if this was something she didn't want. If she stopped, he would have to respect her decision, but now that he'd touched her in such an intimate, non-friend way, he wanted more.

So. Much. More.

Careful not to touch her anywhere else, Reese clenched his fists at his sides. The desire to reach for her, pull her even closer to get the full experience, con-sumed him, but he couldn't pressure her. As much as he wanted to keep kissing her, to touch her, his first prior-ity was to make her feel secure.

He had to be patient or he'd risk everything they had.

When her lips opened beneath his, Reese took that as the proverbial green light and deepened the kiss. Delicate fingers feathered up his arm and sent shivers racing through him.

When had he last shivered during a kiss?

Never. He didn't get all giddy and shaken just from a kiss. He wasn't some hormonal teenager.

The woman was potent, more so than he ever could have imagined. When Josie let out a little sigh, Reese reluctantly pulled back.

Clenching his jaw, along with his fists, he closed his eyes and thought of anything other than how much he wanted to take her into his room and finish this.

A kiss so powerful without truly touching was only a stepping-stone to something else…and it was that some-thing else he wanted to experience with her.

"What was that?" she murmured, her hands fall-ing away.

Trying to lighten the intense mood, Reese smiled. "A hell of a practice kiss."

He didn't want to expose his true feelings, didn't want her to feel awkward, either. She'd just gotten here and he didn't want to send her running.

Josie took a step back and nodded. "Right. Well, you're a hell of a kisser."

Now how could his ego stay low with that type of a compliment? And how could he not want even more?

Just that simple taste had his imagination running even more rampant with endless possibilities.

"Back at ya," he stated with a grin. "I'll get your stuff into a guest room and then we can watch that movie. Which room do you want?"

"Anything with an ocean view," she told him.

Reese nodded and grabbed her suitcase, needing to get a minute to himself to get his head back on straight. As he took the luggage onto the elevator, Reese wondered how the hell he could focus on anything other than that kiss and how soon they would do it again.

Because now that he'd had one taste, he wanted another, and his drive to share more intimacies with her was stronger than ever. Judging from Josie's surprise reaction and then her response, maybe she had similar needs as well.

Focusing on all of this pent-up desire when he had so much else going on should be silly, foolish even, but all he could think about was how powerful it was and how soon he could kiss her again.

An Affair to Remember was not holding her attention and the lack of interest had nothing to do with the fact that she knew each scene word for word. No, her focus was on her still-tingling lips and the man sitting right next to her on the plush sectional sofa. There were plenty of other seats, but here he sat, right by her side.

What the hell had he been thinking, kissing her like that? Touching her with only his lips, yet her entire body had felt that touch. That little niggle of desire he'd launched earlier by claiming her as his fiancée had become something more. She ached with a need she didn't recognize. Never before had a kiss, so simple and sweet, left her wanting to rip someone's clothes off.

But Reese had pulled back and she'd been left with confusion and need.

If that was their practice kiss, she didn't know what would happen if they had to do the real thing for display…this one had felt pretty damn real.

Her cell vibrated against the table and she glanced down at the screen. But it wasn't her phone; it was his. She'd thought for sure it would be Chris again.

Reese leaned forward and grabbed his phone, stared at it for a minute, then muttered something under his breath before firing off a text.

"Everything okay?" she asked.

He shot her a smile and a nod. "Fine. Just work."

"For the Manhattan opening?"

"No, it's about some business I have in Tennessee."

Surprised, she shifted and put her feet up under her on the sofa. "Does this have anything to do with the trip you just got back from, the one you were so secretive about?"

His eyes darted from the television screen to hers. They'd decided to stay in the theater room since the weather was still nasty outside.

When he remained silent, she reached for the remote and paused the movie, instantly silencing the room. She stared at his strong hands still clutching the phone and wondered what secrets he kept locked in there.

Reese blew out a sigh and reached for her hand. The innocent, friendly gesture he'd done so many times before felt oddly different now, after that toe-curling kiss. This was still her best friend…her best friend turned faux fiancé. But they only had to play the game for a few weeks and then they could go back to being friends in all aspects.

She would ignore that little voice asking if being friends was all she wanted. Could she be fearless for now? Could she let Reese out of the friends box, just a little? If she was honest, she'd been wanting…something for a long while now, something different…a change. Maybe she could channel her mother's boldness, just for a while. Since none of this would last, maybe she could grab this chance to pretend to be that bold woman she so desperately wanted to be.

She had such mixed feelings about all of this. How would her heart stand up against playing his fiancée, with all the touching and lingering glances? And how would such acts change the dynamics of their entire relationship? Could they easily slide from one type of intimacy to another without any emotional damage?

She wasn't sure. And yet a part of her wanted to find out.

"I'm not purposely keeping anything from you," he finally told her as his thumb raked over the ridges of her knuckles. "Just sorting through some things. I'll fill you in when I'm ready."

Whatever it was sounded serious. Reese was always the good-time guy. The one who pulled her out of her shell and tried to get her to ditch her planner and do something, anything, spur-of-the-moment. So whatever plagued his mind, it was something big.

The way he kept stroking her hand had even more shivers pumping through her and Josie wasn't so sure staying here at his house was a great idea. At least she was not staying in the same room with him. The hour was getting late and she had to start on a new project in the morning. She was going to need a clear mind and not one filled with passionate kisses and unsettling fantasies about her bestie.

"I'm tired," she told him as she eased away and came to her feet. "I have a busy day tomorrow so I'm going to head up to my room."

Reese stood, too, instantly invading her space by his sheer size. She'd always known he was a broad guy— he did value his gym time—but she hadn't realized just how powerful and sexy he appeared until just now. Her heart beat quicker; her body tingled in ways it shouldn't from just looking at her best friend.

"Are you okay?" he asked, his brows drawn in. "If you're worried about the leaks at your place, my contractor will fix everything and you'll never know there was a problem."

Her leaks. Right. She'd honestly forgotten about that particular mess. Pretty much everything pre-kiss had slipped from her mind. Though she really should try to get back to reality because none of this—not what she was feeling, not what they were pretending—was valid.

Those few seconds of connection with Reese weren't real. He didn't want to build anything with her based on that kiss and he'd already told her this was all for show.

Fine. She could deal with that, but she still didn't know how all of this would work. She didn't have another space filed away for him. He was her rock, her very best guy, the one she could go to for anything. Shifting him somewhere else in her life would only unsettle the solid structure she strived for.

If she failed publicly at a relationship again, she worried how her reputation would hold up. She worried she'd let herself down, because she'd always prided herself on her independence and her control. Thanks to her military father and her regimented childhood, she knew no different.

"I'm not worried about the leaks," she assured him.

Reese reached up and tucked a strand of hair behind her ear, then trailed his fingertips down her jawline. Had he always been this touchy? This affectionate? Was Reese's interest recent or had she taken all of those innocent touches for granted before?

"Is it the kiss?" he asked.

Her heart caught in her throat. Leave it to him to draw out the awkwardness and make it bold and commanding.

"We're still friends," he added. "That kiss didn't have to mean anything."

Josie swallowed and went for full-on honesty as she looked him directly in his daring blue eyes. She was drowning and she had no clue how to save herself other than to just get out of the current situation.

"But it did."

Before the moment could get any more awkward or before he replied that he didn't feel anything, Josie turned and left the room. Maybe that made her a coward, but right now, she was afraid. Afraid for what would happen after two weeks of pretending, when she'd only been here two hours and already had stronger feelings than she should. The fear also stemmed from not knowing how much longer Reese could stay in that friend box she'd so carefully packed him in.

But most of all, she worried that she would never be the same because now that she'd had a hint of what Reese could bring out in her…she wanted to experience even more and that revelation would certainly keep her awake all night.

Five

"Is everything okay, son?"

Reese tightened his grip on the steering wheel as his father's voice came over the speaker in his SUV.

Son. The simplest endearment, one Reese had heard countless times over the years, yet the word only reminded him of all the lies he'd been living for nearly forty years.

Reese turned into Conrad's first location in Sandpiper Cove. This place was as old as he was and the most sought-out restaurant in the state. Many magazines and even television shows showcased Conrad's and its specialty menus and fine dining experience.

All of this belonged to Reese now because he was Martin Conrad's son...or so he'd always believed.

But even having this dynasty passed down to him, Reese wanted to build his own legacy, which was why he was getting the next phase going with his opening in New York.

"I'm fine," Reese replied, pulling into his parking spot. "I'm glad you and Mom are having a nice trip. You both deserve the getaway."

And they did. They had worked every single day for as long as Reese could remember, growing this dynasty from a meager savings account that they'd invested in an old shack. All of that blew up into something amazing and the shack remained, but took on renovation after renovation. Surrounding properties were purchased to accommodate the growth and it wasn't long before they realized they should open another restaurant and then another.

Reese was proud to be part of such a hardworking family; they had taught him so many of his core values. He'd always wanted a family of his own, children to pass this legacy down to someday.

But now? Well, now he questioned everything.

"We're having the best time," his father stated. "Wait… What, Laura?"

Reese waited while his parents held their own conversation in the background. Despite everything he'd learned from that letter, and he was still questioning the validity of revelations from a woman he'd never met, Martin and Laura had raised him. They'd loved him and provided for him, so no matter the outcome of their eventual confrontation about his biological father, they were his parents. He just wished like hell they would've trusted him enough to tell him the truth—if there was a truth to tell.

"Engaged?" his father exclaimed. "Reese, your mother

says you're engaged? She's reading that blog she loves from Josie's magazine. What, Laura? He's engaged to *Josie*? Our Josie?"

Josie had been part of his family for so long. When her father was out of town working or traveling, Josie tended to land at their house. Most holidays during their college days she had spent with them. She was like the daughter his parents never had.

Reese raked a hand over the back of his neck. Yeah, he probably should have told them about this sooner, like last night, but his mind hadn't been on the fake engagement; it had been on Josie and kissing her and her telling him that the encounter had been much more than a simple kiss. He'd wanted to know exactly what she meant by that.

But she'd walked away.

He'd stood in his theater room staring at the empty doorway long after she'd left. Obviously, he hadn't been the only one affected by the kiss and now he had to figure out what to do with this information.

Still, his parents deserved a heads-up. They truly loved Josie like their own…and they were clearly thrilled by this unexpected news.

"Son, are you still there?"

Reese pulled himself back to the call. "Yeah. I'm here. And I was going to tell you today, actually. This all happened so fast."

"Josie is such a wonderful girl," his father boasted. "Hold on, your mother wants to talk to you."

Reese swallowed and listened to the static as the phone was passed around, then he was immediately greeted with his mother's high-pitched squeal.

"Darling," she yelled. "I'm so happy for you guys, though I don't know why I had to read about it online instead of hearing the news from my own son. We will discuss that later, but for now I want to know how you feel. Are you excited? How did you propose? I saw this coming years ago. I cannot wait to throw you guys a proper engagement party."

Reese's mind whirled with one question and thought after another. His mother was always all-hands-on-deck. The woman was only "off" when she was asleep. There was no way he could let her start planning an engagement party. She would get way too wrapped up in this and right now, he couldn't share that it was a sham.

"Mom, let's not order any party decorations just yet," he stated. "Josie is swamped with work and I'm busy with the Manhattan opening. Let's get on the other side of these two weeks and then we can talk. Okay?"

Silence on the other end was all the warning he needed to know she did not like his idea.

"I promise," he quickly added. "You know how important this next opening is. I'm starting a new chapter and I need to focus solely on that. Josie completely understands."

"Of course she does," his mom agreed. "That's why the two of you are so perfect for each other. You're both workaholics."

Well, that was definitely true. Reese took after his father—well, after Martin. He devoted nearly every moment to making sure their upscale restaurants maintained the highest prestige and top-notch reputation people had come to appreciate from them.

"I've asked Josie to cover the event, too," he quickly

told her, turning the conversation toward business. "I figure since she's going as my date, and there's no one else I'd rather give an inside scoop to, this would be a win-win for everyone."

"I can't wait to see you guys," she exclaimed. "You give Josie a big hug and kiss from me."

A hug and a kiss? Sure, no problem. Everything else that came to mind? Yeah, that was the problem.

"We will see you at the opening," she told him. "Love you, Reese."

Emotions threatened to overtake him, but he tamped them down. His mother did love him, that was never in question. But at some point, he'd have to find the right words and the right time to question them.

"I love you, Mom. See you in two weeks."

After Reese hung up, he sat alone with his guilt and tried to tell himself this situation wouldn't last long. Two weeks and he and Josie would go back to being friends. Nobody had to know this had all been a sham, not even his parents.

But he would know.

Every part of him wondered how the hell he could go back to never touching her, never kissing her the way he truly wanted.

And he knew she was affected, too. He'd seen that flare in her eyes and heard that swift intake of breath.

Reese's cell chimed in his hand before he could exit his SUV. He glanced down to the screen to see a message from Josie.

Melissa wants a photo shoot along with the Q&A. She has it all scheduled for tomorrow morning at nine and is hoping to use Conrad's as the backdrop. Want me to make an excuse to postpone?

Reese stared at the message. If they kept pushing forward, how much damage would be done in the end?

But, really, what would a few pictures hurt? The Q&A wouldn't be a big deal. They knew each other better than they knew themselves at times. And the coverage might be good for his new opening, too.

No big deal. We can all meet at the restaurant.

She instantly replied back.

I'm sorry about all of this.

He blew out a sigh and hit Reply.

I'm sorry, too. We'll get through this together.

There was only one thing in his entire life he was afraid of and that was losing Josie forever. Even with everything going on around him, he couldn't lose her. The risk of seeking something more with her terrified him, but he was starting to believe that if he never tried, that would terrify him more.

What if he didn't lose her friendship? What if something magical developed? If he didn't test these new feelings, his fear of the unknown could rob him of the chance at something good.

But… Having a committed relationship really wasn't something he had the time for right now. He was just getting started on this new chapter in his career, and he needed to devote every bit of energy and time to making this next phase a success.

Not only did he demand that of himself, he also didn't want to let his parents down. They'd entrusted their dynasty to him and he'd be damned if he'd get sidetracked.

Reese shot off another reply to Josie.

See you at home tonight.

The message went before he realized how familial that sounded. He certainly wasn't ready for all of that. Maybe someday, but not now. He was too slammed with work and the fact that his personal life from all angles had taken drastic turns.

Yet he couldn't deny he liked knowing Josie would be at his house waiting on him. He'd already asked his chef to prepare Josie's favorite meal and dessert. There was a bottle of her favorite wine chilling and he intended to make this very stressful situation as relaxing as possible for both of them.

Reese stepped from his car and into the hot summer sun that was already beating down. Every single day he came to Conrad's when he was in town, but today he had the urge to blow off work and hit the beach like normal people. He wondered if Josie would ever consider doing something that spontaneous, that out of the ordinary, something that wasn't already scheduled in her planner.

Reese stepped in through the back door, disarmed the alarm and headed for the office he kept on the top floor. The second floor was for VIP guests only and that lounge area was consistently booked. But Reese kept his office on the top floor away from the noise and confusion where he could really work and continually design new ways to grow the company.

As soon as he stepped off the elevator, he pulled up Josie's text again and replied. Tomorrow was a special day and he didn't want it marred by the black cloud of deceit hanging over their heads.

Take the rest of tomorrow off after the Q&A and photo shoot. I have a surprise.

He knew what her response would be. He knew exactly what she'd send back before he even glanced at his screen. So when the phone vibrated in his hand with a new message, he laughed.

I hate surprises. I need to plan what I'm doing. It's like you don't know me.

Oh, he knew her, which was exactly why he wanted to push her beyond her comfort zone, see her live a little. They were both stressed and a day off would do them good. No, he didn't have the time to take off, but nothing was more important than Josie.

Besides, tomorrow was her birthday and he would surprise her with whatever the hell he wanted.

He didn't respond to her message; he just decided to let her think about all the possibilities he might have in store. She'd mentioned working from home today, his home, not hers since there was a crew already at her place working on the damaged roof. He'd already told his chef, Frisco, to take extra special care of Josie and to make sure she was comfortable.

Having her at his house seemed strange, yet right. Reese couldn't help but wonder how she felt being there after last night.

Reese planned on discussing that kiss with her again, finding out exactly how she felt…because he wanted more. More kisses, more touches…just more of Josie, and now that she was in his home, he had the opportunity…but should he take it?

Six

Josie finished her work, leaned back in the chair and stared at the screen. Something felt so off, but she just couldn't put her finger on it. Having an empty wineglass wasn't helping.

It grated that her entire work mode could be tilted off-balance because she'd kissed her best friend. No, he'd kissed her…she'd just enjoyed the hell out of it and still felt the tingling on her lips.

With a sigh, Josie came to her feet and closed her laptop. Thankfully, this piece on new summer cocktails wasn't due for another week. She had all the makings for an amazing article. She even had inspiration photos from the art department with oversize martini glasses filled with pale pink drinks and floating flowers. The recipes shared from various coastal restaurants around the world were in, interviews with restaurant owners were done…but she couldn't find that hook that made everything just come together in an article that didn't sound like a rookie wrote it.

Josie picked up her empty wineglass and left the office. Reese had three designated spots in his home for work and all of them faced the ocean, but she'd chosen the smallest because she preferred to be cozy and quaint…a tough feat in a house of this magnitude.

The moment she hit the top of staircase, a delicious aroma wafted up from the first floor. The chef had only made his presence known once and that was to ask her what she wanted for her lunch. Josie was so used to making her own things or grabbing something from a seaside café that she might get spoiled if she hung around Reese's house too long.

Whatever Frisco had made for dinner smelled like it was going to be divine. The hint of something with peaches hit her as well. There was no way Josie could ever be that masterful in the kitchen; her skills were relegated to her keyboard.

The second she reached the bottom of the steps, Reese walked in the front door. His eyes locked onto hers and Josie gripped the wineglass as she froze. She hadn't seen him since last night, since she fled the room after he'd kissed her. Likely he wasn't awake all night replaying that moment; at least, he didn't look haggard.

That bright blue button-up, folded up on his forearms, showed off not only his tanned skin, but also that excellent muscle tone she knew he worked hard to maintain.

Damn, that kiss had changed everything.

"Looks like you need a refill." Reese broke the silence as he nodded to her glass. "And dinner smells amazing, so this is perfect timing."

He closed the door and tossed his keys onto the accent table before crossing the foyer. Those cobalt-blue eyes locked onto hers and she would have sworn they were more intense than ever.

Yes, that kiss had changed everything.

She'd thought their dynamics had changed with his fake engagement, that first embrace at her door, but that was nothing compared to having his lips on hers. She couldn't seem to put him back in the friends-only box.

Josie had always noticed Reese's striking features and the beauty of his gaze, but she'd never *felt* it before. Josie couldn't begin to share with him what he was doing to her, not when she couldn't even explain all of this to herself.

"I just finished my article," she told him, trying to have what should be a normal conversation. "It's not where I want it, but I can't think anymore today."

Reese reached for her glass. "Let's go have dinner and you can bounce your problems off of me."

Her problems? That was quite laughable considering *he* was the problem. Well, not him physically. No, physically he was the answer, but that was the problem.

Ugh. She was such a mess with her mixed emotions and wayward thoughts. She knew what she meant, but trying to categorize all of her views was proving to be impossible. Josie didn't care for this out-of-control feeling or not being able to maintain some regulation over her own life.

"I'd rather you tell me what's going on tomorrow," she countered, coming down off that last step.

Reese laughed as he started guiding her toward the back of the house. That hand on the small of her back seemed too intimate, but just days ago that would've merely been his friendly gesture. Now she questioned everything…including these newfound emotions.

"We're doing the thing for your magazine and then I have a surprise."

Josie rolled her eyes as she came to a stop. Turning to face him, she crossed her arms over her chest.

"That thing?" she repeated. "You can't be that relaxed about an interview and photo shoot for this fake engagement."

"I'm not relaxed," he amended. "But it's scheduled and there's nothing we can do to change that."

She could call the whole thing off. She could come clean to her boss, just tell her it's a farce, but that would only damage her credibility. If she were going to reveal the truth, she should've done so right off the bat.

"Oh, my mom and dad are thrilled, by the way," Reese added.

Josie gasped. "You told your parents?"

"You know my mother reads your *Cocktails & Classy* blog every single day. I didn't think to warn them off ahead of time."

Guilt overwhelmed her. Josie closed her eyes, pulling in a much-needed deep breath. This lie was spiraling out of control faster than she could keep up. She truly loved and respected Martin and Laura Conrad. What would they think of her after she and Reese "broke up"?

"Hey," Reese said in that calming tone of his. "This

is all going to work out. We just need a couple weeks of make-believe and then we're back to being friends and nobody has to know otherwise."

Two weeks might as well be two years or two decades. With the way she was feeling right now, the end result of this charade would be that she'd possibly get intimately attached; her heart might get even more involved, because she didn't know if she'd have the willpower to put a stop to this madness.

Josie focused back on Reese. "Two weeks," she sighed. "We can do this."

The smile that spread across his face packed a punch and she forced herself to return the gesture. Who knew one kiss could cause so many emotions?

"I believe you said something about refilling my wine?"

He nodded and gestured for her to go ahead. "I had my chef make all of your favorites for dinner, so I hope you didn't have a big lunch."

Josie laughed. "He tried to feed me a five-course meal at noon."

"I told him to make sure you were well-fed and taken care of."

Taken care of. That's exactly what Reese lived for. He was always taking care of his parents, taking care of his staff of hundreds, taking care of her. He was the most selfless, giving man.

Before that kiss, those selfless traits were just part of what she'd loved about him as her friend. But now... well, she couldn't help but wonder how that generosity would carry over into the bedroom.

The instant mental image had her stilling, fantasizing for just a moment. Then she crashed back to reality as she refocused on Reese's gaze.

"I would've been fine with a banana or a smoothie," she told him. "But I appreciate it."

They stepped into the vast kitchen with views of the ocean through the windows, which stretched across the entire back wall. The sun was starting to set, casting an orange glow over the horizon and making the bright blue water sparkle like diamonds.

A million-dollar view.

Josie turned her attention to the long island and nearly gasped. "What is all of this?"

Reese laughed as he went to the wine fridge at the end of the island. "Dinner."

"For all of Sandpiper Cove?" she asked, her eyes scanning each dish.

"I told Frisco to prepare all your favorites and I gave him a list."

And from the looks of things, Reese hadn't missed a thing. There was even a little bowl of Tootsie Rolls, which made her laugh.

"How in the world did he pull off all of this?" she asked. "And the lunch he prepared was insane."

Reese shrugged. "That's why I can never let him leave me. I'd starve, and he's a magician when he's in his element."

Her eyes locked onto his. "You know we can't possibly eat all of this, right?"

"Of course not," he agreed. "Frisco always takes any extras to the homeless shelter, so I don't mind that he goes all out. I know none of this will actually go to waste."

Flowers to the hospital, food to the homeless shelter. Seriously, her best friend was not a typical jet-setting billionaire. She'd always admired his giving nature, or maybe it was that she'd just not seen him in this light before. Because the fact that he always put others first was becoming sexier and sexier.

"What's that smile for?" he asked.

She circled the island and placed a hand over his heart. "You're just remarkable. I mean, I've always known, but lately you're just proving yourself more and more."

He released the wine bottle and covered her hand with his…and that's when the memory of that kiss hit her again, hard. She shouldn't have touched him. She should've kept her distance. Because there was that look in his eyes again.

Where had this come from, this pull between them? When did he start looking at her like he wanted to rip her clothes off and have his naughty way with her?

"We need to talk about it," he murmured.

It.

As if saying the word *kiss* would somehow make this situation weirder. And as if she hadn't thought of anything else since *it* happened.

"Nothing to talk about," she told him, trying to ignore the warmth and strength between his hand and his chest.

"You can't say you weren't affected."

"I didn't say that."

He tipped his head, somehow making that penetrating stare even more potent. "It felt like more than a friendly kiss."

Way to state the obvious.

"And more than just practice," he added.

Josie's heart kicked up. They were too close, talking about things that were too intimate. No matter what she felt, what she thought she wanted, this wasn't right. She couldn't ache for her best friend in such a physical way. If that kiss changed things, she couldn't imagine how much anything more would affect this relationship.

How could she maintain control of her emotions if she let this go any further? She was already having a difficult enough time trying to cope with the current circumstances.

"We can't go there again," she told him. "I mean, you're a good kisser—"

"Good? That kiss was a hell of a lot better than just good."

She smiled. "Fine. It was pretty incredible. Still, we can't get caught up in this whole fake engagement thing and lose sight of who we really are."

His free hand came up and brushed her hair away from her face. "I haven't lost sight of anything. And I'm well aware of who we are…and what I want."

Why did that sound so dangerous in the most delicious of ways? Why was her body tingling so much from such simple touches when she'd firmly told herself not to get carried away?

Wait. Was he leaning in closer?

"Reese, what are you doing?" she whispered, though she wasn't putting up a fight.

"Testing a theory."

His mouth grazed hers like a feather. Her knees literally weakened as she leaned against him for support.

Reese continued to hold her hand against his chest, but he wrapped the other arm around her waist, urging her closer.

There was no denying the sizzle or spark or whatever the hell was vibrating between them. She'd always thought those cheesy expressions were so silly, but there was no perfect way to describe such an experience.

And kissing her best friend—again—was quite an experience.

Reese deepened the kiss, parting her lips and exploring further. She'd stop him in just a minute—she just wanted a little more.

Josie slid her hand from his and gripped each side of his face as he leaned her back a little more. That strong arm across her lower back held her firmly in place. Threading her fingers through his hair, she tilted her head to give him even more access, but those talented lips trailed across her jaw and down the column of her neck.

Any second she should end this, but it felt so damn good she couldn't muster up the strength to tell him to stop. She also couldn't remember why this was such a bad idea.

That hand behind her started shifting; a thumb slid beneath the hem of her shirt and caressed her bare skin. Josie let out a moan, then quickly bit down on her lip to quiet herself. Reese's lips continued to explore her neck, the sensitive spot behind her ear, then down into the vee of her shirt.

There were too many clothes in the way. Her body ached like it never had before and she wanted to feel his skin against hers.

"Reese," she panted, though she didn't know what she was begging for. She just knew she wanted him to keep going, to keep making her feel everything she'd deprived herself of.

An alarm echoed in the room, but Josie ignored it. She didn't want this moment to end…at least not yet.

But the insistent beeping kept going. Reese rested his forehead against her shoulder and she noted his body trembling just as much as hers…if not more.

"I have to get that," he murmured.

Get what? Her mind was still spinning and she didn't know what the noise was, but she wanted it to go away.

Reese slowly released her, holding her steady until she looked up at him and nodded. Her legs weren't quite as steady as she would've liked, so she rested a hand on the edge of the island and willed herself into a normal breathing pattern and heartbeat.

When Reese grabbed his cell from his pocket, Josie realized that hadn't been an alarm at all, but a call. Maybe the interruption was a blessing, because she still wasn't convinced she could have stopped what had been about to happen…and she was already wondering when it would happen again.

Seven

Reese cursed the caller before even looking at the screen. He needed to get in control and back to reality before answering, but he was having a difficult time with that considering he could still feel Josie's sweet body beneath his touch.

Damn it, how far would he have taken things? How far would she have allowed this to go?

Glancing down at the screen, he saw Sam Hawkins's name.

Sam Hawkins, the man who was very likely Reese's half brother and one of the men Reese had gone to see last week. The owner of Hawkins Distillery in Green Valley, Tennessee, was a pretty remarkable guy, considering he was the youngest distiller in the country.

Reese glanced to Josie, who was staring down at

the floor, her eyes wide with shock. He wasn't sure if she was shocked over their behavior or shocked over the fact that she'd enjoyed it so much—because those pants and moans and the way she'd clutched his hair were all clear indicators she'd been more than eager for things to progress.

Turning from temptation, Reese answered the call.

"Hello?"

"Reese," Sam responded. "I hope this isn't a bad time."

Bad time? Reese supposed it could've been worse—like if Sam had called in about ten minutes when clothes were strewn across the floor.

He looked again at Josie, who still seemed to be trying to catch her breath. Yeah, same here. He'd only meant to see if the effect of the kiss last night had been a onetime occurrence, but the moment his lips touched hers, there had been another internal snap that he couldn't control.

"Now is fine," he replied, focusing on the sunset outside instead of the beauty before him. "I didn't expect to hear from you so soon."

"I know. Nick and I were going to give you some time to process everything," Sam stated. "Especially considering you don't know Rusty like we do, it's still a shock to discover your father at our age."

Understatement. Reese hadn't even known there was a father to discover. He thought Martin Conrad *was* his father, for nearly four decades.

"Since Rusty is home from his stint in jail for embezzling from one of our local charities, Nick and I planned on confronting him with the truth."

Reese was well aware that Rusty had been arrested for skimming funds from a charity that Lockwood Lightning endorsed and supported. From all the stories Reese had heard and from the bits and pieces of what he'd dug up online, Reese had drawn his own conclusions that he'd lucked out in life by not having Rusty Lockwood raise him as his child.

"And you want me in on that meeting?"

Reese had to choose his words carefully because he still hadn't explained everything to Josie—they'd sort of been busy pretending to be engaged, fighting a magnetic attraction—and he still wasn't sure how the hell to handle any of this.

"We don't want to pressure you, but I did want to include you," Sam told him. "All of this is still new to us as well. I wouldn't mind getting to know my half brother a little more, but that's going to be your decision."

Half brothers. Reese had grown up an only child and used to wonder how having a sibling would've changed his life. He likely would've been sharing the family business. Having someone else to lighten the load wouldn't be a bad thing. He would've had an automatic friend growing up, too, but he'd had plenty of friends even without siblings.

Friends like the one he'd just groped until she was moaning in pleasure.

Pushing aside those delicious thoughts of Josie, Reese focused on what he wanted to know about Nick and Sam. Discovering two guys who were prominent in their fields of luxury liquor and hospitality—fields surprisingly similar to his own—and who were both eager to get to know him sounded promising, and Reese found that he did want to explore these new relationships.

This whole new chapter in his life would take some time to wrap his mind around, but new ventures never scared Reese. He welcomed challenges... including kissing Josie Coleman.

Again, he shifted his focus back to the call and away from Josie.

"I could make another trip to Green Valley," he told Sam. "Why don't you tell me when would work for you guys? I'm opening a new restaurant in Manhattan next weekend. Maybe we could discuss a possible working relationship as well."

"That would be a solid start," Sam agreed. "I'll talk with Nick and text you. We plan on confronting Rusty soon, though."

Reese swallowed and wondered if tag-teaming was the answer. What good would come from all of them going to Rusty? What did Sam and Nick hope to accomplish? Did they just want to let the mogul know that his sons had all been identified?

None of them needed money and Reese certainly wasn't looking for a father figure to fill a void. He had plenty of love and affection from the amazing couple who'd raised him.

Reese really needed to talk to his own parents before he went to Rusty. He needed all of the history, no lies, no secrets. Reese needed every bit of his life revealed to him.

He needed to understand his true role when it come to Rusty Lockwood. He needed to know where he actually stood in all of his relationships and what the hell he was supposed to feel.

Because his entire world was in upheaval and he honestly had no idea what to think about any of it.

"I'll see what I can work out," Reese replied. "But I can't make promises right now."

"Understood. I'll be in touch soon."

Reese disconnected the call, held his cell at his side and continued to stare out the window. He wasn't ready to face Josie yet, not when his body was still humming from their brief, intense encounter. Their clothes had stayed on. There had barely been any skin-on-skin contact. What would happen when they finally took that next step?

Because Reese had every intention of doing just that. He'd been uncertain before, even after that first kiss, but the way she'd responded moments ago—how could he deny either of them?

There was too much passion here to ignore. There was too much pent-up desire. Who knew how long those feelings had been stirring?

They would never know what they could have if he didn't take the risk. No, he didn't want to lose her as his best friend, but what if things only got better?

When he turned, he found Josie staring straight at him. She'd clearly had time to compose herself, but that hunger was still in her eyes. Her squared shoulders and tight lips, though, were good indicators that she wasn't happy about what she was feeling.

"You're going back to Green Valley?" she asked.

Reese pocketed his phone. "That's not where I thought we'd pick up from where we just left off."

She crossed her arms and stared across the room. "Where did you think we'd pick up? Kissing? Because I'm still not sure that's a good idea."

And that's where they clearly disagreed. There wasn't a better idea, in his opinion.

"You weren't complaining a minute ago," he reminded her—just in case she'd forgotten. "In fact, you were enjoying yourself, if I recall."

Her gaze darted away for a split second before she glanced back to him. "A minute ago, I was sidetracked by, um…"

"My slick moves?" he asked with a smile.

Her eyes narrowed. "Does your ego need to be stroked? I could've kissed anyone and gotten carried away. My eyes were closed, you know, and I happen to like kissing."

Jealousy consumed him as he closed the distance between them. He had her wrapped in his arms and falling against his chest. Her hands flattened on him as her focus was directed straight at his face.

"You think you'd react that way to just anyone?" he asked, tipping her back just enough so she had to cling to him. "Don't throw other men in my face, Josie. I might prove you wrong."

"But…we're friends, Reese."

Something in him softened at her tone, which was laced with confusion—as well as curiosity and desire.

"We *are* friends," he murmured, closing the space between their lips. "Very, very good friends."

Because this was Josie, he wanted to take it slow. He wanted her to recognize this insistent attraction and come to terms with the fact that they had already crossed the friend line. They might as well fully explore this passion.

True, everything surrounding them was in total chaos. But if they didn't take the chance now when they were thrown together, then when would they?

"Reese."

His name slid through her lips as she closed her eyes and tipped her mouth to his. As if he needed any more invitation than that to claim what he so desperately ached for.

Reese wanted her out of this little black dress, he wanted her hair messed up, and he wanted to be the cause of every bit of her chaotic, sexy state.

He'd never wanted a woman so bad in his life.

Her hands came up to his shoulders; her fingertips dug in. Didn't she know? He'd never let her fall.

Reese lifted her up firmly against his body as he spun her around and sat her on the edge of the table. She eased from his kiss and locked gaze with his. He waited for her to stop him, all the while praying she'd let him continue. Touching her was like a drug he hadn't known he was addicted to and now he couldn't get enough.

He reached up to the strap of her dress and eased it down her arm, taking her bra strap with it. Josie trembled beneath his touch and he had to force himself to keep this slow pace. She wanted him, wanted this—that much was evident in her heavy-lidded stare and flushed cheeks. Not to mention she wasn't telling him no.

Keeping his attention on hers, Reese slid the other straps down, earning him a swift intake of her breath as she raked her tongue across her lower lip. There was no way she could imagine the potent spell she held over him—he hadn't even been sure of it himself until now.

Josie shifted and braced her hands on the table behind her, quirking a brow as if daring him to stop. Damn, this woman was silently challenging him in the most delicious way.

Reese started to lean in, more than eager to get his lips on that velvety skin of hers.

"Reese," she whispered.

He stopped, his hands braced on either side of her hips.

"As much as we both want this, tell me it won't change things."

The plea in her tone, in her eyes, had Reese swallowing the truth—because things had already changed. The dynamics of their relationship had started changing the moment he knew he wanted her, which, if he was honest with himself, was years ago. She was just finally starting to catch up.

"You'll still be my best friend," he answered truthfully.

He settled his lips over hers as he grazed his hand up her bare thigh and beneath the hem of her dress. She shifted and rocked back and forth slightly to give him better access.

There was nothing he wanted more than to pleasure her right now. To pour out all of the passion he'd been storing up just for her. No woman could ever compare to Josie—which was why he refused to lose her in his life. Yes, intimacy would change things, but maybe it would make them even closer.

Reese feathered his fingertips along the seam of her

panties, earning him a soft moan and a tilt of her hips. But the moment he slid a finger beneath the silky material, he was the one eliciting a moan.

Josie leaned further back, dropping down to her elbows, but still keeping her eyes on his hand. He'd never seen a sexier sight than what was displayed before him. With her hair a mess, her dress hanging on by the curve of her breasts, those expressive eyes silently begging for more and her spread thighs, Reese didn't think he'd be able to ever have a meal at this table again without getting aroused.

As much as he wanted to roam his mouth over all of that exposed skin, he didn't want to miss one second of the desire in her expression. The moment he slid one finger over her heat, Josie's eyes fluttered closed and her mouth dropped open on a gasp.

Yes. That's what he wanted. That sweet, vulnerable reaction.

Finally, Josie eased back all the way and arched her body as she reached down and circled his wrist with her delicate fingers. Relinquishing control was not his go-to, but he was more than willing to let her guide her own pleasure.

It wasn't long before those hips pumped harder against his hand, before she cried out his name and clenched her grip a little tighter.

Reese took it all in. The passion, the need, the completely exposed way Josie let herself be consumed by her desire.

He'd never forget this moment, not for the rest of his life.

When Josie relaxed against the table and released his

wrist, Reese eased his hand away and adjusted the bottom half of her clothing. She'd gone totally limp and he couldn't help but smile. He'd never seen her so calm, not worried about a schedule or making plans for something else. She was still, quiet…and utterly breathtaking.

As much as he wanted to use her release as a stepping-stone to more, Reese gathered her in his arms and lifted her against his chest. Her head nestled against the crook of his neck like she'd done so a thousand times before.

Reese lifted her bra straps back into place and adjusted the top of her dress.

Josie's hands reached for the zipper on his pants.

"Not now," he murmured, placing a kiss on the top of her head.

Such an innocent gesture when the most erotic thoughts were swirling through his head. Just knowing she wanted to keep going was a victory he hadn't known was even possible. But she was coming off a euphoria she hadn't anticipated and he didn't want her to think he assumed or expected her to reciprocate.

Josie lifted her head, her tranquil gaze locked on his. "Why?"

He said nothing, but he also wasn't ready to just let her go. Gathering her up, he crossed to the wall of glass doors and eased one open with his foot.

"Where are we going?" she asked, looping her arms around his neck.

"You're going to sit out here and relax and I'm going to bring you food."

When he placed her on the cushioned chaise in the

outdoor living area, she simply stared up at him with her brows drawn.

"That's what you're worried about? Food?"

"Oh, I'm not worried," he corrected. "You haven't had dinner."

She blinked and then shook her head and muttered something under her breath about men being more confusing than women. That was an argument he was smart enough to walk away from.

Leaving her outside, Reese went back into the kitchen, and his gaze kept wandering to the now-empty table. Yeah, he'd never be able to eat there again without thinking of her as she'd just been, and he sure as hell wasn't about to tell his chef what had happened in his kitchen.

Reese turned back to the island, rested his hands on the edge and dropped his head between his shoulders. He just needed a minute to get control over his emotions and his arousal. Turning down her advance had been the most difficult thing he'd ever done, but he wanted the time to be right, for her to come to him because that's what she truly wanted and not because she was fuzzy-headed from a recent orgasm.

When he glanced back up, he caught her gaze staring back at him from where she remained outside. There was a vast distance between them, but he recognized so much in her eyes that he couldn't deny. Along with confusion and a hint of frustration, he still saw passion and he wondered exactly what she planned to do about it.

Eight

Josie stepped out onto the balcony off her guest room. The moonlight cast a bright, sparkling glow over the ocean. She had no clue how long she'd been standing out here letting her thoughts roll through her mind.

Chris had texted only a little while ago and she'd finally responded, telling him this was her final correspondence, she had moved on and she wished the best for him. Then she blocked his number.

She didn't know what to make of everything that had happened earlier with Reese and she couldn't worry about Chris's feelings at this point. It was her slipup on the phone with him that had started this entire ordeal and toppled her life out of control.

All of those neat, tidy boxes that had compartmentalized every aspect of her life were now completely obliterated.

From the way Reese made her feel, to the fact that she'd never felt such a rush of emotions, to the way he'd eased back when she'd reached for him. Everything was different now and she had no idea how she could juggle all of these feelings and still remain calm.

Josie crossed her arms and rubbed her hands over her skin. The breeze off the ocean washed over her, tickling her and doing nothing to dampen her arousal.

And she was still aroused. True, Reese had brought her to pleasure, but she wanted more. He'd left her wondering what else she could experience with him. What would happen if they managed to get all of their clothes off? If they were skin to skin and not worried about anything else beyond physical intimacy?

How would this change their relationship?

Not only that, if she completely let go and gave in to her desires, there would certainly be no controlling where it led. She'd never felt like she was floundering before, but that's exactly where she was right now. The decisions she should make collided with the decisions she *was* making and all of it was confusing the hell out of her.

A sickening feeling settled deep in her stomach over the possibility of losing her very best friend. She couldn't afford to be without him. She couldn't imagine even one day without texting or talking to him. He literally knew her secrets; he was her go-to for everything.

And he'd made her eyes roll back in her head and her toes curl with a few clever touches as he'd laid her out on his kitchen table.

Shivers racked her body as she recalled every talented trace of those fingertips. Who knew her best friend had such moves? And who knew she'd love it so damn much?

Dinner earlier had been strained. Josie wasn't sure if things were awkward because she was still aroused or because their relationship had shifted so far away from something she could recognize and label.

Regardless, Reese and his chef had outdone themselves with all of her favorites. She only wished she could've enjoyed them more.

Josie turned back toward her room and closed the patio doors at her back. She had to get up early and look refreshed for her Q&A and photo shoot. Considering it was well after midnight, she wasn't sure how fresh she would be able to make herself. There was only so much carefully applied concealer could do.

The silk of her chemise slid over her skin as she padded her way back to her bed. Every sensation since she'd felt Reese's touch only reminded her of how amazing he'd been. Every moment since her release, she'd ached for more and didn't know how to make that happen.

But didn't she know? She was just as much in charge of what was going on as he was.

But was she as brave? Nothing scared or worried Reese. That was the main area where they were 100 percent opposite.

In that kitchen earlier, though, they had been completely and utterly perfect.

Except for that one-off with Chris, Josie had never done something so spontaneous in her life. She made plans for everything and typically got irritated when her plans were shifted or canceled. Some might have even called her a nerd, but she preferred to be described as "structured."

Right now, though, she preferred to finish what Reese had started. Or maybe she'd started this? Regardless of who'd started what, the fact was, nothing had been finished.

And maybe she opted to break out of her perfect box because Reese made her feel things she'd never felt before. Maybe, if she was being honest with herself, she liked experiencing her reckless side with him because she knew she was safe. Reese would never let her get hurt.

Was he in his room thinking about what happened or was he fast asleep without a care? Knowing Reese, he'd fallen right to sleep, and she wasn't even a thought in his mind right now.

Well, too bad, because there was no way she could ignore this and certainly no way she could go to the Q&A and photo shoot while feeling such turmoil.

She didn't know if she was making the best decision or the biggest mistake.

There was only one way to find out.

Arousal and nerves clashed inside her as she tiptoed down the hallway toward Reese's bedroom.

This was insane, right?

She should just go back to her room, read a book or play on her phone or anything until she could push him from her mind.

But one step led to another and she found herself standing outside the double doors leading to the master suite. Josie placed her hands on the knobs and eased the doors open. Moonlight flooded the room, cascading a beam directly onto the king-size bed across from her.

She couldn't do this. She shouldn't be here.

What was she thinking? This was Reese. Her very best friend from school who had seen her at her absolute worst—when her prom date dumped her, when she had that dumb idea to get a perm and he told her she was beautiful anyway, when she broke out in hives from some new facial cleanser she'd tried for an article and he ordered in dinner so she didn't have to go out in public.

He was her rock, her support…not her lover.

Josie turned back toward the hall.

"Stay."

The word penetrated the darkness and had Josie reaching to grip the doorknob again for support. Her heart beat so fast, so hard in her chest, unlike anything she'd experienced before.

"I shouldn't be here," she murmured, still facing the darkened hall. Too late to slip out now.

"You want to be here or you would've stayed in your room."

Why was he always right?

"That doesn't mean this is a good idea," she told him.

The sheets rustled behind her and Josie pulled in a deep breath, willing herself to finish what she'd come for. This was what she wanted; this was exactly why she'd made that short trip from her room to his.

He knew full well why she'd come, so denying it now would only make her look like a fool.

Josie turned, not at all surprised to see Reese standing behind her. Bare chest with a sprinkling of hair, broad shoulders, his dark hair messed up from his pillow and those hip-hugging black boxer briefs were not helping her resolve.

"Who's to tell us this is a bad idea?" he countered in that husky tone of his.

Well, no one really, but shouldn't she be the one saying this wasn't smart? Shouldn't she insist that they were friends above all else?

Yet she'd come to his room because she wanted to forget that common sense logic and remember exactly how amazing she'd felt in his kitchen.

"Stay."

He repeated the simple command, and something just clicked in place—something she hadn't necessarily planned or given much thought to. For the first time in her life, she didn't care about her plans. She only cared about her wants.

And she wanted Reese.

Everything about this felt out of control, and yet safe at the same time.

That moment when she took a step forward, she saw Reese's shoulders relax, a smile spread across his face. There was something so intimate and arousing about the darkness, the quiet of the night and the moonlight streaming through the windows. There was no need to even pretend she didn't want to be here. It was time she owned up to exactly what she needed and not make excuses or apologies.

When this was over, there would be no room for regrets. Regrets would only lead to the downfall of their friendship, and she refused to let him slip from her life.

Josie reached for Reese and she could have sworn she heard him mutter something like "finally," but she wasn't positive. Her heart beat too fast, the thumping rhythm drowning out anything else.

All at once his hands were on her, his mouth covered hers, and he cupped her backside, lifting her against his firm body.

Every thought vanished as she let the overwhelming sensation of passion consume her. An unfamiliar feeling overcame her and all she could think was that this felt too right to be considered wrong.

Reese turned and moved them through the room, never taking his lips from hers. Josie laced her fingers behind his neck and held on as anticipation built and her body ached for so much more.

She tilted and landed softly on the comforter as Reese came down to rest on her. The weight of his body pressed her deeper into his warm bed.

The way he settled between her thighs had Josie tipping her hips, silently begging him for more. Reese's lips left hers and roamed over her jaw and down the column of her throat. She arched her back, granting him access to anything and everything he wanted.

His weight lifted off her as he eased his way down her body. Strong hands tugged at her chemise and Josie reached down to help him. She shimmied the silk up and over her head, tossing it aside without a care, leaving her only in her lace panties.

Reese came up to his knees, and in the glow of the moonlight, she didn't miss the way his heavy gaze raked over her body like this was the very first time seeing her.

He'd seen her plenty—in all kinds of outfits, in a bikini—but never like this and never so intimately. She wanted to freeze this second, to remember his look forever. She'd never felt sexier or more beautiful than right now.

Josie lifted her knees and came up onto her elbows. She wanted him to touch her with more than his stare. She needed skin to skin, and she was done waiting.

In a flurry of movements, she worked off her panties and assisted him in taking off his boxer briefs. Reese slid off the bed for a moment and procured protection before coming back to her.

This was really happening.

Josie should have been worried, but all she could think of was how much she wanted him to join their bodies, to make them one. Nothing felt weird or awkward, even though this was Reese.

Actually, she was surprised how perfect it felt.

He braced his hands on either side of her head and leaned down to glide his lips over hers.

"Be sure," he murmured.

Josie wrapped her arms and legs around him, guiding him to exactly where she wanted him. The second he slid into her, Josie's body bowed as she cried out. Her fingertips dug into his shoulders and Reese immediately set a rhythm that did glorious things to her.

With his strong grip on her hips, Reese eased up and stared down at her while he made love to her.

No. They weren't making love.

This was sex. She hadn't planned for anything more.

"Get out of your head," he told her. "Stay with me."

He eased back down, slowed his pace and smoothed her hair away from her face. She didn't know how he always knew what she was thinking. He was just amazing like that.

Speaking of amazing, the way he moved his body over hers, glided his lips across her skin, had her body climbing higher. Josie gripped his hair as he covered her mouth with his. Her ankles locked even tighter as her climax hit.

He didn't release her lips as he swallowed her moans. Her knees pressed against his waist as every possible emotion overcame her. The intense pleasure and utter serenity completely took over. Josie lost herself in the moment, the man.

Nothing could ever compare to this right here.

Before she could come down from her high, Reese pulled his lips from hers, pumped even harder, and she watched as his jaw clenched. Those bright blue eyes locked onto hers as his release rolled through him.

Josie had never seen a sexier sight.

This was the only side to Reese she had never seen, and she honestly hadn't known she could get turned on so much even after her body had stopped trembling.

But seeing him come undone, well, Josie figured she'd be staying the night in this bed because she wasn't finished here.

Reese eased back down, shifting to the side and gathering her in against his side.

"Stay," he whispered.

Again, such a simple word that held so much meaning, so much promise.

Josie turned, tipping her head up to his as she raked a finger across his jawline. "I'm just getting started," she whispered back.

Nine

"Who were you referring to when you said you couldn't be her?"

Reese didn't mean to break the silence with that question, but he'd been wondering for some time now and obviously Josie wasn't going to be forthcoming with the information.

Just in the past two days he'd discovered there was much more to her than he'd ever realized. Clearly, she'd held this secret, but she'd also been hiding a passion that matched his, which he hadn't even considered.

Knowing they were compatible in more ways than just as friends blew his mind.

Having Josie in his bed had been more than he'd ever imagined...and he had a hell of an imagination where she was concerned. But realizing they were so damn compatible was just another confirmation that a physical relationship had been worth the risk.

The silence stretched between them as she sat on the edge of the bed with her bare back to him. The sun hadn't even come up yet and she was trying to leave. She'd spent the night here, they'd gotten little sleep, and they had to get ready to go to this interview at his restaurant and attempt to fake an engagement.

Reese would rather stay in this bed and figure out what was really going on between them, to know what she was thinking. Physically, she was here, but he wasn't sure she was with him mentally.

"What do you mean?" she asked, glancing over her shoulder.

That long, silky black hair fell down her back and he had the strongest urge to reach up and feel those strands slide between his fingertips.

"In your closet the other day," he reminded her. "The one with the leak. Who were you referring to when you said you couldn't be like her?"

Her eyes darted down, but even from her silhouette, he could see the sadness in her expression. Reese eased closer, but didn't touch her. He still didn't know where they'd landed in this postcoital moment, and he didn't want to make things awkward. He wanted her to feel comfortable enough to answer his question.

"My mother," she murmured. "I don't remember much about her, but I do remember her always wearing bright colors. She loved blues and reds. She always had on red lipstick, too."

Reese had never met Josie's mother, and actually hadn't seen many pictures of her, either. But he did recall seeing one photo, years ago, and Josie looked exactly like her mother. The long, dark hair, the doe eyes, the petite frame and the flawless, light brown skin tone.

"I remember Dad saying that when he first met mom during his travels to the Philippines, when he first joined the army, he fell in love with her on the spot. He loved how bold and vibrant she was. She challenged him and made him work for her affection. They were so in love."

Reese wanted to erase that sorrow from her tone, but he wasn't sorry that he'd asked. This was a portion of Josie that she'd kept locked away from him. They'd been friends for so many years, yet he'd never heard her talk of her mother this way and he sure as hell hadn't had a clue that she'd kept a shrine to her in her closet in the form of unworn clothes.

"Were those clothes hers?" he asked.

"No." Josie came to her feet and slid back into her chemise before settling back down and turning to face him. "I buy them thinking I'll take the plunge one day and just step out in something bold like she always did. But I'm not her. I'm boring, predictable and more comfortable in black. Besides, that's how my readers know me—classic black. Any photo I'm in or any event I attend, I'm always in black. It's my signature look now."

She attempted a soft smile, but that sadness still remained in her eyes. Had she always had that underlying emotion? Did he just take for granted that she was okay with how her life had turned out? He couldn't imagine losing his mother, but he doubted Josie would ever feel whole with that void in her life.

He was still trying to figure out how he felt regarding

the fact that he was adopted. Now he had three parents and his world was all over the place. Even so, this was nothing like what Josie had gone through.

"You can wear whatever you want whenever you want," he informed her. "Be yourself. If that's a bright red dress, then do it."

She gave him a sideways glare, that typical Josie look when he suggested something she thought was a completely moronic idea.

"I'm serious," he urged. "There's no dress police. Maybe that could be your next article. How to revamp yourself—or some clever title you'd come up with."

Josie laughed and relief washed over him. He always wanted to hear her laugh, to see her wide smile and know she was happy.

"I wouldn't use something so trite as the word *revamp* in my title. I'm beyond college days when I was too tired to come up with something catchy."

She came to her feet again and smoothed her hair back from her face with a sigh. "Besides, I'm not getting the equivalent of an adult makeover, so this plan is irrelevant. I'm fine with who I am, I just sometimes wonder what it would be like. That's all."

Reese sat up in bed, the sheet pooled around his waist. He kept his eyes on that body he'd worshipped nearly all night. He wanted to know if she'd join him again tonight, because one night wasn't nearly enough, but he wanted to leave that next step up to her. He wasn't ready for a long-term commitment and he didn't want her to misunderstand what was happening here. It was up to her to continue what they'd started. She'd come to him once before…he had to believe she would again.

"I'm going to get ready," she told him. "If we leave early, we can swing by Rise and Grind. I haven't had an iced mocha latte in forever."

"You had one last week. I picked it up for you and brought it to your house and even delivered it into your home office."

Her brows drew in as if she were trying to remember, but then she shrugged. "Well, a week is too long."

Reese shoved the covers aside and rose. Josie's eyes immediately landed on his bare body and then darted away.

"You're not going to act embarrassed, are you?" he asked, purposely not grabbing his clothes.

"No, no." She glanced anywhere but at him. "Nothing to be embarrassed about, right? We're both adults and last night was…it was…"

Reese bit the inside of his cheek to keep from laughing at her stammering and her focus darting all around the room like she was trying to find something to land on other than him or their night together.

He rounded the bed and came up behind her. Not touching her took a considerable amount of willpower, though.

"No regrets," he told her.

Josie jumped, clearly unaware he'd moved closer.

"I don't have regrets," she stated, still without looking at him. "I have concerns."

Might as well be the same thing, but he wanted to alleviate any worries.

"Nothing we did was wrong," he told her, taking her shoulders and turning her to face him. "You know that, right?"

Her eyes caught his as she nodded. "I just don't want things to change."

"How would they change? We both had a great time, we both enjoyed it...if your moaning and panting my name were any indicators."

She rolled her eyes and smacked his bare chest, which was the exact response he wanted. He needed to lighten the mood so she didn't feel like this was anything more than what it was...sex between friends. He didn't want her worried or afraid that they couldn't still be the best of friends.

They were both on unfamiliar ground here. And he wasn't sure how the hell to even start setting boundaries. All he knew was that he wanted her on a level he'd never wanted anyone before...the rest could sort itself out later.

"We won't start comparing notes," she said with a smile. "You did your fair share of that sexy clenched-jaw thing so I know you had a good time."

"Sexy jaw thing?" he asked. He had no idea what that meant, but he'd had a good time. He decided to zero in on the fact that she'd called him sexy.

Maybe they would be right back in his bed tonight.

"Your ego needs no help from me," she told him as she took a step back. "And I need to get ready. Coffee is on you this morning."

She sashayed out, but not before tossing him another grin that punched him with a heavy dose of lust. He had no idea how this interview would go or what they'd be expected to do in the photo shoot, but none of that mattered.

Reese was already counting down the time until they came back here, and he could get to know more of that sweet body of hers.

"And if you could slide the back of your fingertips down her cheek," the photographer suggested.

Josie stilled, her palms flat against Reese's chest. He had one arm wrapped around her waist and had her flush against his body, while he used the other hand to obey the photographer's commands.

"Now lock eyes," the photographer added. "Like you're dying to kiss, but you can't."

Well, at least that part wasn't fake. With Reese this close and her hormones still in overdrive from last night, she desperately wanted to feel his lips on hers... sans an audience.

Was that normal? Should she want to strip down her best friend? She wasn't even sure what to call this new-found relationship they'd created, but she also knew if she read too much into it, she'd drive herself mad.

Maybe she just needed to create a new box, one without a label but still a nice, neat area to keep these emotions in for now—until she knew what to do with them.

"A little closer," the photographer stated as she snapped away.

She moved in closer and Josie tried not to break eye contact with Reese, but the lights and the people standing around watching were a bit unnerving.

They'd set up just inside the stunning entryway of Conrad's. With the serene waterfall wall, the suspended glass bulbs showcasing pale greenery, the place seemed simple, yet classy, and perfect for a photo where the photographer wanted to focus on the couple.

"Breathe," Reese whispered.

Her eyes held his and that desire staring back at her had her heart beating even faster. Having sex and being in the dark was one thing, but pretending to be in love with lights and cameras all around was definitely another.

Melissa stood off to the side, smiling like a mother of the bride. Guilt settled deep. All of this had started simply because she wanted her ex to move on.

One failed marriage was embarrassing enough. She didn't want to be known for another unsuccessful relationship. Perhaps she and Reese would fool everyone with these photos of a couple in love and then once they announced they were better off as friends, people would see them in public together, and everything would go back to normal.

She hoped.

"Oh, wait a minute."

Josie jerked away from Reese when her editor interrupted the clicking of the camera.

"Where's her ring?" Melissa asked. "We can't do photo shoot about the engagement without the ring."

Josie froze. The ring? Damn it, she hadn't thought that far ahead. Reese had joked about it, but that had just been him trying to annoy her in that playful way of his. They weren't actually going ring shopping. Good grief, that would be absurd, but she couldn't think of a lie right off the top of her head.

Her eyes darted back to Reese's, who was reaching into his pocket.

"Right here," he stated, producing a ruby set in a diamond band. "I cleaned it for her this morning and we were in a rush to get here, so I slipped it into my pocket."

Josie's attention volleyed between Reese's sexy grin and that ring she'd never seen before in her life. Was he serious? How in the hell did he just procure a ring—a rather impressive, expensive-looking ring—out of his pants pocket? Even Reese wasn't that powerful...was he? How had he made this happen and why hadn't he clued her in on it?

"Here you go, babe."

Reese lifted her left hand and slid the ring into place and the damn thing actually fit like it was made for her. Had he known her ring size, too?

"Let me see," exclaimed her editor.

Josie was busy examining the rock herself because this was seriously a piece of art. When her editor grabbed her hand and squealed, Josie couldn't help but laugh. She glanced back to Reese, who merely winked, as if he'd had everything under control from the start.

Again, the man took care of all the details and never acted like he was put out or tired. How did he do all of that without a planner, a spreadsheet, a personal assistant?

Okay, he had assistants, but Reese was also very hands-on. There was no way he'd send an assistant to get an engagement ring, not even a fake one.

"You two are so lucky," Melissa stated, glancing between Josie and Reese. "Okay, get back to the shoot. I just had to see what he chose and it's absolutely perfect."

Josie glanced around at the crew staring and waiting on them to continue. "Um, could Reese and I have two minutes?"

Everyone nodded and Josie grabbed Reese's hand and pulled him toward the back of the open room. There wasn't much privacy to be had, but she had to use what she could.

She turned so that Reese's broad frame blocked her from the rest of the audience.

"Where did you get this?" she whispered between gritted teeth.

Reese smiled. "I couldn't let my fiancée be without a ring. That wouldn't say much about our love, now would it?"

She narrowed her eyes at his sarcasm.

Of course he only smiled and replied, "I bought it."

He bought it. Like he'd just gone out and gotten a pair of shoes or a new cell phone. She didn't even want to know what this ring cost.

"Can you return it?"

Reese's brows drew in. "Return it? Why?"

She couldn't say much with their current lack of privacy, so she merely widened her eyes and tipped her head, knowing he could practically read her mind most times.

"It's yours, Jo. Think of it as a birthday present if that makes you feel better."

That soft tone of his had her heart melting and she firmly told her heart not to get involved. Whatever this was going on with them had to be structured or the entire faux engagement would explode in her face, taking her heart in the process.

"I'm sorry, but we still have to get to the interview," Melissa chimed in. "We do have deadlines, you know."

Yeah, Josie was well aware of deadlines—when it came to work *and* Reese.

Less than two weeks now.

Josie glanced down to the ring on her finger, the symbol of so much more than what was actually going on. There was another layer of guilt because each day that went by, she found herself deeper into this lie.

The deep red stone stared back at her and she wondered what on earth made him choose one so bold instead of a traditional diamond. She also wondered what the hell she'd do with an engagement ring once the engagement ended.

Reese lifted her hand and kissed the spot just above the ring as his eyes remained locked onto hers.

"Ready?" he asked.

Was she ready? She didn't know how to answer that because she had a feeling he wasn't talking about the pictures.

The ring weighed heavy on her hand as they went back to the crew. This farce was almost over. She only had to hang on until after the Manhattan opening and then they could go back to the way things were before… if that was even possible.

Ten

Reese had never been more relieved than when that interview was over. There were some questions he and Josie definitely had to fudge, but they'd sounded believable and that's all that mattered.

And when he'd asked her to take the rest of the day off, he'd never thought she'd actually do it. Yet here they were, leaving her house after she wanted to pick up a few things and check on the progress of the work.

Reese's crew said it would be at least another week because they'd run into some other issues they were fixing while there. Fine by Reese. He was in no hurry to get her out of his bed.

"I assume you're taking me somewhere for my birthday and it has something to do with the beach."

They both loved being outside whenever possible. Their schedules were so demanding, and nothing relaxed them quite like the gentle waves and the calming winds off the ocean.

Reese pulled out of her drive and said nothing. He wanted this evening to be all about her and he wanted her to relax without worrying about the fake engagement, the article, the renovations on her house…nothing.

He also needed a break from his thoughts and issues. Josie was always the answer when he needed some space from reality.

"I'm not telling you what the surprise is," he stated. "We already went over that."

"That was yesterday. I'm going to find out soon anyway."

"Then that's when you'll know and not a minute before."

He didn't even care that she pouted and turned her attention out the window. He'd planned a perfect birthday evening and she would love it.

"You're coming to the opening with me next weekend, right?" he asked as he turned down his private road.

"I wouldn't miss it."

"I want you to cover it, if you don't mind multitasking as my date and my journalist."

Now she glanced toward him with a smile on her face. How did her smile turn him on? It was such a simple gesture, yet packed such a lustful punch. Maybe that's why he always wanted to make her smile.

"I am quite capable of doing both," she informed him. "So my surprise is at your house?"

Laughing, Reese pulled up and waited for his gate to open. "Something like that."

She remained silent as he parked and gathered her things.

"Follow me," he ordered as he followed the path around the back of the house, leading toward his dock.

"Oh, a ride on the yacht," she exclaimed. "Fun. It's a beautiful afternoon."

A perfect day for relaxing…and maybe more. He'd planned this birthday surprise well before last night, so now he couldn't help but wonder if they'd pick back up where they'd left off.

Reese assisted her down the dock and onto the yacht. His chef stood at the entrance to the cabin and nodded as they stepped on board. Frisco wasn't just his chef, though that was his main position and what he'd been hired for, but the man did absolutely everything Reese asked and typically a little more. He was invaluable.

"Good afternoon, Reese. Miss Coleman."

"Thanks for setting everything up, Frisco." Reese slapped the man on the back. "That will be all. Take the rest of the day off."

"Thank you, sir."

Once Frisco left them, Reese gestured for Josie to step on into the cabin.

"Go change," he urged. "I'll get things ready to go."

"Don't you want to change, too?"

He took a step closer, but didn't reach for her. "Is that an invitation?"

Her eyes clouded with desire, a look that had been new to him only days ago, but now he knew it all too well. Even though they'd only spent one night together, he wanted so much more. One night was not nearly enough time to explore all things Josie.

"Isn't that why you sent Frisco away?" she asked, quirking a brow.

"I sent him away because I want to spend your birthday with you, under the sun and then the stars, out on the water, without anyone around. He's done all I needed him to do."

Her eyes raked down him in a way that he hadn't experienced before. Reese liked this side of Josie and had to admit his ego swelled a little—okay, more than a little—knowing he had a hand in drawing out her passion.

"Maybe I need help changing into my suit," she purred as she reached for the hem of her black pencil dress.

She pulled it up and over her head, tossing the garment to the side. Josie stood before him in only a matching black silky bra-and-pantie set and those little black heels. With all of that dark hair pulled back, he wanted to yank the pins out and mess it all up.

"You surprise me," he told her. "That's not something I ever thought I'd say with you."

Josie shrugged. "I may like to plan everything, but I also know what I want."

Arousal slammed into him.

"And what's that?" he asked.

With her eyes firmly set on his, she reached for the snap of his dress pants. "More of last night."

Reese shoved her hands away and wrapped his arms around her waist, hauling her up against his chest as he claimed her mouth. He needed no further permission to take what she so freely offered.

Josie locked her ankles behind his back as Reese

crossed the living quarters. The accent table on his way stopped him, though. He wasn't going to make it to the bedroom, not with the way Josie was clawing at his shirt.

She jerked his shirt up as he dropped his pants and boxer briefs to the floor. Josie laughed as he attempted to toe off his shoes and kick his clothes aside. A few random strands of her hair had fallen across her face, but he wanted her even more out of control.

Reese reached behind her and released the fastener holding her hair up. The silky strands instantly fell around her shoulders and her laugh quickly sobered as she stared up at him.

He gripped her hips and scooted her closer to the edge of the table. When he slid a finger inside her panties to pull them aside, she curled her fingers around his shoulders.

"Protection?" she asked.

He glanced toward the bedroom where he'd been heading. "In there," he nodded.

She bit down on her lip and jerked her hips against his hand. "I trust you. I just had a checkup and I'm on birth control."

Reese swallowed. Never in his life had he gone without a condom, and knowing he had the okay to do so with Josie was a hell of an unexpected turn-on.

"I'm clean," he assured her. "I'd never do anything to hurt you."

She locked her gaze with his and nodded, giving him the silent affirmation to go ahead.

Holding the thin material aside, Reese slid into her, earning him another of her slow, sultry moans.

He gritted his teeth, taking just a fraction of a moment to relish the fact that no barriers stood between them. This was a first for him.

But the urge and the overwhelming need to have her took hold again and he couldn't remain still. Josie lifted her pelvis against his, urging him on, and Reese was more than ready to comply.

Josie lifted her knees against his sides, wrapped her arms around his neck and covered his mouth. He might physically be in the dominant position, but she held all the power. He was utterly useless when it came to her, and she could do anything she wanted.

There was frantic need coming off her in waves, a feeling he couldn't quite identify, but now was not the time to analyze her every thought or motive. All he wanted was more of this reckless, unrestrained Josie.

Reese reached around and flicked open her bra. Never removing his lips from hers, he fumbled enough to get the bra off and away so he could claim handfuls of her breasts. He wanted all of her, as much as she would give, and he was so damn glad he didn't have to hide his desire anymore.

"Reese," she murmured against his lips.

Her body quickened and he slid a hand between them to touch her at her most sensitive spot, knowing it would drive her over the edge.

Her gasp against his mouth and the way her entire body tightened had him pumping even faster, working toward his own release. Josie cried out and dropped her head to that crook in his neck. Reese used his free hand to press against the small of her back, making them even more flush for the best possible experience.

That's when euphoria took over and his body started

trembling. Josie's warm breath hit the side of his neck, only adding to the shivers consuming him.

Her fingers slid through his hair as she placed a kiss on his heated skin.

Reese blew out a slow breath when his body calmed. It took another minute for him to regain the strength to pull away, but he only eased back slightly to look down at her.

"Still need help with that suit?" he asked.

"I think I need some water," she laughed. "And maybe food if that's any indication of how my birthday surprise is going to go."

Reese smiled. "That's not exactly what I had planned for your birthday, so we're both surprised."

Reese took a step back and helped her from the table. He still wore his shirt and nothing else, while she still had on her panties, which were now very askew.

Fast, frantic sex had never crossed his mind when it came to Josie. He'd always thought he'd take his time and explore every inch of her. He hadn't rushed last night, but he still hadn't taken the time he wanted. And just now? Yeah, that was the fastest sex on his record.

But he wasn't sorry.

Josie had set the pace; she had wanted him here and now. Who was he to deny her…and on her birthday no less?

Reese unbuttoned his shirt and went to pick up his other clothes strewn over the floor.

Josie slid out of her panties and gathered her things, throwing him a smile over her shoulder as she headed toward the suite.

Reese barely got to enjoy the bare view when his

cell chimed in the pocket of his pants. He shuffled the pieces in his hand until he could find the phone. Clutching everything under his arm, he glanced to the screen and contemplated letting it go to voice mail. He really didn't want any interruptions, but his parents couldn't just be ignored.

And he was going to have to tell them what he'd found. They were going to be at his new opening, but he needed to talk to them before that. His big night in Manhattan certainly wasn't the time to tell them he was aware of the adoption and knew who his biological father was.

With a sigh, he slid his finger over the screen.

"Hey," he answered. "Still enjoying the mountains?"

"Hi, sweetheart," his mother answered in that smiling tone she had. "We are actually heading back home. We're on our way to the airport now."

"Home?" he questioned. "I thought you were only coming to New York next weekend. Are you guys okay?"

"We're fine," she assured him. "You know how your dad is. He just feels useless if he's not doing something productive."

"He retired," Reese reminded her. "He's supposed to be useless right now, relaxing in some amazing location that will give you guys all the drinks and massages you want."

His mother laughed. "Sounds good to me, but I think he misses you. I mean, I do, too, but he worries you're taking on too much and he just wants to support you and be there if you need advice."

Reese pinched the bridge of his nose and closed his eyes. "I've been doing this my whole life. I've got it covered."

"I tried to tell him that, but you have to remember he doesn't know what to do with his days right now. Just, maybe give him a little piddly job or, I don't know, ask his opinion on something?"

There were a million things involved in running a successful chain of upscale restaurants, and that was before adding in a brand-new opening. Reese could no doubt find something for his father.

Josie came back through wearing a one-piece black bathing suit that shouldn't have his body revving up again, but…well, it did.

"I'll see what I can do," Reese told his mother without taking his eyes off Josie. "Could you and Dad come to the house tomorrow?"

"I'm sure we can. Everything all right?"

Reese tore his eyes from Josie. He hadn't meant to just blurt out that he needed to see them, but now that he had, he'd follow through. As uncomfortable as this conversation was going to be, he wanted the truth.

"I'm fine," he assured her. "I just have something I don't want to discuss over the phone."

"Well, I'm intrigued. We'll be there around one if that works for you."

"I'll have Frisco prepare lunch. Have a safe flight. Love you, Mom."

He hung up and clutched his cell at his side. Should he just leave this letter alone? He and his parents had a great relationship; there was no reason to pull all of this past out in the open.

But he had two half brothers that he wanted to pursue a relationship with and he had to be honest with his parents about the events that had happened since they'd been gone.

"Are you skinny-dipping or putting on trunks?"

Josie's question pulled him back to the moment. He glanced toward the glass doors overlooking the sparkling ocean and back to the woman who expected him to follow through on this birthday celebration.

She deserved it all, and he wasn't going to let this unexpected bomb in his personal life affect her day.

"Do you have a preference?" he asked with a wink.

She merely laughed and shook her head. "You sounded serious with your mom. If this fake engagement is getting to be too much, you can go ahead and tell her the truth."

"What? No, that's not it." He sat his clothes down on the curved sofa and pulled on his boxer briefs. "I just have something to discuss with them that I don't want to wait on since they're coming home early."

Josie tipped her head, her ponytail sliding over one shoulder. "Is it the restaurant opening? You haven't acted like you're worried about it."

"I'm not," he assured her truthfully. "My team is on it and I was just up there. I know that night will be perfect."

Her brows drew in. "Oh, I didn't know there was something else bothering you. I just assume if something is wrong that you know I'm always here to listen."

Well, now he felt like a jerk.

Reese stepped forward, wanting to console her, but selfishly wanting his hands back on her body. He found the more he was with her, the more difficult it was to keep his distance…especially now that he knew exactly how she felt and how she trembled beneath his touch.

"I do tell you everything," he assured her. "You're my best friend, Jo. Let's just enjoy your day and talk tomorrow. Deal?"

He really needed to talk to his parents before he opened up to her. He owed them that much, giving them the courtesy of explaining their side and listening to what they had to say.

Josie reached up and patted his cheek. "Ignore me. You don't owe me an explanation. I just want you to know I'm here anytime."

His settled his hands on the dip in her waist and pulled her closer. "I'm well aware you're here. But today, let me pamper you. Now go out and lounge on the sundeck. I'll get changed and we'll take off. I'll join you in a bit."

She looked like she wanted to say more, but she nodded and stepped away. When she hit the steps leading up, she turned back.

"Hurry. I need someone to rub sunscreen on my back."

That was an invitation he couldn't ignore. For now, he was just going to focus on Josie. He wasn't going to think about the father he'd never met, telling his parents he knew the truth and he certainly wasn't going to think about the way the words *best friends* sounded wrong when he'd said them because they were more.

He just had to figure out how the hell to keep both of them from getting hurt when this all went back to platonic, because after he had his opening in Manhattan when they needed to be seen arm in arm, they would have to face reality.

And the reality was…all of this was temporary.

Eleven

Josie barely recognized herself. First, she'd ditched work, then she'd lain around the yacht letting Reese ply her with mai tais, and now she was enjoying a candlelight dinner on the deck with the full moon shining down on them.

She had to admit this birthday was turning out to be pretty awesome.

"You're going to spoil me," she told him as she reached for her wineglass.

Reese sat his napkin on the table and leaned back in his chair. "It's your birthday. I'm supposed to spoil you."

Josie didn't mean just today or in this moment. She meant in general. Reese had always been the one to comfort her, to make sure she was happy, to have her back at all times.

Hence the faux engagement.

But the undercurrent in this relationship had shifted and she was discovering that it was difficult to find her footing. She should feel guilty for wanting more sex, for enjoying it as much as she was, because there would come a time when they had to revert back to being just friends. They couldn't go on this way forever. At some point, Reese might want to find someone and settle down and have a family. That's how he was raised; that's all he knew—family and business.

Oh, she knew he dated and jet-setted around with multiple women, but none of those relationships lasted and he'd never claimed to have been in love before. He'd also never acted like he wanted to marry anytime soon, which had made that engagement months ago all the more shocking, but Josie knew the day would come. Reese's genetic makeup was that of a family man, of heritage and legacy. Those were just traits ingrained in him.

She, on the other hand, knew nothing of that type of commitment or long-term bond and the idea terrified her. Her family had been ripped apart, and then the emotional walls went up. Reese had been the only one she'd firmly clung to.

She was proud of herself, though. She'd stepped out of her comfort zone and been bold enough to take what she wanted. But how did she go back to what she'd been once everything was done? When they didn't need to show their faces to the public and they could just be Reese and Josie, best friends? Was that even possible?

So, sex was good. It was great, in fact. Josie figured she'd just enjoy herself, enjoy this bit of freedom she'd never allowed herself to have, and hope nobody got hurt in the end because she still needed that rock her best friend provided. She always had.

Josie glanced down to the ring on her finger and couldn't deny how much she loved the sparkling piece. The oval ruby surrounded by twinkling diamonds. She'd never given an engagement ring much thought before.

"Looks good on you."

She turned her attention to Reese, who nodded toward her hand. "I knew a ruby would look good on you."

"You were just dying to get some color on me," she laughed. "It's beautiful, but you know I can't keep this."

"Sure you can. I told you, consider it your birthday gift, but for now the public can believe it's your engagement ring."

"Reese—"

He reached across the table and grabbed her hand, stroking his thumb over the stone. "A friend can't buy another friend a nice birthday gift?"

She didn't know why every time he threw out the word *friend* she felt a little…off. Josie couldn't quite find the right word for how the word made her feel, but it certainly wasn't settled.

She hated disruption in her life. She'd grown up with a very regimented, standoffish father, and all of that rearing had carried over into her adult life. Everything had changed after her mother passed because, looking back, Josie realized that it was her mother who had been doting and loving, while her father demanded structure and obedience.

Josie still craved that safe zone, the comfort of knowing every aspect of her life was in the proper place.

"I got you something else," he said, hopping up from the table.

"I don't need anything else," she laughed. "The cruise, the dinner, the ring. I'm good, Reese."

He smiled down at her. "Trust me, this was not expensive, but I couldn't resist."

Now she was intrigued. She waited while he stepped down into the cabin and then came back holding a small, narrow box that was so small there was no bow. Just simple wrapping.

"It's really not much," he repeated, handing the gift over. "But I hope you'll put it to good use."

She took the gift, but kept her eyes on him. "It's too small to be a sex toy."

Reese laughed. "I'm all the sex toy you need right now."

Right now.

Josie let the words wash over her. She tried to brush them aside, but they wiggled their way right past the giddiness that consumed her and hit her heart. The simple term took hold, threatening to penetrate and cause pain.

She refused to let their current situation hurt her or damage their friendship.

Ignoring thoughts of the future, Josie tore the paper and discovered her present.

"A tube of red lipstick?"

She glanced up to Reese, who stood there smiling.

"I figure if you're not comfortable wearing the clothes, maybe we could ease you into the color."

She stared at the name brand and was actually impressed he'd known what to purchase. "I'm not sure bright red lips would be easing into wearing color."

"Just try it," he told her. "Don't let fear win, Jo. That's all this is. Fear. It's a tube of lipstick. I'm not asking you to skydive."

Josie took the cosmetic from the box and slid the lid off. Turning the base, she stared at the vibrant shade and wondered how the hell she could pull that off. Her makeup regimen consisted of mascara, black of course, and sometimes a sheer gloss if she wanted to be extra.

"Listen," he told her as he pulled his chair around the table and next to hers. He grabbed her hands and set the tube on the table. "I'm not trying to make you into someone you're not. I'm not trying to make you uncomfortable, but you have all of this inside of you. If you want to channel your mother or pay tribute to her in some way, then do it. Do it for you, and who gives a damn what other people think."

She stared into those bright blue eyes and wondered how she'd never gotten lost in them before. How had she never noticed just how remarkable Reese was? Not just to look at, because she'd known for years how hot he was, but he was her friend…right? She shouldn't have had lustful thoughts.

Yet now she did.

They'd been intimate a handful of times and she already had enough fantasies to last a lifetime.

Beyond his looks, though, there was that heart of gold. He dominated everything around him, but not in an asshole kind of way. Yes, he demanded respect, but his loyal circle of friends and employees loved him and would do anything for him. That was the sign of a true leader.

"Why did we never date when we were younger?"

she asked before she could stop herself, because they weren't even dating now.

His brows drew in as he released her hands and sat back in his chair. "I asked you out."

Confused, Josie racked her brain, but drew a blank. "You did? When?"

"In college," he told her as if she should remember. "I was helping you move from the dorm into your first apartment and I asked you out."

She recalled when he'd helped her. They thought they'd never get her hand-me-down couch up that flight of stairs to the second floor. They'd laughed, argued, shared a horrible pizza for dinner.

Oh yeah. That's when he'd asked her.

"I thought you were joking," she finally stated, but caught the sober look on his face. "You were serious?"

Reese didn't smile. He didn't make a move as he continued to stare back at her. "I'd never been more serious."

Oh. Well.

What did she do with that information?

She couldn't exactly go back in time, but if she could, would she have said yes? Josie had never thought of Reese as more than a friend until recently, but the word *more* was such a blanket term. It could be applied to anything.

She didn't know how to reply to his statement, but he had clearly thought about this over the years because he hadn't forgotten the moment. Obviously, there had been a bigger impact on him than her.

What exactly did that mean? Surely he didn't want to take this beyond best friend territory…did he?

"Reese, I—"

He leaned forward and cut her words off with a kiss. She melted into his powerful touch, completely forgetting anything she needed to say.

"No more talking," he murmured against her lips. "I want you wearing nothing but that ring and the moonlight."

Shivers raced through her at his sexy command. Anything they needed to discuss or work out with this relationship could be done later, because Reese was stripping her clothes off and she had a feeling she was about to get another birthday present.

"I discovered I'm adopted."

Josie's gasp over the warm night air seemed to echo.

It was well past midnight, so technically her birthday was over. They were on their way back to his place, fully dressed, and he found he couldn't keep the news from her any longer. The only people who knew that he knew the truth were strangers. Reese needed her advice and her shoulder to lean on. That was the main thing he valued about their relationship. Even when he was trying to be strong, to put up a front of steel, he could let his guard down around her and she never criticized or judged him.

He'd wanted to tell his parents first. He really thought he owed them that. But the other part of him needed Josie's advice on how to handle such a delicate situation. There was nobody he trusted more with this secret.

"Adopted?" she repeated. "Reese, how... I mean, who told you? Are you sure?"

He guided the yacht toward his dock. In the distance,

his three-story beachfront home lit up the shoreline. He always loved this time of night when the water was calm and quiet. He needed a stillness in however he could manage to gain one, in order to keep his sanity.

"I'm pretty certain," he told her, still keeping his eye on the dock. "I also found out I have two half brothers in Green Valley, Tennessee."

"That was the reason for your trip."

He nodded as he felt her come up beside him. The wind whipped her hair, sending strands drifting over his bare arm.

"Who are your birth parents?" she asked.

Reese shrugged. "I received a letter from a woman who I found out was my half brother's mom. She was dying and before she passed, she sent three letters. Even her son didn't know who his father was growing up, but she wanted to clear the air, I guess. Anyway, I don't know about my birth mother, but my biological father is Rusty Lockwood."

"Lockwood," she murmured. "As in, Lockwood Lightning?"

"Yeah."

"Wow." Josie laid her delicate hand on his arm for support. "Have you met him?"

Reese slowed the engine as he neared the dock. "No, but I've not heard pleasant things about him and in my own research, I've read some disturbing news. He's certainly no comparison to Martin Conrad."

The gentle squeeze from her touch had a bit of his anxiety sliding away.

"Nobody is Martin Conrad," she agreed. "Do your parents know you found this out?"

"No. That's what I want to talk to them about to-morrow."

He still didn't know how to approach the topic other than just showing them the letter and giving them a chance to explain.

"Do you...um, do you need me there?" she asked, her tone low, uncertain. "I mean, I don't want to step over the line and make you uncomfortable, but if you need someone—"

Reese reached up and slid his hand over hers as he glanced her way for a brief moment. "I want you there."

She seemed to exhale a breath and her body relaxed against his. "I don't even know what to say, but I'll do whatever I can for you."

He knew she would. He knew no matter what decision he made, she would stand by him.

"I'm going to Green Valley in a few days." He steered the ship expertly between the docks. "I'd like you to come with me if you can get away."

"I'll make the time, and I can always work on the road," she told him. "Or are we taking the jet?"

"It's going to be a quick trip," he stated, killing the engine. "We'll fly to save time."

She nodded and smiled. "Tell me when to be ready and I'll be there."

Once the yacht was secure and he'd assisted her off the dock, Reese blocked her path to head back to the house. He framed her face with his hands and leaned closer.

"You said I would spoil you, but I think it's the other way around," he murmured against her mouth. "Maybe I'm the one getting spoiled because I don't deserve all I want to take from you."

Reese wrapped his arms around her, pulling her against his chest and claiming her lips. He didn't want to talk, didn't want to think, didn't want to consider tomorrow or even the day after that. Right now, he wanted to take Jo back to his bedroom and show her just how much he ached for her.

Because their two weeks were slowly coming to an end, and he wasn't quite ready to let this physical relationship go. And maybe there was more, maybe there was something beyond the physical. Reese wasn't sure if he was getting the friendship bond confused with something more or not...he only prayed nobody got hurt in the end.

Twelve

"Darling, you look so happy."

Reese cringed when his mother wrapped her arms around him and then stepped back to examine him and Josie, who stood at his side.

"I cannot tell you how thrilled I am that the two of you are together," she went on. "I've known for years you were the one for my son."

Josie's eyes darted to his, but Reese merely smiled. He had bigger things to deal with right now than this fake engagement. He was about to crush the two people who loved him more than anything, who'd raised him like their own, who'd given him the life he lived today.

But they all deserved for the secrets to come out so they could move forward. He'd had time to deal with the truth. He knew his parents were good people and they likely had done what they thought was in his best interest.

"Can we at least get inside before you start smothering them?" Martin asked as he stepped into the foyer.

Reese stared at the man he'd always thought of as his father. He'd never given it much thought, but other than the fact that they were both tall with broad shoulders, there were no other similarities.

Laura reached for Josie and wrapped her arms around her, too. Reese hated the guilt that layered in with his anxiety. He'd never held on to this many secrets at one time in his life.

Between the engagement and the news about his biological father, Reese had to get something out in the open before he drove himself mad. The only saving grace in all of this was that Josie was finally in his bed, where he'd wanted her for longer than he cared to admit. Granted, now he didn't know how to take a step back with her into that friend territory. He honestly wasn't sure he wanted to, but they'd agreed that after his opening, they would make an announcement that they were better off as friends and call off this fake engagement.

What did it say about him that he wasn't ready for that announcement?

"Oh, my word, that ring is gorgeous," his mother declared, holding Josie's hand. "So unique and perfect."

"It's really beautiful," Josie stated, but Reese didn't miss the tightness in her tone. "Why don't you guys come on in? Frisco set up lunch out on the back deck."

Reese was thankful Josie took over and turned the attention away from the engagement, but that meant the next topic was another he didn't want to get into.

Lunch flew by with chatter and laughter, but Reese knew time was ticking and he'd have to just pull the letter from his pocket and share.

Josie's fingertip drew a pattern over the condensation on her water glass and he knew she was feeling all the nerves as well. He met her gaze and she offered him a reassuring smile.

"I'm glad to see you guys," Reese started. "But there's something I need to discuss."

His mother sat back in her seat and shifted her attention. "Yes, you have me intrigued. Is this about New York? You're not moving, are you?"

Reese shook his head. "I love it here and I'm fine with traveling wherever I need."

"Is something wrong, son?" his father asked, resting his elbows on the arms of the dining chair.

Reese reached into his pocket and pulled out the letter. He passed it to his father.

"I received this right after you were released from the hospital and I didn't want to bring it up," he added. "And then I wanted you guys to enjoy your trip, so I kept it to myself until I could sort things out."

Martin Conrad's eyes darted from Reese down to the folded letter. He opened the paper and started reading. It didn't take long for the color to drain from his face.

"Martin, what is it?"

His father remained silent as he finished reading, but ultimately he handed the letter across the table.

Reese's heart beat so hard, so fast, but he tried to remain calm. This was the best move in the long run; there would just be some painful hurdles to overcome.

Surprisingly, his mother didn't get upset. She squared

her shoulders and placed the letter on the table, running her fingertip along the creases in a vain attempt to smooth it out.

Her dark brown eyes finally came up to his.

"I want you to know we did everything we could to make the best decision at the time," she told him. "We went through an agency, but the birth parents wanted to remain anonymous."

"That's when we decided not to tell you about the adoption because we had no more information to give," his father added. "You were our son from day one. Blood didn't matter."

No, it didn't. These were his parents and there had never been any doubt the lengths they would go to to make him happy and show their love.

"Do you hate us?" his mother finally asked. "I don't think I could stand it if you were upset with us. We just wanted to give you the best life."

Reese scooted his chair back and went around to his mom. "Never," he said, leaning down to wrap his arms around her. "I could never hate either of you. I just didn't want to keep this from you. I may always wonder why you didn't tell me before, but I respect that you have your reasons. I've never been a parent or in your shoes, so I can't judge."

"Well, now you have the birth father's name," his dad chimed in. "Have you reached out to him?"

Reese straightened, but kept his hand on his mother's shoulder. "No. I wouldn't have done that before talking to you. I did go to Green Valley, Tennessee, though. I've met with my half brothers. Nick Campbell and Sam Hawkins."

"Sam Hawkins," his dad murmured. "He's the son of Rusty Lockwood, too?"

Reese nodded. "And Nick is a major investor and renovator. He's opening a resort this fall in the Smoky Mountains. A project his late mom started."

"Sounds like all the boys turned out well," his mom said. "I don't know Rusty, other than through the Lockwood Lightning name."

Reese glanced to Josie, who had given her silent support this entire time. He wasn't sure what all to get into regarding Rusty, but he knew he didn't want to think about it right now. He'd let the secret out; that had been his main goal.

"I plan on going back to Green Valley," Reese added. "Sam and Nick want to confront Rusty. All of us together."

His mother inhaled sharply and glanced up at him. He saw the fear in her eyes, but she remained strong. Two of the strongest women he'd ever known both had their eyes on him.

"I only want to meet him, maybe see if he knows the name of the woman who gave birth to me."

Now Laura Conrad's eyes did well up. The last thing he wanted was to cause her pain.

"I may not do anything with the information," he assured her. "I honestly don't know. All I know is this is still new to me and you guys have had years to process. I'm asking you to trust me to do what is right for me now."

Martin came to his feet and eased around the patio table. "Of course we trust you, son. You do what you think is best. We'll support you."

Reese nodded, worried if he said too much, emotions would clog his throat and overcome him. This delicate situation demanded control.

His father reached out and wrapped his arms around Reese. Patting his back, Reese took the embrace, this one meaning so much more than any in the past.

"Will you keep us posted on what you find?" his mother asked.

Reese turned back to face her and smiled. "Of course. Josie and I are going to Tennessee in a couple of days. I'm not sure how long we'll be there, so we may just go on to New York from there."

His mom came to her feet and opened her arms. He gathered her in, recognizing as always how petite yet resilient she was.

"I hope you find what you're looking for," she whispered. "I just don't want this to change us."

He eased back and held on to her slender shoulders. "You guys are my parents. Nothing can change that."

Over his mother's shoulder, Reese caught Josie swiping a tear. He didn't even think of the emotional impact this would have on her. Having a distant relationship with her father and no mother, this had to be difficult, seeing him with such a strong bond with both of his parents.

"I'll just leave you guys and start cleaning up." Josie eased her chair back and started reaching for the dishes. "I'll bring dessert in a few minutes."

"Don't clean up," Reese told her, but she was already stacking plates and carrying them away.

"You've got a good woman there," his father declared. "It's going to take a strong woman by your side to do the work we do."

Reese was well aware of that, but he hadn't thought of Josie by his side in that sense for the long term. They were friends…friends enjoying the hell out of each other and helping the other out during a difficult time.

Would his parents be disappointed when he told them he and Josie weren't actually going to get married? Maybe, but he would have to cross that bridge when they got to it.

And it wasn't like Josie was going anywhere, right? She would still be by his side as his friend. Her support was all he needed—the intimacy was just the fulfillment of something he'd been fantasizing about.

He had so many career goals to achieve before thinking of anything long-term with a woman. Besides, Josie never acted like she was ready for a commitment, either. So why was he stressing? Why was he feeling a heaviness, knowing the end of this farce was near?

"I was also thinking we could do a live timeline piece."

Josie had been taking diligent notes about the new spring options for her column. Even though they hadn't reached fall yet, the industry was always looking ahead at least one or two seasons. They had to stay ahead of other competing journalists, bloggers and magazines. The entire industry was one big race to see who could reveal the next season's hottest styles, fashions, dinner party themes and so much more.

"I'd like to document your journey to the aisle," Melissa stated with much more glee than Josie was feeling.

Josie stared down at the ruby. She couldn't stop staring at it. When she worked, there it was. When she drove, there it was. When she was sipping her morning coffee, there it was.

Always a reminder of this farce she'd started.

"I've got so much other material to cover," Josie stated. "I'm super excited about the fall spread I'm doing on various ciders and pairings. I think it will be great to incorporate those with a coastal feel since not everyone can have a bonfire and hoodies."

"Yes, yes," her editor agreed. "I love that idea, too, but I'd like to hand that one off and have you solely focus on this engagement."

Josie closed her eyes and took a deep breath. What could she say? Until the Manhattan opening, she and Reese were playing the part of lovers in love.

She had the lover part down, but she didn't know about the "in love" part.

Did she?

No. That would be silly. They weren't in love; they were just friends. Sure she loved him in that best-friend way, but what did she know about being in love with someone? She'd never experienced any such emotion.

She blew out her breath and attempted to relax. Once this was all over, she wouldn't be so anxious and have to take so many calming breaths…she hoped.

"That's fine," Josie reluctantly agreed.

She'd still get that fall piece back once Melissa realized there wasn't actually going to be a wedding, so there was nothing to worry about. Josie would just keep those notes saved on her computer and continue to work silently on that project.

"Would you be opposed to me sending a photographer with you when you look at dresses?" she asked. "Obviously, not taking shots when you find the one."

Dresses? Um, she wasn't going to go quite that far in this charade.

"I won't be looking at dresses for a while." Josie felt a little better about that true statement. "Reese is so busy with his opening in Manhattan, and we are taking a short trip to Tennessee before that. We can discuss the dress situation when I return."

And that would buy the time she needed to come clean.

"I can work with that time frame, but we'll need to post some things on the blog. Maybe you could share some of your favorite places where you'll be registering or we could do a fun poll on where viewers think you should honeymoon."

Registering and honeymoons were definitely not on her radar. Josie wanted out of this conversation and off the phone so she could start packing for her trip. She was both anxious and excited to go away with Reese. She wanted to meet Nick and Sam and she was more than ready to get away.

"Maybe a poll of favorite flowers?" Josie suggested. "Something simple, but not too much."

"Great idea. I'll get something put up tomorrow, but make sure you interact with the viewers." Her editor laughed. "Why did I tell you that? Of course you will. This is the happiest time of your life."

Josie glanced to the ring again. Maybe not the happiest, but definitely the most interesting.

"I'll be sure to hop on over the next few days," Josie promised.

She finally ended the call and sat back in her chair.

Pushing aside all the wedding talk and engagement whirlwind was going to be best for this trip. None of this was real, so letting it occupy space in her mind would only drive her crazy.

Josie came to her feet and shifted her focus to the trip. She needed to be Reese's support system for this. When he'd told his parents, Josie had been surprised at how well they took the news that Reese had discovered the truth. She'd been overcome with emotion at their precious bond, at the hurdles they faced as a team and conquered together.

She shouldn't feel sorry for herself. Maybe her entire life would've been different had her mother lived, but that was not the way things were meant to be. Josie knew her father loved her. He just had closed in on himself and become even more regimented since he'd retired from the military, and that was okay. She could look back now and see that he had struggled. Everyone dealt with loss differently.

Josie headed to the bedroom she had been sharing with Reese. The work on her house was almost done, but she wouldn't be staying there until she and Reese returned from New York. When they returned, the farce would be over, the engagement would end and they'd go back to being just friends.

The looming deadline weighed heavy on her. She didn't know why. They'd been friends before; they'd be friends again.

But now that she'd been intimate with him, how

could she give that up? They'd grown closer than she'd ever thought possible. But there was no future for them as an actual couple. There was no reason to be delusional about the truth.

Nope. Reese would go right back into that best-friend box and one day they would look back at this engagement and just laugh.

Right?

Thirteen

Reese slid his hand into Josie's as they made their way toward the entrance of Hawkins Distillery. This time walking in was no easier than the first, but at least now he had her by his side.

True, he'd already met the guys, but now there were more details to discuss and their lives would continue to intertwine.

Sam had arranged for a private dinner after closing hours so they would all have privacy and could freely talk. Apparently, Sam's and Nick's significant others were going to be here as well, so Reese was doubly glad he wouldn't be the fifth wheel.

"I've never heard you this quiet," she murmured as they neared the main entrance.

"How can you hear me being quiet?"

She laughed and slapped his arm. "You know what I mean."

He did and he appreciated her concern. Giving her hand a gentle squeeze, he stepped to the entrance and gripped the wrought iron door handle as he turned to face her.

"I know what you mean, but I'm fine. Nervous, but it helps that you're here." He tipped his head, his eyes darting to her lips. "You still haven't worn that red lipstick. Saving it for a special occasion?"

She rolled her eyes. "I can't just wear red lipstick, Reese."

"You can," he countered. "We all have to face our fears, Jo. Step out of our comfort zone sometimes to see what or who we can become."

Josie stared at him, then leaned in and gently kissed him before easing back. It took quite a bit to surprise Reese, but her spontaneous show of affection, when they didn't need to put on a show or weren't heading into the bedroom, surprised him.

"Since you're facing your fear, you looked like you needed it," she told him with a smile before he could question her.

Releasing the door, he framed her face and gave her a proper kiss. There was no gentleness, no lead-in. This woman was an addiction he couldn't let go of anytime soon.

When he eased back, still holding on to her, her eyes remained closed and her mouth open. He stroked his thumb across her lower lip.

"I always need that," he murmured.

Her lids slowly lifted as she refocused on him. "What's happening between us?"

A knot in his stomach tightened. He had no clue how to answer that because he wasn't quite sure himself. He knew she was his best friend, knew that they were more than compatible in the bedroom and knew she'd always stood by his side. But he wasn't sure beyond that. In his world right now, he had a mess that needed to be cleaned up before he could think too much about anything else.

"Let's curb this topic for later," he suggested.

She stared another minute before ultimately nodding. He kissed her once more before letting her go and opening the door. He gestured for her to go ahead of him and then he followed her in.

"Wow," she muttered as soon as they were inside.

Reese had to admit, the place was spectacularly done in an industrial, modern yet old-charm combination. The exposed brick walls, scarred wood floors, and leather-and-metal chairs in the lobby area were perfect. Definitely masculine, rustic, very Smoky Mountains and spot-on for a distillery.

"I've never been to a distillery," she told him. "I may just have to do an article on Hawkins because this place is amazing, and I only just walked in. Think I could get a guided tour?"

"Of course you can."

Reese turned to see Sam striding toward them. He reached out and shook Reese's hand, then turned his attention to Josie.

"I'm Sam Hawkins," he stated. "I'll give you a tour anytime you want. After dinner, if you have the time."

Josie's smile widened and nodded. "I'm Josie and I'd love that, but I should tell you I'm a journalist, so I ask all the questions."

Sam laughed and folded his arms across his chest.

"I'm aware of who you are, and you can ask all the questions you want."

Of course Sam had done his research. He'd invited virtual strangers into his space, strangers who were near family. Reese had done his share of looking into all parties in attendance as well.

Sam's fiancée, Maty Taylor, was an attorney. Actually, she had been Rusty's attorney, so Reese had to assume that's how Maty and Sam met.

Then there was Nick and his fiancée, Silvia Lane. Silvia was expecting a baby and the two were finishing up a spectacular resort in the mountains. Reese had every intention of booking their best suite once it opened.

"We'll discuss a possible article later," Josie promised.

Sam nodded. "Sounds good. Everyone is already in the back if you guys want to follow me."

Josie slid her hand into Reese's. The fact that he didn't even have to ask for her support just proved how in tune they were with each other. He might be a bundle of nerves on the inside, but having her with him during the most difficult, worrisome time in his life was absolutely invaluable.

They headed all the way into the back where a large enclosed dining area had been set up. The three exterior walls were all windows, providing a breathtaking view of the mountains.

"This is our main tasting room." Sam directed his comment to Josie. "I can set you up with a tasting after the tour, too, or you can try anything you want with your dinner."

Josie's smile beamed once again and Reese could

feel the excitement rolling off of her. This was why she excelled at her job. She truly loved what she did, and it showed through her enthusiasm and her research.

Reese turned his attention to the other three in the room. They stood in a group near the table all set up and he found that their smiling faces put his nerves at ease. Instinct had gotten him far in business and he had a good feeling about today, about the future.

"You must be Reese and Josie." A slender woman with long blond hair approached them and extended her hand. "I'm Maty Taylor, Sam's fiancée. We're really glad you both could join us."

The other two came around the table as well, and Reese felt the nerves slip away as all of the introductions were made. There was something so ironic that the three men were all broad and powerful and each of the women they were with appeared to be bold, confident. Reese wondered what other underlying similarities they all shared.

"I'm Nick Campbell and this is my fiancée, Silvia Lane."

Silvia had a small baby bump and Reese felt a twinge of jealousy. What would Josie look like pregnant with his child?

But immediately, he shut that question down. He wasn't ready for long-term with her or anyone else. He and Josie were forging their way through this new territory and the thought of a child terrified him.

That one-day-family idea he'd had wasn't coming anytime soon. He had too many plans he wanted to have in place before he started thinking about his legacy.

"I have to be honest," Maty said, leaning toward

Josie. "Silvia and I are giddy with excitement that you're here. We absolutely love your column."

Reese watched as Josie simply beamed. "Thank you so much. I love meeting readers one-on-one. Writing can be a lonely industry."

"And congratulations on the engagement," Silvia added. "Isn't it funny how life works? The guys all discover they're brothers and we all have recently become engaged."

Josie glanced to Reese and he literally saw the proverbial shield come down, masking her true emotions. Nobody knew her like he did, so her reaction wouldn't be noticeable. Still, he hated they were in a position to lie.

He also hated that he'd heard Chris had still been leaving notes and flowers on Josie's doorstep. His construction crew had kindly informed Reese of that fact, and Reese had sent Chris a not-so-subtle text telling the guy to move on or face harassment charges.

Hopefully that was the end of the issue.

The women seemed to shift and congregate discussing weddings and babies…neither topic appealed to Reese, so he moved toward Nick and Sam.

"Thanks for making the trip," Nick said. "I'm sure this is still a shock to you."

Reese tucked his thumbs through his belt loops and nodded. "I'm getting used to the idea. I spoke with my parents, so that was the toughest part."

"I can't imagine," Nick added. "Sam and I have a meeting set up with Rusty tomorrow evening at seven. We're actually meeting in his office."

Reese listened to the details about how the charges

of embezzlement were sticking, how Rusty was about to lose everything and how Sam had never revealed to Rusty that he was Sam's father.

"So Rusty only knows of you?" Reese asked Nick. Nick nodded.

"I didn't want anything from him," Sam chimed in. "I didn't want money or to merge our businesses, nothing. I didn't want to give him any inkling that I was his son, but after thinking it over, I don't care if he knows. He's tried to buy my distillery for years now and I'm more than happy to show him just how powerful I've become. He's got nothing on me."

Well, Rusty was in for one hell of a surprise when he discovered he had two more bouncing baby boys.

Laughter from the women filtered through the open space and Reese couldn't help but smile. Josie fit into every single aspect of his life. He wondered what that kiss meant earlier, the one just outside when she'd claimed it was because he needed it.

Was she developing stronger feelings? Was he?

He glanced over his shoulder and she happened to glance his way. She sent him a wink that packed a punch, but not of lust. There was something building between them, something he wasn't sure he was ready for.

Regardless of what happened once their two-week sham was over, Reese knew he would never be the same.

"That was so much fun," Josie exclaimed as she and Reese made their way into the cabin they'd rented. "I cannot believe I got a tour, a tasting and an invite to come back to watch firsthand production."

Reese unlocked the door and ushered her inside the

spacious mountainside cottage. Well, this particular cabin was called "Cozy Cottage" but there was nothing tiny about the four-thousand-square-foot space. Josie didn't realize how much she would love the mountains until she and Reese had driven up to this secluded rental. No wonder people always wanted to vacation here.

She might be a beach girl at heart, but she had a feeling the mountains would be calling her name again and again.

"And here I was worried you'd feel left out," Reese joked as he tossed his keys onto the table by the front door. "Sam seemed pretty anxious to let you interview him for a piece."

Josie smoothed her hair back and crossed her arms. "You're not jealous, are you?"

Reese held her gaze and cocked his head. "Should I be? Sam was named one of Tennessee's most eligible bachelors not that long ago."

Josie took a step closer. "Well, I think he's pretty in love with Maty and I'm—"

She stilled. No, she wasn't in love.

That was absurd. She was just getting caught up in all of this engagement fiasco.

"You're what?" Reese prompted.

Josie dropped her arms and squared her shoulders. "I'm not looking for a man," she told him.

Reese reached for her, his hands already working the zipper hidden on the side of her dress. "Is that so? Well, I wasn't looking for this, either, but here we are."

What did that mean? She wanted to ask, but his hands were moving on her, ridding her of all her clothes as he walked her backward.

"Have you checked out the deck?" he asked, a naughty gleam in his eye and a cocky smile to match.

"No. Should I?"

Her hands went to the buttons of his black dress shirt and she had him out of it before he could answer.

"There's a hot tub," he told her, firmly settling his hands at the dip in her waist. "There's also a flatbed swing. Both perfect for stargazing."

Josie smiled, raking her fingertip over the lines of his abs. "Is that what you're undressing me for? Stargazing?"

"You shouldn't get into the hot tub with your clothes on," he said.

Josie let him lead her outside, where she finished undressing him. The wide deck did provide a spacious hot tub and on the other end, a wide bed on a swing, perfect for lounging with your lover.

And that's the word she'd been looking for all this time. Reese had moved from best friend to lover, but she wasn't sure where his head was with all of this. What would happen once they decided to publicly call off the engagement? Would they still sneak a rendezvous here or there? Would he still want this physical intimacy? Because she wasn't sure she could give this up now that she'd experienced Reese.

"You're letting your mind take you away again," he accused.

Before she could defend herself, he picked her up and hauled her over his shoulder like she was nothing more than a blanket. Mercy, his strength was sexy.

He climbed into the hot tub and gently set her down. The warm water instantly had chill bumps popping up.

He reached over and tapped a button, instantly turning the jets on…as if she needed more stimulation to her already-aroused body.

When he turned back to her, he had that look again, the one that promised she was in for a good time.

"About that kiss earlier," he started as he reached for her. He sat down and pulled her onto his lap, giving her no choice but to straddle him. "Want to tell me why you're kissing me when nobody was looking?"

Yeah, about that. She'd told him he looked like he needed it, but in reality, she'd just wanted to. The pull toward him was growing stronger and stronger. She'd had to make up something quick because she didn't want to reveal her true feelings…basically because she wasn't even sure what her true feelings were.

"Maybe I like kissing you," she said, looping her arms around his neck. "Maybe I'm enjoying myself with you, despite all the chaos around us."

His hands eased up her thighs and around to cup her backside. "We do seem to draw the attention to us, don't we?"

She leaned into him, her breasts flattening against his chest. How could he keep carrying on a conversation? Her body was ready to go and he seemed to be taking his time.

Josie shifted a little more until she settled over him at the exact spot she ached to be. With her eyes locked onto his, she sank down, smiling when he moaned and closed his eyes.

Being in control where Reese was concerned wasn't an easy task. The man thrived on staying dominant at all times. But now his head dropped back against the edge of the hot tub and Josie braced her hands on his shoulders as she began to move.

Reese lifted his head and closed his mouth over her breast. She bit down on her lip to keep from crying out. Between his hands, his mouth and that rock-hard body moving beneath hers—oh, and those jets—Josie wasn't going to last.

When his lips traveled up to her neck, Josie dropped her head back and arched her body into his. He murmured her name over and over as she rocked against him.

All too soon, her body started climbing. As much as she wanted to make this moment last, she was fighting a losing battle.

Reese kept one hand on her backside and gripped her neck with the other, easing her down so he could claim her lips. She threaded her fingers through his hair and let every wave of emotion wash over her, through her.

His body tightened beneath hers as he joined her. Josie kept herself wrapped all around him, taking in the passionate kiss as her body came down from the high.

Reese's hold lessened as he nipped at her bottom lip, then rested his forehead against hers. The water continued to pulse around them, relaxing Josie even more. She didn't want to move, didn't want to face reality. She only wanted to stay in this moment that seemed so right because all too soon she would have to face the fact that she had to let Reese slip back into that friend box.

But for now, for tonight, she was in his arms.

Tomorrow he would meet his biological father and Josie wanted to give him as much comfort and peace as possible…and she prayed she could keep her heart from tumbling into love for her best friend.

Fourteen

"Are you ready for this?" Sam asked.

The three brothers stood outside the Lockwood Lightning Distillery. The sun was just starting to set behind the mountains, the tours had all ended, and the place was closed. Rusty was expecting them and Reese had a ball of nerves in his gut.

"Are you ready?" he countered to Sam. "Rusty isn't aware that you're his son, either."

Sam shrugged. "I honestly don't care if he ever finds out about me, but I'll stand with you guys as a united front."

Reese could understand and respect that. They were all at different places in their lives, but ultimately the deathbed confession of one woman had brought them all here. He also understood why Nick's mother had sent those letters. She hadn't wanted her son to have no family once she was gone.

"Let's get this over with," Nick stated. "I don't like spending any more time with this bastard than necessary."

Reese had dealt with some shady jerks in business before, but he hadn't imagined someone could be as terrible as Rusty was rumored to be. Clearly, he was getting ready to find out.

Sam reached up and pressed the intercom button next to the side door of the offices. Seconds later the door clicked and Nick reached for it.

He opened and gestured. "After you guys."

Reese stepped inside and the mixed scents of leather and alcohol hit him. The atmosphere was quite different from Sam's distillery. Here things seemed older, definitely a vibe from twenty years ago, where Sam's distillery seemed fresh and cutting-edge with the older themes complementing the decor.

"Gentlemen."

Reese turned toward the staircase and stared up at the landing, at Rusty Lockwood. He seemed older, heavier, in person than the photos Reese had seen online. Or maybe Rusty was just tired and run-down after being arrested and investigated regarding some serious charges.

Having your life and company on the brink of collapse would certainly wreak havoc.

Rusty's eyes scanned the guys, but ultimately landed on Reese.

"Recruiting new allies?" he asked. "I don't even know him, so I doubt he wants to see my demise."

Sam snorted. "You're about to know him. Are you coming down or standing there lording over us?"

"Are you staying long or will this meeting be short?" Rusty asked as he started to descend the steps.

Reese's first impression was that the man didn't like that he was being overrun. He didn't even bother with an introduction, as most people would when meeting someone new. He clearly didn't have any positive feelings toward Sam or Nick.

"Trust us, we don't want to be here any longer than necessary," Nick stated. "But there are some things we need to discuss."

Rusty came to the bottom of the steps and crossed his arms over his chest.

Reese couldn't stand it another second. "I'm Reese Conrad," he said, extending his hand.

Rusty stared for a second before giving a firm shake. "I've heard your name. You own those restaurants."

Those restaurants, like there was something wrong with being a restaurateur. Like people didn't have to book reservations at least a month in advance for a table, and even longer for the private lounge.

Rusty clearly had the mentality that he was above everyone else.

"I own eight restaurants and I'm opening my ninth in New York this coming weekend," Reese amended.

Rusty grunted and turned to Nick. "So what's this all about?"

"You recall my mother left me a letter about you being my biological father."

Rusty nodded. "And?"

"She sent letters to two of my brothers as well," Nick added.

Reese watched as Rusty processed that statement, then the man turned toward Sam, then Reese. His eyes showed absolutely no emotion. Nick might as well have told him the sky was blue for the lack of surprise on his face.

"So is this a family reunion?" Rusty asked. "And how do I know any of this is true?"

Sam took a step forward. "I don't give a damn if you believe us or not. We're just letting you know that you do have children. We want to clear the air and you can decide what to do from here. I don't believe any of us are looking for fatherly advice or holiday invites."

"I'm actually going to offer to buy Lockwood Lightning from you," Nick stated.

Reese jerked his attention to Nick, who only had his sights set on Rusty. From the way Sam reacted, he was just as surprised by Nick's offer.

"Buy me out?" Rusty scoffed. "When hell freezes over."

Nick shrugged and slid his hands into his pockets. "I knew that would be your first reaction, but that's why you're failing right now. You aren't thinking like a businessman. Instead, you're letting your emotions override common sense."

Rusty glanced at each of them. "Is that why you all came here? To gang up on me and get me to sell? You think I'm just passing down all I've built because I supposedly fathered you?"

"Bloodlines have nothing to do with this decision,"

Nick amended. "You don't need to answer me now, but I will own this distillery."

"What do you know about running a distillery?" Rusty mocked. "You renovate buildings and sell them off for others to run."

"He doesn't know about distilleries," Sam agreed. "But I do, and I'll be his partner."

"You think I'd sell to either of you?" Rusty asked. "After I tried to buy you out for years and you turned me down? I supposed your third crony is going to want in on this, too?"

Reese shrugged. "Always looking to expand. I'd go into business with them."

Rusty puffed up his chest as he pulled in a breath. The buttons on his shirt strained against the movement.

"If that's all you guys wanted, you wasted your time." Rusty started to turn back to the steps, but stopped himself. "I won't sell my distillery to any of you and I'm not really looking for children who will inherit my legacy. You can see yourselves out. The door will automatically lock, so don't come back."

And with that warm parting, Rusty went back up the steps to his lair or office or hellhole.

Nick and Sam both turned to Reese and he honestly didn't know what to say about the anticlimactic, not to mention fast, meeting they'd just had.

"Well, I guess that settles that," Reese said. "Clearly, he doesn't care about his sons, so I'm done here."

Nick glanced toward the empty steps and back to his brothers. "I meant what I said. I'm going to buy this place. It was something I'd thought about, but the minute I saw him, I knew. If you guys want to join me, we'd make a hell of a team."

Reese didn't make rash business decisions, but this was one thought that held merit. An already-established distillery run by three brothers who had all already made names for themselves in the hospitality and real estate industries was a no-brainer.

"We should discuss this elsewhere," Sam stated as he started toward the main door. "Let's head to my place where we can talk. I have a feeling this is going to take some strategic planning."

Reese followed, already pulling out his phone to text Josie and tell her what had happened and where he was heading. Odd that his first instinct had been to contact her and not his parents, but he would talk to them in person. He missed Josie when he wasn't with her and wanted to fill her in on everything going on in his life.

After last night, between the hot tub and then falling asleep holding her on the swinging bed under the stars, Reese couldn't help but wonder if maybe he was ready for more. Maybe the thought of commitment and long-term had always scared him in the past because the right person hadn't come into his life.

But she had.

She'd been there all along.

As things started to settle in his personal life, maybe long-term included Josie as well. Maybe she was settling right into the spot she was meant to be.

Reese had so much to think about regarding his brothers and Josie. There was a whole host of things he needed to weigh in his head before he made any life-changing decisions.

One thing was certain, though: the life he'd been living only a few weeks ago no longer existed. He was facing a new chapter and hell if all of this didn't scare him to death.

"I put an offer in on a house here."

Josie shifted and turned over in the swing bed, shocked by Reese's words. They swayed as she moved.

"In Green Valley?" she asked.

With one arm braced behind his head, he toyed with the ends of her hair with his other hand. His eyes held hers and she truly wished they could stay right here forever.

But that was a fantasy. They were friends, doing each other a favor, and they'd tumbled into bed in the process.

It was as simple and complex as that.

He grinned. "What do you think of this place?"

"You put an offer in on this cabin?"

Reese tucked her hair behind her ear, then rested his hand over hers, which was on his chest. "I love this outdoor setup overlooking the mountains. The interior would need to be updated to my tastes, but that's just cosmetic. I love the layout and the setting."

"Was it for sale?"

His brows drew in. "Did it need to be? I want a second home and for the right price, I bet the owners would be all too happy to find another cabin to buy and use as a rental."

That was Reese. Find something, make a plan, obtain it. He'd done the same with his Manhattan restaurant. He wanted to move on to a broader customer base and he'd done it without thinking twice.

"I don't know what's going to happen with Sam and Nick or even if this distillery of Rusty's is even going to be an option, but I want to be present when I'm needed and I'm growing to really love the mountains."

Yeah, she was, too. This was their third night here. They were flying to Manhattan in the morning, but they'd shared some special memories here… memories she'd have to keep locked away once all this was over.

"I invited the guys and their fiancées to the opening," Reese went on. "They said they'd be there."

Josie smiled. "You're really bonding with them. I'm glad. You all seem to really mesh well together."

"It's like we're old friends," Reese stated. "It's strange, really, but I'm comfortable around them."

"Have you talked to your parents about them?" she asked.

He nodded. "I called them earlier while you were in the shower. They're happy for me, that I'm forming a relationship with Nick and Sam. They apologized for how the meeting with Rusty went and I realized I had no expectations for that meeting, so it's not like I'm let down. I have the greatest parents of all time."

Josie couldn't argue there, but she didn't want to get swept up in thoughts about her late mom or her absent dad. She wanted to focus on the positive and the happiness that was stemming from all of this chaos.

Reese's finger slid over the ring on her hand. She cringed, feeling like a fraud every time she looked at it.

"Why did you marry Chris to begin with?" he asked.

The words hung between them and Josie didn't want to give him the truth. If she gave him the truth, that would just be another shove away from being "just friends."

Risking more terrified her. She'd rather have Reese back in that friend zone than to keep moving toward something that could crumble. She wasn't the best with relationships; she'd never had anything serious that lasted, so what did she truly know?

"Jo," he prompted.

She blinked her focus back to him. "It was a rash decision."

"Obviously, but what snapped inside that head of yours and made you rush to the courthouse? You had only dated him a few months."

Maybe she *should* be honest. Maybe that would be the best therapy and they could discuss what exactly was going on with all of these emotions. They'd talk and figure out why it was best that they just remain friends.

"You were engaged," she stated simply. "It made me realize that we were entering new chapters in our lives."

She stared down at him, wondering how he'd take her response. But that was the truth. She'd realized she might not be the only woman in his life forever. There would be someone else he'd share secrets or inside jokes with.

And she had gotten jealous.

There. Fine. She could admit it…to herself. She was human and she didn't like sharing, okay?

"Making a rush in judgment isn't like you," he told her. "You plan everything. Hell, you have an alarm to check your planner. But you married someone because I was engaged?"

"I made a mistake," she defended herself, sitting up a

little more. She crossed her legs in front of her, needing just a bit of distance between them in this small space. "I wasn't in love with Chris. He was a nice guy, I feel terrible that I hurt him, but honestly I don't think he loved me, either. He just wanted to be married because his family had been putting pressure on him."

Completely the truth.

"Why did you get engaged?" she retorted.

Reese shrugged and stared up at the starry sky. "I was taking over Conrad's full time and starting to wonder about my legacy and who I would share it with. I know I want a family someday, but once I got engaged, I realized I wasn't ready and she wasn't the one."

Josie placed her hand on his chest and smiled. "Sounds like we both dodged bigger mistakes."

"Speaking of, Chris has been leaving notes and stopping by your house," he told her. "My contractor informed me several days ago, so I reached out to Chris."

Josie stilled. "What? You should let me take care of this."

Reese's gaze came back to hers. "I let you try that, we ended up engaged and he still didn't back off. I told him if there was any further contact there would be harassment charges filed."

Josie didn't want a keeper. She didn't want anyone, especially Reese, fighting her battles.

"This engagement wasn't my doing," she informed him. "I told Chris I had moved on. You're the one who threw out I was your fiancée."

"He needed something stronger than just dating," Reese replied in that calm tone of his. "I could've said we'd already eloped."

Josie pulled in a deep breath and closed her eyes. The opening was in just a couple days and then they would go back to normal. Hopefully Chris would still keep his distance.

"I'm tired," she told Reese as she rolled off the side of the swing and came to her feet. "I'm going in to bed."

Reese continued to lie there, staring up at her. "We can stay out here," he suggested. "When I buy this place, I plan on staying out here as much as possible."

Josie smiled, but her heart was heavy.

She wanted things to go back to the way they were a few weeks ago. She wanted to ignore the way her heart shifted when Reese talked about lying with her, holding her or when he spoke of the future. They didn't have a future, not in the way they'd been playing house these past several days.

"You can stay out here," she told him. "I'll be fine."

She turned and stepped into the house, closing the patio door behind her. Maybe he'd come in and maybe he wouldn't. Right now, she needed time to think.

Reese had never acted like he wanted more with her. He seemed content with just the physical, which was fine. It had to be. If they tried this whole relationship for real, she didn't know how long that could or would last. If he tired of her and moved on…that would definitely ruin their friendship.

That was a risk she couldn't take, no matter how much she might be falling for her best friend.

Fifteen

Reese adjusted his tie, more out of nerves than anything else. The opening was due to kick off in less than thirty minutes, but that wasn't what had a ball of tension in his belly.

The restaurant business was in his blood; he wasn't worried in the slightest about failure or mishaps. Manhattan had been his main goal and here he was. Getting the building in the exact location he wanted had been the most difficult part. Everything from here on out was in his wheelhouse.

He stood on the second-floor balcony where he had a clear view of the first-floor entrance and one of the bars. For this location, he'd gone with old-world charm. Black and white, clean lines, clear bulbs suspended from the second floor to the first, a glossy mahogany bar. He'd wanted to keep this place upscale like the others, but really appeal to that classical era he associated with New York.

Josie had accompanied him from the penthouse he'd purchased a month ago. He wanted to keep a place in town because he planned on visiting quite often now. Their conversations had been a little strained since they'd left Green Valley a couple days ago. She was pulling back, and he was losing her.

The fear that continued to grow and develop inside him stemmed from that distance, from this fake engagement, from the fact that after tonight they wouldn't have to pretend anymore.

He'd just wanted to get through this opening, but now…well, he wasn't so sure he wanted things to end.

Oh, she wanted to go back to the friendship they'd once had, but that was impossible now. He knew her too intimately, had let her into that pocket of his heart he hadn't even known existed, and he'd seen her in a whole new light.

After being best friends for twenty years, Reese hadn't even known it was possible to still learn more about her, but he had. He'd actually discovered more about himself, too.

Like the fact that he wanted to give this relationship a go in every way that was real.

A flash of red caught his eye and he turned his attention to the bar area below. He knew that inky black hair and those killer curves.

But red?

When they'd arrived, she'd been wearing a long black gown with a high neck and an open back. This dress was…damn. This was the hottest thing he'd ever seen.

That dip in the back scooped dangerously low, and when she turned, he got an eyeful of a deep vee in the front as well. Classy, sexy and a hell of a shock to his entire system.

Hadn't he just thought that he'd finally seen all sides of Josie?

She glanced around the open space and he couldn't maintain the distance another minute. He made his way down the steps from the VIP area and crossed the tile floor.

"This is not the same woman who came with me," he stated.

Josie spun around, a wide smile on her face. Her dress wasn't the only thing red—she had her lips painted and it was all Reese could do to contain himself and not cover her mouth and mess that all up.

Damn, she was the sexiest thing he'd ever seen— and for the time being, fake or otherwise, she was his.

"I wanted to surprise you, so I had some things sent over so I could change here," she told him. "And I figured if I was going to go all out, I might as well do it all."

She gave a slow spin with her arms out wide. "What do you think? Can I pull off color?"

He took a step closer and reached for her hips. "I think I'm going to have to cut this night short and get you alone as soon as possible."

That red smile widened. "You can't mess me up, so keep those lips and hands to yourself. I have a dutiful hostess role to play as my fiancé is having a grand opening."

"He's a lucky bastard," Reese murmured as he leaned in and grazed his lips up the side of her neck.

She shivered beneath his touch and his grip on her hips tightened.

"We still have time," he whispered into her ear.

The waitstaff bustled around getting last-minute flutes of champagne and appetizers set out at various tables, but if they saw him and Josie in a passionate embrace, that would just make them look like more of a couple.

And right now, he didn't care who saw him doing what. He wanted her alone and he wanted her now.

"Other than the fact I want to rip that dress off and show you how much I need you, you do look so damn amazing, Jo."

She looped her arms around his neck. "I feel…good. I was worried once I got here I'd chicken out and keep on the black dress, but once I slid into this, it felt right."

He took a step back before he made a complete fool of himself and took her hands in his. His thumb slid over her ring.

"And it matches perfectly," he told her.

Her smile faltered a bit.

"What is it?" he asked.

Her eyes went from their joined hands back up to his face. "Have you seen the blog?" she asked. "It's up now. I just scanned through it when I was in the back."

"I haven't seen it," he told her. "Is something wrong with it?"

She pursed her lips for a moment before shaking her head. "No, nothing wrong. It just looks so real. Even I almost believe we're engaged."

Reese's breath caught, but he quickly recovered. Taking her hand, he ushered her off to the side where nobody could overhear. He kept his hands firmly locked with hers because he wanted to get this out; he wanted her to listen to everything he had to say.

Mercy, this was the riskiest move he'd ever made and he didn't care. If he let this moment, this woman, go without speaking his mind, then he'd regret it forever.

"You're scaring me with that look in your eye," she joked.

"What would you say to keeping the ring?" he asked.

Her brows drew in. "You insisted I keep it when I told you to return it. You claimed it could be my birthday gift, but it's a bit extravagant for that."

Reese swallowed the lump in his throat. "It's not extravagant if it's a real engagement ring," he suggested. "Keep it, keep me. Let's do this, Jo."

Her eyes widened on her gasp and she jerked her hands from his. "Do this? You mean, stay engaged?"

His delivery and proposal really needed work, but he was so damn nervous he hadn't really prepared his exact words.

"When we were talking the other night, it occurred to me that maybe we hadn't found the right people because we *are* the right people."

Josie continued to stare at him like he'd lost his mind, and maybe he had, but he still had to take this chance.

"Think about it," he went on. "We have always been there for each other. No matter what has happened, good or bad, we have each other's backs. Right? We trust each other. We're a hell of a team in bed and out."

"But you're my best friend," she countered, her voice holding no conviction. "We agreed…"

He took a step closer. "That was before everything changed. I love you, Josie."

"I love you, too," she said. "*As my best friend.* We can't do this, Reese. Just because we grew intimate doesn't mean we can build a life together."

"Your fear is showing," he murmured. "We've already built a life together."

"My fear?" she questioned. "It's common sense. We wouldn't know how to live together, to really forge our lives together like a husband and wife. Have you really thought about this or did you just get caught up in the role?"

"The only thing I've gotten caught up in is you. You can't believe I would ask if I wasn't serious. I want to try this with you."

Her eyes misted as she took another step back. "Trying leaves room for failure, and I love you too much to lose you as my friend, Reese. I'm sorry."

She turned and walked toward the back of the restaurant, leaving him completely confused and shattered.

He'd known before he'd asked that she'd be scared, but he'd had no clue she would completely shut him down. Did she really believe he'd let her get hurt? Didn't she trust him, trust *them*, more than that?

Chatter from the front doors pulled his attention back to the moment. Nick, Silvia, Sam and Maty were all smiles as they were the first to arrive. Right behind them, his parents.

This was his family. All of these people right here were here to support him on the most important night of his life.

Josie might have had to put distance between them, and that was fine, but he would regroup and stick around.

He wasn't going anywhere now that he knew exactly what he wanted...*who* he wanted.

Josie smiled and nodded, she shook hands and answered questions. Nobody knew the truth, that her insides were shaking, that her head was ready to explode with all the thoughts ramming together in there, and her heart was aching in a way she'd never known.

How dare Reese spring that on her? A real engagement? Was he out of his ever-loving mind?

"You look absolutely stunning."

Josie turned to see Silvia and Maty. The two women were beaming, which lightened Josie's mood somewhat. She needed a distraction and perhaps these were just the ladies she needed to chat with.

"I know you always wear black for your column and appearances," Maty stated, "but that red is gorgeous with your dark hair and skin tone."

"Thank you," Josie said, sipping her champagne. "I was worried it was too over-the-top, but I wanted to do something special for Reese. He's always on me about stepping out of my comfort zone."

Is that why he'd proposed for real? To get her out of that comfort zone? Because that wasn't just stepping out, that was jumping off a cliff without a parachute.

"I just saw the blog right before we came in." Silvia clutched her glass of sparkling water and leaned in to Josie. "Girl, you two are so adorably in love. I can't wait to see your journey to the aisle."

"I still can't believe we're all getting married," Maty said with a wide grin. "It's such an exciting time."

Josie wanted to correct them; she wanted to confide in someone that this was all a farce and there was no way she could marry Reese.

He didn't actually mean what he'd said. He'd gotten caught up, that's all. He would realize once he had time to come down from this high of the opening that they were better off as friends.

That nice, safe zone they'd lived in for so long was just waiting for them to return. Josie wanted that normalcy back because being in limbo with her emotions, her hormones, her heart…it was simply too much to bear.

She'd felt so brave wearing this red gown, but when it came to her feelings regarding Reese, she wasn't feeling so bold anymore. She'd tried. She wanted to be that daring woman. But…what if the risk was too great? What if they destroyed the life they'd built during all those years of friendship?

"I see the guys are talking with Reese's mom and dad." Josie nodded to the bar area. "I'm so glad this is all working out for him."

Silvia nodded. "Nick was worried if the third brother came forward that he would be like Rusty. I'm just grateful they've all found one another. Nick said he's going to do everything in his power to buy out Rusty, and Sam and Reese are joining forces."

Reese had mentioned that to Josie. She couldn't believe he was adding more business ventures to his plate, but that was Reese. He lived for success and to her knowledge, he'd never failed at anything.

Maybe that's why he didn't want to let her go. Would he see this public announcement calling off their engagement as a failure, like she had said at the start?

"Is everything all right?" Maty asked, placing a hand on Josie's arm.

Josie blinked back to the moment. "Oh, yes. Sorry about that. It's been a long couple of weeks."

Understatement.

"Would you two excuse me?" she asked.

The ladies nodded and Josie stepped aside to go get some fresh air or a moment to herself. Even with all the chaos of the successful opening, she was having a difficult time concentrating on anything other than this ring weighing so heavy on her hand.

The ring that Reese wanted to mean more than it could.

Josie made her way to the private office Reese kept in the back. Once inside, she closed the door and leaned back against it. She just needed a minute to compose herself, that's all. Then she could go back and play the dutiful, proud fiancée.

Because at midnight, this Cinderella story was over.

Sixteen

Reese stood on the second-floor balcony once again, staring down onto the empty first floor. The launch had been a huge success. The reservations were all booked up for the next three months and several reviewers were already talking about them during some prime spots on their social media accounts.

He wondered if Josie took mental notes or if she'd just checked out after he'd dropped that bomb on her.

Reese trusted her. He knew she'd still cover the event and make a good article for *Cocktails & Classy*.

Which reminded him, he still hadn't seen their post on the blog. Part of him didn't want to see it, if the images had impacted Josie so much. Was that why she'd been so scared? She'd seen the photos and realized what they had was real?

Reese pulled his cell from his pocket and quickly found the site. He skipped the dialogue; he knew exactly what they'd said during their interview. That had been the easy part.

The first image he came to was the one where Josie had her eyes closed, her head turned toward her shoulder and he had placed a kiss on her head. The tender, delicate picture made him smile.

He scrolled through more words and stopped when he came across the picture of when they had to lean in for the "almost" kiss. His fingertips splayed over her jawbone and neck as he tipped her head back. Josie's eyes were locked onto his, her lips slightly parted.

Even though he'd been right there in that moment, he'd had no clue what this shot had actually looked like. They definitely looked like they were in love, like they were literally half a breath away from closing that narrow gap between them. She'd been nervous, worried what this would do to them.

If only she'd let those fears go and see what she had right in front of her.

Heels clicked on the tile below and Reese glanced from his phone to see Josie step into view. She immediately glanced up and caught his gaze.

"I thought you took a ride back to the penthouse," he told her.

"I was going to, but I couldn't leave."

Reese glanced from the phone back to her. "I was just looking at the announcement online. We look good."

She crossed her arms over her chest, giving him a delicious view from this angle.

"We do," she agreed.

The tension in that vast gap between them was charged and Reese felt it best to keep a good distance. If he got too close, he'd want to touch her, hold her, tell her every reason why they should be together, but she had to come to that realization on her own.

"I know you think it's a good idea to keep going," she started. "But I can't marry you, Reese."

So they were still at that stalemate. Fine. He was a patient man and Josie was worth waiting for.

"You have to understand," she added.

"I understand you're afraid. I understand this isn't what you had planned, but you have to see that none of this is new."

She jerked like he'd surprised her. "Not new? We've only been faking this for two weeks and we've crammed quite a bit into that short time frame. It's all quite new."

He couldn't stand the distance anymore. Reese came down the steps and stood at the bottom of the landing, his eyes meeting hers across the way. She still wore that red dress, those red lips. She still took his breath away whether she had on black, red or nothing at all.

"None of this is new," he explained. "Everything between us has always been there. We are just now bringing it to the surface."

Her arms dropped to her sides as she shook her head. Her fear and hesitancy made him want to reach for her, but he also recognized he needed to give her some space.

She glanced down to her hand as she toyed with the ring. He stared, knowing what was coming, hoping he was wrong.

But she slid the ring off and held it out in her palm.

When her eyes came up to meet his, there was no way she could hide the unshed tears.

"I'm not taking it back," he told her. "I bought it for you."

"You never bought me something this expensive for my birthday before."

He stared at her for another minute, but knew which battle he wanted to fight. He didn't want to be a jerk about this, and she obviously needed time to think. Fine. He'd hold it for her until she was ready.

Sliding the ring into his pocket, he extended his hand.

"How about we head up to the rooftop, take a bottle of champagne and relax?" he suggested. "We've both had a rough few weeks and I could use some quiet."

She looked at his hand, then back to his face; her brows drew in as she cocked her head.

"That's it?" she asked. "We're just going to move past the fact that you wanted to marry me and now we're going back to being buddies that fast?"

Damn woman was confusing him...and herself, which was probably a good thing. If she was confused, then that meant her mind wasn't completely made up.

"Isn't that what you wanted?" he asked. "I still need my best friend. Do I want more? Of course. But I'm not pushing you out of my life simply because we don't agree on the future."

Her lips curved into a grin as she reached for his hand. "One glass," she told him. "And no sex."

She was killing him.

"That dress was made for sex," he informed her, leading her to the elevator.

As they stepped into the elevator, she slid her hand from his. "I can't, Reese. As much as I want you physically, I can't risk my heart. I need a clean break from this, or someone is going to end up hurt."

Too late. Her rejection stung, but he wasn't giving up and he had to believe she wanted more and was just too worried to grab hold of what was right in front of her.

Her actions said more than her words ever could.

She'd stepped out of her structured life to take a chance with him; she'd worn the red dress, the red lipstick...she did want to be bold and brave, but he knew she was afraid.

He respected her and knew she would realize what they had... eventually.

"Fine," he conceded. "Champagne on the rooftop with our clothes on to celebrate a successful night."

She nodded. "Deal."

Reese led her up to the rooftop with flutes and an unopened bottle. If she wanted to slide back into friend territory, then that's what they'd do. He hoped she realized he never backed down from a fight, and having Josie permanently in his life was the one fight he would never give up.

Josie stared at the blue bikini. Should she? She was home in her own element and going to her own private beach. Who would even care? Besides, she'd donned that red dress for everyone to see and she had to admit, she'd felt pretty damn good about it.

After flying back to Sandpiper Cove, Josie had moved back into her own home since the renovations were done. The crew had put everything back the way it had been before. Her spare closet needed to be reorganized, but at least the mess was completely gone and nothing had been ruined.

Josie needed to spend the day on the beach, to decompress after a whirlwind trip, meeting Reese's new family in Tennessee, his opening in New York and the proposal that never should've happened.

It shouldn't have…right?

Yes. She had made the right decision to save them further hurt down the road. Not only the hurt, but she was also saving them from destroying a friendship that she could never replace. He was her one constant. She needed him to always be there, and if they married and decided it didn't work or he grew tired of her, where would she be?

Alone with only her work to keep her company.

Josie stripped from her pajamas and pulled on the blue bikini. To hell with it. For two weeks she'd been so happy. Perhaps that was due to taking chances and being that bold woman she'd always thought she could be, a bold woman like her mother had been.

She grabbed the matching sheer cover and her straw hat. After sliding into a pair of gold sandals, she stepped from the closet and caught herself in the mirror. Well, she didn't look terrible, just different. But she was keeping it and spending the day in the sun, with a cold beverage and a good book.

Though with the way her mind was spinning, she wasn't sure any book could hold her attention.

The alarm from her driveway dinged. Who would be coming here? She wasn't expecting anybody.

Reese. Had to be.

She glanced at her reflection one more time, but decided not to change. He'd seen her in a bikini countless times over the years. Just because they'd been intimate didn't mean she had to do things differently. They were back to being just friends and a bikini was something she'd wear with a friend. Besides, this was her house. She could wear whatever she wanted without worrying about unexpected guests.

Josie headed down the hall and to the foyer just in time to see Chris pull his car up near the steps. On a sigh, she pulled her wrap around her and stepped onto the porch.

The second he got out of his car, he caught sight of her. Thankfully, he remained in the drive and didn't make his way to her.

"I'm not going to bother you," he promised with his hands up. "I just wanted to come by and tell you I'm happy for you."

Confused, Josie took another step until she was at the edge of the porch. "You couldn't text?"

"After all we've been through, I needed to see you one last time. I saw the blog and I realized that you and Reese have something I could never have with you. As much as I hate it and wish we were still together, I know you two belong together. Too bad we didn't realize that sooner."

She didn't know what to say, so she remained silent.

"Anyway, congratulations," he stated. "You deserve to be happy."

Josie could tell he truly meant it. "Thank you. I want you to be happy, too, Chris."

He offered her a smile and stared another moment

before he waved and got back into his car. She watched as he drove off and she wondered what he'd seen in those images that she hadn't. True, she'd stared at the blog longer than necessary; she'd even pulled it up again this morning.

She and Reese did look happy, but they *were* happy. They had a bond that was unmistakable. But they were going to have to discuss a mutual press release regarding their "breakup" and make it sound like they were still ridiculously happy and loved each other…they were just not in love.

The thought tugged at her heart and she pushed the emotion aside as she went back into her house. She reset the alarm and went to the kitchen to whip up a mai tai.

Just as she was pouring her blended drink into a large travel cup, her cell rang. Josie sat everything down and reached across the island to her phone.

Not Reese. How silly that she'd been expecting him to call or come by. True, they'd just gotten in yesterday, but it'd been over twelve hours since she'd seen him.

Her editor's name lit up the screen and Josie knew she still had to pretend the engagement was on.

"Hello."

"Jo, the blog is breaking records," Melissa squealed. "Have you seen? The comments are astounding and we are getting emails that we can't keep up with."

When she'd gotten online this morning, she hadn't even looked at the comments—she'd been too wrapped up in the photos.

"That's great news," Josie stated.

"We'd love to keep this momentum going," her editor tacked on. "Do you know when formal engagement pictures will be ready or when you will be dress shopping? If we could do a weekly wedding update, I think that would be best. There are so many details that we could easily make this work."

Josie rubbed her forehead. "Let me think about this, okay? Reese and I just got back last night and I'm still a bit fuzzy."

"Yes, of course. Oh, and honey, that red dress was fabulous," she praised. "Great move on your part to branch out at your fiancé's grand opening. You two looked absolutely perfect."

Guilt weighed heavy on her, but another emotion overrode the guilt. Regret.

Had she made the right decision turning Reese down? Since the moment she'd slid that ring off, everything had felt wrong, out of place.

"Thanks," Josie replied. "Let me think on weekly blogs and I'll be in touch."

"Sounds great. I'm just so happy for you guys. You really look like you're in love and that's so rare to find these days."

Unable to handle anymore, Josie said her goodbyes and hung up. She grabbed her drink, ignored her phone on the counter and slid her beach bag from the kitchen chair and onto her shoulder.

No phone, no uninvited guests at her door; she just needed peace and quiet and the ocean. That's all. The space in her head was filled to capacity.

And the man who occupied each and every thought was the man who claimed to love her, who wanted to spend his life with her.

Josie pulled in a deep breath and headed out to the

beach. She had so much thinking to do and serious decisions to make. Was she ready to take that leap? Was she ready to take the biggest risk of her life and create a brand-new box?

One where she and Reese were together forever?

Seventeen

A shadow came over her and Josie squealed.

"Good grief, Reese," she scolded as she jerked her legs over the side of her lounge chair. "You scared the hell out of me."

"Well, you scared me, because I've been texting and calling. Usually, you are glued to your phone."

She adjusted her hat and stared up at him. "I wanted some time alone and didn't want to be interrupted. What are you doing here?"

"I was going to see if you wanted to take the boat out?" he said. "Nick, Sam, Silvia and Maty are at my house."

"They are?" she exclaimed. "Did you know they were coming?"

"We had discussed it, but it was kind of a last-minute thing. I invited them yesterday before we left New York and they came this morning. Frisco is going to work up a shrimp and crab boil. I know how much you love that."

Josie came to her feet and reached for her cover-up, but too late. Reese's eyes raked over her barely clad body and every one of her nerve endings sizzled with arousal.

Well, clearly this was going to be a problem. Now that she'd had him, she couldn't simply turn off that need.

She slid her arms into the sheer material and stared back at him. "We aren't engaged anymore," she reminded him. "So how is this going to work?"

Reese shrugged. "I would have asked you as a friend even before we did this fake engagement. Nothing has changed there, Josie. I want my best friend by my side and I figured you'd enjoy the day out. You seemed to really hit it off with Maty and Silvia."

"I did. They're amazing."

Reese smiled and her heart ached. "So you'll come? I can take you over if you're ready now. It looks like you're all set for a day on the boat."

This was weird. He made no move to touch her. Except for that wandering gaze, she would swear he was right back in that friend zone.

Had he moved there so easily? Had he already forgotten that he'd told her he loved her?

Reese picked up her sunglasses and book and shoved them into her beach bag, then lifted it up.

"What do you say?" he asked.

What did she say? Josie shook her head, as if that would somehow put all these jumbled thoughts back into place.

Melissa thought she and Reese looked in love; her ex-husband had said the same. Reese professed his love and Josie…was confused.

"Something wrong?" he asked. "If you don't want to come, no pressure. We can tell them about this whole friend thing. Believe me, they're discreet with secrets, so they won't say anything until we can make an official statement."

Josie continued to stare at him. "That's it? Less than forty-eight hours ago you said you loved me and now you're good with being friends?"

"I do love you," he informed her without hesitation. "I also respect your decision. What do you want from me?"

The question was, what did she want from herself? She wanted to be able to trust her feelings, to trust that if she took this leap, he'd be holding her hand the entire way. She'd been slowly moving toward this moment, and now she was going to reach for the life she wanted…the life they deserved together.

"I want it all," she murmured before she could stop herself.

Her eyes dropped to her feet as a wave of fear coupled with relief washed over her.

She'd let out her true feelings, but now what?

Reese's fingertip slid beneath her chin as he forced her to meet his gaze. "Say that again, Jo. I didn't quite catch it."

She closed her eyes.

"No," he demanded. "Look at me. I've waited for this for a long time."

"How long?"

His smile softened. "Probably since I met you, but at least a few years."

Years? How had she taken so long to catch up?

"Tell me what you're thinking," he told her. "I don't want any confusion."

He still hadn't reached for her, so she reached for him. She placed her hands on either side of his face and stepped into him.

"As much as I love our friendship, I love you more," she told him. "All of you. I want to be with you, but I'm terrified."

"You think I'm not?" he asked with a laugh. "I just know that never having you again sounds like pure torture and I need you, Jo. I need you in my house, in my life, as more than a friend."

"What happens if we can't—"

He covered her lips with his. Her bag slipped to the ground, landing at her feet as he wrapped his arms around her and pulled her flush with his body.

"We don't fail," he murmured against her lips. "That's not who we are, and we love each other too much."

Her fear melted away little by little. He was right. They were both so strong, they'd always held each other up and she knew going into a deeper relationship would be no different.

"So do we get the ring back on this finger?" he asked.

Josie nodded. "Yes. Let's go back to your house since your family is waiting on you."

"Our family," he corrected. "They're our family now, Jo, because you're mine."

Epilogue

Six months seemed like a long time, but in the grand scheme of things regarding legal doings and commercial sales, it was lightning fast.

Reese smiled. Lockwood Lightning was now officially under new ownership. Sam, Nick and Reese were in the moonshine business.

"This has been a hell of a ride," Nick stated as he poured five glasses of moonshine and one glass of apple cider for his very pregnant fiancée.

The guys had signed papers yesterday and this morning they were making things official. Rusty had been so strapped for cash between the embezzlement, the lawyer fees and back taxes he'd "forgotten" that he'd had no choice but to sell. The guys offered more than anyone else would have and now they were all starting this new chapter as one unit.

"I'm glad I could be part of it," Reese said, sliding his arm around Josie's waist.

Since that day she'd come home with him six months ago, she hadn't left. She'd sent for her things, moved in and they were officially planning a wedding. The weekly blogs were getting to be exhausting, but she was loving every minute of it and he wanted nothing more than to see her happy.

Nick doled out all of the glasses as they stood in a circle in the main tasting area of Lockwood Lightning.

"To new beginnings," Sam declared as he raised his tumbler. "This is just the start of a new dynasty."

"And with the resort opening in a few weeks, we are slowly taking over Tennessee," Nick added.

"I'll drink to that," Sam laughed.

Silvia gasped. "Oh, no."

Everyone turned to see her holding her side.

"I think I'm having a contraction." She grimaced. "I mean, I think I've had them all morning, but this one seems strong."

"All morning?" Nick asked. "And you're just now telling me?"

She scrunched her face and handed over her glass. Josie quickly reached for it before it dropped.

"I knew this was such an important moment for you guys," she defended. "But I'm pretty sure I need to get to the hospital."

Reese nodded. "Go. We'll take care of things here."

Nick ushered Silvia out the door and Reese turned, catching Josie's eye. She smiled and something he didn't quite recognize glinted in her eye.

She tipped back the cider that had been Silvia's and handed him her moonshine.

"You might want to do another toast to new beginnings," she told him. "And I'll take another cider."

Her statement, her actions, finally hit him.

"Jo?"

Her smile widened and she nodded. "About ten weeks now."

"Ten weeks?"

"Surprise," she exclaimed.

Maty laughed and turned to Sam. "Don't look at me. I have no news, but I wouldn't mind getting a puppy."

"Deal," Sam agreed.

Reese took the empty glass from Josie and handed it to Sam. He pulled her against him and couldn't help the tears that clogged his throat. All these years he'd thought about a family, but never knew where to start.

Now he knew.

The woman he'd been waiting for had been in his life for so long. She'd agreed to marry him for real six months ago and now they were going to start a family. Nothing could have made him happier.

"I love you," he whispered into her ear.

"I love you, baby." She held on to him and he thought he heard a little sniff. "We're going to kill this parenting gig."

He eased back. "We are," he agreed. "But can we not tell your editor? I'm afraid of what she'll have us do next for the magazine."

Josie eased back, her eyes filled with unshed tears as she smiled. "We'll hold her off as long as possible."

Good, because Reese needed his family all to himself for now. He'd waited a long time and he finally had everything he'd ever wanted.

* * * * *

BACK IN HIS
EX'S BED

JOSS WOOD

Dedicated to my own "Wilfred Seymour," my dad.
You taught me to love books and writing and that
there's always a plan to be made. I miss you
every day. Love you always.

One

Beah Jenkinson exited the black taxi at the swanky entrance to Claridge's, grateful for her long vintage cashmere coat. Ignoring the light drizzle, she paid her fare, tucked her designer clutch bag under her arm and sucked in a deep breath.

She could do this; she *had* to do this…

It was only dinner with one of the most important and elusive art collectors in the world.

And her ex-brother-in-law Carrick.

And her ex-husband, Finn.

Who also happened to be two of her three bosses. Not a big deal.

Liar. It was *such* a big deal…

"Good evening, madam."

Beah returned the black-frocked doorman's greeting with a distracted smile and walked through the doors and into the lobby of the impressive hotel. Allowing her coat to swing open, she resisted the urge to turn and check her reflection in the glass doors, to reassure herself that her off-one-shoulder, tight-fitting cobalt blue cocktail dress with its ruffled hem was suitable.

She knew she looked fine; she always did, and her dress was a perfect combination of business chic and dinner sexy. As per usual, she'd pulled her Orphan Annie curls into a tight chignon and she'd covered her much-hated freckles with expertly applied makeup.

She was thirty years old and looked like what she was, a woman confident in her body and her looks. She had an amazing career, a wonderful life. It was only when she was faced with meeting Finn Murphy that she felt like the insecure, clingy, desperate-to-be-loved young woman she'd been nine years ago.

So annoying.

Needing a minute to regulate her breathing, to slow down her over-fast heart rate, Beah ducked into the plush ladies' room and sat on the edge of a velvet-covered stool, staring down at her classic nude heels.

Resting her head against the wall, Beah closed her eyes.

You can do this, Jenkinson. It's just business.

Needing reassurance, Beah pulled her phone out of her clutch bag and hit one on her speed dial. It was early afternoon in Boston, but if she was lucky, her best friend would answer her call. Beah held her breath as the phone rang. And rang. Dammit, Keely was busy; she wouldn't be able to talk Beah down from this ledge.

"Hi, Bee."

Beah's heart settled as air flowed into her lungs. Keely's voice, as it always did, steadied her, made her feel connected. She'd met the small blonde through the Murphy brothers and they'd instantly clicked. When

Beah and Finn announced their divorce, Keely had rocked up on her doorstep with wine, pizza, chocolates and open arms.

"Why are you here?" Beah had asked her, tears streaming down her face. "I thought the Murphys gained custody of you in the divorce."

"Finn has his brothers. You need someone."

That's what Keely had told her as she swept into her life. Although they lived on either side of the Atlantic Ocean these days, they were as close today as they'd ever been.

"Bee? Talk to me, honey."

Beah straightened, leaned back into the chair and tipped her face up to look at the molded ceiling. "I'm sitting in the ladies' room at Claridge's."

Keely waited for a beat. "Would you like to tell me why?"

Beah turned her head to the right, saw her reflection in the massive mirror and wrinkled her nose. She looked as pale as a ghost. "I'm about to have a working dinner with Finn, Carrick and Paris Cummings."

"Ah. Are you feeling nervous?"

Not exactly. "Off-balance, maybe. I'm good at my job, Keely, and I meet clients all the time. And I speak to Carrick and Ronan a few times a week. Finn…"

"Finn what?" Keely asked, sounding amused.

"Finn—"

"Hold on a sec, Bee. My PA has a question…"

It was a temporary reprieve, but it gave Beah time to think. Memories tumbled as Beah waited for Keely to return her attention to their conversation. She'd been twenty-one and had left London for New York, excited to work in a new city. With honors degrees in both economics and fine art, she secured an internship at

Murphy International—a world-renowned art auction house. Within days, she'd she met the brilliant, terribly sexy Finn Murphy, a stunning combination of geeky nerd and sexy jock.

A few months later she'd hurtled into marriage with the youngest Murphy brother, hauling along a cruise liner's worth of baggage, all rational thought doused by their hectic sexual attraction.

Like moths to a flame, rivers flowing to the sea and stars burning out, her landing in Finn's arms and in his bed had been inevitable.

Beah was terrified that on meeting him face-to-face again, history might repeat itself.

Since their divorce they'd both made a silent but concerted effort to avoid each other, even though they both still worked for Murphy International. Living on two different continents helped, and on the few occasions she'd needed Finn's expert opinion on a painting or an objet d'art, she sent him detailed photographs or, if that didn't suffice, he met the client on his own.

They'd made avoiding each other into an art form.

"Look, I know you can't possibly be nervous about having a business meeting because you're nothing like the girl you used to be," Keely said, returning to their conversation. "You're head of acquisitions, responsible for advising Murphy's rich clients on their collections, about what they could acquire and what they should dispose of. You're smart, funny and gorgeous."

This was why every woman needed a best friend, someone to shore up her defenses when the cracks started to show. "You need to remember how far you've come, what amazing things you've done, Bee."

Beah closed her eyes, happy to let her friend talk.

"You walked out of your marriage and soon afterward you moved back to London, joining Murphy's UK office. You worked your tail off, clawing your way up the ladder to become one of the most powerful people in the organization. Murphy's is lucky to have you, Bee, and that's why they pay you the very big bucks, because they know your clients are loyal to you and will walk if you walk. Hell, you could open your own art consulting company right now and you'd have a list of wealthy clients as long as your arm."

Yeah, about that…

"Um, actually, that reminds me of something I've been meaning to tell you," Beah said, and asked Keely to switch to FaceTime. When Keely's face appeared on her screen, she smiled at her brown-eyed, blond-haired friend. "There you are…"

Keely waved her words away, eyes bright with curiosity. "What? Have you met someone?"

Beah rolled her eyes. "I don't have time to date."

"No, you don't *make* time to date because you use your busy work schedule as a shield. You think that if you keep busy, you won't have time to feel anything for anyone."

Okay, a bit too close to the truth. And not something she wanted to think about right now… "Do you want to hear this or not?" Beah demanded.

Keely handed her that patented, I'm-so-smart smirk. "Sure, go for it. But we will revisit this topic at a later date."

Not if Beah could help it.

"Michael Summers. Have you heard of him?" After Keely shook her head, Beah continued. "He's a prominent art adviser, consultant and dealer. One of the most respected in the world. He has decades of experience and is an art guru…"

Beah twisted her vintage flower ring around her middle finger. "He wants to retire and he's looking for someone to run his business, to start taking over his client list."

"You?"

"Me." Beah nodded. "It's a hell of an opportunity, Keels. He's a legend and I'm honored he wants me to join him. But…"

"But it would mean leaving Murphy's." Keely tapped her finger against her cheek. "Could you still work with Murphy's or would you be persona non grata?"

Beah tasted panic in the back of her throat. Murphy's was the only place she'd ever worked, all she knew.

Beah pushed her fear away; she was just scared of the unknown. Change was never easy and she hadn't signed an oath in blood or a lifetime contract to work for Murphy's.

She was allowed to move on. "Not that they ever would, but they would be stupid to blackball me because a lot of Michael's clients purchase art from Murphy International. They'd be cutting off their nose to spite their own face."

"And I presume Murphy's has had other employees leave, other salespeople, nicking their clients?"

"Sure, it happens all the time."

"And Murphy's has survived?" Keely persisted. "So in this context, you are not thinking of yourself as an employee but as a Murphy, as Finn's wife."

"Ex-wife." Beah corrected, feeling the familiar pang in her chest. She'd loved adding Finn's surname to hers. Beah Jenkinson-Murphy felt damn right.

Had felt right.

"If you were working for any other company, would

you be hesitating?" Keely demanded, as forthright as always.

"Probably not. This is a hell of an opportunity. And an even bigger commitment. If I take this position, I might be able to schedule dinner with you in, maybe, five years or so. My life will go into hyperdrive."

"Mmm, interesting."

Beah knew that when Keely said "interesting" in that tone of voice, she had many, many thoughts on the subject. Beah glanced at her watch and grimaced. "Condense your thoughts into two sentences, Keels, or I'm going to be late."

"Why haven't you jumped at Michael's offer if it's so amazing, Beah? I suspect it's because you are letting your personal feelings for your ex and his family cloud your judgment, which is strange because you profess to be very over Finn Murphy."

Beah was over him. After nine years, she *had* to be.

"Also, apart from the prestige of working for someone of his stature, Michael's offer also intrigues you because you'd be so busy you wouldn't have time to think, to feel, to date. It'd be another excuse for you not to engage in real life."

This? Again? Beah loved Keely, she did, but her best friend was both opinionated and stubborn. And sometimes, an attack was the best defense. "And you? Are you dating?"

Keely didn't flinch at her accusation. "This conversation is about you, not me." Keely cleared her throat and Beah knew her next words might have the potential to sting. Keely, forthright and honest, rarely pulled her punches.

"While I hate that you, and Finn, were hurt by your divorce, it was, in many ways, good for you, Beah. You learned to stand on your own two feet, to ask for what you want, to chase down a goal. Though I sometimes do think you've become a little too independent."

"Is that even possible?"

"Let me put it this way… I worry you push people away, that you don't allow anyone to get close."

Because that was what Finn had done to her.

"I'm close to you," Beah protested.

"Mostly because I push and pry and keep pounding on the door when you slam it close," Keely replied.

Beah couldn't argue with her.

Over the past nine years, Keely had been her North Star, her compass point, her bedrock. She didn't need anything more than to know she was standing in her corner. Keely's friendship was the equivalent of having her own thirty-girl squad. "I have *you*, Keels."

"But as fabulous as I am," Keely replied with asperity, "I do not have a pair of big arms, a low voice and a non-female point of view. You need *love*, Jenkinson, and God knows, you need *sex*. When did you last go on a date? And for the love of God, do not tell me the last person you had sex with was Finn Murphy," Keely demanded.

Beah shook her head. She'd had sex since divorcing her ex. Not often and not great sex, but it still qualified. Just.

Beah glanced at her watch and grimaced. If she didn't hustle, she would be late and she was never late. She stood up and tucked her clutch bag under her arm. It was a fantastic excuse to end this frustrating conversation. "I need to go, Keely. My bosses won't be impressed if I'm late, and Paris Cummings hates tardiness."

"I suppose I should know who Paris is but I don't," Keely said, sounding peeved.

"Art collector, old money, a property developer. Re-clusive and grumpy." Beah said, heading for the door. Paris Cummings was an art collector she'd been pursu-ing for years, and she had to attend this dinner and help woo the stubborn collector to their side of the fence.

And that meant sitting at the same table as her ex-husband, pretending they hadn't spent the best part of a decade avoiding each other.

Beah blew Keely a kiss and tucked her phone back into her clutch. She placed the bag under her arm and pulled an insouciant smile onto her face.

She was no longer the impulsive wild child who, within a week of meeting Finn Murphy, moved into his luxurious apartment and married him in Vegas on the three-month anniversary of the day they met.

She was successful. She was confident. She was in control…

At the entrance to the very upmarket restaurant, Beah smiled at the maître d' and surrendered her coat. Resisting the urge to check that no red curls had escaped her smooth chignon, she looked over the exquisitely decorated dining room, her eyes immediately going to the best table in the room.

As if he could feel her eyes, Finn jerked his head up and their gazes clashed.

Beah's feet felt glued to the floor and she couldn't pull her eyes off his masculine, oh-so-handsome face. There was a hint of the nerd he'd once been, in the wire-rimmed glasses over sharply intelligent eyes and a slow-to-smile mouth. A close-cropped, super-short beard covered his cheeks and jaw; his dark blond hair was overlong and could do with a trim but his shoul-ders were wide in a designer suit, exquisitely tailored for his tall frame.

Finn pushed his way to his feet, unfurling his long, muscled body. He wore a black shirt without a tie and his eyes, a light green, remained on her with laser-like intensity.

He used to look at her like that while they were making love, as he was about to slide into her. Like she was a puzzle he didn't understand but needed to complete...

"Ms. Jenkinson? Ma'am?"

Beah heard her name being called from a place far away and wrenched her eyes off Finn onto the concerned face of the maître d'.

"The Misters Murphy are expecting you and, I'm sure, delighted to have you join them." He gestured her to precede him.

Beah forced herself to cross the room, to keep her face impassive. Yeah, she could pretty much guarantee Finn Murphy was *not* delighted to see her.

She wasn't thrilled to see him, either.

Fifteen minutes earlier...

It was just another dinner with another client in a swanky restaurant. While he wasn't a fan of the concept, he'd attended more than a few as an owner of Murphy International.

There was no reason to feel nervous.

Finn Murphy lifted his hand to loosen the tie cutting off his air supply and silently cursed when he realized he wasn't wearing a tie and the collar to his black shirt was open.

He was *not* nervous. Stressed maybe, but not nervous. He and his brothers were in the final stretch of preparing for one of the biggest art auctions in a generation and it was his responsibility to ensure every piece auctioned—including paintings by the old masters, impressionists and cubists, negatives by Ansel Adams, and one of the best collections of Jade in the world—was beyond question and reproach. Every provenance for roughly eight hundred items needed to be checked, verified, collated.

If his nerves didn't play up when he was falling off three-hundred-foot buildings BASE jumping or flying down black-diamond ski runs, then he had no reason to feel jittery while waiting for the arrival of one of the wealthiest art collectors in the world.

And his wife.

Ex-wife, dammit.

Finn picked up his water glass, put it down again and reached for his glass of red wine, lifting the crystal rim to his lips. He would not look at his older brother, not just yet. Carrick could look past Finn's devil-may-care attitude to the rolling mess below his seemingly steady surface.

He didn't want to talk about how the thought of seeing Beah again, even if it was just a business dinner, made him feel nerv—a little tense. They'd once been as close as two people could legally be; now they were little more than across-the-pond work colleagues, vague acquaintances.

"Take a deep breath, Finn."

Finn narrowed his eyes at Carrick. His oldest brother looked calm and controlled, but amusement flickered in his light green eyes. Finn considered, as subtly as he could manage it, flipping off his brother. At fifteen, when he'd been the biggest rebel and pain in the ass, that might've been his reaction. At thirty-three, he was way past acting like a child. Or he should be.

But the urge was there.

"Why are you acting like a cat on a hot tin roof?" Carrick asked, picking up his tumbler of whiskey.

"I'm fine," Finn replied through gritted teeth. "You know I prefer to be left out of these client dinners. I'm not good at making small talk."

It wasn't a lie—he really wasn't. Carrick and Ronan were able to charm and coerce, to make small talk, but Finn tended to be too terse, too abrupt. His bluntness was legendary throughout Murphy International. There was a reason why he preferred to work alone, why he buried his head in books and texts and research. He was better with art and objects than he was with people. Inanimate objects didn't talk back, dammit.

He was the company nerd, the brain, the Murphy recluse. He had no problem with any of those descriptions. They were all, to a degree, true.

Carrick's gaze was steady. "You are here because Cummings wants to meet you. Apparently he's quite a fan."

Finn snorted. "He's a fan? You make me sound like the front man of a boy band."

"He was very impressed that, despite being blasted by every authority on D'Arcy, you refused to cave when the art world insisted you were wrong."

This again? Years ago, fresh out of college with a PhD in art history, he'd published a paper suggesting the painting *Thief in the Night*, by the celebrated French artist, was painted by one of his apprentices and not by the master himself.

He'd been called an upstart and arrogant and worse, but he hadn't cared then and didn't care now. He knew what he knew and was rarely proved wrong. It had taken a year, and a series of forensic tests, for the art world to accept he was right. The owner of the D'Arcy, whose painting lost millions because Finn refused to budge, was still not a fan. But as Murphy International's head of world art, Finn's responsibility was to the art, not to the owners.

"Anyway, Paris Cummings was impressed by your research and your steadfastness under intense pressure."

Finn picked up his wineglass and swirled the liquid around the bowl. "I don't regret sticking to my guns but I do regret the bad PR around that incident."

His arrogant attitude hadn't helped. Back then he'd been particularly impressed with himself, thinking his double degree in art and forensics, and his ability to speak a half dozen languages, made him special, and he'd liked his reputation for being something of an art genius. He most definitely hadn't liked being questioned. Admittedly, he'd been a bit of an ass.

These days, after a failed marriage and a decade to grow the hell up, he wasn't so quick to tell people he was better, smarter, quicker. He'd come to realize that while he was smart in certain areas—he excelled at anything book-based and was naturally sporty—he was shockingly bad with people.

Unlike his brothers, he wasn't emotionally intelligent. Concepts were easy; people weren't.

People, and their sticky, complicated psyches, were a complete mystery to him. He didn't think that would change anytime soon.

Finn leaned back in his chair and glanced at his oldest brother. His brother and Sadie—the art detective he'd hired to do a deep delve into a painting that might be a lost Homer—were engaged and besotted with each other. The air crackled whenever they were in the same room and the glances they exchanged were blowtorch-hot.

Ronan, the middle Murphy brother, was also currently distracted by his, so he said, inconvenient attraction to Joa, his temporary nanny.

Finn's brothers' preoccupation with their women suited Finn; it took their attention off him—*BASE jumping, Finn, are you mad? Shark diving without a cage? You take too many risks*—and he was grateful for the reprieve. They didn't understand his need for adrenaline, his willingness to push the envelope.

He didn't understand why, after experiencing divorce and death, they were even flirting with love and commitment, so he considered them even.

To Finn, handing over his heart was the biggest risk of all. Allowing oneself to be vulnerable was, to him, the most dangerous thing one could do.

He'd tried love once but hadn't allowed himself to go all the way, to risk everything, with Beah. And, not surprisingly, their marriage had crashed and burned.

Carrick pulled back the cuff to his designer jacket to check his watch. "Cummings will want to talk art with you. He's a bit of an art history and science buff. Just go along with it. Beah and I will jump in if you start getting…impatient."

Finn knew Carrick wanted to add *irritated*.

But holding an intellectual conversation with one of the world's wealthiest collectors of art, in front of Beah—the woman who still starred in his every sexual fantasy—was going to be a challenge.

"I saw your email saying you are wanting to take some vacation time in a few weeks. Where are you going?" Carrick asked.

"Ice climbing in Colorado."

Three, two, one…

"Is that safe?" Carrick asked, frowning.

Well, no. Because if it was safe, Finn wouldn't be doing it. Half the fun of adventure sports was the risk. He couldn't, wouldn't, risk his heart, but he had no problem putting his body on the line.

Because when he stood on the knife-edge of danger, that was when he felt most alive. And, yeah, he liked the excitement of achieving something exceptional. The complete focus the sports required also switched off his washing-machine brain, and it was his way to stop thinking, analyzing, planning.

And the dopamine rush kicked ass…

"Aren't you scared something will happen?"

Finn considered the question. Sure, it was a factor, but he didn't let fear stop him. "You know we can't control the future, Carrick. Bad things happen."

Carrick didn't reply and Finn knew he was thinking of their past, the many tragedies the Murphy siblings had been forced to handle. The world saw them as this successful, rich, we-have-the-world-at-our-feet family but people rarely remembered the hell they'd walked through, hand in hand.

But they'd stuck together and yeah, here they were. Scarred, battered, but still a unit, still stronger together than they could ever be apart.

Yet their pasts had shaped them, had molded him. All his siblings had their issues; Finn didn't like how love made him feel vulnerable and he knew it was better, easier, less risky, to hold back than to love someone completely.

It was better, safer, to keep his distance than to love someone and lose them.

Rolling his shoulders, Finn sent Carrick a reassuring smile. "Don't worry so much, Carrick. Nothing is certain, so we might as well live in the present and not worry about the future. Besides, I plan on being around for a long time, if only to keep annoying you and Ronan."

"Cummings is here," Carrick said, standing up. "Play nice."

Finn rose to his feet and buttoned his suit jacket. He rearranged his face into what he hoped was a genial smile as he watched the tall, thin man cross the room. Catching a flash of cobalt blue behind him, Finn moved his gaze from the art collector to the bold redhead talking to the maître d', wild curls pulled back into a ruthlessly tight chignon.

Her makeup was perfect, hiding the spray of freckles on her nose and cheeks, and her once-lush, curvy body was fifteen pounds lighter.

Finn felt his stomach twist. Beah looked older, sleek and sophisticated, every inch the successful London businesswoman. Wildly attractive but cool, remote…

He couldn't help wondering whether anything remained of his arty, curly haired, impulsive wife.

Ex-wife.

You speak many languages, Murphy, you can remember she's your ex-wife.

Two

Beah accepted Carrick's brief kiss on her cheek, heard his low-pitched "good job" and smiled. Earlier Paris Cummings had verbally agreed to move his artwork through Murphy's and she'd helped to persuade the billionaire Murphy International was the right avenue to dispose of some of his lesser artworks, including a small Lowry.

Sure, they didn't have a written agreement, but in the art game, bigger and bolder deals were solidified on a handshake. Trust was imperative in the world they operated in.

Tomorrow she would meet with Finn and Paris at his Hyde Park house and they'd trawl through his collection, making the final decision on what he was prepared to sell, and give estimates on what returns he could expect to realize. Yes, that would mean another face-to-face with Finn, but to land a client as important as Paris Cummings, she'd meet with the devil himself.

Beah watched Carrick escort Paris out of the restaurant, intensely aware of Finn at her side, the fabric of his designer suit brushing her bare shoulder. He smelled like he always did, of sunshine and fresh air, sex and sin, and Beah felt her head swim.

Maybe she shouldn't have had a second glass of prosecco.

Oh, who was she kidding? It wasn't the wine making her head swim, it was the presence of her hunky husband...*ex-husband.*

Acting professional throughout their meal had nearly killed her. She'd done nothing more than move her food around, conscious of those incredible green eyes on her, of every movement he made. She noticed his strong hands and remembered feeling them sliding over her bare skin. She noticed the way the subdued lighting turned his blond hair to gold...his broad shoulders, the way his black shirt fell down his wide chest and over what she remembered to be a six-pack stomach.

He still made her feel squirmy and whirly, and his effect on her—the throbbing deep inside her, the heat between her legs—frustrated her. She was not the young, high-on-great-sex girl she'd been at twenty-one. She shouldn't be feeling anything for him...

Not anymore.

Beah touched her chignon, checking that her curls were still under control. She hated her hair. When she allowed it free rein, she instantly looked ten years younger, wild and out of control. And her wild curls reminded her of Finn raking his hands through and burying his nose in her hair.

It was a memory she hated. And loved.

But these days, she always, always kept her hair pulled back. It was easier to maintain, control...

Control was important.

"You look good, Beah."

At his unexpected compliment, Beah lifted her face and her eyes slammed into Finn's. To the casual observer, he looked relaxed, urbane and debonair. But she knew him well enough to see the tension in his tight lips, his slightly raised shoulders. She knew Finn hated these meet-and-greet dinners and suspected the past two hours had been as difficult for him as they had been for her. But for completely different reasons.

Beah started to respond, to return his compliment, but then pulled her words. What was the point? She'd respond, he'd reply and within a minute they'd run out of conversation. Conversation had never been their strong point.

Beah lifted her fingertips to her forehead, conscious of the pounding behind her eyes. "We don't need to exchange inanities."

Finn's eyes darkened with what she suspected was irritation. "It's been a while, but you should know the one thing I don't do is inanities."

He made her sound churlish. "Thank you for the compliment." She pushed the words past her teeth.

Finn gestured to the exit. "Let's head for the bar, have a drink."

"Why?" Beah asked, conscious of his light touch on her back. It didn't mean anything; it was just Finn being his well-mannered self.

Except his touch made her skin sizzle, sent sparks dancing across her skin. Why was she still reacting to him like this? So much time had passed, but Finn could still rocket her from controlled to capricious in ten seconds.

Beah edged away from him, putting some space between them. Their intense chemistry was a good reminder of why they needed to keep an ocean between them, why they could never work in the same city, in the same building. On the same continent...

Finn made her feel off-kilter and off-balance and she didn't like it, dammit. She'd worked very hard to create her calm, orderly world, but one dinner and five minutes' conversation with Finn and she was feeling flustered.

Damn him.

On exiting the restaurant, Beah turned to Finn and shook her head. "I'm going to skip having a drink with you. I'm tired and I still have work to do tonight."

Finn pushed his jacket back to jam his hands into the pockets of his suit pants. He tipped his head to the side. "Coward," he quietly murmured.

Beah narrowed her eyes at him. "You think I'm scared to have a drink with you?"

How dare he imply she was a chicken? She'd divorced him, refusing to take a cent from him, moved back to her home country and worked her butt off to claw her way up the corporate ladder. She'd never asked for any favors from either her ex-husband or her ex-brothers-in-law, and few people within the organization, especially those in the UK, knew she'd once been married to one of the owners of the company.

Rising through the ranks, using her maiden name, had taken guts and hard work...how dare he imply she lacked courage?

Finn's green eyes were locked on hers. "Let's think about this logically, Beah."

Implying that he was always logical and she was not... *Grrrr.*

"Beah, in three months we are going to be holding

the spring sales and auctioning off the Mounton-Matthews collection. The PR is about to go into overdrive and you are going to have a hundred questions for me from about as many collectors regarding the various items up for sale. We both know this is the most important collection to be auctioned in a generation, maybe two. We can carry on exchanging cold, quick emails or we can get over ourselves and try to be friends, establish a working relationship that actually *works*. We were married a long time ago. Don't you think it makes sense for us to try to find a new normal?"

Beah suspected he was using the collective "we" when he actually meant *her*. And it really irritated her that he was acting like the attraction was all one-sided, as if his eyes never went to her lips, to her breasts... pretending he had absolutely no sexual interest in her at all.

Oh, he might be a Murphy owner, might be one of her bosses, but holy crap, he needed a reality check.

She wasn't riding this roller coaster of lust by herself, thank you very much.

Beah walked over to the bank of elevators, hit the button and waited for the doors to slide open. She could either call him on his statement or she could sit through a drink, maybe two, and make small talk. They could discuss the upcoming auction, art, their clients and what she thought they would be interested in, what the art market was doing these days.

Yeah, they could do that...she *would* do that. She would not let Finn Murphy suspect she still craved him, that she missed his sexy body, that she occasionally woke up at night, her body flushed, on the edge of orgasm because a naked Finn had visited her in her dreams.

She never missed her uncommunicative, emotionally distant husband, but damn, she did miss her skilled lover.

The elevator doors slid open and Beah stepped inside, conscious Finn was right behind her, his big body dwarfing her. Two couples stepped in after them and then another couple, and she found herself wedged into the corner of the elevator, Finn's huge body shielding her from the other occupants of the tiny space. Her breasts brushed his chest and her dress flowed over his strong thighs.

Then Beah made the mistake of lifting her eyes upward, noticing the strong cords of his neck, his soft blond stubble. His sexy mouth should be registered as a weapon. Looking into those eyes, edged with long lashes and framed by strong brows, could prove addictive.

He was all man, heat and sex and desire.

Finn's eyes darkened and his hand came to rest on her hip, his fingers pressing through her dress to burn her skin. His thumb brushed over her hip bone and his eyes darkened, took on a golden hue. He wanted her.

Beah could see it in his eyes, in the way he kept looking at her mouth… Oh, and the hard ridge in his pants was a solid clue, too.

Finn lifted his other hand to hold the side of her face and Beah held her breath as his mouth descended toward hers. She needed to know whether he still tasted the same—sex and sunshine and wind and heat—and she placed her palms on his chest, her fingers curling around the lapels of his jacket. If he didn't make the connection, she would.

Beah closed the last inch of space between them, standing on her toes to close the gap. His mouth brushed hers and she released a tiny, just-for-him moan. She felt his smile, inhaled his scent and then his lips covered hers, his short beard tickling her lips. Beah felt his hand slide around her to her back, and he pulled her closer so her stomach pushed into his erection. Dizzy from lust and want and need, she opened her mouth and Finn's tongue slid inside to tangle with hers, heating her from the inside out.

She was lost, in his smell, in memories, in the sheer masculinity of this man she'd never been able to forget...

From a place far away, Beah heard the doors to the elevators slide open, the chatter of guests leaving. She should pull her mouth off his, put some distance between them, but it had been so long and he felt so damn good.

Finn pulled his mouth off hers, half turned, and Beah peeked around him to see a family heading toward the elevators, determined to join them. She needed to get out of here, walk across the lobby and go home.

This was foolish, a special type of stupid.

But Beah couldn't move, and not only because Finn's bulk caged her in. She knew that if she gave him the slightest push, if she even hinted at feeling uncomfortable, Finn would back off; he would release her and let her be on her way.

But she didn't want to go anywhere. Right now, being in Finn's arms was exactly where she needed to be...

Finn used the side of his fist to hit a button and the doors to the elevator immediately responded, sliding shut on the astounded faces of the family heading their way.

Finn looked from her to the panel and back to her. "Three choices, Bee. I can open these doors again and you can step out into the lobby, or we can go to the bar and have a drink."

Beah looked up at him, touching the corner of her mouth with the tip of her tongue. "And choice number three?"

"My room," Finn said, his voice raspy with need. He placed a finger into the band of the bodice of her dress and tugged. "And the instant you step through the doors to my suite, this is coming off. Everything will come off."

She shouldn't. This was such a bad idea, but she'd been a good girl for a long time. "You promise?" Beah asked, dropping her hand to his waist and sliding it under his jacket. She tugged his shirt from the waistband of his pants and she sighed when she finally felt hot skin covering hard muscles.

Yeah, this. *Finn*.

"As long as you get naked, too."

Beah saw a flash of relief in his eyes, and Finn punched the number to his floor. And then he returned to kissing the hell out of her.

Because, yes, this was the way they communicated best. The only way they could.

Keely Matthews walked out of her bathroom and looked at the huge mass of male gorgeousness lying facedown on her California king and sighed. Dare Seymour, broad back, wide shoulders, muscular legs and an ass that was pure perfection, lay with his head in his arms, asleep.

There was nothing she wanted more than to curl up beside him, rest her head on his shoulder and drift off.

She was tired, too, pleasantly so. Two bouts of stupendous sex had her feeling loose and relaxed and a little affectionate. She didn't mind one and two; three was unacceptable.

She was not going to allow herself to go all gooey-eyed over Lawyer Seymour. He was too masculine, too attractive, too sigh-worthy, and Keely wasn't the type to go all mushy over men.

Especially men she didn't think she liked.

Or men she liked too much.

Oh God.

Keely leaned her shoulder into the doorframe and rubbed her temples with her fingertips. She should never have started sleeping with Dare, but resisting him was impossible. The man had superior kissing skills. His skill at French kissing was exceeded only by his skill in the bedroom.

And because sex was a fine way to catch feelings, she often found herself slipping into affection, thinking about him when she shouldn't, spending far too much time reliving their naked time.

She had to take a step back. Keely did not want a relationship and she most especially didn't want a relationship with someone as hardheaded, stubborn and bossy as Dare.

There was only room in a relationship for one bossy person, and that was normally her role. Keely knew she wasn't to everyone's taste. Her managing ways and her bull-in-a-china-shop approach frequently didn't win her any friends. As a teenager and young adult she'd genuinely tried to be less bossy but her good intentions always dissolved after a week, or month, or two.

She couldn't help it if she saw issues clearly, if the solutions to problems just popped into her head. And yes, maybe she could keep her opinions to herself, but why should she watch the people she cared about suffer when she had the answers?

Keely knew she was difficult; she'd been told that many times on many occasions. And all her relationships followed a similar pattern—her lovers told her they could cope with a strong woman, that her assertiveness turned them on, and she took them at their word.

But after two months, three, they all started complaining, telling her she was too over-the-top, too managing, too *much*.

And they packed up their stuff and walked out of her life, leaving her not-so-tough heart shredded.

After many tears and having her heart dented and dinged, she'd learned to keep all her love affairs on the surface and bed-based; that way she couldn't get hurt. And Dare Seymour, her lumberjack-looking lawyer, was not going to be the latest in a long line to drop-kick her heart.

Walk over to him, wake him up and kick him out. C'mon, Keely, you can't let him sleep over...

"Let me guess—you are about to kick me out." Dare's words were muffled but she heard his aggravated mumble. He rolled over and pushed his way up in the bed, looking ruffled and sexy. Keely fought the urge to straddle him, to place her mouth on his and taste him again...

Dare ran his hands through his hair, his blue eyes sharp. "We've been sleeping together for six weeks, Keely. Surely I can sleep over without the sky falling down?"

Keely stared at her bare feet. Sure, he could, but sleepovers were for people in relationships, not for casual lovers. And she had to keep Dare very casual indeed.

Keely lifted her chin and met his eyes. "I don't like people in my space."

Dare linked his arms across his flat stomach and Keely was grateful the sheet covered his groin area. A bare-chested Dare was distracting enough; Dare in all his glorious nakedness would be too much to resist. "Cut the crap. You're just scared."

Keely forced herself to lift one, just one, arrogant eyebrow. "Nothing about you scares me, Seymour."

Dare had the temerity to smile. "Oh, honey, *everything* about me scares you."

Keely tipped her head to the side and ignored her tumbling heart. "Are you experiencing a rush of blood to your head? An aneurysm? A little brain episode? Because you're acting weird."

"You're using sarcasm to avoid the subject. You're scared of me because I'm strong enough, man enough, to cope with your sharp tongue and pushy personality."

That's what they all said, and she'd trusted them enough to believe her previous lovers. Then they bailed. They *always* bailed.

She wasn't stupid enough to believe Dare would be the exception to the rule.

Keely placed her hands on her hips, annoyed with him and equally annoyed with herself for wanting to believe him. Keely made herself wave at the bed, dismissing their lovemaking with her hand. "It's just sex, Dare. You're seeing something that isn't there."

Dare flung back the sheet and gracefully rose to his feet, supremely confident in his nakedness. He loomed over her but Keely met his hard stare with one of her own. "You can BS yourself, Keely, but don't try to BS me. I see your eyes when I touch you, I hear your moans, the way your voice softens when you say my name."

"That's what women say in the heat of the moment," Keely protested. "Don't take my words seriously."

"Don't lie to me," Dare responded. He cupped her chin in his hands and Keely narrowed her eyes at him. "I can read you, Keely, and you're not half as tough as you think you are. Something is bubbling between us and it's more than sex."

Keely's stomach rolled over. Oh God, not again. She couldn't do this again. "It's only sex, Seymour. You're getting the physical and the emotional confused."

"The hell I am," Dare muttered, dropping his hand. He took a step back and sent her a slow, sarcastic smile, lifting those incredible shoulders in a small shrug. "Cool. Then find someone else who can give you the same buzz."

Horror at the suggestion must've jumped into her eyes because Dare's expression turned from sarcasm to satisfaction. "Not keen on that idea, huh?"

Keely placed her hands behind her back and pulled an implacable expression onto her face. She would not let him get the better of her in this argument. He won most of the arguments they had, usually by using logic to get his point across. It was very annoying.

"This conversation is ridiculous and it's time it ended," Keely told him, walking across the room to pick up his suit pants from the floor. She tossed them onto the bed and plucked his dress shirt off the occasional chair, resisting the urge to put the fabric to her nose, inhaling his unique smell.

Dare found his boxer briefs, pulled them on and reached for his pants. Keely didn't like the contemplative look on his face, knew that his sharp brain was working a mile a minute behind those gorgeous navy eyes. Yeah, he was up to something and she suspected it wouldn't be anything she liked...

She hated to be kept waiting. "Just spit it out, will you?" Keely demanded.

Dare pulled on his shirt and left the sides unbuttoned, pushing the tails back to slide his hands into the pockets of his pants. He sent her a steady look. "Do you want to stop sleeping with me?"

"No! Hell, no!" Okay, maybe she should not have responded so quickly, been a little cooler, played a little harder to get.

"Good to know." Dare's mouth tipped up at the corners. "The thing is, Keely, I still want to sleep with you, too, but I also want more."

More? How much more? Oh, crap. Keely lifted her hand to her throat, feeling her windpipe constrict. "Uh...what...um..."

"I've rendered you speechless. I'm impressed," Dare commented. He lifted his hand at her hot stare. "Okay, here's the deal..."

She didn't like the determined look in his eyes, the tension behind his genial expression. "I'm a guy, so obviously, I don't want to stop sharing your bed and exploring your amazing body..."

"But?" Because an enormous *but* had just strolled into her bedroom and plopped itself down, looking expectant.

"*But*, if you want to sleep with me, you're going to have to give me something first."

Ah, like what? Did she even want to know? Keely wasn't sure she did, mostly because she suspected there wasn't a hell of a lot she wouldn't do for sex with Dare.

Damn him.

"If you want sex, then I want a date."

A date… *What?*

Keely wrinkled her nose, confused. "What the hell are you talking about?"

Dare tucked his shirttails into his pants, did up his expensive ostrich-skin belt. "For every hour we spend in bed, I want two hours where we talk, dance, interact."

Keely's eyebrows shot up into her hairline. "Do you dance?"

"I can shuffle." Dare walked over to where she stood, gripping the back of her chair for support. He picked up her hand, skimmed her knuckles with his lips. "You look like I've just asked you to experiment with whips and chains and leather chaps."

"I… I…" Dammit. Where had all her words gone? She was never at a loss for words.

"You are determined to keep our relationship bedroom-based, Keely. I'm determined to take it up a notch."

"How much more?"

"I want to marry you and for you to have my babies."

Shock must've jumped into her eyes because Dare laughed, his blue eyes turning softer, gentler. "Okay, the look on your face was priceless. I'm just kidding, Killer."

Keely narrowed her eyes at his use of the nickname, but then quickly turned away, hoping he couldn't sense her disappointment at the quick retraction of his marriage-and-kids offer. Because it was her dearest dream. Marriage and a family were all she'd ever really wanted.

A proper place to belong…

Dare rolled his big shoulders, looking pensive. "We're not kids anymore, Keely, and the enemies-with-benefits thing is getting old. I just want to see if the spark can build into a fire."

She'd experienced many sparks, a few fires, but they'd been quickly smothered or doused by her strong personality or her partner's inability to deal with it.

No, she couldn't do this. Not with Dare. Not with this man who would, she was convinced, make mincemeat of her heart. "It won't work, Dare."

Dare slid his thumb over her bottom lip. "Of course it will, Keels, just trust me."

She couldn't; she had too much to lose. Her heart had already taken far too many knocks. She had to protect herself.

Keely pushed steel into her spine, stepped away from him and wrapped her arms around her torso. She made herself shrug. "Okay, no deal." She held out her hand for him to shake. "It was fun while it lasted."

Dare had the temerity to grin. He took her hand and yanked her into him, his lips sliding across hers. Keely was about to sink into the kiss when he pulled away. "I don't think so, sweetheart. You want what I do, you're just too stubborn and scared to admit it. I bet you won't last two weeks before you call me up and invite me to dinner."

"When pigs fly."

Dare kissed the tip of her nose, still openly amused. "And I expect you to pay for dinner and for us to talk, Keely. Only if I think you've tried will I allow you to have your way with me."

Keely wanted to slap him senseless. "You are such a jerk!"

"Because I'm done with you dictating the parameters of this relationship?" Dare asked, and she saw the hint of the ruthless lawyer he was. "Because I want more than just your body?"

"Because you're *pushing* me."

"I'm pushing you because you are braver and better than this, sweetheart." Dare bent down to pick up his shoes and sent her a tight smile. "I'll wait for your call."

"When hell freezes over." Keely tossed the words at his back.

Dare stopped and looked over his shoulder, sending her a slow, sexy smile. "Is that before or after pigs fly? I look forward to seeing both."

Argh. Keely released a wail of frustration and noticed her hairbrush on the side table. By the time she picked it up and launched it in his direction, the infuriating man had left her room.

She would not call him, buy him supper, spend hours talking to him. He was out of his mind if he thought she was that weak…

But dammit, the thought of not seeing him again made her heart feel empty, hollow and cold.

But that was better than having her heart broken.

Three

Beah felt Finn roll out of the bed, and as soon as the bathroom door closed behind him, she left his bed and looked around for her clothes. Not finding her dress or her underwear—clothes had flown as soon as she'd stepped into his massive luxurious suite—she pulled Finn's black shirt over her head, grateful when the tails hit her knees. Picking up a glass of water off his nightstand, she tipped the glass against her lips and allowed the water to slide down her parched throat.

She'd kill for some coffee. Beah pushed her curls back from her forehead, wincing as she remembered how Finn had pulled her pins from her hair, wrapping his hands in her out-of-control curls. Beah knew most of her makeup had either been kissed or rubbed off and her freckles would be on full display, making her look like the young woman she'd once been, instead of the woman she was now.

Her makeup and hair were shields, some of the many she kept up as barriers between her and the world. And she'd keep them up. She wouldn't let a hard-bodied, superbly-talented-at-making-her-scream man sneak through her defenses again. She'd worked too hard to transform herself, to become financially and emotionally independent. She couldn't allow herself to slide back. Finn had taught her that the only person she could trust, the only person she could rely on, was herself.

No, she needed to make it clear to him this was only about sex. They'd shared a night exploring each other's bodies and that's as far as they could ever go.

They had chemistry, not a connection.

As the door to the bathroom opened, Beah reached up to scoop her long hair off her back. She wished she had some pins or a band, but having neither, she twisted it into a messy knot, thinking anything was better than looking like a wild Irish waif.

Conscious of Finn's eyes on the tops of her thighs, Beah dropped her arms and the shirt fell a couple of inches. Trying to act cool, likc having soul-shattering sex was something she was accustomed to, Beah rocked on her feet. She needed to say something clever or, at the very least, utter a casual greeting but…man.

How could anyone act casual when she was confronted by six feet three inches of sculpted muscle? Beah allowed her eyes to dance over his ridged stomach, across his chest lightly covered with blond hair, over those huge arms. He didn't have an inch of fat on him and, if possible, was stronger and fitter than he'd been in his midtwenties. His narrow hips were covered by a white towel and Beah lifted her fingers to her mouth to check she wasn't drooling.

Shake it off, sunshine.

He wasn't perfect; he never had been. He was aloof and distant and while he was supersmart, his communication skills needed work. A lot of work...

Finn walked over to the bedside table and picked up the phone. Beah stared at his bare back, heard him order coffee and thanked God one of them had their priorities straight. A shower, a quick cup of coffee and she was out of here.

Finn replaced the phone in its cradle and turned to face her. He gestured to the bed, and his green eyes, mysterious and unfathomable, pinned her to the floor. "That was..."

It wasn't like Finn to look for words. "Fun? Interesting? A mistake?" Beah attempted to fill in the blanks.

Finn folded his arms across his chest. "One and two. A mistake? Not if we don't want it to be."

Finn was a master of speaking in riddles. "Meaning?" Beah snapped.

"It only becomes a mistake if we allow it to be one," Finn slowly responded. "In my head, it was a great night spent with a woman I once adored."

Adored, not loved. Hearing him speak about his feelings in the past tense shouldn't have hurt, but it did. Beah straightened her shoulders, more annoyed with herself than she was with him. They'd been divorced for so long, but he still could prick at her. It was ridiculous. *She* was ridiculous.

Finn glanced at the door and then back at her. He gestured to the vacant bathroom behind her. "Would you like to take a shower? I'll find your clothes while I'm waiting for room service."

Oh, it was obvious he couldn't wait for her to leave, that while he loved her body, he wasn't keen on her company. It was fairly obvious not much had changed in a decade.

But she wouldn't let him see even a hint of discomfort. She would not make this out to be anything more than a night of shared pleasure. "A shower sounds great, and I'll have a quick cup of coffee. I still have to get home before making it to Paris's house by nine."

"I can handle Paris if you want to skip the meeting."

Oh hell no. She'd been trying to get her foot into the door with Paris Cummings for years now and she wouldn't let Finn do her job for her. She would join Finn at the meeting and she'd get Paris to sign an official Murphy International document and she would add another collector to her already impressive client base.

And when she saw Finn again, nobody would suspect he'd licked her from tip to toe, that they'd brought each other to orgasm after orgasm with startling regularity.

Nobody would suspect a damn thing.

Because it was one night, not her life.

"Take your time."

Finn's words jerked her back to the present and she nodded. *Right, head on straight, Jenkinson. Be cool.*

As she crossed over from the window to the bathroom door, she heard Finn's phone ping with an incoming message. Hers probably had a dozen emails and another dozen messages, all from clients needing advice, wanting to sell or needing to buy.

Shutting the door behind her, Beah resisted the impulse to find her phone, to see what she'd missed. Fifteen minutes wouldn't make a difference. She was allowed a little time to enjoy this luxurious shower and the upmarket lotions and potions the hotel provided its guests.

Beah pulled Finn's shirt over her head and dropped it to the floor, stepping into the glass shower enclosure. She sighed as the hot water hit her shoulders, her neck, releasing the tension in her lower back. She loved her apartment in Notting Hill, but the water pressure was terrible and her showers were more like soft drizzles than hard, warm summer storms. She might not leave his shower, not ever.

Hearing the door open, Beah looked over her shoulder to see Finn leaning against the bathroom counter, staring down at the expensive phone in his hand.

"Hey," Beah protested, keeping her back to him.

Finn glanced up, looking distracted. "Bee, I saw every inch of you last night. That horse has bolted."

True. Beah turned, looked at him and noticed his preoccupation, the worried frown pulling his thick eyebrows together. "What's the matter, Finn?"

Finn waved his phone at her. "Do you remember Ben?"

Of course she did. Ben was Finn's oldest friend. Ben and his girlfriend, Piper, had been the only people invited to Finn and Beah's spur-of-the-moment wedding. Then Ben and Piper split up and, after the divorce, Beah lost touch with both of them. A pity, because she'd liked them both.

"I lost contact with them. I'm glad you didn't," Beah said, pouring a healthy amount of the body wash into her hand.

"Ben and I talk every couple of months," Finn replied. "He's still in Hong Kong, working as an investment banker."

Beah waited for him to continue, knowing it wouldn't help to tell Finn to hurry up with the explanations. He'd do it in his own time, or not at all.

"He wants a favor," Finn said, rubbing the back of his neck.

Finn wasn't the most social of men but once he made a friend, he rarely lost them. It didn't escape her notice that Finn held on to his friends, but he'd let her go easily.

Go away, hurt and disappointment. There's no place for you in my head.

"He and Piper are getting married. In six weeks."

Well, there was some lovely news. Beah grinned. "That's awesome. When did they get back together again? Is she in Hong Kong?"

"They reconnected about a year ago and Piper moved to Hong Kong to be with Ben."

All good news, so why was Finn in the bathroom with her? "Well, what does the message say?"

Finn glanced down at the screen. "'We're getting married. Need a hell of a favor,'" he read. "That's weird, because Ben isn't the type to ask for anything."

Beah frowned as she rinsed the soap off her body. "What sort of favor?" she asked. "And do you have a spare toothbrush?"

Finn reached for the handle to the drawer next to his hip, looked down and grabbed a toothbrush, still in its plastic cover. He put his phone on the counter and stared down at it as he wrangled the toothbrush out of its cover. Reaching for the paste, he squeezed some onto the head of her brush before yanking open the shower door and handing her the brush.

It was all very normal, so domestic, like it was a routine they had down pat. But nothing about this situation was normal…

Beah popped the brush into her mouth and shut off the water. She took the towel Finn held out and wrapped it around her torso, tucking the ends into the material under her arms. Out of the corner of her eye, she watched Finn's fingers tap out a message and within a minute, he had a reply.

Beah nodded at his phone. "So?"

"He wants me to call him," Finn replied.

Beah finished brushing her teeth. Her hair was a mess, so she pulled it out of its knot to allow it to spill down her back. Some of the curls brushed Finn's wrist, his shoulder, and he immediately picked up a curl and wrapped it around his index finger. "It's much longer than it was," he murmured.

"I need to cut it. It's too long," Beah replied, finger-combing it back from her forehead. She quickly started pulling the strands into a tight braid, another way to control the curls.

"When you get my clothes, can you also find my bag?" she asked. "There's a band in the side pocket."

Finn nodded, his eyes darting from her hair to her mouth. For a brief moment, Beah thought he might kiss her again, her mouth, the ball of her shoulder, the tiny patch of skin where her neck met her ear. She couldn't allow that to happen. If she did, both their towels would come off and they'd be back on his bed, or in the shower…

Either way, they'd end up naked, intertwined and late.

The night was over; this was a new day, and they had to move on.

Needing to break the spell, Beah bumped him with her hip. "Forget it, Murphy, the moment has passed."

"Bet I could bring it back," Finn said, the back of his knuckle running up her bare arm.

Sucker bet, Beah thought. *Be strong, Bee. One of you has to be sensible.*

A knock on Finn's hotel door penetrated the heat swirling between them. Finn cursed and scowled at her in the mirror. "I'll get the coffee."

"And my clothes. And my hairband." Beah pulled an insouciant smile onto her face, trying to pretend she hadn't been a heartbeat away from yanking his towel down and plastering her still-wet body against his.

She waited a minute, then another, wondering what was taking Finn so long. When she was sure the server had left, Beah took another ten minutes to rub lotion over her body, to comb her hair out. Then, still just wearing her towel, she walked into the sitting room of Finn's lavishly decorated suite and saw him sitting on the edge of a chair, his forearms on his knees staring at the carpet.

Beah halted, knowing something was wrong.

"Finn? What happened?"

Finn raised his head to look at her, his eyes filled with misery. "I just spoke to Ben. As he said, he and Piper are getting married back in the States, in six weeks."

That was happy news, so why did Finn look sick to his stomach?

"Ben has asked me to take care of the arrangements, basically to organize the wedding. Neither he nor Piper has family who can do it for them. I've agreed to help them."

She still didn't understand; pretty much everything could be done on the internet or via Skype. Hell, Piper could get on a plane and spend a week in Boston and organize everything herself. While she admired his willingness to help, Beah couldn't understand why he was agreeing to help with this wedding when he had so much else to do. The Mounton sale, for instance. Finn was an integral part of the most anticipated sale of the last decade. Plus, there was this upcoming meeting with Paris Cummings and the authentication of Keely's possible Homer.

Why did a friend's wedding skip to the top of the list?

"Piper wants to get married, in Boston, in six weeks." Finn repeated his words, his voice flat and his eyes haunted. "She has stage four pancreatic cancer. Ben says she has, at the maximum, six months to live."

Beah dropped down to sit on the arm of the closest chair, feeling like someone had punched her in the stomach. She lifted her fist to her mouth, her eyes instantly filling with tears at the thought of Piper—lovely, bold and vivacious—trying to make sense of her future.

Or lack thereof.

Beah pulled her bottom lip between her teeth, biting down on the tender skin. "How can we help? What can we do?"

Finn's eyes slammed into hers. "You can help her by helping me organize a wedding that will be remembered in this lifetime. And in the next."

Beah walked over to the tray of coffee and lifted the heavy pot and poured the fragrant liquid into two bone china mugs. Ignoring the milk and cream, she lifted the mug to her lips and took a sip, sighing when the heat hit her lips and her tongue.

Man, she needed this hit of caffeine, almost as much as she needed to leave.

But she couldn't do that until she was dressed. Beah looked around the lounge and saw her dress on the floor. Picking it up, she shook it out before taking another sip. Scooping her panties off the back of a chair, she bunched them in her fist, thinking she'd go back to the bathroom, change and leave.

That was a good plan, a sensible plan. If she left now, she could have an hour or two to herself, to regain some much-needed perspective, to make sense of what had happened last night.

"Where are you going?" Finn demanded, his voice a low growl.

Beah sighed at his shocked and pale face. Finding out an old friend had minimal time to live was devastating to hear and she knew he needed time to process the idea. When she'd heard that her mom was on borrowed time, she'd fallen apart.

She sympathized; it was crappy, awful news. Finn needed time to digest Ben's news, and knowing how self-sufficient and reticent Finn was, he'd want to do that alone.

Beah lifted her coffee mug, then her dress. "I'm going to get dressed and then I'm going to leave."

"But we need to discuss Ben and Piper's wedding."

Beah's eyes widened in surprise. Okay, he'd thrown out a suggestion that she help him organize their wedding, but she'd thought it was a throwaway comment, a statement made on the spur of the moment.

She hadn't, not for a moment, thought he was being serious, as she told him now.

"I seldom make statements I don't mean, Beah," Finn said, standing up to pour himself a cup of coffee.

"Look, I feel really sorry for Piper, and Ben. I know how awful it is. I lived through it myself." Beah rubbed her face with her hands, trying to push away the memories of her mom's skeletal frame, her pale face, her labored breathing. "But Finn, I haven't had any contact with them for nine years. Ben is your childhood friend and I only met Piper a couple of times after Vegas. I don't *know* her."

"But you know how to organize a wedding. You've done it before."

Beah frowned, puzzled. "What are you talking about?"

"You organized Nell's wedding."

Nell—now there was someone she hadn't thought about in years. They'd been fellow interns at Murphy's and Beah, in between working and getting naked with Finn, had helped her organize her wedding. Beah shook her head at Finn's computerlike memory. "Wow, I can't believe you remembered that."

"I remember everything," Finn stated, his eyes not leaving her face. He rubbed the back of his neck and shifted from foot to foot. "Look, I'm good at many things but...weddings? Not my strong point. He's my best friend and he's going through hell, so will you help me?"

Beah clamped her bottom lip between her teeth, holding back the hard "no" hovering on her tongue. She didn't have the time to work on a wedding. She had clients to see, trips to make. Just today she had to meet with Paris Cummings, meet another client for lunch at the Ritz, and she'd been invited to attend a West End show with a Kuwaiti princess.

But truthfully, there was another bigger, bolder reason why she had to say no...

Simply stated, she couldn't afford to spend more time with Finn Murphy. Because being around him made her feel vulnerable. She'd worked damn hard to create the life she wanted, and Finn made her question her choices.

Those oh-so-familiar questions rolled around her head. What if she'd fought harder for him, for their marriage? What if they'd gone for counseling? What if she'd given him more space, been a little less demanding?

But she wasn't solely responsible for the demise of their marriage. What if he had been a little more communicative, more understanding? What if he'd put her first instead of his work or his need for solitude?

Beah pushed her hair off her face with the back of her wrist. The sex was great but the walk down memory lane? Not so much.

Fact: their marriage was over. The night they'd just spent together, as wonderful as it was, was over. They needed to go back to being work colleagues who communicated via email.

She was allowed to say no to this request, allowed not to become involved. That didn't make her a bad person. She was just trying to protect herself.

Beah pushed her shoulder into the frame of the door. "I don't have the time and, might I point this out, I live here in London, not Boston. Even if I agreed to help, there's little I can do from here."

It was the truth, but it wasn't the whole truth. But Finn didn't need to know that.

Finn took a large gulp of coffee, then another. "We both know you could relocate to Boston for a couple of weeks if you wanted to."

"But I don't *want* to, Finn. My clients are here. My work is here."

I can't spend any more time with you, Finn, she silently added. *I can't take that much of a risk.*

"I don't know anything about organizing weddings!" he said.

"You did book two tickets to take us to Vegas," Beah pointed out, and winced at the sarcasm in her voice.

Ten years and a divorce later and she still felt cheated

because she'd never had the pretty dress, the prolonged excitement, feeling like a princess on her wedding day. That trip to Vegas had been a last-minute decision, and carrying on with the theme of impulsivity, their decision to marry had been a spur-of-the-moment thing, an impetuous decision by two stupid kids. She'd bought an off-the-rack dress from the hotel shop and stole some roses from the chapel garden for her bouquet. No planning had been involved. That might have been why she'd agreed to help Nell.

Finn banged his cup down on a heavy silver tray. "When did you become so stubborn?" he demanded, frustration on his masculine face.

Beah pulled in a long breath, looking for patience. "I learned to say no when I divorced you, Finn. I learned to do what was right for me, to not be pushed around, to not bend over backward to make people happy. I feel really sorry for Piper, I *do*. But I'm not helping you organize their wedding," Beah told him.

She couldn't; being around Finn made her *feel*. He also made her lose control, and she had to retreat to solid ground.

She needed to get back to her apartment and they needed to go back to ignoring each other. It was the safe choice, her *only* choice.

Beah walked back into the huge bedroom and threw her clothes onto the plump king-size bed. Dropping her towel, she yanked her panties up her legs, over her hips. Her eyes burned and she blinked back traitorous tears.

Breathing deeply, she ran through the conversation in an attempt to reassure herself that she'd made the right decision. It was true, she was busy, crazy busy, with Murphy business, preparing her clients for a series of sales, starting with the massive Mounton-Matthews sale at the beginning of spring. She also had meetings with her lawyer, with an accountant, and after she'd picked their brains, she'd meet with Michael to discuss his incredible offer.

Beah glanced at the closed door and bit her lip, fighting the wave of guilt, for saying no to Finn, for letting Piper down and, because she was on a roll, for wanting to walk away from her position at Murphy International. It wasn't a defection. She was allowed to do something else, join another company, restructure her business life. She'd once been married to a Murphy but she wasn't a family member, for goodness' sake. She didn't need to remain with Murphy's "'til death do us part."

It had taken her a long time to accept that she had a right to look at new opportunities, to find a new challenge, to enhance her career. Men did it all the time.

She had a right to put herself first, to protect herself. So if that was true, why was she not only fighting tears but also the urge to run back to Finn and tell him she'd help him organize an amazing, albeit last-minute, wedding?

Beah hurried back to her apartment in Notting Hill and after changing, she poured herself another cup of coffee and walked into her sun-drenched living room. She loved her apartment. It was colorful and cozy and the only place where she could fully relax.

Beah looked over to the mantelpiece and smiled at the large photograph of her and her mom, taken just before she got her diagnosis, when life still made sense. Two weeks after that photo was taken, their lives fell apart and everything changed forever.

Beah sighed, thinking that Ben and Piper's lives had also been flipped over and around. She wondered how they were coping with the harsh reality of a terminal illness diagnosis.

Beah had no regrets about her mother's death… Wait, that was wrong. Of course she regretted her mom's death; she still missed her every day, but she had no misgivings or regrets about her mother's final days. Though Beah had been young, just nineteen—nearly twenty—she'd given her mom the best possible send-off. In those final days and months, they'd loved each hard: up, down and sideways. She'd taken six months off from school to care for her mom and she'd do it all again without hesitation.

They'd always been a team and while they'd had their fights—what mothers and daughters didn't argue?—they'd been brutally honest with each other, utterly authentic. They'd struggled through her dad's leaving, together, both equally hurt and astounded and side-swiped by his lack of integrity.

They'd turned to each other for comfort, a rock-solid team of two. Up until the last few days, when her mom slipped into a coma, they'd laughed and wept and hugged. They shared happy memories and, in their own unique way, said goodbye. Back then, having watched her mom die, Beah understood life was meant to be lived, every second of every day.

That was why she jumped, both feet first, into love with Finn, moved in with him at the first opportunity and married him in Vegas. She'd been determined to wring every drop of happiness from her life.

But somewhere between her divorce and today, she'd lost that willingness to jump, to catapult herself into a situation. She'd been badly bruised when her marriage collapsed and trying to reconnect with her dad shortly after she signed the divorce papers had, in hindsight, cemented her need to protect herself.

Beah jumped when her phone rang and she scooped it up, smiling at the familiar number.

"Why are you still awake?" she asked Keely, automatically calculating the time difference. "Have you just kicked someone out of your bed and sent him on his way?"

"Basically."

Beah's eyes widened. "Well, wow. Who?"

"That's a long and complicated story," Keely replied, her tone blasé. Beah, because she knew Keely so well, also heard the not-ready-to-talk-about-that subtext.

"You didn't text me to tell me how your dinner went. Did you and Finn resist the urge to kill each other?" Keely asked.

"We behaved until he stripped me naked."

It took a moment for Keely to fill in the missing blanks. "Hopefully not while you were at still at the dinner table," Keely drily responded. "So you slept with him?"

"No, sleep didn't feature much. Earth-moving sex did."

Beah heard the tint of bitterness in the words and sighed.

"I'm not sure what to say, or how to react to that," Keely said.

"You and me both."

Beah pulled in a big breath and a torrent of words accompanied her exhale. She quickly and, hopefully accurately, summarized Finn's request to help her with the wedding, how she felt about Piper's diagnosis and how she felt bombarded by memories and the stinging return of past hurts.

"And now, because I'm a masochist myself, I'm re-membering how my father wasn't thrilled to see me after I returned to London after Finn and I fell apart," Beah muttered, hearing the rasp of tears in her voice.

During that awkward conversation with her dad she learned he'd moved from her childhood home into the one owned by the woman he'd been having an affair with while her mom had been taking her last breaths. On the mantelpiece was a photo of her stepmom and her dad on their wedding day, a scant four days after her mom's funeral.

While Beah had been nursing her sick mom, her dad had been off playing happy family with his mistress and her then-six-year-old daughter, who called him dad.

Something died in her that day. Maybe it was her na-ivete, her innate belief that people were mostly good, that love was meant to make you happy, that the men she loved were supposed to love her back.

But those horrible years long ago did teach her to be strong, to be independent, to not rely on anyone else to do what needed to be done. People, especially the peo-ple who were supposed to love you the hardest, always let you down.

"I can't stop thinking that in Hong Kong, a couple is coming to the end of their time together, that a life is drawing to a close," Beah told Keely, swiping at the tears rolling down her face. "I'm scared to spend time with Finn, Keels. He ties me up in knots, but my heart aches for Ben—I know what it feels like to watch some-one you love die. He will be veering between hope and despair, trying to be strong and stay strong…"

"Oh, honey."

"And Pippa wants a pretty wedding, a celebration of their love, a wonderful memory to hold on to. Hell, I'm as healthy as a horse and I wish I had that memory. I wish Finn and I had that perfect day!"

Pippa and Ben needed that memory, something wonderful to hold on to as their time together wound down, as her strength started to fade. And Beah had refused to help because…yeah, her reluctance to become involved started and ended with Finn.

Beah rested her elbows on her knees and pulled the tiny rake through the white sand of her minuscule meditation garden on her coffee table. She'd thought sex with Finn would be just that, good sex. But dammit, it had been more…

It had been both sweet and hot, familiar and strange, tender and steamy. It was everything great sex should be. And great sex like that didn't happen to strangers; it happened between two people who had a connection, who knew each other well.

Beah knew she could not afford to deepen her connection to Finn Murphy. Thank God she lived in London; if she lived in New York or anywhere on the East Coast she'd have to see Finn more often, upping the chance of her falling back into bed with him.

Maybe back in love with him, which would be an untenable situation.

"I'm weak and Finn is hot, Keely, and I don't want to start feeling something for him again."

"And you think you will if you help him organize this wedding? How would that happen?"

"Via emails and phone calls, I suppose. He's going back to Boston and I am staying here."

"Sadly," Keely quipped. "So, with you in London and him here, in Boston, if you offered to help him help Ben and Piper, you'd exchange a few emails, maybe a couple of calls?"

"Yes, brief calls, even briefer emails, I'd keep it completely professional."

"So where's the problem and how would it be different from what you've been doing for the past nine years?"

Not a hell of a lot.

"You're clutching at straws, Jenkinson. Are you going to help Ben and Piper or not?" Keely demanded in her forthright manner.

"I don't think I could live with myself if I didn't."

"Attagirl," Keely said. "My work here is done. Love you, bye."

Beah shook her head at Keely's abrupt goodbye and placed her phone on the coffee table. She rested her forearms on her knees and admitted that she wanted Piper to have the wedding Beah didn't have, the memory of a perfect, glorious day, saturated with love.

And really, Finn would need help choosing menus and flowers and deciding on the order of ceremony. He was, after all, the guy who'd thought it was a great idea to get married by Elvis in a tacky chapel in Sin City.

Beah swallowed down her resentment, reminding herself that she'd said yes; she'd gone along with his impulsive suggestion. She'd been damn happy to be getting married, so scared that Finn would change his mind that she'd eagerly agreed to anything he wanted, as long as he put that ring on her finger.

But secretly, she'd really wanted to walk down an aisle in a fantastic dress, holding lilies and roses, saying their vows in front of family and friends and a priest who took the ceremony seriously.

But she'd missed her chance at a fairy-tale day. She didn't want Piper to miss her chance, too. There wasn't much Beah could do from London, but she could find

out exactly what Piper wanted and pass her requests
on to Finn, who could put them into action in Boston.
With detailed instructions, he couldn't go too wrong.
She hoped…

Beah pulled her laptop toward her and punched Ben's
name into her social media accounts. Through friends
of friends, she found out where he worked and within
another few minutes had Piper's contact details on her
screen.

Social media was awesome.

An hour later, she ended her call to an ecstatic Piper,
who thanked her, over and over, for agreeing to help.
Like Beah, she'd doubted Finn and Ben's ability to pull
off a romantic wedding. They were good guys, she'd
said, but men who didn't understand the importance
of throw cushions and fresh flowers shouldn't be in
charge of weddings.

Two minutes after Beah ended her call to Piper, her
phone dinged with a text message from Ronan.

As we kick into high gear preparing for the Mounton-
Matthews sale, Carrick and I think it's best if you relocate to Boston for the next eight weeks. You're needed
here. ASAP.

Crap.

Beah stared down at her phone, panic tightening her
throat. It was true—no good deed went unpunished.

Finn exited the taxi outside Paris Cummings's house
and glared at the handsome, obviously old house—
Georgian, maybe? Paris Cummings had a hell of an
address. As he'd told them last night at dinner, he had
views of St. Paul's Cathedral, an underground swim-

ming pool, and Hyde Park was practically on his door-step. Finn pushed his hands into his hair and watched the ubiquitous black London taxicab roll away. He rolled his shoulders to dispel his tension and pushed back the cuff of his coat and sweater to look at his vintage Rolex. It had been his grandfather's and it still, sixty years on, kept perfect time.

It told him he was ten minutes early for his appointment. Thinking he'd take the time to connect with Ben again—their earlier conversation had been cut short because Ben needed to attend a meeting—he dialed his friend's number, leaning against the cast iron railing separating the property from the sidewalk.

His phone rang and Ben's face appeared on his screen, looking ten years older than Finn remembered. Finn, not great at conversation at the best of times, didn't know what to say, what comfort to offer, but Ben just smiled and waved his halting words away.

"She's going to beat this, dammit," Ben told him, try-ing to sound upbeat. "I refuse to accept that she's just come back into my life to be taken from me so quickly."

Finn nodded. Thanks to consulting Dr. Internet ear-lier, he now knew that the chances of Piper beating pancreatic cancer were slim. Practically nonexistent.

"Piper wanted me to thank you for agreeing to or-ganize the wedding. She'll be finished with her chemo and radiation treatments by then and hopefully will be able to enjoy the day without pain and the side effects," Ben said. "We'll be flying in earlier that week."

Ben picked up a pen and tapped his desk with the end. "Thanks for doing this, Finn. Piper doesn't have any family, and as you know, I can't trust mine to do it right."

Finn nodded, remembering that Ben's home life had

been hopelessly chaotic, with his parents either flush with cash or practically destitute. Thanks to their see-saw financial situation, Ben spent a great deal of time at Finn's house in Beacon Hill.

"Can you send me a list of what Piper wants?" Finn asked, thinking back to Carrick's wedding to Satan's bride, Tamlyn, and Ronan's marriage to Thandi, Finn's much-adored but now deceased sister-in-law. They'd both been grand affairs, with hundreds of guests, a forest of flowers, an open bar and many hot, single bridesmaids.

"Do you know if she has any ideas about flowers or food? Music? Do you want a band?"

Ben hesitated. "Maybe, with Piper being fragile, we should keep it simple. And because she tires easily, on the short side?"

This would be much easier if Beah had agreed to help him. As Finn recalled, she'd done a brilliant job organizing Nell's wedding, and Nell and her fiancé hadn't had lots of money. She'd thrown herself into the role of wedding planner and sometimes acted like she was planning her own wedding.

Was that because they'd married in Vegas, with him blithely telling her that they didn't need the hoopla of a formal affair?

He hadn't been interested in the church and party deal. Had Beah agreed or had she wanted a fairy-tale wedding? Funny how he could remember Nell's details but not Beah's reaction to their own choices. *Selective memory, Murphy?*

And why was it worrying him now? They'd had a fun wedding, with Piper and Ben there to witness it, and a helluva weekend in Vegas. And their marriage, as she'd coolly reminded him earlier, was over.

"I'm thinking about hiring a wedding planner to help me organize everything," Finn told Ben, rubbing his forehead.

Ben grimaced. "I tried to do that, thinking it would be the most logical solution. But everyone I called is booked solid. Apparently spring is their busiest season and nobody has the time, or the inclination, to organize a hastily planned wedding. Being in Hong Kong for so long, I don't have any contacts in Boston anymore and have no strings to pull."

As a Murphy, part of the most famous family in the city, Finn always had a string, or ten, to pull. But Finn also knew that Sadie, Carrick's fiancée, had decided to postpone her and his oldest brother's wedding because everyone and their mother got married in May and June.

"I know it's a big ask, bud, but my hands are tied. We can't leave Hong Kong right now. Piper needs to finish some treatments and I need to be with her." Ben's stress blazed from his haunted eyes and Finn could see that he was clenching and unclenching his fist.

Finn would make this work; he would. He would not let Ben and Piper down. A wedding planner was a long shot but Beah wasn't.

Ben and Piper needed her to help him and he wasn't afraid to push that button. They were adults; they could learn to deal with the past and their red-hot chemistry.

"Send me any ideas you have," Finn told Ben. "And Ben... I am sorry. This is, God, sucktacular."

It was a word from their childhood, something so dramatic and impressive that it surpassed all imagined levels of suckiness.

Ben managed a small, sad smile. "It really, really is, bud."

Finn disconnected and pushed through the wrought

iron gate and walked up the steps to the white front door to Paris's house, wondering if Beah was inside. Damn, this process would be much easier if she'd just said yes initially. The Beah he remembered, the one he'd been married to, would've jumped to help him, would've been eager to please him. Back then, when he said jump, Beah jumped.

Finn cursed. God, he'd been a helluva jerk.

These days, she was very much her own person, a little fierce and a lot independent. And because she was now both, even more intriguing.

Finn didn't have time to be intrigued, wasn't interested in the concept. Especially when the one being intriguing was his ex-wife.

Four

Dare Seymour frowned at the email on his computer, thinking his client had rocks in his head. It was far too late in the day—hell, it was past eight—to deal with this particular client's attempts to circumvent the law. His patience had run out hours ago.

Dear Sir,
You are being a dick. Actions like this will land you in an orange suit, shacked up with an inmate named…

Dare sighed, cursed and hit the backspace on his keyboard to delete the correspondence and closed his email program. He'd deal with his idiot client in the morning when, hopefully, he'd have more tact. When he felt this pissed off, this frustrated, it was time to leave the office. Food, a workout or exceptional sex normally went a long way to restoring his equanimity.

Food and a workout he could organize—probably

sex, too, if he headed to a bar and put out some feelers. The problem was, he didn't want stranger-sex; he
wanted Keely.

Annoying, infuriating, stubborn woman that she
was.

Dare glared at his phone lying on the desk, willing it
to ring. He hadn't heard from her for days, and he was
very tempted to call her. In ten minutes, he could be in
his car on his way to see her; in forty minutes he'd be
naked and so would she.

Dare rubbed the back of his neck. And after a few
bouts of amazing sex, they'd be back to where they'd
been before, having amazing sex. Which wasn't, on
the surface, a problem—he loved sex and he was good
at it—but he wanted more, dammit. For the first time
in his life, he wanted something deeper than a physical connection, something more tangible. He wanted
Keely's mind as well as her body…

But the brown-eyed blonde was more stubborn than
a pack of mules.

Well, he could be stubborn, too, and he wasn't going
to give in. This standoff was damned frustrating but
Keely had to realize he was the one person in her life
who wouldn't buckle under the force of her personality,
who wasn't intimidated by her bossy, managing streak,
who was strong enough to deal with her. She was smart,
determined and willful but, dammit, so was he.

He wanted more from her, from them—what *more*
consisted of he wasn't quite sure, but it definitely included some sort of emotional commitment, some sort
of mental connection—and he was going to get it.

Just watch him.

Dare pushed his chair back so hard it hit the cre-
denza behind him and rose to his feet, stretching. He

pushed down the lid of his laptop, slid it into its cover and idly wondered if one of his many brothers—and partners within the law firm—were still around and interested in joining him in the ring for a sparring session and then dinner. He really didn't feel like being on his own tonight.

Dare reached for his phone to put a message on the family group chat and stopped when he heard a gentle rap on his office door. He looked over his shoulder and Keely stood in the doorway, long blond hair tumbling over her shoulders, a wicked look on her face.

Well, well, well…and to what did he owe this pleasure?

Dare saw it in her eyes as she approached him, the burning desire, the flush on her cheeks. Oh, yeah, she wanted him as much as he wanted her. Good to know.

Dare—his can't-rock-me expression on his face—perched on the edge of his desk, legs spread apart, gripping the sleek wooden edge with white fingers. He had to hold on or else he'd grab her and the desk would see a great deal of non-law-based action.

"Keely, this is a surprise."

Keely walked up to him, stood between his legs and grabbed his loose tie, pulling him down. Dare allowed the space between them to close, needing to taste her.

"Hi, lover."

Dare smiled against her lips, amused by Keely's attempt to seduce him. Then her lips met his and her small tongue traced the seam of his lips, silently encouraging him to open up. If he did, if they started to kiss, to really kiss, he didn't know whether they would stop. And he needed to stop. He had to keep the upper hand.

He kept his lips closed.

Keely pulled back and he saw the annoyance in her

eyes, followed by a flash of determination. "Stop playing hard to get, Wilfred."

Funny how he loved hearing his old-fashioned birth name on her lips. Nobody called him Wilfred. He'd been Dare from a young age, and on her lips, his name sounded like an endearment. Sometimes she also made it sound like a curse, but he was ignoring those times.

"I *am* hard to get, Killer," Dare murmured back. "You know the stipulations…"

"Shut up." Keely placed her hand on his chest and renewed her assault against his lips. He wasn't going to touch her, lift his hands off the desk. But his resolve was tested when Keely's hand skimmed down his chest, over his stomach and came to rest on the bulge in his pants.

She stroked him and Dare gritted his teeth. Then she slid down the zipper and pulled down the band of his underwear to rest her hot, warm, greedy fingers on his erection. Man, best feeling ever.

"Don't you want this, Dare? Don't you want me?" Keely asked, her words punctuated by little kisses to the corner of his mouth, along his jaw.

Of course he did. He was a man, not a machine.

Keely growled her frustration and pulled her hand out of his shorts to attack the clip holding his suit pants together. When the flaps to his pants opened, she delved back in, both her hands enveloping him.

She was killing him.

Keely swiped her thumb across his tip and sweat broke out on his forehead. "I checked the offices as I walked down the hall. You're the last one here."

That was not unusual. He was frequently the last person to leave.

"And that means we can have hot office sex, preferably on your desk, with no one to disturb us." Keely's smile turned wicked again. "I like the thought of you working here and remembering what you did to me as you are talking to a client."

And if that happened, his efficiency and IQ would drop fifteen points.

Keely stepped back and Dare nearly cried when her hands left him. She shrugged off her coat and then, smiling, started to slowly unbutton her blouse. Dare watched as one button, then two popped open on her black silk shirt to reveal the edges of an emerald green bra. Sexy, lacy and transparent.

God, she wasn't playing fair. Then again, he'd never expected her to.

But if he didn't stop this, right now, he was toast. And Keely would've won their battle of wills.

Keely picked up his hand and placed it on her breast, and Dare couldn't help testing her weight, rubbing his thumb across her very responsive nipple. Man, she had the best breasts, full and high and exquisitely tender. He knew he could make her come just by touching her breasts...

Get with the program, Seymour, and shut this down. Now, while you can.

Dare pulled his hand back, pushed it through his hair before standing up and jamming both hands into the pockets of his pants. When her action pushed his pants down his hips, he cursed and quickly pulled up the zipper, wincing as the material closed over his straining erection.

Wow, uncomfortable.

Keely frowned. "And now?"

Be strong, Seymour. You're a grown man; you can refuse sex.

"And now you take me to dinner, we have wine, and

we chat. After that, and depending on how the evening goes, we might, or might not, have sex."

It took a minute, maybe more, for his words to sink in. And had Dare not been fighting his body's urge to strip her and do her on the wall, floor or table, he might've laughed. He'd never seen Keely discombobulated, utterly lost for words, and he was sly enough to enjoy what he knew would be a rare occurrence.

"I… You…"

And Keely never spluttered. This was only getting better. Dare moved farther away from her—being a man not a machine—and risked sending her a small smile. "It's not like you to mumble, Killer. Normally you have better language skills."

He saw a tide of fury, red and bright, skim up her throat, into her cheeks. "Are you seriously still playing hard to get?" she demanded, slapping her hands on her gently rounded, gorgeously feminine hips.

You could be holding those hips, sliding into her…
I'm delaying gratification.
But what if you don't win this one in the end?

"I'm not playing at anything, Keely. I'm holding you to the agreement we made. If you want sex, you're going to have to date me."

"I don't want to date you! Or anybody else," Keely shouted, her eyes wild and furious.

Dare tipped his head to one side. "Why not?"

"Because it never works out!" Keely retorted. She pushed her hands into her hair, holding the heap of blond hair back. "Why can't we keep this simple? What is *wrong* with you?"

Dare lifted one shoulder, his eyes steady on her face. Keely was afraid…of what? He searched her eyes and saw the fear, the healthy dose of vulnerability.

"What are you scared of, Keels? Getting involved? Commitment? Being loved?"

Keely released a low growl. "This conversation is pointless. You don't want a relationship with me, Dare, not really."

"How do you know?"

"*I* don't want a relationship!"

"And again, why not? Because you are scared? Of what? Getting hurt? That comes with the territory, Keels."

Keely released a small screech before bending down to pick up her coat. Without bothering to do up her open blouse, she jerked the garment on, muttering about stupid men, she was an idiot for coming here, she'd find what she needed somewhere else. Dare knew she wouldn't; Keely would never leave him to go trawling.

She didn't want sex. She wanted sex with *him*. And despite her fury, he knew she was intrigued by the possibility of "more;" she was just too damn stubborn to take the step.

But she would.

Because he knew he could out-stubborn her. It wouldn't be easy, but she was worth it.

Dare was coming to believe she was worth pretty much everything and if he had to drag her to that realization, he would.

Keely reached for her bag and jerked it over her shoulder, looking like a furious warrior woman. Risking a slap, or a kick to the shins, he approached her and slowly, because he was the only one who was going to see her amazing breasts in her sexy bra, began to thread buttons through the holes of her shirt.

When he was done, he sent her a crooked grin. "Sure

I can't change your mind? I'm starving and am craving pizza."

He knew pizza from the Italian place a block over was her weakness. As he expected, Keely's eyes narrowed. "Are you trying to bribe me?"

"Is it working?"

Keely responded by grinding the pointy heel of her boot into his big toe. It took all of Dare's willpower not to grimace, not to react. He wouldn't give her the satisfaction. When she released the pressure, he forced a smile. "Is that a no?"

"It's a *screw you, no*!" Keely hissed, turning around with a snap, every inch of her curvy body radiating fury. "You're going to pay for this, Seymour."

"How?" Dare asked, intrigued. This should be good.

When she spun around, hair and eyes wild, the moisture dried up in his mouth. "I don't know, but you will."

He grinned, excitement coursing through him. "Can't wait." He reached for his jacket, trying to act sanguine despite his throbbing toe. "Sure you don't want any pizza?"

Keely threw up her hands, flipped him off and stormed out of his office.

Yep, Keely was the woman his heart wanted. Dammit. Life was going to be hella interesting with her in it.

And she would be in it. *Guaranteed*.

The eight-foot door to Mounton House swung open and Beah smiled when Keely wrapped her arms around her waist and squeezed tight. Keely always gave the best hugs, but because she was clutching an expensive bottle of champagne—Moët, courtesy of her Kuwaiti princess—and Belgian chocolates, another gift from another client, Beah couldn't hug her back.

Keely eventually stepped aside and allowed Beah into the impressive hall. Beah was grateful because, while there were hints of spring back home in London, Boston was still damn cold.

"It's so nice to have you back in Boston!" Keely said, tugging her inside.

Beah placed the champagne and chocolates on the hall table—eighteenth-century, French—and allowed her enormous tote bag to drop to the floor. "It's just temporary, Keels. I'll be back in London by the end of May. Thanks for letting me move in here."

Keely snorted. "Like I would let you move in anywhere else, and it's not like I don't have the room. Especially now that the film crew have vacated the place."

Beah remembered Keely and Joa had recently lent out the turn-of-the-century fifteen-bedroom house—complete with many reception rooms, two libraries, a ballroom, two dining rooms, a media room and servants' quarters—to a director who was filming a horror movie. "Any problems with them?"

Keely shook her head. "A couple of broken glasses, a broken vase, thankfully nothing valuable."

Keely picked up the champagne and the chocolates. "Let's open these and have a drink."

"Good plan," Beah agreed, following Keely through the huge mansion to the kitchen at the back of the house.

Once there, Keely reached for two flutes—crystal, of course—and gestured for Beah to open the champagne. Beah, not wanting to waste a drop of the exceptional vintage, eased the cork out with a discreet pop.

After they'd toasted each other and taken a sip or two, Keely cocked her head, looking concerned.

"How are you feeling about being back in Boston?"

Beah knew what Keely was really asking—how did

she feel about seeing Finn again, on a daily basis? She wanted to lie, to Keely and to herself, but couldn't. "It's not ideal but I have no choice. They want me here, so here is where I am."

"And what's happening with your job offer from that Winters guy?"

"Summers, Michael Summers," Beah corrected her. "He wants an answer and is pushing me for one. I'm trying to delay making a decision until after your sale."

"Why?"

Beah sipped her champagne. "It's a chaotic time, Keels. The Murphys are under immense pressure. Your sale is highly anticipated. I don't think you and Joa actually understand how important it is. PR is ramping up. We are in constant contact with our biggest clients and all the agents of clients we don't represent directly. If the art world heard I am jumping ship, even that I am considering moving on, it would cause ripples and give rise to questions neither the Murphys, nor I, have the time to answer right now. Speculation and gossip would run rampant and it would dilute the massive PR campaign. I can't let that happen."

"You're that important?"

Beah didn't take offense at Keely's skeptical question.

But yeah, she was a powerful person in the organization, and her leaving would be discussed. And gossiped about. Stories would be swapped, embellished, made up. She didn't want any of it touching the spring and summer sales, the busiest time in the world of high-end art. "I am."

Keely nodded, understanding. "Well, nobody will hear a word of your plans from me."

Beah knew that; she trusted Keely implicitly.

"And you and Finn?" Keely asked.

There was no her and Finn. They'd had sex; it wouldn't happen again. She couldn't afford for it to happen again. She had too much to do and couldn't be distracted. Besides, she was more than a little annoyed with her ex.

A week ago, she'd sent Finn a detailed list of what needed to be done about Ben and Piper's wedding but when she asked for a progress report—yeah, she was checking up on him—she'd found out he'd accomplished next to nothing.

High up on her to-do list was to light a fire under Murphy's admittedly delectable ass.

Keely grinned. "I bet you a hundred bucks you won't be able to keep your hands off his—" she grinned "—admittedly delectable ass."

Beah groaned. "Did I say that out loud?"

"You did. We'll get back to Finn and his ass but—" Keely reached across the island counter for her phone "—give me a second to cancel my plans for tonight."

Beah placed her hand on her wrist. "What plans? Do you have a date?"

Keely frowned. "Yes. No… Sort of."

Keely threw half the contents of her glass down her throat and Beah lifted her eyebrows. "What's going on, Keels?"

Keely rubbed the tips of her fingers against her temple. "That damned lawyer Wilfred—Dare—Seymour."

Beah topped up her glass, intrigued by the frustration on Keely's face. Her friend was incredibly confident, amazingly self-assured, and a lawyer had her in a froth? Interesting…

"You're going on a date with him?"

"Not by choice," Keely muttered. When Beah

frowned, she waved her words away. "God, no, he's not forcing me to date him, as if he could! He just challenged me to spend a couple of hours with him. And we're not allowed to discuss anything to do with work. Or Isabel. Or art. Or this house."

Beah was now intrigued. "And why did he issue this…*dare*?"

Keely glared at her for her deliberate choice of the word. "Because he says the only reason I keep snapping and snarling at him is that I'm scared that if I don't, I might jump him."

Beah nearly snorted champagne out through her nose. When she felt she could talk, she schooled her features—damn, it was nearly impossible not to smile—and asked the obvious question. "And can you resist him?"

Keely sent her a red-hot, I'll-slay-you-where-you-stand look. It lasted only three seconds and then her shoulders slumped and her face crumbled. "No. Probably not."

Tread softly now, Beah. "And why would you want to resist him?"

Keely looked at a point past Beah's shoulder. When she returned her attention to Beah's face, she looked rueful. "We've been sleeping together for a while. I keep telling him it's just good sex. He keeps insisting it's more and that I am too stubborn to admit he's right. He's put this ridiculous rule in place… Crap, I can't believe I am telling you this."

Beah leaned forward. "If you stop now, I swear I'll slap you. What rule?"

Keely blushed. "If I want sex, I have to date him first. He's not putting out until I've bought him dinner and spent some time emotionally engaging with him."

Beah slapped her hand against her mouth to keep

from laughing out loud. Oh, she really wanted to make a comment about tables and the turning thereof…

"I didn't think he was the kind of man to pass up an opporunity to have no-strings sex. What is he doing?" Keely demanded.

"I haven't the faintest idea," Beah lied, convinced Keely was A) not ready to hear Dare Seymour was obviously head-over-heels in love with her and B) not ready to face the life-changing realization she might be head-over-heels in love with him, too. They needed to work it out themselves; Beah didn't want to spoil their fun.

"The nerve of the man," Beah stated, silently laughing.

Keely tipped her glass at her, frowning. "Why do I think you are laughing at me?"

Beah placed her hand on her chest and tried to look innocent. "Not me."

"Pffft." Keely drained her glass. She looked at her watch and winced. "I'm going to be late if I don't hurry."

It appeared that changing her plans was no longer on the agenda. Okay then. Beah grinned, knowing Keely was going to have a long, lovely night ahead of her, especially if she bought Dare dinner. "Okay. I'm going to head over to Murphy's. I need to talk to my bosses about your auction."

Keely pulled her bottom lip between her teeth. "I still feel like Isabel's turning in her grave at us selling her beloved collection."

"The dead are dead, Keels. It's up to the living to live." Beah knew this; she lived it every day. "And the money you raise is going to Isabel's foundation. That's a very good thing."

Beah stood up and drained the last of the champagne from her glass. "I'm going to freshen up. And you need to get ready for your *date* with your hot lawyer."

Keely hopped off her chair and pinched Beah's side. "You are enjoying this a bit too much, Bee."

Beah grinned. "But remember, just because you buy a guy dinner, he's not obligated to sleep with you."

"I hate you so much right now," Keely said, picking up the box of chocolates and holding them to her chest. "I'm confiscating these because you're being snarky."

Beah laughed, kissed her on the cheek and left. While she enjoyed watching Keely flail around in relationship confusion, she had no intention of doing it herself.

Then why did the thought of seeing Finn again cause the butterflies in her stomach to take flight?

It was nearly six by the time Beah walked into the lobby of Murphy International. The receptionist, someone Beah didn't recognize, was packing her bag to leave and when Beah showed her Murphy International identification badge, she was told Finn was in his basement office, a sprawling space he'd had remodeled shortly after he joined Murphy's straight out of college.

Beah placed her thumb on the panel to the lift that would take her to the secure areas of the company, including the storeroom where multimillions of dollars' worth of art was housed. It still bemused Beah that the Murphys trusted her as they did and, yeah, she felt guilty about her plans to leave them.

She made good money with them, very good money, but leaving Murphy's to join Michael wasn't about the money. She wanted the freedom to make her own decisions, to see whether she could cut it on her own in this hard, secretive world of trading art and priceless antiques.

When she left Murphy's, she would finally feel totally independent, answering to no one. Only then would she know if she would sink or swim. It was the ultimate test of her ability to stand on her own two feet.

To show herself she didn't need a father. Or a husband. A *man*. It was a way to keep busy, and hopefully, a new challenge would satisfy her restless spirit, the part of her that was always looking for something else, something more…

Something to fill the holes in her life she didn't like admitting she had.

Her life hadn't turned out the way she'd planned. She'd thought she would be a mom by now, happily married, settled. Still working, naturally, but easily switching among being a wife, a mom and a business-woman. Yeah, her life was nothing like that. And now she couldn't imagine being immersed in a family, purely because she now understood, on a fundamental level, that people left when one needed them the most. The three people she'd loved the most had all left her—at different times and in different ways—but no matter whether they'd wanted to or not, they'd still left.

She'd never put herself in that position again. Ever.

And no matter how sexy her ex-husband was, how much she desired him, she would never be fool enough to expect more from him than he could deliver. Besides, she didn't need anything from him; her life was good. She felt fulfilled.

Didn't she?

Feeling a little irritated with herself, Beah barged into Finn's basement office, allowing the door to slap closed behind her.

He stood by the bookshelves filling the back wall, black-rimmed glasses over his green eyes, holding a thick open book in his big hands.

Sexy nerd. Brains and muscles were a killer combination.

Annoyed with where her thoughts went, Beah reined them in and slapped her hands on her hips. "Have you contacted the florist? Confirmed the time for the ceremony at the chapel? Told the caterer how many people to expect?"

Finn closed the book, replaced it and slowly, oh so slowly, walked past his desk, past his beat-up leather couch to where she was standing. As he walked, Beah appreciated his long-legged stride, the way his black Henley skimmed over his chest and dipped into the curves of his muscled arms, fell over his flat stomach. His long legs, covered in faded denim, ate up the space between them, his flat leather boots not making any sound on the expensive hardwood floor.

Okay, to amend her previous statement: she might not need him, but she wanted him.

Instead of speaking, Finn placed his palms on either side of her face, tipped her head and took her mouth in a hot, hard kiss. Beah considered, just for a moment, objecting. Instead she let his tongue push past her lips, touch her tongue, and then she fell into his kiss.

Holding his wrists, she arched her back, pushing her breasts into his chest, sliding her tongue over his, welcoming his taste and touch and smell. His hand moved down her cheek, her neck, and settled on her breast, his thumb sliding over her nipple, supersensitive beneath the expensive lace of her bra.

Beah wanted her clothes off, she wanted them to be naked, and she wanted it now. Taking a step backward, pulling Finn with her, she reached behind her and fumbled for the lock on his door, eventually turning it so they couldn't be interrupted.

Finn pulled his mouth off hers, his green eyes glittering in the low light of his freestanding lamps. "Here? Now?"

"Yeah."

Beah wound her arms around his neck, placed her mouth against his, eager to get back into the kiss. She nibbled his bottom lip and took a minute to realize Finn's fingers were digging into her hips but he wasn't responding to her kiss.

Feeling like she'd jumped into an icy pond, she pulled back and allowed her hands to drop to her sides. "Problem?" she asked, trying to act casual.

Finn's eyes didn't leave hers. "Ronan scheduled a meeting in—" Finn glanced at his expensive high-tech watch "—ten minutes."

Right, that was why she was here at Murphy International. To meet with the Murphy owners and her bosses. *Ack.*

Beah dropped her head, feeling heat seep up her neck and over her cheeks. One look at Finn and she'd lost all sense of propriety, all sense of place. And time.

"I like the fact that I can knock you off your game," Finn said.

Beah really wanted to smack the smirk off his face. She looked at the door, considered the size of his head and squinted at the door. "Are you certain your monstrous ego can fit through the door?"

Finn grinned. "I manage." He sat down on the corner of his desk and stretched out his long legs, crossing his feet at the ankles. "Do you always walk into offices and start kissing the hell out of your colleagues?"

"Do you always start your conversations with your colleagues with a French kiss?" Beah volleyed back.

"Touché."

Beah needed to get this conversation—and her thoughts and her damned priorities—back on track. Damn Finn for having this effect on her, for being able to shut down her brain and send her spinning.

"I came down here to talk to you about the wedding..."

"Thank you for helping me out, by the way."

"I'm doing this for Piper and Ben, but mostly for Piper. Every woman deserves a fairy-tale wedding."

Finn nodded. "Fair enough." He picked up a baseball from his desk and tossed it from hand to hand. "So you stormed down here, a few hours after you landed at Logan, to talk to me about the wedding. Are you that much of a control freak, Beah?"

"I am not a—" But yeah, she was. Keeping control was how she now managed her life; everything was put into boxes and corralled and contained. It would be much easier if she took over all the arrangements for the wedding; then she knew everything would be done to her exacting standards.

Having Finn involved made her feel like a three-year-old was rummaging in her just-tidied box of toys and tossing stuff over his shoulder. Beah shuddered.

Beah jammed her hands into the pockets of her slim-cut, straight-legged trousers. She would not lose her temper but really, did he not realize the wedding was in four weeks? That Piper and Ben would be here in three and everything had to be in place by then? Piper did not need any additional stress; she just needed to enjoy every aspect of her big day. It had to be perfect...

"Flowers? Chapel? Caterers?" Beah pushed the words out.

"For someone who wasn't going to help with the wedding, you have become very involved." Finn linked his fingers against his flat stomach. "Why?"

"Because I don't trust you not to get involved in some research and leave everything to the last minute. Or for you to run off on one of your adventure trips and leave their wedding un-arranged," Beah snapped.

"That's not fair, Beah. I readily admit I wasn't the best husband, but I never shirked my responsibilities or broke my promises."

But he had. He'd promised to love her until they died but when their marriage no longer worked, when it got too much to handle, he bailed. His need to be free had been more important to him than she was.

And it still hurt, dammit. It shouldn't, but it did.

But what she wouldn't do was rehash their old arguments or fling blame. They were divorced. Their marriage was long over, so it shouldn't matter anymore.

But it—

No, enough. Move on, Beah. Stop flogging this very dead horse.

Before she could change the subject, Finn spoke again. "Are you trying to help Ben and Piper because it reminds you of what you went through with your mom?"

She was trying to keep perspective but she couldn't help the surge of anger and resentment. No, he didn't get to mention her mom, not now. How many times had she tried to talk to him about what she went through watching her mom die? But every time she reached out, he shut her down, changed the subject, distracted her with sex. "Subject closed, Finn."

"Why?"

Beah sent him a hard look. "You couldn't talk to me about her when I most needed you to, Murphy. I worked through my issues around my mom's death—and my dad leaving—on my own, without help from you. Or anybody. Why would I want to rehash now and why would I want to do it with you?"

Beah thought she saw regret in his eyes, remorse on his face, but the light was too low and the emotion too subtle for her to be certain. Besides, it didn't matter—this conversation was over.

She lifted her hand and pointed a finger at Finn. "Don't go there, Murphy. We might still be attracted to each other and, yes, I was quite keen to sleep with you just minutes ago. But chemistry is all there is between us. I have no interest in talking about the past, yours, mine or the brief time we shared together."

Instead of responding, Finn just stood up, picked up a folder off his desk and walked over to the door. He turned the lock, opened the heavy door and stepped back before gesturing her to take the lead.

Beah started to walk toward him, annoyed by his lack of response and confused by the thoughtful expression on his face. It didn't matter; she'd made her point and also put up a strong barrier between them.

Shrugging, she walked into the hallway, thinking she had to go back to ignoring Finn Murphy because nothing good came of being in the same space as him.

Beah turned to see what was keeping him and winced when she saw him picking up her tote bag and her coat from where she'd tossed them before she'd started kissing him. Beah rubbed her temples with her fingers. Finn still had the ability to mess with her head, to knock her off her stride...

To make her lose control.

Five

Finn followed Beah into the elevator, feeling disconcerted and off-balance. He wasn't the type to look back, never had been, preferring to put his past behind him. Of course he'd thought about Beah over the years, probably more than he should—he often remembered how amazing the sex was, the way her hair glinted with streaks of gold in direct sunlight, her whiskey-colored eyes, open and filled with love, as she first looked at him in the morning—but up until Beah's recent reappearance in his life, he'd never spent a lot of time analyzing their marriage, preferring to believe they had been too young and too dumb to have made such a lifetime commitment.

Beah's phone rang and she pulled it from a side pocket of her bag, lifting it to her ear. "Your Highness, how nice to hear from you."

Beah wasn't being facetious; Finn could think of at least five of their clients holding royal titles.

"I'm sorry, I'm in Boston, but how can I help you?"

Finn tuned out of Beah's conversation, silently admitting that he was mostly responsible for them crashing and burning. Yeah, Beah had been clingy and emotionally demanding, but had he been more mature, a little less selfish, he would've realized any woman who'd lost her mother to cancer and her father to abandonment would need extra reassurance.

"He's a Moroccan sculptor working in glass. He's phenomenal," Beah stated.

It both shamed and irritated him that he'd never given her the space to talk about her mom, about what she went through as a teenager. On the few occasions he did try to listen, he hadn't known what to say, how to respond, how to comfort her…how to make it better.

Because he found talking hard, because he found emotion difficult, he'd chosen not to engage at all. Why was so it tough with her? Was it because hearing about her mom reminded him of his own losses—his birth mom, then his stepmom, Raeni? Or was it because he couldn't change her past and he felt incapable?

"But do you like his work, Princess Sofia? Or are you buying it as an investment?"

Whatever the reason, he knew the man he'd been—that selfish boy—had failed her. He'd brushed over her pain and attempted to slap a Band-Aid onto a gaping wound. Finn rubbed the back of his neck. If he could, he would go back and kick his own ass. Hard.

He'd messed up and he owned that. But what could he do about it? What did he want to do? What did he want from Beah this time around? And more importantly, what could he give her?

The thing was, while he might be a bit more self-aware these days, he hadn't changed much. The thought depressed Finn because he was educated enough to know age should bring some sort of emotional growth, but he still wasn't comfortable with emotion; he still liked his own space. He still thought it was better to hold back than love someone completely.

But he liked Beah, enjoyed her, loved what they did to and for each other. When he made love to Beah, he felt like he was flying over fresh powder, felt the same rush of dopamine as he did when he donned a wingsuit and flew off a cliff.

With Beah, he felt intensely alive.

And that scared the crap out of him.

"He only produces a few sculptures a year and they get snapped up pretty quickly. I can put out some feelers, ask if he's interested in doing a commission. I can also contact a few collectors who own his work to see if they want to move any along."

She was so smart, knowledgeable and personable. And she was so good at her job.

Finn shot a look at her pretty profile, idly noticing her spectacular hair was pulled back into another of her complicated smooth twists. He wanted to find those pins, yank them out and feel those pretty strands on his fingers, over his hands, his stomach and his thighs…

"Okay, we'll chat soon. Thanks so much for the call and my regards to your family," Beah said, ending her call.

Finn banged the back of his head against the metal skin of the elevator. He needed all his determination not to blow off their meeting with Ronan because he desperately wanted to slowly undress her and go back downstairs to bend her over the arm of his sofa.

See how easily he was distracted by her? One minute he was thinking about how much he'd failed her, how alive she made him feel, and two hops and a skip later and he was thinking about her naked...

That, he suspected, wasn't going to stop.

But God, he should apologize for being such a selfish prick all those years ago.

"I'm sorry," Finn forced the words out, keeping his eyes closed.

"What are you sorry for, Finn?" Yeah, he heard the ice in her voice, the thread of irritation.

"For blowing you off when you wanted to talk about your mom." Finn forced his eyes open, forced himself to look at her. "I should've listened more."

Astonishment flickered in Beah's copper-colored eyes and she opened her mouth to speak, but no words came out. She tried again with the same result.

Shaking her head, she lifted her hands. "I—"

Before she could finish her sentence, the elevator stopped and the doors opened and Carrick stood in the hallway, looking impatient. Carrick, immediately sensing the tension, placed his hand on the door to keep it open and briefly kissed Beah's cheek. "Hi, Bee. Nice to see you again."

His brothers had always adored Beah and had given him a hard time about the failure of his marriage, frequently telling him he was making a mistake by letting her go. But Finn was, like them, as stubborn as hell and he'd genuinely believed the divorce was for the best.

Carrick darted a look between them, a tiny frown appearing between his dark brows. "I can catch another elevator if you two need to talk."

Beah gestured him inside. "No, come on in."

Carrick stepped inside, the elevator resumed its ascent, and Carrick stood between them, a solid shield.

Finn darted a look at Beah and saw she was staring down at her feet, her arms crossed over chest.

Yeah, this silence was as awkward as hell. Thank God they only had to endure another twenty seconds of tension. When the elevator opened, Carrick looked from Beah to him and shook his head.

His oldest brother sighed. "It's going to be a long couple of long weeks," he said before stepping out.

Beah started to follow him but Finn's hand shot out to grab her elbow, halting her forward momentum. He waited until Carrick was out of earshot before meeting Beah's eyes. She looked down at his hand clasping her arm and very deliberately stepped away.

"Oh, please, just now you had your hand in my pants." Finn shot the words out and immediately regretted them. Yep, he went *there*. God, he really wasn't good at talking. Finn released a frustrated growl and linked both his hands behind his neck. He released a low curse. "Okay, sorry, again."

Confusion and frustration jumped in and out of Beah's eyes. "Let's just go find your brothers, Finn."

Finn took the risk and grabbed her fingers, linking them in his. "Just hold on a second, Beah, let me get this out." He looked for the right words, mentally tested and discarded a couple of sentences, and went with his gut. He'd either flame out or not, but Carrick was right—it was going to be tough if they didn't find a way to deal with each other.

They all had important jobs to do and a show to put on, art to sell. "Can we try, at the very least, to be friends?"

"This again?" Beah tugged her fingers away. "Seriously, Finn? After everything, you want us to be friends?"

Finn lifted one shoulder and let it fall. "I wasn't a good friend to you while we were together, Bee. I'd like to change that."

Beah looked astounded and he didn't blame her. Hell, he barely understood the request himself. "Well, what do you say?"

Beah looked at her watch, hauled in a breath and gave him a what-the-hell look. "Okay, whatever. Give it your best shot," she told him, her voice saturated with doubt. She expected him to fail, Finn realized, as he followed her down the hallway to the conference room.

At the door, she turned and lifted her fine, arched eyebrows. "And what are we going to do about our still ridiculously strong chemistry?"

Finn grinned at her as he reached around her to open the door. "I'm sure you've heard the phrase *friends with benefits*?" He immediately noticed her shock but managed to swallow his laughter. He placed a hand on her back and gestured for her to precede him. "After you."

Carrick, standing just a couple of paces from the door, looked from him to Ronan and grinned. "And so it starts."

Finn's eyes jumped between his brothers' smirking faces. And what did Carrick mean by *that*?

Finn pulled up in front of Mounton House, cut the engine to his Porsche Cayenne and took a moment to look at his ex-wife, walking down those stone steps. He'd texted her early this morning, telling her he needed her input on the upcoming wedding, and asked if she would spend part of the morning with him. He'd expected her to say no but here she was, heading toward his vehicle. Finn leaned across his seat and pushed open the passenger door. She took the hand he held out and he gently tugged her into the car, casting an eye over her beautiful face.

"I miss your freckles."

Beah sent him a surprised look. "What?"

He shrugged, punched the start button and his powerful car roared to life. "You cover your freckles with makeup, but I like seeing them."

She touched her nose. "You do?"

"And I also miss your curls."

"Fire-red curls and freckles make me look like I'm fifteen and it's not how I need my clients to see me," Beah said, crossing her legs. She looked incredible in a bulky oatmeal sweater worn over tight black jeans tucked into knee-high boots.

Finn pulled out into traffic and turned down the heat, thinking this was one of the first sunny days Boston had seen for a long, long time and he could actually feel some heat in the sun. It had been a long winter and he couldn't wait for spring.

"What's on the agenda for today?" Beah asked.

Before he could answer, Beah's phone rang and she dug in her tote bag, pulling out the expensive device. Since he'd stopped for a red light, he looked at her as she stared down at the screen, obviously debating whether to answer her call.

He wanted to peek at her screen to see who'd put the excited but hesitant look on her face.

"Hi there."

Okay, not Beah's standard way of greeting anybody, making him think she didn't want him to know who was on the other side of the call. Which just, dammit, made him even more curious.

The light turned and Finn accelerated.

"I'm good, thanks. Just very busy," Beah said, and

was silent for a while, her concentration fully on the person on the other end of the call. "I'm not sure when I'll be back in London but I promise you, as soon as I know, we'll get together."

A potential date? Another lover? Finn felt acid flare up in his gut. Yeah, he couldn't deny it, he felt a green monster gnawing on his backbone.

"I can't answer your question right now," Beah said after another long silence. "But you know it's something I'm thinking about."

Hell, what was she being asked to do? Take a holiday? Go on a date? Sleep with someone? Move in with someone? Finn's hand tightened around the steering wheel and he glared at the back of the sedan in front of him.

He felt Beah's eyes on his profile and heard her softly spoken words. "I'll call you…when I can talk."

Yep, there was definitely something she wasn't telling him. And why did she feel the need to keep secrets from him?

Oh, that might be because you two are no longer married, and you've barely spoken for the past nine years.

Beah disconnected the call and put her phone back into her bag. He wasn't going to ask; he didn't have the right to pry. He'd lost that right when he filed for divorce.

"Who's the guy?"

Hell of a thing when your mouth no longer obeyed your brain.

"None of your business," Beah replied. And it wasn't; it really wasn't.

"Are you sleeping with someone else?" Finn asked, trying to sound casual but missing by a thousand miles.

"Would it bother you if I was?" Beah asked, and he heard the amusement in her soft question.

This wasn't funny, dammit. "Damn right it would. I don't like sharing."

He turned his head and caught Beah's nod and the thoughtful look on her face. "I don't like sharing either so, fair enough. Just for the record, I'm not sleeping with anyone else."

Finn felt the monster retreat and stretched the fingers on his right hand, then his left. "Okay." He waited for her to explain and then waited some more. But no explanation came.

Crap. He didn't like being kept in the dark. Not about her. And he knew, at a gut level, whoever had been on the end of the call was damn important to Beah.

Who? Why? What was she up to?

Before he could push, Beah changed the subject. "Where are we going first?"

The moment had passed and Finn knew he wasn't going to get anything out of her until she was ready to spill. And she might never be ready. Not the nicest thought he'd ever had.

Finn pushed his irritation way and signaled to turn right. *Get your head in the game, Murphy. You have no right to push and pry.*

How would you feel if she was pushing you?

Finn wished, just for a second, that she would. He wanted her to go there, mentally encouraging her to pry, so they could start breaking down the barriers between them.

And why did he want to do that? He had no intention of falling even a little in love with her again, so what was the point?

Crap, she confused the hell out of him. And he wasn't a man who was easily confused.

"Finn? Agenda?"

Finn dragged his thoughts back to the present and dragged a hand over his face. "Right. I haven't been completely useless, wedding-wise. I have been in contact with vendors and last night I sent various emails to various people—the florist, the cake baker and the wedding coordinator for the chapel—asking to meet this morning."

"And they agreed at the last minute?" Beah asked.

He couldn't blame her for sounding skeptical; it was primo wedding season, and few people in the wedding industry had time for last-minute demands. But being a Murphy had its occasional perks, and immediate attention was one of them.

Finn shrugged. "I'm a Murphy and our name grabs attention. No doubt my wedding planning inquiries have the rumors flying about my impending marriage. When I rock up with you, the rumor mill will go into hyperdrive, so do not be surprised if you see a headline tomorrow suggesting we are getting remarried. Would that be a problem for you?"

He was fishing because he was still curious about her call, but Beah, dammit, was too smart to take the bait.

"Are we going to tell the vendors that it's Piper and Ben getting married, not us?"

"If it comes up. I'm not in the habit of explaining myself and I really don't care what people say or write about me."

He'd learned that lesson from Carrick after his ex-wife Tamlyn fed malicious stories to the press about Carrick's alleged verbal abuse and his numerous affairs. None of it had been true, but the truth didn't matter when it came to selling stories.

As a result, Carrick never explained or issued comments.

"But," Finn said, thinking out loud, "it's a helluva sensitive time for the company right now and we cannot afford any bad publicity. Maybe we should just tell people we are organizing this for our friends. We'll keep it simple, saying they are in Hong Kong and we're doing the legwork for them."

"Are you really worried about adverse press attention?"

He felt Beah's eyes on his face and turned his head to send her a quick look. He frowned, feeling a swirl of apprehension in his stomach. "You know we are, Bee. The sale is huge and we can't afford anything to take the attention off it."

Beah nodded and looked out her window. Finn wished he could see her eyes, wished he knew what was going on behind those copper-colored depths. Because he sure as hell thought something was.

Beah played with the funky antique silver bracelet on her left wrist and he wondered if it was the same one he'd given to her their first Christmas together. It looked like it, but he couldn't be sure.

"I'm sorry for assuming you hadn't made any arrangements," Beah said. "I'm a bit of a control freak and it's really important to me that Piper has her fairy-tale wedding."

Because she didn't have one? Before Finn could ask that question, Beah started to speak. "There wasn't much my mom wanted when she was dying, except to be with me. But she did want one last holiday by the sea, so I packed her and her morphine drip into my car and we headed for Devon. She couldn't do much more than sit in her wheelchair on the pier but I saw the peace on her face. I still remember her lifting her face to the sun and smiling." Beah's voice cracked and Finn swallowed down an unexpected rush of emotion.

"It's important to me that Piper gets her version of a seaside holiday and if this wedding is what she wants, then that's what I'm going to give her. We've become pretty close in the past couple of weeks, maybe because I've experienced watching someone with cancer and I know how devastating it can be." Beah lifted her slim shoulders before allowing them to sag.

Finn thought she'd exchanged a few emails, maybe spoken to Piper on the phone once or twice. He'd never expected her to become emotionally involved with Piper, especially with Beah's history of nursing her own mom through her death. He admired her courage for giving this to Piper, and for nursing her mom, especially since he still felt uncomfortable talking about her mom and her battle with cancer.

"I'm sorry."

Out of the corner of his eye, Finn saw her tense, saw the same expression on her face that he'd seen last night. But he needed to say this again, make her understand.

"I should've listened to you when you wanted to talk about your mom. I shouldn't have changed the subject or distracted you. That was wrong of me."

Beah half turned to face him, pushing her glasses onto the top of her head. "Why did you push me away? I've never understood."

He couldn't tell her she made him feel too much, that getting emotionally close to her, as close as two people should be when they were married, scared him.

"I'm not a great talker, Bee." Finn glanced out the window and felt the pressure in his head, in his chest. "That being said, I should've tried harder. To understand. To, at the very least, let you talk."

"You were supposed to be my best friend, Finn." Beah's quiet words ripped his heart in two.

"I know, and I failed you." Finn reached across the expanse between them to place his hand on hers, squeezing her fingers gently. "I really am sorry."

He didn't know if it helped but the words were out there. He'd managed to say what he needed to. Beah didn't speak but she did, eventually, turn her palm upwards and link her fingers in his. "I appreciate you saying that, Finn. But our marriage was a long time ago and I'm over it."

He heard the determination in her voice. His head understood their time had passed but damn, his heart wasn't completely on board.

And his libido had never forgotten her. She was still the best he'd ever had.

"If we could get past wanting to rip each other's clothes off, we could be friends," Beah mused.

Finn lifted his hand to return it to the wheel. Why couldn't they be friends and have sex? For as long as she was around? It sounded like a win-win solution to him.

Beah took a long time to respond to his suggestion. "I don't know, Finn," she said, twisting her hands together. "The last time we hopped into bed we ended up getting married and divorced within a year."

"We were young and dumb," Finn replied. "We're older, wiser, less impetuous."

"We started kissing in a lift and ended up naked ten minutes later," Beah pointed out.

Okay, that had been pretty impetuous, but they were

allowed one slip, weren't they? "We're not going to end up doing anything stupid, Beah."

They weren't going to confuse love and sex again, weren't going to hand over their hearts and exchange rings and vows.

"But friends with benefits, Finn?" Beah sounded skeptical. "I kind of thought you were kidding last night."

He never joked about sex. And especially not with her.

"Why not? We're single, consenting adults who enjoy each other's bodies." So much. "We have art in common and Murphy's in common. We're both committed to the company and our careers."

Finn braked at the red traffic light and turned his head to look at her, his curiosity caught by the strange look crossing over her face. It was a combination of guilt and determination, mixed with a healthy dose of "oh, crap."

What the hell was that about?

"What's the problem?"

Beah tipped her head, looking puzzled. "I'm not sure what you are getting at…"

Good try, Beah. "What aren't you telling me? And don't say nothing because I know something is up. We might not have seen much of each other over the years, Bee, but I know when you are hiding something."

Beah slipped her glasses back onto her face and sent him a tight smile. She gestured to the traffic light, which had turned green. "Let's move on, Murphy."

Finn knew she wasn't only talking about their trip but also the direction of their conversation. He also realized she wasn't going to open up, and her reticence annoyed him.

His ex-wife seemed to have more secrets than Vatican City. And he didn't like not being part of the inner circle.

By lunchtime, they'd visited the chapel, decided on a white chocolate and raspberry cake, and met with the florist. They were due to meet with the caterer to finalize the menu and had booked a string quartet. The wedding reception would take place in the ballroom at Mounton House, the only place they could find able to hold fifty-plus people at very short notice.

They were making progress, Beah thought, making notes on her iPad. Piper and Ben's wedding was on track. All the bride and groom had to do was rock up and be happy.

Beah made a final note, looked up and noticed Finn wasn't heading in the direction of Murphy International.

"Where are we going?" she asked.

"Detour," Finn replied.

"I need to get back to work, Finn," Beah said, twisting in her seat to face him.

"It's only noon. We can be back in the office by two or three." Finn's placed his big hand on her knee and squeezed. "Come home with me, Bee. For an hour, maybe two."

Beah pulled her bottom lip between her teeth, caught between temptation and sensibility. If she did this, if she said yes, it would take whatever they had from a one-night stand to a fling, to something not so easy to dismiss.

Oh, she wasn't going to allow it to go deeper than a brief affair, that wasn't an option, but it would still be more than a heated, impetuous night.

She should think about this, work out the pros and cons.

Finn pulled over into an empty parking space, just a mile from the Charlestown Navy Yard, where he owned a condo on Constellation Wharf. He'd bought it, so she heard, shortly after their divorce, fulfilling his wish to live on the water.

"If you are unsure, I'll do a U-turn and take you back to Murphy's," Finn told her, his voice low but his tone sincere. He rested his forearms on the steering wheel and turned his head to look at her. "I don't want you to feel pressured into doing something you don't want to do."

She was nearly thirty years old and nobody pushed her around, especially when it came to her body. "I'm perfectly capable of saying no, Murphy."

Finn grimaced. "I know, Bee." He shoved his hand through his hair, frustration jumping in and out of his eyes. "You're not the young woman I married, but can't you see I'm also trying not to be the jerk I used to be?"

Beah considered his statement. The old Finn would've just driven her home, not giving her much of an option, teasing, charming and persuading her into doing whatever he wanted. Grown-up Finn was giving her a choice and she appreciated it.

But she still didn't know if going home with him was a good idea.

"Jeez, Finn, I don't know. This could become complicated."

Finn's green eyes were steady on hers. "You're overthinking this, Bee."

Was he right? Was she overanalyzing the situation? Sleeping with Finn didn't mean anything had to change; she would still be the same person she was before. She'd just be Beah with a sex life.

Sleeping with Finn didn't mean she'd have to make

any compromises or change her thinking. He was asking to share her body, not her life. A good thing, since she wasn't about to give up her independence for anyone, to rely on anyone, ever again.

"Maybe this will help you decide," Finn murmured before she could give him her answer.

He cupped the back of her neck and his lips touched hers in a surprisingly tender kiss. Beah murmured her approval as he softly, gently explored her mouth.

It was a first kiss, a getting-to-know-you-again kiss, a kiss with no beginning and no end. Beah forgot she was sitting in his car just a mile from his condo. It felt like she was sitting on a moonlit beach in Santorini, in an isolated treehouse in the Pacific Northwest. It was sweet and sigh-worthy and persuasive.

She wanted this, she wanted him…

Had she ever stopped? No, not really.

She was going to say yes.

Six

At his harbor-view condo, Finn didn't bother giving Beah the tour. In true Finn fashion, he looked single-minded and determined, and Beah was left in no doubt as to where he wanted her.

In his bed, naked.

As Beah followed Finn through his luxurious house, her hand swallowed by his, she caught glimpses of his deck, the harbor, expensive yachts and boats through the floor-to-ceiling glass of his living room on the bottom floor. They went up a floor and a sleek kitchen, den and dining area occupied the open-plan space. Finn didn't stop to let her take in his eclectic collection of art, he simply led her up the stairs to the third floor, finally stopping in the spacious hallway. He turned to look at her, placing both hands on her hips.

"Study to your right, master bedroom to the left. Guest rooms on the next floor," Finn told her, his eyes on her mouth. "Last chance, Bee."

Beah placed one hand on his chest, the other on his right cheek. She slid her thumb over his full bottom lip. She didn't need to think about this. She knew exactly what she wanted, and that was him. Above her, around her, in her.

"Take me to bed, Finn."

Finn didn't hesitate. He wrapped his arm around her waist and opened the door to his room. Beah's attention was immediately caught by the view. How awesome would it be to wake up to boats bobbing in the blue-green sea? The sun was shining and there wasn't a cloud in the sky and she felt like she could step from his bed onto the deck and from there onto a yacht.

Beah gestured to the view. "Wow, love the view, Murphy."

Finn didn't answer and when she turned her head to look at him, she immediately noticed the gleam in his eyes. Eyes that had yet to leave her face.

"Mine is better," he solemnly told her. Beah felt warm and squishy, like she had when she was newly married to him, caught up in the romance and emotion of being appreciated by the man she adored.

Don't go there, Beah. He's not your husband anymore and no matter how wonderful he makes you feel, this is only sex, just sex.

This was an hour or two out of her day, not a gateway to something more, something important.

Don't you dare forget that.

She had to stop thinking, so Beah sat down on the edge of his California king and pulled off her boots, then her thin socks. Conscious of Finn watching her, big arms crossed and biceps bulging, she stood up to shimmy her tight jeans down her thighs.

He watched her movements with those soul-melting eyes, his intensity raising sparks on her skin.

Beah arched an eyebrow at him. "Are you just going to stand there?"

"I'm enjoying the show," Finn told her, the corners of his mouth edging upward. She loved his half smile, half smirk; it was as sexy as hell. Finn rolled his finger, silently telling her to keep going.

Okay, if that was how he wanted to play it. Feeling sexy and dainty and oh-so-feminine, Beah turned her back on him, slowly pulling her cable knit sweater up her torso. She glanced out the window, wondering if she was giving the yachties a free strip show. Hesitating, she looked over her shoulder at Finn, whose eyes were on her butt. She briefly wondered if he liked her sunshine-yellow thong.

The huge bulge in his pants assured her he was liking everything.

That was all good and well but Beah had no intention of sharing this very private moment with anyone who happened to be looking out their portholes. She wasn't into public displays of affection, and the idea someone might be watching made her feel creeped out.

"Can we have some privacy?"

"We can see out but nobody can see in. But I can lower the blinds if you feel uncomfortable."

Trusting his word, and only dressed in a skimpy half-cup bra and the matching yellow thong, Beah walked over to the window and placed both her hands on the glass.

"Sure nobody can see what I'm doing?" she said, purely to tease.

She waited, heard rustling behind her but didn't turn, knowing Finn was shedding his clothes. Beah shuddered when she felt Finn's bare chest against her back, his erection pushing into her lower back, their skin separated only by the thin material of his boxer briefs. Then his big hands slid around her waist, one hand on her stomach, pulling her into him, the other moving up her torso, stretching his fingers to cover as much of her breasts as he could.

"You are so damn sexy, Beah Murphy."

She wasn't a Murphy anymore, but Beah didn't correct him, not wanting to spoil the moment. A rose by any other name and all that. Besides, the time for words had passed. She now needed him to touch her, to taste her, to make her scream.

Beah reached behind her and covered his erection with her hand, squeezing his hard shaft. He was big, impressive and, despite making love to him on countless occasions, she still wondered how he fit.

Beah felt his mouth on her shoulder, and his fingers slid over her right breast to find her already-hard nipple. She tipped her head back and stared at the bright blue sky, feeling like she was part of the water, of the sky, immersed in Finn.

Finn unsnapped her bra and the material dropped to the ground. Spinning her around, he tugged her toward the bed, pushing her down to the edge. He stood between her knees, not touching her with anything but his eyes.

But Beah needed more than hot eyes and appreciation. "I need you to touch me, Finn."

"In a moment," Finn said. "Let down your hair, sweetheart."

Beah didn't think about objecting, she just tugged on the band and tossed it away, not caring where it fell. Finn gently pushed so her back hit the cool linen on his bed. He knelt beside her on the bed and pulled his fingers through her curls, spreading them out to lie against the snow-white duvet.

"You have no idea how many times I've imagined you here, like this."

She believed him because she'd also, back in London, thought about him in her bed, often wished he was there. At one point they'd meant the world to each other; it was natural to miss the best parts of your life.

That didn't mean anything. She wouldn't allow it to mean anything.

She was so tired of thinking, of overanalyzing. But when Finn touched her, her overloaded brain shut down and there were only feelings, delicious sensation. Needing to lose herself in him, she reached for him, touching his muscled shoulders and chest, fingers skimming over his flat nipples.

She needed to stop thinking and this was, bar none, the best way to do it.

Lifting her torso to a half-sitting position, she pushed her fingers under the band of his underwear, looking for his heat and hardness. Finn looked down and licked his lips, his eyes closing as she wrapped her fingers around his shaft. He was so smooth, so deliciously, wonderfully male...

Beah knew she was wet and so ready for him. She tugged at the fabric, trying to push the briefs down his right hip. "Off, now."

Finn stood up, shed his underwear and gently pushed her thighs apart, looking down at her most private places. Beah felt the urge to cover up, to squirm, before remembering he'd seen all of her before.

Finn dragged a finger through her short red curls, slipping inside to test her readiness. "So hot, so wet."

"Finn." Beah panted, reaching for his neck and dragging his mouth to meet hers. His tongue slid past her teeth as his erection scraped her sensitive spot. Beah thought she just might come if he did that again.

Finn muttered a curse, leaned across her, his tip probing her entrance, and yanked open the bedside drawer. Beah heard him curse, heard a book hitting the floor, and then the drawer bounced off the hardwood. Finn released a few more curses and then a sigh of relief.

He sat back, ripped the packet open and rolled the condom down his gorgeous length, stroking himself as he did so. Man, there was nothing sexier than a man touching himself, his big hand wrapped around his hard shaft. Beah groaned and Finn's eyes slammed into hers.

"That's hot," Beah told him, looking for any moisture in her mouth.

"This?" Finn stroked himself again and Beah nodded. If he didn't touch her soon, spontaneous combustion was a possible outcome.

Unable to stop herself, her hand sneaked between her legs, but she had no time to pleasure herself because Finn released a hard curse, slid his hand under her butt and lifted her up to push inside her warm, wet channel until he was buried to the hilt.

She welcomed every inch of him, loved his heavy, reassuring weight. The smell of his cologne mingled with the heady scent of sex and her perfume. Beah sighed and, needing more points of contact with his hard body, arched her back to rub her breasts against Finn's chest. Finn, not moving, gritted his teeth.

Beah, not sure why he was waiting but fixated on her own happy ending, lifted her hips in a rhythm designed to ramp up her pleasure.

She didn't know if she could wait for him, didn't

much care if he was with her or not. Beah felt the tips of Finn's fingers pushing into her butt, the look of pain-pleasure on his face, the jumping muscle in his jaw. He didn't move, allowing her to set the pace, to take what she needed.

Time stood still, galaxies collided as the stars ducked and dived and planets spun around each other. Beah arched her back, reached for more and when she found her soul-shattering release, she spun away, hurtling from star to star, passing through the sun, shattering the moon.

When she started to float back to earth, Beah gripped Finn's big biceps and stared up into his forest green eyes, burning with a golden fire. He was still inside her, hard and heavy.

Finn slowly smiled as he pulled a loose curl out of her eye. "Was that good?"

Beah, having lost her ability to talk, just nodded.

Finn pumped his hips and Beah felt another spurt of pleasure, deeper and slower but no less wonderful than before.

"Good." Finn smiled, his eyes intense. "Now I want you to come again."

It was one of the few orders Beah was happy to obey.

Ten days later, Beah was trying to get Finn to con-centrate on making decisions about Ben and Piper's fast-approaching wedding but Finn, standing behind her office chair, kept distracting her by nibbling her neck or playing with her hair.

Beah felt his clever fingers tracing the edges of her collarbone and slapped his hand away. "Finn Murphy! Concentrate! These decisions are not going to make themselves and the wedding is three weeks away."

Finn responded by sliding his hand down her chest, under her top and cupping her breast, his fingers playing with her nipple. Beah tipped her head sideways, keeping an eye on the door, on the glass walls, leaning her temple against his forearm, taking a minute to enjoy the ripples of lust running through her.

"I haven't seen you for ten days, and you're asking me to concentrate on flowers and fripperies. Not a chance." Finn bent down to murmur in her ear as his thumb swiped over her nipple, making her harder than she believed was possible.

"Someone might see us."

"Relax, honey, I'll hear someone walking down the hallway before they see us," Finn told her. "But there's an easy solution to your dilemma. Come down to my office. We can lock the door and hide away for an hour. Maybe two. Or three. Hell, let's just ditch work—it's after four."

Man, she was tempted. So tempted. But she couldn't. She had a meeting with one of her newest clients, a dot-com millionaire who was flying in to see her, wanting to talk about starting an art collection. And she had to remind herself, Finn's house was not home. Her home was her apartment in Notting Hill, even though she hadn't been back to London in nearly a month.

It was true, she could work from anywhere.

Her client was due in—Beah glanced at her Cartier watch—five minutes. He could be walking down the hallway at this very minute. Dammit, no time to do anything interesting. And by interesting, she meant running down to Finn's basement office and stripping him naked and exploring his ripped body with her tongue and teeth.

Beah sighed and reluctantly pulled Finn's hand from

beneath her top. Finn wasn't the only one who was as horny as hell.

Beah stood up, glanced through the glass walls of the office. Seeing no one in the hallway outside, she dropped a quick, hard kiss on his sexy mouth. "Later. Now behave!"

Beah stepped back and tried to move the chair but Finn kept it in front of him. When she tried to push it beneath the desk, he raised his eyebrows and shook his head. "Give me a minute, honey. Nobody needs to see the steel pipe in my pants."

Ah, no, they didn't. She blushed but met his eyes, knowing hers reflected the same desire he was feeling. "We'll have our own private party later, I promise."

"My place? As soon as you can get away?"

She couldn't resist him, nor did she want to. It had been too long. Nearly a fortnight ago Ronan sent her to São Paulo to meet with the board of directors of a private museum in the city. They were thinking about thinning out their collection and wanted Beah's opinion on what art they should sell and keep and whether they, and Murphy's, could strike a deal.

From São Paolo she'd taken the opportunity to travel to Bariloche, a quaint Alpine town in southwest Argentina. A resident of the town had, a few months back, sent a photograph of a possible Renoir via the contact form on their website and it looked enough like the real deal to warrant the trip to the pretty town.

Much to the owner's disgust, she'd decided the painting was a fake, a good fake, but still a forgery. The volatile owner of the painting had yelled and screamed and told her she was going to get a second opinion and Beah shrugged, left her card and left town.

It wasn't the first time she'd told a family their much-treasured piece of artwork, passed down through generations, was a fake and worth nothing. It wouldn't be the last, either.

But while Beah was away, she'd thought about Finn often—okay, all the time—and missed him intensely. Her dreams were hot and filled with memories of his hands and mouth and the way he loved her...

"Seriously," Finn growled, "if you don't take that look off your face, I'm going to place you against the nearest wall and kiss you senseless. And to hell with anybody watching."

Beah shook her head and held up her hand. Right! That was for later. Beah sucked in a breath, walked around the desk to put some space between her and Finn—better safe than sorry—and pointed to the stack of wedding magazines on the desk. She grabbed the nearest one and flipped it open to a page she'd marked with a bright yellow Post-it.

"White roses and jasmine or bright, cheerful gerbera daisies?"

Finn looked at the pictures, frowned, then shrugged. "I don't know."

Men. "It's simple, Finn, which one do you prefer?"

"Either. Both. I'm sure Piper will love both," Finn replied. "Why don't you ask her?"

Beah frowned. "I've sent her a couple of emails and text messages but she hasn't replied. Have you spoken to Ben recently?"

Finn shook his head. "Actually no, not for a week or so. But I've been slammed."

Weird. Beah chewed on her bottom lip. But they were running out of time to organize their big day and they couldn't wait for Ben and Piper to get in touch. "We have to make the decision today. The florist needs to get the order in."

Finn pushed the chair away and placed his hands on his hips. "I trust your judgment, Bee, and they did ask us to organize this wedding. Make the call."

Flowers were a big deal and a very personal choice. This was too much pressure. "Why don't you?" Beah wailed.

Finn gestured to his clothes. "I wear black and denim all the time because it matches and I don't have to think about it. My place was decorated by an interior decorator. This isn't what I'm good at. Just choose, Bee."

Okay, then. Beah's eyes danced between the pictures in the magazine. The daisies were fun but roses and jasmine were romantic. Those were the flowers she would choose if this was her wedding. "Okay, jasmine and roses. Next, the cake."

Finn grinned. "We decided on raspberry and white chocolate. Three tiers because my brothers will be there and they'll demolish a tier each on their own."

"And you'll eat the other tier." Beah joked, making a note in her diary.

"Have you managed to look at the menus the caterers sent over?" Beah asked, looking at the next item on the list.

Finn winced. "Yes, I did. Sadly, they don't have time to prepare a tasting menu."

The man was always thinking about his stomach. Or sex. "Due to the short time frame, we are going to have to trust them to deliver. What menu did you choose?"

"The one featuring roasted duck. I'd just be happier if we had the opportunity to do a taste test."

"They are one of the best companies in Boston. Their food will be exemplary," Beah told him, making a mental note to cross "food" off her wedding list. "You're just thinking with your stomach again."

"When you bend over the desk and show me the edges of your very pretty pink bra, that's not all I'm thinking with…"

Beah slapped her hand against her top and her eyes slammed into his. Lust, want, need… Man, she had to cut this meeting short and take care of this raging fire burning between them.

If she didn't, they might set Boston on fire.

"Jeez, Finn, stop looking at me like that."

"Not possible," Finn growled.

Beah heard the ding of an incoming text message and saw that it was from Eli, telling her that he was on the way with her client. Beah held up her phone to show Finn the message and he pulled a face and stepped behind the back of her chair again. Right, he needed another minute. She could do with a couple herself to get her composure back, too.

The thought both thrilled and scared her. She had to get whatever was burning between them under control. Because if she didn't, it was going to incinerate her.

But she could work on her lack-of-control issues later; right now she had a job to do, a client to talk to. Business to conduct. And she had a decision to make. Beah glanced down at her phone, thinking about the email she'd received from Michael Summers en route from São Paulo to Boston. He needed a definite answer and he needed it soon. She was pretty much out of thinking time.

It was all a bit too much. Between the upcoming sale, her demanding clients, Michael, traveling and organizing the wedding, her plate was overloaded. And then there was Finn…

Built, gorgeous and sexy. And, despite his flirty banter, still as emotionally remote as he'd ever been. Right now, she felt 3 percent human and 97 percent stress.

Stressed or not, she had a job to do. Beah hauled in a deep breath, touched her hair to make sure her curls were under control and smoothed her hands over her hips. Pushing back her shoulders, she walked over to the closed door, pulled on a smile and opened the door.

She greeted Eli, Ronan's PA, before holding her hand out to Marshall Ford, her newest client. He was six foot something, built like a linebacker and not like anything she'd imagined he'd look like. Weren't computer nerds supposed to look nerdy?

Marshall Ford was, well...*wow*.

If she didn't have a sexy ex-husband in her bed, she might be tempted to flirt. Or more...

"Beah, this is Mr. Ford," Eli said. "I can organize coffee and pastries if you'd like?"

Beah shook Marshall's hand and lifted her eyebrows. "Coffee and pastries, Mr. Ford?"

"Please call me Marsh and yes, both would be good," Marshall replied in a deep, clear voice. "I'm starving."

"For me, too, Eli, thanks."

Beah heard Finn's voice behind her and wrinkled her nose. Was Finn planning on sticking around? Why? Beah narrowed her eyes at him as he approached them. Finn ignored her, holding out his hand for Marsh to shake. "Finn Murphy, director."

Beah wanted to roll her eyes but didn't. Finn normally introduced himself as their head of art, emphasizing his position rather than emphasizing his, well, Murphy-ness.

Could her ex be feeling a little threatened, a bit jealous? The thought amused her since she hadn't thought him capable of that particular emotion.

But, jealous or not, she would not let him hijack her meeting. This was her turf and he was not welcome. Beah turned back to Eli. "Finn will have his coffee in his office, Eli, since he was on his way out."

Finn opened his mouth to object but Beah sent him a shut-the-hell-up look and spoke before he could. "I'll talk to you later, Finn."

Beah turned her attention to Marsh Ford and gestured for him to enter the office. "Come in and take a seat. Maybe you'd be more comfortable sitting on the sofa than at the desk."

When his back was turned, Beah slapped Finn's arm and gestured for him to leave. He sent her an annoyed look but did, thank God, step into the hallway. Eli, Beah noticed, was trying not to laugh.

Beah rolled her eyes at both of them, shut the glass door behind her and, when she turned back to Marsh, knew Finn's eyes were burning into her back. She kept her expression pleasant and released a small sigh of relief when Eli tugged Finn down the hallway.

"Marsh, welcome to Murphy International. Let's talk art."

Finn dumped the Thai prawn curry—a favorite of Beah's—into a storage container and slapped on the lid. He emptied a pot of water into the sink and put the packet of egg noodles away.

Thank God he'd yet to open the champagne. He'd taken the effort to cook Beah's favorite meal and he was annoyed he'd wasted both the food and his time. But having a bottle of two-thousand-dollar champagne—

Bollinger 1996 Vieilles Vignes Françaises—go flat would've upped his blood pressure.

Finn pulled the bottle from the ice bucket and put it on the granite island.

Opening the fridge, he reached for a beer and popped off the cap, then headed for the deck, snuffing out the scented candles on the dining table.

So much for the romantic welcome-back dinner he'd planned.

Finn stepped onto his deck and placed his forearms on the railing, resting his beer bottle against his biceps. The mist rolled across the calm sea, shrouding the boats. It was slightly warmer tonight; maybe winter was finally releasing its grip on Boston. Finn couldn't wait for spring, and for summer. Not only would the pressure of the Mounton-Matthews sale be over and they could all, somewhat, relax, but he could go white-water kayaking, kitesurfing, get back into the water.

He swam at the gym's pool, but it wasn't the same as spearfishing or free diving.

Finn felt the tingles of restlessness dancing across the back of his neck. He'd forgone his second trip to the mountains—snowboarding—because Beah told him she would be back in Boston this week.

He'd stuck around because he'd missed her. More than he should.

Finn took a deep draft of his beer, feeling stupid for making a romantic meal for his once-upon-a-time wife. They hadn't made any firm plans for tonight but he'd assumed, judging by their sex tinged, I-need-you-bad banter earlier, that they'd be spending the night together.

But her meeting with Marshall Ford had obviously rolled, as he knew her meetings often did, into drinks and then a meal. Entertaining clients was part of Beah's job, he understood the concept, but he didn't have to like it.

He liked it a hell of a lot less when her client was a good-looking son of a bitch, with more money than God, young and single. And, yeah, he'd looked up Ford as soon as he got to his office…

His jealousy was pathetic.

This was why he'd avoided Beah for so damn long, he thought. Obviously, and subconsciously, he'd realized their attraction was too strong, their magnetic pull too great, and it was easier to keep their distance than to revisit their always-bubbling desire. Having a major ocean between them helped.

Once the sale was over, life would go back to normal. Beah would return to London permanently, their affair would be over, and his life would settle down.

But dammit, just having her around made him feel lighter, brighter, less serious. Beah could always take him out of his head, lighten his mental load, make him laugh. And maybe that was why his younger self couldn't deal with her, couldn't cope with what they had. Sure, they'd married quickly, but he'd known her; his soul had recognized her. She was like a warm, tropical wind blowing fresh air through the bad parts of him—those closed-up, calcified caves and grottoes devoid of air and light for the longest time.

He worried that the longer she stuck around, the more he'd start to rely on her, start to lean on her. Because life had taught him the women he leaned on, loved—his mom, his stepmom, even Thandi, Ronan's wife, to an extent—had all left him.

Tennyson had it backward: it was better *not* to have loved than to have loved and lost.

But was that really true? Or was he just a yellow-bellied coward? Sure, he could jump out of helicopters onto virgin snow at twelve thousand feet, dive from buildings with a parachute on his back and minimal space between him and the ground, fly down steeply angled paths on his dirt bike…but love and relationships took a special type of courage.

And Beah was the only woman who'd ever made him feel the way he did when he was flying down a black diamond run or bailing out of an airplane.

Breathless, scared, exhilarated, utterly focused.

No wonder she scared the crap out of him.

Adventure sports could break his body, but he'd risk that possibility any day of the week. A broken heart? No thank you.

And Beah was the only woman who could snap him like a twig.

Finn heard the faint snick of his front door opening, heard the clunk of her tote bag hitting the floor, the tap-tap of her heels across his hall. Finn didn't turn around but his body immediately reacted to her presence; his loins tightened and his heart bounced off his chest, careened around his rib cage. She was here.

It was about damn time.

Her gorgeous scent enveloped him first and then her arms came around his waist as she laid her cheek on his shoulder blade. Finn's heart settled and sighed and he couldn't help reaching around to grip her lower thigh with his free hand.

"Hey, sorry I'm late."

He wasn't going to ask; he really wasn't.

"How was dinner with Marsh?"

He felt, sensed, Beah's wide smile. "Lovely. His partner Alex joined us. He's a clothing designer in LA and he's been pushing Marsh to start collecting. He was supposed to join us at Murphy's but he had to meet a fabric supplier across town and his meeting ran late."

Marsh Ford was gay. Finn didn't know whether to feel relieved or foolish. He could do both at the same time. Finn turned around and gathered Beah to him, smiling when she reached up to drop a kiss on his jaw-line.

"Sorry I didn't let you know, but my phone battery ran out of juice. I forgot to charge it when I got to the office."

He wanted to tell her it was okay but he was still a little pissed that he'd made a meal, waited for her, wondered where she was.

Beah tipped her head to the side, her eyes on his. "You okay?"

"Sure, why?"

"Just checking." Beah sniffed. "Did you make Thai prawn curry for supper?"

"Yeah."

"Did you save me any? If you didn't, I'll be pissed. You know how much I love your Thai prawn curry."

Yeah, he did. That was why he'd made it. But she didn't need to know how much effort he'd gone to. He felt enough of an idiot as it was. Finn hoped she didn't notice, or comment on, the wet, superexpensive bottle of French champagne still dripping condensation all over his kitchen counter and the candles on the dining table.

Well, there was one tried and tested way to distract her. Finn cupped her face in his hands and bent his lips to cover hers. He'd meant his kiss to stay gentle, at least initially, but Beah immediately burrowed in close, her lips parted, and the world ignited.

Then Beah's tongue stroked his and Finn's world rocked, then settled. Holding Beah felt normal. But better than normal, it felt right. She was the only one who'd ever made him feel both excited and comfortable at the same time, like he was leaving earth in a spaceship while wearing his favorite pair of jeans. There had been other women between then and now—he was divorced, not dead—but nobody had ever held him like she did, touched him like she did.

Nobody tasted as she did.

Nobody, he suspected, ever would. She sipped, then sucked and then, to mix it up, swirled her tongue around his. Finn's stomach dived as he took control of the kiss, gently biting her bottom lip, before soothing the sting with a touch of his tongue. And he couldn't help his hands moving over her body...

It was what they were made to do. Beah had beautiful bumps in her spine, a surprisingly full bottom, and he bent his knees slightly to trace the back of her thighs, up and over her butt cheeks, smiling when he felt the cord of her thong. His woman wore sexy underwear and he loved it. Finn moved his hand between them and he skimmed her mound, happily swallowing her moans of encouragement. They'd barely started but he could feel her heat, her happiness at being in his arms.

Did this feel right to her, too?

Beah pushed his hand away and flipped open the catch of her pants, pushing the zipper down. The pants hung on the curve of her hips and he took the invitation and slid his fingers over the lacy material, finding the edges of her tiny triangle. Beah wiggled against his hand as he slid his finger under the seam, slipping through her heat and wetness to Beah's tiny bundle of nerves.

Beah sank against him, her knees dissolving, and Finn tightened his arm around her back, pulling her to him as her legs widened, allowing him deeper access. He pushed into her. One finger, then two, and his thumb was brushing her clitoris.

"Beah, you are so very sexy," Finn muttered against her mouth, staring into her foggy-with-lust eyes.

"We should stop." But her words were accompanied by a push against his fingers, encouraging him to go deeper, so Finn decided to listen to her actions, not her words.

They didn't need to stop. All the lights in his house were off, they stood in the shadows and the yachties were inside, warm and toasty.

They were doing this. Here. And now.

Nothing was more important…

"Take this moment, Beah, and lose yourself. Lose control."

Beah dragged her eyes up to meet his. "I don't know if I can."

Finn bent his knees, just a little, to level his gaze with hers. He tapped his fingers against the inside of her channel and Beah sucked in a sharp breath. Yeah, she liked that. "You can come. And you will."

He could see the doubt hovering on her lips but he stopped her words with a hard kiss, a flick of his thumb against her clitoris. She pushed even closer to him.

Hampered by her pants, he shoved them down her hips and hooked his foot around the leg of the low wooden table to drag it closer.

Finn cupped the underneath of Beah's thigh and placed her foot on the table, opening her up to his gaze and giving him complete control. Leaving her mouth, Finn looked down at her, pretty in the moonlight. He pulled her thong to one side and stared, pulling his fingers out of her to trace her small red strip of hair with one finger, ramping up her pleasure by delaying the inevitable.

Finn transferred his gaze to Beah's face, to find her watching his actions, completely turned on.

Beah lifted her hand up to his jaw, pushing her fingers into his skin to make him turn his head. She stood on her tiptoes and kissed his mouth, her tongue telling him exactly what she wanted his fingers to do. She was now completely caught up in her own pleasure; she had no thoughts for him and what he needed and it didn't matter.

Because what he most needed was to watch her fall apart in his arms, completely and utterly lost in what he could do to her.

And for her.

Beah's pleasure was all that mattered...

And talking about her pleasure, Finn started to fully concentrate on what he was doing, sliding his finger over her clitoris and into her vagina in a slow, steady, orgasm-building rhythm. He needed more—he wasn't sure what, so he lifted his other hand to push open the sides of her coat, impressed he still had enough blood flowing to his brain to undo the buttons of her shirt, leaving it to fall open and show a hint of her ivory bra. His tanned hand was dark against her lighter skin—and then it disappeared beneath the cup of her bra to cover her breast. Instantly her nipple swelled into his palm, demanding attention.

He aimed to devastate her control—fingers in her panties and fingers rubbing her nipple—and he was rewarded by the sound of her harsh breathing, which told him her whole world had narrowed to this moment. She was completely entranced by what he was doing to her. Beah rested her forehead against his collarbone, a gooey, melty mess in his arms, and he felt her climbing up and up, looking for her release. How was it for women? Finn briefly wondered. Did it start, as it did with him, in the base of their spine? Was it a rush, a bold, intense light shooting through their system? Or was it like a warm wave?

However it felt, he'd never seen anyone sexier than Beah looked, right this minute, her lips parted and her face flushed. Her hair was falling out of her knot, and her eyes were a deep, dark, mesmerizing gold. She looked wild.

"You're close, Beah, and damn pretty," Finn growled in her ear. "So very, very sexy."

She liked the words, he could tell. He gave her some more. "I could come just by looking at you as you fall apart."

It was the truth. He felt like he was about to blow and she'd yet to touch him.

"Finn, I need…"

"Me. You need me, doing this," Finn muttered, pushing another finger into her and pushing his thumb against her clit. Beah moaned. Then shuddered.

"Come for me. Right now."

At his command Beah fell, and fell, instinctively bucking against his fingers as she milked every last sensation from her orgasm. She didn't notice he'd pulled his hand away from her breast to shove it down his own pants. He just needed one tug, maybe two and yep, he was there with her, his hand warm and sticky as he orgasmed.

Their harsh breaths bounced off the water and Finn closed his eyes.

He'd been determined to make Beah lose control but in doing so, he'd also lost his.

Seven

It was their sixth date since his ultimatum, and Keely had yet to see Dare naked again. But she was damned if she was going to ask him when and where they would have sex. She wasn't that desperate.

Okay, she was more than desperate, but she refused to let him in on her little secret. A girl had her pride. Then why, if she wasn't getting great sex as he'd promised, had she agreed to join him for a casual meal at his favorite bar? Because she—dammit and damn him—really enjoyed his company. Dare was smart, witty and occasionally deep and Keely loved talking to him. And she liked the feeling of being wooed, charmed, flirted with and thought about. She liked the flowers and the text messages, the way he phoned just before eleven to say good-night.

She *liked* him.

But she had to get them back on track, back to all

they could be, all they could have. The truth was, she was enjoying dating Dare a bit too much. And that was unacceptable. She was not going to fall in love with Wilfred Seymour. Not, not, *not*.

Tonight, because she needed to protect herself, and her tender heart, she was going to give him an ultimatum. It was either back to the bedroom or break up…

Keely slid into the booth and sighed when Dare sat on the same side of the table as her, shoulder to shoulder, his thigh pressed against hers. A waitress approached them and Keely couldn't blame her for not being able to pull her eyes off her date…off Dare, she corrected.

Dare ordered her a glass of chardonnay and himself a beer and when the waitress finally left, he gently jammed his elbow into her side. "You're quiet. Everything okay?"

Keely shifted on the bench to sit in the corner of the booth, putting a healthy amount of distance between her and the man who kept her awake at night and, when she did manage to fall asleep, was the star of her fairly dirty dreams.

She could do this; she had to do this. And this bar—down to earth and unpretentious—was the perfect place to have this conversation. "We need to talk."

Dare nodded. "I've been expecting you to say this and the answer is no. We're not going back to the way we were." He had the balls to tack a smile onto the end of his statement and Keely felt her temper spark.

"You're not the only person in this relationship," Keely shot back.

"I'm the only one with some sense," Dare retorted, leaning back. He closed his eyes and shook his head. "I'm tired, Keels. I've had a hell of a day. And I'm horny. Let's not do this tonight, okay?"

She'd noticed the blue smudges under his eyes, the deeper grooves around his mouth. She wanted to know why he looked shattered, what had caused his stress, why he looked unhappy. But she couldn't allow herself to go there; it was too dangerous.

"I can take care of the horny," Keely told him, using her most seductive voice and putting her hand on his thigh. She could do sex. It was emotion that scared her stupid.

Dare looked disappointed and then anger flashed in his eyes. "Such a predictable response, Killer. And boring."

Boring? Okay, that stung. Keely jerked her hand off his leg and narrowed her eyes at him. "I'm boring?"

Dare rolled his eyes. "I didn't say you are boring, I said your response was."

"What do you want me to say, Wilfred?"

The waitress strolled across the room with their drinks and when she got to the table, she darted a glance to Keely and then Dare, obviously sensing the tension between them. Dare ignored her curiosity and reached up to pinch the bridge of his nose with his index finger and thumb. "Do you have any aspirin?" he quietly asked.

Keely, caught on the back foot, nodded and pulled her bag onto her lap. She shoved her hand inside, looking for the small tin in which she kept a few tablets. Finding it, she opened it and shook the contents into her hand.

"How many do you need?" she quietly.

Dare picked three pills off her hand, threw them into his mouth and chased them down with a few gulps of beer. Placing his beer back onto the table, he half turned to face her.

"I've had a shitty day. I lost a court case and one of my oldest clients was arrested for fraud, which pisses me off because I warned him. My favorite paralegal quit to join another firm and I have the headache from hell," Dare quietly told her. "And instead of asking me what's wrong, the person I couldn't wait to see, the one person who always brightens my mood, immediately reduces what we have to sex."

Okay, he was seriously pissed. And judging by the pain in his midnight blue eyes, hurt. She hadn't meant to hurt him; she was just scared.

But scared or not, she should've asked him about his day, tried to sound like she cared. Because she did, so much. Keely took a sip of her wine and wondered what would happen if she stopped creating distance between her and Dare, if she allowed herself to enjoy his company, to enjoy this flirty, wonderful, exciting time.

But what if she fell in love with him? What then?

Maybe he'd catch her. Maybe she wouldn't fall and smack her head. Maybe she wouldn't feel like every bone in her body was broken. Maybe she'd be okay.

Maybe…

"You know what, you might be right."

At his sober words, Keely pushed her spine into the vinyl booth, every muscle in her body suddenly as tight as a newly erected barbwire fence. She kept her eyes on his somber face, on the disappointment in his eyes.

"Maybe we should go back, but not to sex. Maybe we should go all the way back to when we were lawyer and client, casual acquaintances," Dare said, his voice cool. Keely placed a hand over her heart, hoping she could stop her heart from ripping in two.

"Dare…" She didn't want that. She couldn't bear it.

"I've tried with you, Keely, done my damn best to

show you we could be good together, that we could build something." Dare stood up and jammed his hands into the pockets of his jeans, his jaw rock hard and his eyes narrowed. He had his courtroom face on, was wearing his don't-mess-with-me look.

He was going to walk away...

"But this isn't a one-way street and I need something, too. I'm thirty-five years old and I want a partner, a friend, someone I can lean on. But you're determined to believe I'm going to hurt you. You are throwing away something with the potential to be amazing because you're scared."

Of course she was! Didn't she have a right to be?

"I'm scared, too, but I'm done with being the only one who is fighting for us. I'm tired of being the only one who believes in us. I don't believe in soul mates. In a world of eight billion people there has to be more than one person I can be happy with. Since you don't want to join me on this ride, I'm going to find someone who will."

His words were like a punch to her heart, a Taser to her soul. Keely opened her mouth to speak but couldn't find air, her tongue unable to find the words. After a minute of staring at her, Dare yanked his wallet from the back pocket of his jeans, fished out some bills and tossed them on the table. "Right. Thanks for nothing."

Keely wrapped her arms around her stomach and watched him walk away, wishing she was brave enough to call him back, wishing she could throw caution to the wind and love him.

He was walking away, but this time, and unlike all her previous lovers, she'd pushed him to do exactly that.

Unable to sleep, Beah, dressed in Finn's shirt, walked out of his bedroom onto the smooth deck and leaned her forearms on the railing, looking down onto the harbor. It was chilly, sure, but Beah welcomed the icy breeze on her bare legs. She'd always liked the cold, liked how alive it made her feel.

Hot sex with Finn Murphy had the same effect on her. She'd been in Boston for a while now and she'd had a lot of sex, and all of it was fantastic. While she kept a few items in her room at Mounton House, most of her clothes were hanging in Finn's closet, her shoes were mixed with his on his rack, her toiletries cluttered the surface of the bathroom cabinets. She'd all but moved in.

It was going to be hard to go back to London and her empty apartment. She'd never considered herself to be particularly lonely in London, but she suspected she would be when she returned. In Boston, she'd become—because Finn was close to his brothers and their partners—friends with his sister Tanna, his brother's significant others, Joa and Sadie, and she'd met the Brogan twins and their partners. She'd been invited to lunch and to girls' nights out, or to join them for a "before work" cup of coffee. They were smart and funny and, despite being Boston's A-listers, very down to earth.

She had friends…and she liked it.

Work was also, currently, fun. She liked working out of the Boston office, being down the passage from her direct boss, Ronan. Email exchanges and telephone calls had worked but she liked being able to pop her head into Ronan's office, to chat face-to-face about a client or a pitch. Working out of Murphy headquarters made her feel less isolated.

Yep, going back to London was going to suck. But she'd soon be moving into Michael's upmarket offices in Kensington and she'd have a new challenge, new clients, and would be too busy to think and feel.

And that was how she liked to live her life...

Wasn't it?

Beah heard Finn step out onto the deck and smiled when he wrapped his arms around her and rested his chin on the top of her head. Beah lifted her hands to hold his wrists, sighing as his heat warmed her back, butt and the backs of her thighs.

Finn, big and bold, gave the best hugs. He made her feel treasured and safe and protected. The way she did ten years ago before they fell apart.

Don't get used to it, Beah. This isn't a long-term thing.

"It's freezing out here, Bee."

He'd never been a fan of the cold. "Just a few minutes more."

"Don't blame me if our fingers fall off from frostbite."

"Stop being dramatic, Murphy," Beah replied, amused. She looked across the harbor, sighed at the luxury boats. "Do you sail? I can't remember."

"Levi, Tanna's fiancé, owns a marina and a couple of boats. I go out with him occasionally, but it's not something I'm passionate about."

Beah dropped a kiss on his wrist below the cuff of his sweatshirt. "And you still love risky sports?"

Finn hugged her closer, shivered, and Beah took pity on him. Stepping out of his arms, she walked to the sliding door and back into his warm bedroom, the covers messy from their lovemaking.

Finn closed the door behind him, picking up the conversation. "Yeah, I still ski and parachute."

Such tame words for what he really did.

"Double black diamond runs and BASE jumping?" Beah heard her words, grateful she didn't sound accusatory or shrill. God, they'd had many arguments on this subject, about him risking his life, about his need to escape. Hindsight was a great tool and she now realized that more than wanting him to give up his pursuit for adrenaline, she'd just wanted him to give her as much attention as he did his sports. She'd wanted him to turn to her, to open up, to spend *some* of his free time with her.

Finn led her out of the bedroom and down the stairs to his light-filled, airy kitchen. After asking her if she wanted coffee and powering up his machine, he raised an eyebrow. "You're not going to lecture me?"

Beah shook her head. "I'm not your wife anymore, Finn. I have no right to comment on how you spend your free time."

A strange expression crossed Finn's face, one Beah couldn't decipher. Was it sadness? Relief? Confusion? Who knew? Finn turned his back on her and opened the fridge.

"But I never understood why you loved it." *And why you preferred risking your life to talking to me.*

"Are you hungry? I'm hungry."

Beah stared at the back of his head as he looked in his fridge for something to snack on. It was classic avoidance behavior. He didn't want to discuss the matter so he changed the subject.

Some things never changed and she was a fool for thinking, hoping, they would.

Beah walked over to the cupboard, grabbed a glass and filled it with water. After taking a few sips, she rested the cool glass against her forehead, wishing she could stop wishing.

She wanted things to be different...but mentally and emotionally, she was back where she'd been so long ago. Despite her promises to herself to keep this simple and bedroom-based, she still—why?—wanted Finn to *open up to her*.

And she might be a hair's breadth away from falling in love with him again—a terrifying possibility but one she could no longer avoid.

Finn straightened, closed the fridge and Beah noticed his hands were empty. He leaned his shoulder into the stainless steel appliance and rubbed the back of his neck. "Exercise takes me out of my head," he said, his expression thoughtful. "It clears out the junk and allows me to see situations clearly."

Wow, he was talking. This was new.

"I don't have a death wish, Beah. I don't go out there thinking I could die. Sure, death and injury are a risk, but it's not something I think about because I don't want or intend to die." Finn hesitated a moment before continuing. "When I jump off a building or free climb, I sink or swim or fall by *my* own choices. It's the only place I feel like I am in complete control."

"I don't understand."

"And I don't know if I can explain it to you."

Beah felt Finn's eyes on her face, heard his sigh. Beah expected him to shut down but he continued to talk. "One of my earliest childhood memories is of people asking me questions, trying to talk to me, but I never got a chance to respond because Carrick and Ronan jumped in and spoke for me. I guess my reticence started then because I didn't, apparently, talk much, or at all. I suppose it became a habit."

Okay, that made sense. Finn worked out his problems

on his own. He never shared his inner thoughts with anyone, not even her. Stupid that it still hurt.

"I still don't understand why you think it's a good idea to throw yourself off buildings," Beah stated. Finn walked over to her, took the glass from her hand, filled it up with water and downed the contents. He looked out the narrow window to the dark night beyond.

"It makes me feel alive, it reminds me to live. I've seen death often—my birth mom, Raeni, Thandi, even Tanna came damn close to dying—that I feel like I need to *feel* life. What I do requires total focus, immense concentration. I have to push aside the crap, the minutiae of life and only think about what I'm doing in the moment. And it's in those moments that I feel I am truly one with the world, tuned in," Finn added. He smiled his quirky, ovary-rolling smile. "And yeah, I enjoy the rush."

"Thanks for explaining it to me. I understand better now." Beah rested her hand on his warm forearm and squeezed. "I appreciate you opening up."

Finn lifted his hand to push a curl behind her ear, to run the pad of his thumb over her cheekbone. "I can't help but notice you don't talk half as much as you used to."

Yeah, she'd been a spiller, telling him anything and everything, thinking if she opened up, so would he.

Beah, not able to look at him, walked over to the coffee machine and opened the cupboard doors above the machine to look for cups. "I used to be a talker, now I'm a bit more like you. I tend to work things out by myself."

"Did I do that to you?" Finn asked.

Beah shrugged. He hadn't *done* it to her; nobody had that much power. But after their divorce, she'd *chosen* to retreat, to become more emotionally isolated. It didn't hurt so much when you looked around for emotional comfort and found none. "We choose our actions, Finn."

She didn't want to spoil what had been a lovely day by talking about the past, so Beah changed the subject. "This is a really nice place."

Finn looked around and nodded. "I enjoy it."

Beah, from memory, fixed Finn a cup of coffee before making her own. She sipped, sighed and rolled her head, trying to work out the tension in her neck.

Finn slid onto a modern stool at the island and wrapped his big hands around his mug. He looked at her, green eyes intense. "Talking about talking, I sense you are wrestling with something, that you are trying to make a decision… Can I help?"

Beah looked down at her bare feet, her toes tipped with red. Wow, Finn paid more attention to her than she'd thought. Her first instinct was to lie, to tell him he was allowing his imagination to run riot, but that was a cop-out. He'd been honest with her; she could—to a point—be honest with him.

But she couldn't tell him everything, not yet. She held up her hand in a silent request to give her a moment to think.

When the spring sales were over, she'd ask for a meeting with the Murphy brothers and explain her reasoning for wanting to go out on her own. Until then, she'd keep her plans under wraps. None of them needed the additional stress—the sale was too important, too once-in-a-lifetime to distract her from providing the best service to her clients…

Clients she hoped would leave with her when she left Murphy's. And why did she feel a rush of guilt at that thought? It wasn't like she would be telling them not to deal with Murphy's, it just meant they would become *her* clients and not Murphy's clients. She could deal with other auction houses, grow her income and her business…

Not that she needed much more than she already had. She owned her house and another she'd bought as an investment property. She had a solid, extensive portfolio of stocks and investments, a huge retirement fund. All her needs, and most of her wants, were covered by her monthly salary and the huge commission she earned from Murphy International.

Why was she doing this if it wasn't for the money? Beah ignored Finn's quizzical expression and walked out of the kitchen, past the dining area and down the steps into the sunken lounge, to look out Finn's huge windows and onto the water. Why was she determined to own her own business, to set up something new?

Because, maybe, she was hoping a new venture, a new challenge, would fill the hole inside her, would quiet the nagging voice frequently reminding her something was missing. She wanted a new challenge so she didn't have time to think of anything else, her rogue thoughts drowned by her work…

She wanted to be busy so she didn't have time to miss her marriage, to mourn her dreams of being part of a unit, of having her own family to love and laugh with.

Beah sipped her coffee and heard Finn behind her. Instead of reaching for her, he placed his shoulder against the glass pane, sensing she needed time. And space.

"I can see you have a lot on your mind, Beah," Finn quietly stated. "How can I help?"

He couldn't. Because what she most wanted from him he couldn't give her. Not back then and not now.

Beah gave him a quick shake of her head. "I'm not

going to lie to you and tell you I'm not wrestling with something. I am. But I can work it out myself."

Finn opened his mouth and she expected an argument. Instead, he sent her a wry smile. "I'm here if you need a sounding board, Bee. You know that, don't you?"

"Because we are friends with benefits?" Beah demanded, wincing at the bitterness she heard in her voice.

"Because I still care for you," Finn quietly said.

He still cared for her. *Whop, whop, whop.*

She was on the edge of tumbling back into love, of handing her heart over, and he just *cared* for her. Well, wasn't that a metaphorical bucket of cold water? Finn sipped his coffee, staring at the dark water beyond the deck. "How is your dad? Do you ever hear from him?"

Beah frowned, a little off-balance at his abrupt change of the subject. Beah ignored the cold hand gripping her heart. "Nope, such an action would require him making an effort and my dad never excelled at putting himself out."

Finn walked over to the nearest chair, sat down and placed his feet on the coffee table. "You sound bitter."

Of course she was. She had a right to be! "My father left my mom when he realized how much care and support she'd need. He left me to cope with a terminally ill parent. He moved in with his long-term mistress, a woman whose child he adopted as his own, the woman he married a few days after my mom's funeral. Do I not have a right to be bitter?"

Finn just handed her a gentle, understanding smile. "I'm bitter, and angry, on your behalf. What a prick."

Beah almost smiled at Finn's matter-of-fact tone of voice. And he was right—her dad was a prick. "What about your stepsibling? Have you met her? Does she know about you?"

The grip on her heart tightened, iced up. "Nope, we were never introduced. She'll be fifteen, sixteen this year."

"Does she know about you?" Finn asked.

"I have no idea. Probably not," Beah admitted. She looked at her watch, feeling uncomfortable with the depth of the conversation. They were just exes having sex. They weren't supposed to be talking.

Sex was uncomplicated, easy. Sex didn't require anything more than a mutual exchange of pleasure. Sex didn't need words or emotions or conversations.

And these types of conversations made her think she might, just might, mean something more to him than a bed buddy, someone he cared about. Conversations like these gave her hope and hope was, as she knew, damn dangerous.

She had to shut this down, to reerect any emotional barriers she'd constructed between them. She had to protect herself. She would not open herself up to Finn again and find herself in the same position she did years ago, needing more from him than he could give.

Nope. Not happening.

She knew of a great way to distract them both. Beah put her coffee cup on the table and slid her leg over his thighs and her arms around his neck. She looked at his mouth, dragged her fingertips through his soft beard. Sex they could do, and do well; talking was dangerous.

"I love your eyes," Beah told him, admiring the darker green ring holding in that lighter shade.

Finn lifted an eyebrow and his hand rested on her bare thigh, sliding up and over her hip.

"I love all of you."

Beah's heart bounced off her rib cage and she quickly reminded herself he was talking about her body, cautioning herself not to read too much into his comment. She cursed herself for her earlier stupidity. She was not the same idealistic, unrealistic girl who'd married him so long ago.

Beah dropped her head to kiss the side of his mouth, to nibble on his jaw. This was not an emotional connection, a rejuvenation of a love affair.

They were work colleagues, two people who were attracted and were acting on their attraction.

Nothing more, nothing less. This was cut-and-dried, simple.

They. Were. Done.

But she needed to make sure they were on the same page, reading from the same book. "You mean you love what we do to each other, right?"

Finn just held her face in his hands, handed her an enigmatic smile and pulled her down to take her mouth in a fierce kiss.

It was only much, much later Beah remembered that he never answered her question.

Eight

Beah sat in Paris Cummings's overly decorated sitting room, staring at her hands instead of the amazing art on the walls. She had a tiny chip in the pale pink polish on her right hand, and the diamond ring she wore on her right hand—her mom's engagement ring from her dad—needed a cleaning.

She wished a dirty ring and a tiny chip in her nail polish could keep her occupied but a million thoughts buzzed around her brain, chief of which was how much she missed Finn.

She'd left Boston in a hurry early yesterday morning because one of her oldest clients, a Russian oligarch, told her he would be in London the following day and he could only see her at three the next afternoon. He was, he'd also told her, in a buying mood.

Because it was her job, Beah caught the next plane out of Logan International and upon meeting Yuri, and his new, very young wife, was told he wanted to start a jewelry collection. Beah wasn't fooled. Yuri didn't care about jewels, but his new wife—wearing a ten-carat diamond ring—obviously did.

But, because he was immensely powerful and stupidly rich, Beah kept her mouth shut, put a pleasant expression on her face and took notes. Yuri, being Yuri, wasn't interested in easily obtainable pieces, no, he wanted famous jewels, fabulous jewels, items worn by kings and queens and Hollywood icons and Indian princes. He wanted the exceptional and the outstanding and it was her job to find them for him.

Which wouldn't be easy because those types of items rarely came up for sale. She could see many phone calls in her future to collectors, asking whether they were prepared to sell their much-treasured pieces. She already knew the answer would be no.

Or a hell no.

If you owned Catherine of Russia's emerald and diamond necklace and matching earrings, or Elizabeth Taylor's Krupp diamond ring, you held on to them because you'd never get the chance to own the magnificent pieces again. Yuri, she was afraid, was going to be disappointed.

Before making it back to her apartment after a long day yesterday, she'd also had a dinner meeting with Michael Summers and she'd informed him she was very interested in joining him and was excited about a new challenge and that while she wasn't saying yes just yet, she probably would.

As soon as she said the words, she'd felt her stomach cramp, panic close her throat. Michael had clapped his hands in delight, kissed her and ordered champagne, obviously not noticing she was close to tossing her cookies.

Michael was much more enthusiastic about her coming on board than she was. What did that mean? Why wasn't she more excited about this amazing opportunity? Why was she hesitating? Why did she suddenly feel like Michael's offer was not what she really needed or wanted?

Why was she starting to think that only a hot, reticent man and a life spent with him in Boston would fill up the empty holes in her life and her heart?

Beah's phone rang and she glanced at the door before lifting it to her ear. "This is Beah."

"Hey, sweetheart."

Beah smiled and looked at her watch. It was just past six in Boston, which meant Finn was just waking up. It made her feel warm and wonderful that she was the first person he thought of when his eyes opened.

"How is your day going?" Finn asked.

"Good, thanks. You still sound half-asleep."

"Mmm. I was having an X-rated dream."

"Was I in it?" Beah asked, dropping her voice and keeping an eye on the door.

"Only you. When are you coming home?" Finn demanded.

Home. The word rolled easily off his tongue and it was tempting to believe he meant it. But Beah knew that essentially nothing had changed. Finn hadn't given her the smallest hint he wanted to take their relationship to the next level, to make any sort of commitment. They were just bed buddies who'd once been married.

Finn still needed distance and she still needed intimacy...

Beah heard the door opening, told Finn she had to go, assuring him she'd talk to him later. She stood up, buttoning her black jacket over her black silk shirt.

She shook Paris's hand, asked about his health and sat back down on the nineteenth-century chesterfield sofa and crossed her legs, one hand on the folder next to her. She accepted Paris's offer of coffee and smiled her thanks at his butler.

Paris sat down in the chair opposite her—a rare, nineteenth-century Howard & Sons wingback, covered in the original blue-and-white fabric, totally gorgeous—and draped one leg over the other and pinned her to her seat with intense eyes. Thoughts of Finn and his sexy dreams were pushed to one side as Paris interrogated her about the items in the upcoming sale, asking her what she thought he should buy, what price the items would reach and what items in his collection he should consider selling.

Beah's brain kicked in and they spent the next hour running through the Mounton-Matthews collection and the artworks Paris owned, talking prices, values, returns.

Paris eventually stopped grilling her and leaned back in his chair. "My butler will be here with hot coffee soon." He picked up the plate of pastries and a small side plate. "Have something to eat. You look pale."

"I'm a redhead, I always look pale," Beah said.

Paris's smile hit his eyes and, for a moment, he looked ten years younger. "Have a piece of lemon cake. It's fabulous."

Beah picked up the tiny square and popped it into her mouth, where it melted on her tongue. She moaned and immediately reached for another square. "Oh, the cake is just amazing. Light and full of flavor. Please give your cook my compliments."

"Thank you."

Beah tipped her head to the side, instantly suspicious

when she saw a touch of red on his cheekbones. "You baked the cake?"

Paris shrugged. "And the chocolate éclairs, and the brandy snaps."

"Really?"

"Baking helps me relax, helps me think. I've been baking since I was a kid."

Wow. Now that was something she'd never expected to hear. Her reclusive art collector was a world-class baker. Keeping her eyes on him, Beah popped the tiny éclair into her mouth, chewed. Then she picked up a brandy snap, ate it and leaned back, placing the small plate on the side table next to her. "The lemon cake is even better than the other two, which were excellent."

She waited, her heart in her mouth, for Paris to smile and eventually it came, along with a hint of approval. Yay, they were on their way to being...well, not friends, but not serf and lord, either.

The butler arrived with fresh coffee and after drinking a cup, Beah started to gather the papers she'd placed on the sofa next to her. She was putting her laptop back into its bag when Paris's next question sent chills galloping over her skin.

"Tell me, are you really going to leave Murphy's to join Michael Summers?"

Beah felt her laptop start to slip and she grabbed it, feeling like the air in the room had disappeared. If Paris knew about her plans, who else in the art world did?

Did the Murphy brothers know? Had someone told them? But how would they know since her discussions with Michael were private? Whom had he told? And how far had the rumors gotten?

Pretty far, if Paris Cummings, reclusive as he was, knew about her plans.

"Uh…"

Paris held up his hand. "I see the thought has crossed your mind. Are you unhappy at Murphy International? Do they not treat you well?"

That wasn't why she was leaving. They'd been good to her, as Beah quickly explained. She could see the question in Paris's eyes, his lack of understanding.

A few weeks ago, she would've had a pat answer for him: she felt constrained, she wanted the freedom to make her own business decisions, to work with other auction and art houses. She wanted to spread her wings. But for some strange reason, she tried to give Paris the full truth. "I need something more, something different…"

"And you think going on your own, cutting your ties to the Murphys, will help you find what you are looking for?"

Beah rested her elbows on her knees and placed her chin in the palm of her hand. She should shut down this conversation, tell him she hadn't made any irrevocable decisions yet, but the kind, almost paternal look in his eyes pinned her to her seat.

"Are you sure you will find what you need by changing your career?" Paris asked.

Beah frowned at him, not understanding. "Sorry?"

"Maybe you are looking for a change in the wrong place. Maybe more work isn't what you need."

Beah straightened and squared her shoulders. "Work is all I have, Paris." And she wasn't sure whether she was reassuring him or herself.

Paris stood up and slid his hands into his expensive suit pants. He sent her a slow smile. "Then, my dear, you are going to end up like me. Living in a fancy house with an incredible collection and more money than I can spend."

Beah followed him to her feet. "That doesn't sound bad," she quietly stated.

"It's not. Until you find yourself in your kitchen at three in the morning, baking because you are so damn lonely you can't breathe." Paris surprised her by dropping a kiss on her cheek. He pulled back and gripped her shoulder. "You're not going to find what you're looking for by working more, Beah. Trust me, I know. Benson will see you out."

Beah stared at him, both flummoxed and touched by his obvious concern. At the door, Paris turned and pointed his finger at her. "Talk to the Murphys about your plans. Because if I've heard the rumors, they will have heard them, too. And if they haven't, they will. And soon. Get ahead of this, Beah. You owe them that."

Paris slipped through the door and Beah folded her arms across her chest and rocked on her heels. She cursed softly, fighting her need to panic. But knowing deep down in her soul that Paris was right.

She needed to get ahead of this, no matter how hard it was to do.

In the conference room, Finn glared at Ronan when he raised another issue to add to today's agenda and cursed his brother's chattiness. Ronan used to hate meetings as much as Finn did, but these days he was the only one trying to keep these directors meetings short and sweet.

And he needed short and sweet, because he'd just received a text from Beah telling him she was back in Boston, back in her office down the hall. He couldn't wait to see her and Ronan was running on about a new website designer.

Finn resisted the urge to bang his head against the

desk and mentally begged Carrick to call an end to the meeting...

But chatty or not, Ronan was far happier than Finn had seen him in years. With the death of his wife, Thandi, Ronan had gone through hell and back, trying to raise his two boys while dealing with grief. Joa was breathing new life into Ronan, and his nephews and Finn would never be able to thank her enough. Sadie had also turned Carrick's life upside down and inside out and both his brothers walked around with smirky, I've-got-the-world-in-my-hands grins.

They did, and Finn was happy for them. *He was.* And he was a little jealous his brothers had the guts to try again, to commit their lives to their women, to take the risk. He didn't think he could do it. Not again. He'd tried once with Beah and failed.

But had he really tried? He hadn't opened up to her, hadn't given all of himself. He'd kept her at an emotional distance, running away from deep emotion, scared of being vulnerable and choosing numbness over the richness of loving and being loved.

What if he chose to be brave, what if they went all in and gave it another shot? Would he also end up sitting at this table with a sappy look on his face? God, he wanted that. He wanted the same happiness his siblings had.

Sure, it was a risk, his heart was on the line, as was Beah's. Finn acknowledged she needed someone who could communicate, someone who could open up. He could try to be that man. Oh, he doubted he'd be Mr. Outgoing, but he could talk more. And more importantly, he would listen to Beah. Really listen, even when the conversation turned tough. If he could fling himself off a mountain only wearing a wingsuit, he could take a chance on love...

Because, yeah, he loved Beah.

Had he ever stopped? She'd always been on the periphery of his mind. Was that why he felt guilty every time he slept with someone who wasn't her? Divorced or not, he still considered her his wife. *His.*

And if he didn't make a move, do something to convince her to stay, in a few weeks—three to be precise—she would be back in London.

Finn didn't know how he would function without having her in his life. And he wouldn't be satisfied with a weekend here and four days there. He wanted to see her most days, to hold her when she slept, to wake up to her on weekdays as well as weekends. He needed to be in Boston; his family and his work were here. Would Beah consider relocating to Boston?

Would that even be a possibility?

If he told her he loved her, if he offered her more than sex—marriage? babies?—would she consider giving him another chance?

"There's only one way to find out and that's to ask." Carrick's words jerked Finn back to the conversation and he sent his brother a hard look.

"What did you say?" Finn demanded, needing to make sure he'd heard what he heard.

Carrick frowned at him. "If she isn't asked, we won't know the answer."

Finn pushed his chair back so hard it slammed into the wall behind him. He slapped his hands on the desk and grinned at Carrick. "Exactly."

Finn left his laptop and notes on the table and walked past Ronan to slap his hand on Carrick's shoulder. "Thanks, brother."

"Uh…for what?"

Finn didn't bother answering him since Carrick

wasn't the person he needed to speak to. Talking to Beah was all-important.

Behind him, he heard Carrick's dry comment. "I was talking about the new web designer but it's pretty obvious our youngest brother wasn't on the same page."

"I agree," Ronan replied, amused. "His light is on but someone is playing with his dimmer switch. And that's not something I often get to say about our favorite genius."

Finn hurried down the hallway to the office Beah had claimed as her own two months ago. He looked through the glass walls to the immaculate space beyond and saw Beah sitting at the large desk, tendrils of hair falling out of her loose bun, black-rimmed glasses on her nose. She was reading a thick document and her concentration was intense.

Finn stopped, jammed his hands in the pockets of his jeans and rocked on his heels. She was beautiful in an Irish goddess type of way, clear skin, fine features, that deep red hair. And while she was heart-stoppingly beautiful, he was also proud of the woman she'd become. She'd made a name for herself as being one of the best art consultants in the business and she'd done it with hard work and without name-dropping. Few people knew they'd once been married. No, Beah's success had been all her own, and he was incredibly proud of her.

He also loved her, more than he ever did before.

Finn stepped up to her door, knocked and opened the glass door. Beah frowned at the interruption and then she smiled. It was a smile that didn't reach her eyes.

Beah wasn't as happy to see him as he was to see her—why not? His heart rate inched upward and his stomach pulled itself into a tight knot. Was he doing the right thing? Should he raise this love-and-staying-in-Boston question now or should he give her time to decompress, to relax? This was their workplace and maybe it wasn't the right time or place…

Finn bent down to brush his lips across hers and when he pulled back, he saw a strange emotion in her eyes, one he couldn't identify. Fear? Trepidation?

Or was he just seeing in her eyes what he thought might be in his?

"Hi, sweetheart."

"Hi back," Beah replied, her voice as subdued as her eyes. Okay, what was going on here? And why did he suspect it was something he really didn't want to hear?

Facing her, Finn rested his butt on her desk and stretched out his legs. "Everything okay?"

"Yes, no… We need to talk."

Words to freeze a man's blood. Finn forced a cocky smile onto his lips. "I'd far prefer to kiss the hell out of you."

And that wasn't a lie.

Beah didn't smile at his quip and desire didn't jump into her eyes. Crap, something really was wrong. Finn placed his hands on the desk and forced the words past his lips. "What's wrong, Beah? And don't tell me nothing because I can clearly see something is eating you up inside."

"I need to talk to you and it's not going to be an easy conversation." Beah placed her elbows on her desk, linked her hands and touched them to her lips, obviously looking for the right words. Finn frowned. Was she going to call it quits, end their relationship?

"I saw Paris Cummings when I went to London."

Her statement wasn't a surprise. He'd assumed a meeting with her newest client was in the cards.

"Okay. And how is the old curmudgeon?"

"He isn't old and he isn't very curmudgeonly." Beah wrinkled her nose. "Is that even a word?" She waved her question away. "Anyway…"

Beah stopped talking and Finn held his breath, knowing he wasn't going to like the next words out of her mouth. It was something to do with the guilt on her face, in the way she couldn't meet his eyes. Oh, yeah, he was about to hear whatever Beah had been hiding from him, and he wasn't going to like it.

And waiting wasn't something he did well. "Just tell me, Beah."

Beah rubbed her temples before sitting up straight and gripping the edge of the desk. "For the last couple of years, Michael Summers has been asking me to join him."

Everyone in the art world knew of Michael Summers. He was one of the world's most influential art consultants, someone who was respected, even revered. He was the go-to guy for high-net-worth individuals who wanted to start or expand their art collection.

Finn needed to make sure he understood her correctly. "Explain."

"He's wanting to semi-retire and he wants me to take over his business. He's offered me a partnership and I think I'm going to take it."

Beah wanted to leave Murphy's? What the hell? She was a Murphy. She couldn't leave! Finn stood up and slapped his hands onto the surface of her desk. "Not happening."

Beah's eyes cooled. "You do know you have no say about who I work for, right?"

"You're a Murphy. Your loyalty is to us," Finn ground out, feeling the world shifting beneath his feet.

While he'd been thinking of her moving in with him, of love, of their future, she'd been obsessed with going back to London, jumping ship.

It was amazing how someone with a decent IQ could be so intensely stupid.

Beah stood up, echoing his stance by placing her hands on the desk and leaning toward him. "I'm not a Murphy anymore, Finn. You gave me up when you asked for a divorce, remember?"

The stupidest thing he'd ever done, period. But he couldn't tell her that because while he was thinking about a future with her, she'd been making plans for a future that didn't include him. It really had been just about sex for her. Well, hell.

So this was what being run over by a train felt like.

Anger, hot and sour, bubbled. So this was all about her career? Okay, then. "We have employed you, paid you a massive salary, promoted you."

"That's crap! I took back my own name and worked my butt off for everything I got! You didn't give me anything I didn't deserve."

She was right, of course she was. But he couldn't tell her that, not while his heart was sliding through a mincing machine. He wanted to ask her not to take the offer, to stay with Murphy's, beg her to choose him.

What if she didn't share his feelings; what if this really was just a bed-based relationship? Had he read more into this than what there was?

Highly possible. This was, after all, Beah he was dealing with. She'd always managed to mess with his head. And maybe he was wanting more because he was jealous of his brothers' happiness and contentment. Maybe he didn't want to give up the great sex. Maybe it was because he was tired of being alone…

Maybe he didn't love her. Maybe he was just over-reacting, not thinking straight.

But whether he was or not didn't change anything. She was still walking away from him. And the thought scared the crap out of him. And Finn loathed feeling scared. Since he never felt fear hanging by his fingertips off a rock face or cliff diving, it annoyed him that a tiny redhead could make him feel this way.

"I wanted you to know before word spread."

"If the rumor hadn't gotten out, would've you told me?" Finn demanded, his voice as cold as those ice waterfalls he loved to scale.

"I was planning on talking to Ronan after the Mounton-Matthews sale," Beah replied, straightening.

"You were going to talk to Ronan and not me?"

"I'm talking to you now, Finn." Beah cursed when her desk phone rang. She ignored the incessant buzz and held his eyes, as if daring him to say something. Anything. Should he? Should he take a chance, persuade her to stay?

The phone stopped and Beah sighed. She opened her mouth to speak and the damn phone rang again. She snatched it up, barked a greeting and then handed the phone to him. "It's Eli. He says it's important."

Nothing was as important as this, as her. Screw Summers. Beah's place was at Murphy's, with him. She was his and as soon as he got rid of his caller, he'd set her straight.

"Eli, I'm not taking calls."

"Finn, it's me. Ben."

Finn frowned. He immediately looked at his watch and did a calculation, it was shortly after three in the morning in Hong Kong. Why was Ben calling so late? Oh, God, *no*.

"Ben, what's happened? Is it Piper?" Finn's eyes collided with Beah's and he watched the color drain from her already-pale face.

"She's not doing good, Finn." Ben's voice broke.

Finn released a long breath and leaned across the desk to hit the button to put the phone on speaker.

"Beah's with me, Ben. Talk to us, bud," Finn said, resting his right butt cheek on the desk. "What's going on?"

"She hasn't been feeling as well as she was a few months ago. She's really weak and in pain. I took her back to the oncologist today and she had another scan." Ben's voice broke. "It's spread, the cancer. It's now in her spine and in her organs. She has less time than we thought."

And they hadn't had much time to begin with.

Beah winced and abruptly sat down on the edge of her chair. Finn saw her tears and felt his eyes burning. He tried to speak but the words got stuck in his throat. Jesus, this was why love sucked so much, why it should be avoided. Why loving someone was so damn risky.

"How can we help you, Ben? Is there anything we can do?" Beah asked, her voice steady despite the tears rolling down her face.

Ben took a long time answering. "As you know, we were supposed to fly in soon, we wanted to spend the week before our wedding with you."

God, he'd forgotten all about their wedding.

"We still want to get married but Piper is too weak to fly. We are just going to have a quiet ceremony here, in our apartment. I'm terribly sorry but I need you to cancel all the arrangements you made."

Finn swallowed, trying to dispel the hard ball of emotion in his throat. "I can do that. Do you want me to fly out, be at the wedding?"

"Oh, God, yes, please. Piper's sister is flying in and we'll invite a couple of our close friends," Ben said, his voice a croak. "But can you come soon? I want to get my ring on her finger."

"You tell me when and I'll move heaven and earth to be there," Finn told him. No matter what was on his plate, he'd be there if Ben needed him.

"Day after next."

That soon? Okay, then. "I'll see you soon, bud."

Finn disconnected the call and ran his hands over his face. He'd heard the desolation in Ben's voice and couldn't believe Piper, young and vibrant, vivacious and bold, had less than a few months to live. How was Ben going to get through this? How was he going to cope?

This was why it was better to hold back from loving someone completely, why it was important to keep Beah at a distance. *Because when you lost love, no matter what form it took, it eviscerated you.* How stupid he'd been to even think about trying to solidify what he and Beah once had, because love always, always left.

Beah's hands gripped his biceps and he opened his eyes to look down into her sad, sympathetic eyes. "Oh, Finn. I'm desperately sorry. I'll make the arrangements for us to fly to Hong Kong, book the hotel, just leave it to me."

Finn squeezed his eyes shut, thinking he needed distance.

"I'm going alone," he told her, his voice harsh.

Beah's eyes widened with shock. "But, Finn...you can't."

Finn picked her fingers off his arms and stepped away. "Sure I can. You don't need Murphy's or me, and I sure as hell don't need you. If you can walk away from me and Murphy's, I don't need you to hold my hand at my friend's wedding."

"That's not fair," Beah whispered, looking like he'd punched her. "You didn't ask me not to join Michael, didn't give me a reason why I should stay at Murphy's. Why I should stay with you?"

Finn, fighting the wave of vulnerability crashing over his soul, hardened his heart and his tone. He shrugged. "You shouldn't. We're bed buddies, Beah. There's nothing more to us than sex."

"BS!" Beah shouted. "You know that's not true. If you gave me a good reason to stay, to move to Boston, I would."

Finn looked at the door and wished he was walking through it. He hated these emotion-laden, fraught conversations. They were messy and ugly and he remembered now why he avoided them. "I only want you to stay in Boston so you can keep sleeping with me. That's basically it."

Finn saw Beah's flushed face, saw her hand close into a fist. Then she dropped her head. Finn bent his knees and saw tears sliding down her cheeks.

He grimaced, fighting the urge to take her in his arms. He could handle yelling but her tears unmanned him.

He was halfway to the door when Beah's softly spoken words stopped him in his tracks. "All I ever wanted you to do was love me, Finn."

He turned and saw her looking at him, her heart in her eyes, and his heart crashed and exploded.

"Back then and now, all I wanted was for you to love me, to talk to me, to maybe lean on me. I told you about Michael hoping you'd persuade me to stay in Boston, to try to make us work. But there is no us because you won't let there be."

Beah wiped her tears away with the balls of her hands and stared down at the wet streaks. "I should never have slept with you, should never have let you back into my life. Because you haven't changed, Finn. Yeah, you're bigger and maybe even more good-looking but you haven't grown up at all, not where it counts. You're still emotionally stunted, still scared of me and the way I make you feel."

Every word was another slap, every tear another punch. Finn watched Beah as she straightened her spine, shook her head. She pointed to the door. "Go, Finn, walk away, because it's what you do best."

He couldn't help the question because he needed to know. "What are you going to do?" he demanded, his voice hoarse.

Beah managed a small smile, cold enough to freeze the balls off a steel statue. "Don't worry about it, Murphy. What I do, or don't do, has nothing to do with you. Your job is to protect yourself and to hell with anything else! Be like that, but I will see you in Hong Kong. I will be there for Piper. I *will* witness their vows."

"I don't want you there."

"*I. Don't. Care.* This isn't about us or our crumbling relationship. This is about Ben and Piper and not spoiling their wedding ceremony." Beah pointed to the door. "Go, Finn. You know you want to. And after Hong Kong, I'll leave your life, professionally and personally. And permanently."

Finn, knowing that he couldn't stop her from traveling east, threw up his hands in defeat. She was right. Piper and Ben's wedding wasn't about them. "I'm going to use the company jet to fly to Hong Kong. A driver will collect you. I'll text you with the time."

Beah's glare slashed through him. "I'd rather swim

to Hong Kong, thank you very much." Beah brushed past him and her elbow accidently-on-purpose jabbed his stomach. "See you in Hong Kong, Murphy. And when we meet again, do me one last favor?"

He raised his eyebrows and Beah nailed him again with her sharp words. "Don't bother talking to me. There's nothing left to say."

Nine

Finn stormed back down the hallway and when people quickly stepped out of his way, he knew his expression was thunderous. Blocking off the memory of Beah's tears, of the hurt he'd put on her face—again!—he slapped his hand onto the door of the conference room and pushed it open, glaring at the people sitting around the table.

Carrick was the first to react. "Finn? What's the matter?"

Ronan stood up, placed his hands on the table and sent him a hard stare. Finn dropped into a chair and placed his head in his hands before pushing the balls of his hands into his burning eye sockets.

"What's going on, Finn?" Carrick repeated his question.

God, he felt like a ten-day smoldering heap of trash.

From a place far away, he heard Carrick ordering the staff to leave and when Ronan shoved a cup of hot black coffee under his nose, he dropped his hands to push the cup away.

"What happened?" Carrick asked, worry in his eyes.

"We are calling off Ben and Piper's wedding. She's sicker than we thought and she's too weak to fly to Boston."

"I'm really sorry to hear that," Carrick said, placing his hand on Finn's shoulder. Finn shrugged it off and abruptly stood, needing to pace.

"How much time do they think she has?" Ronan asked.

"Not as much as we thought." Finn's heart broke for Ben. "I couldn't ask for specifics. But I need to go to Hong Kong. They are still getting married and I told Ben I'd be there."

"When do you want to leave?" Carrick asked. "I'll contact our pilot and get him to file a flight plan."

"Today, tonight, as soon as possible," Finn replied, trying to think. "I'm going to go home, pack and then I'll head to the airport."

Carrick nodded and picked up his phone to send a text. Finn linked his hands behind his neck and caught Ronan's eye. He bristled at the sympathy he saw in those eyes so like his own. "What?"

"Is Beah going with you?" Ronan asked.

Finn released a sound that was a cross beneath a laugh and a growl. "Why would you think that?" he demanded, surprised at his jumping heart. He'd thought that organ was dead and gone.

"Because you were organizing the wedding together. Because you are sleeping together. Because you love her. Because we don't want you to be alone," Ronan said, using his calm-down-client voice.

Finn glared at his brother. "We're bed buddies,

Ronan, nothing to get excited about. There's nothing between us but sex."

If he could start to believe what he was telling himself, really take it on board, maybe he could function without Beah.

Ronan let out a bark of laughter before rolling his eyes. "You are talking such crap, Finn, and you know it. Beah should be with you—you need her."

"I don't need anyone!" Finn pushed the words out. "I'm perfectly fine on my own."

Carrick and Ronan exchanged a long look and Finn debated which of them to hit first. Did it matter? Releasing some of his roiling anger—this sticky, sour hurt— via his fists connecting with his brother's faces would make him feel much better.

"You punch us and we'll punch you back," Carrick told him, in a super-reasonable, super-genial tone. It just made Finn want to smack him harder.

But he didn't have time to rumble with his brothers and he didn't want to rock up at the wedding, even if it was low-key, with a black eye or split cheek. He had to get his brothers off his case, move them onto another subject, and he knew exactly how to do that.

Yeah, it meant throwing Beah under the bus but what the hell.

"Beah is thinking about leaving Murphy's and joining Michael Summers."

Neither of his brothers looked surprised and Finn felt his temper, already bubbling, heat a few degrees. "You knew?"

Carrick shrugged. "We've been hearing rumors."

"And you didn't tell me?"

"You and Beah are divorced," Ronan pointed out.

He knew that, dumbass. "I'm still a partner in this firm."

"I heard about it the morning after we met Paris Cummings for dinner in London," Carrick explained, pulling out a chair and dropping into it. "I was going to tell you but any idiot could see you and Beah spent the night together. You actually looked happy for a change. I decided not to rock the boat."

"Carrick told me and we decided to bring Beah to Boston, thinking that if she worked out of Boston, she might change her mind about wanting to move on," Ronan added.

Finn couldn't understand their reasonable tone, their lack of anger. "Why aren't you more upset about this?"

Ronan lifted his bone china coffee mug to his lips. "Frankly, I'm surprised she lasted this long with us. She's well respected in the industry and has amazing connections. Her clients love her. And her moving doesn't mean we'll never deal with her, it just means we have to reorganize the way we pay her since she earns most of her income via her commission structure."

"She belongs here," Finn insisted, wondering why he was arguing. Wouldn't it be easier if Beah just moved on, if they made this split between them final and complete, if they severed the last cord binding them together?

"No, she belongs with *you*, not the company," Carrick replied. "The company has no hold on her. And even if you were together, I'd still have no problem with her joining Michael Summers. You're thinking with your heart, Finn, not your head."

Of course he was, and that never went well. When he allowed his stupid, emotional organ to rule, he only hurt himself. And Beah.

Would he ever learn? It was official—he was stupid when it came to dealing with people. He was far better off alone. He did alone quite well.

And he was tired of talking. He looked at Carrick. "Did the pilot respond?"

Carrick checked his phone and nodded. "Yep, you're all set."

Finn nodded his thanks and headed for the door. He placed his hand on the frame and turned. "I'll be in Hong Kong for a few days—two, three? When I come back, I might head to Aspen or the Arapahoe Basin in Colorado. I need..."

Finn saw the disappointment in Ronan's eyes. "You need Beah, but because you are too stubborn to go there, you're going to throw yourself down a slope to prove to yourself you are alive, that you are free. True freedom comes with courage, Finn, with deciding what you want and working to get it. And maybe you and Beah won't make it work a second time but it would be the adventure of your life if you did."

Finn didn't need an emotional adventure; he needed a physical one. He'd far prefer to end up with a broken body than a broken heart.

The dented and dinged organ barely beating in his chest was hard enough to handle.

Beah dropped into her office chair, turned her back to the glass wall and hoped her waterproof mascara was up to the job. Waving her hands in front of her face, she tried to think of work, tried to concentrate on making a mental to-do list to get her mind off the fact that Finn had, once again, walked out of her life.

The tears rolled again.

Beah wrapped her hands around her waist and leaned

forward, accepting that she couldn't brush off this pain. She was such a fool, thinking Finn had changed, that he was wiser, older and, maybe, finally, able to love her the way she needed to be loved.

His scars were too deep, his fear too great. Ironic that he was fine with risking his body but not his heart.

You've been here before, Beah; you will survive this. You survived your mom's death and your dad skipping out; you survived loving and losing Finn before.

You can do this. And even if you think you can't, you have to.

Because it wasn't going away and it wasn't something she could change.

You have to work with things the way things are, not how you want them to be.

Beah lifted a hand to her throat, feeling like a razor blade was slicing the cords in her neck. She hauled in a breath, feeling like there wasn't enough air, and tried to fill her lungs again. All she wanted to do was lie down on the carpet, pull her knees up to her chest and weep hot, hard tears. But she still needed to leave this office with a modicum of dignity, without anyone suspecting Finn had ripped out her heart and tossed it out the window to be squished by the wheels and heels using the road below.

The razor blade moved down her throat and into her chest, coming to rest in her stomach, where it widened the hole she'd been living with for the past ten years.

It was now bigger and deeper and wider than ever before.

She hadn't needed work or a busy life to fill the void; she'd needed Finn. In the past few weeks, being with Finn—loving and laughing and working with him—

she'd felt happy and fulfilled and, yeah, complete. The hole had almost closed…

Only to be ripped open, bigger and bolder than before.

I only want you to stay in Boston so you can keep sleeping with me.

Bastard! And such BS!

But Finn needed a reason to walk—run!—away and her telling him about Michael's offer, and then Ben's phone call, had spooked him. Instead of planting his feet and taking a chance, he'd grabbed on to the two excuses he'd been offered and bailed.

She was incredibly mad at him, furious at herself for handing her heart over to him again. When would she ever bloody learn?

She was smart and savvy, she knew this, so why was she intensely stupid when it came to Finn?

Maybe she could figure it out on the sixteen-hour flight to Hong Kong.

Keely looked at her red-eyed, red-nosed friend and wished she could just hug Beah until she felt better. But as she knew, Beah needed to cry, to weep for what she couldn't have. When she was done, she could start picking herself up and moving forward.

Because that's what strong women did. Life could break their wings but they always, always found another way to fly.

Keely dumped some wine into her glass and sat down next to Beah on the couch in the least formal of Isabel's sitting rooms. She wrapped her arm around Beah's shaking shoulders and congratulated herself on managing to avoid feeling like this. Because this was exactly the way Dare would've made her feel, in ten months or ten years.

She missed him, Keely admitted, sipping her wine. But this sort of pain, this gasping, soul-shattering feeling, wasn't worth a few months of bliss. Because as experience had taught her, Dare would tire of her in a few months…they might make six months; eight would be a record.

By then the wonderfulness of sex would wear off and he'd find himself annoyed by her strong personality and her bossy ways, her definite opinions. He would be sick of arguing with her, tired of feeling emasculated.

She was not the type of woman men stuck to or with. Men needed someone softer, calmer, easier to deal with.

She would never be what Dare needed.

Yep, they'd been smart to call it quits before anyone got too hurt, before they felt like their souls were being shredded.

Keely watched as Beah reached for her wine, took a healthy sip and wiped her tears away with the tips of her fingers. "I've cried more in days than I have in… well, since Finn told me wanted a divorce."

Keely sent her a sympathetic smile, thinking it wouldn't help to tell her the best predictor of what would happen in the future was what happened in the past.

Men dumped her; Dare would, too. She knew this as well as she knew her signature.

But this wasn't about her. "It'll get better, Bee."

Beah's eyes were flatter than she'd ever seen them. "So they say."

"Give it time." Keely pulled her arm away and put her feet onto the edge of the coffee table. "Have you been in to work since you came back from Hong Kong?"

Beah shook her head. "Before I could ask for some

time off, Ronan emailed me and told me he wanted me to take a vacation." Beah's lips almost lifted into a smile. "It was a two-sentence message, something along the lines of his brother being as ass and he didn't want to see or speak to me for at least a week."

"Nice of him," Keely said.

"It was, especially the part about his brother being an ass."

"How was the wedding?" Keely asked, ignoring Beah's sharp intake of breath and the tears rolling down her cheeks.

"Sweet, tender, wonderful. Piper and Ben are so in love, utterly besotted with each other. She looked… wonderful." Beah choked out the words, her hand on her heart. "Ben is taking some time off to be with her and I think that's a good thing. They seemed to appreciate us, me, being there."

"And how was Finn?"

Beah shrugged and pushed back into the chair, as if trying to get away from the question. "We greeted each other and then went back to doing what we do best— ignoring each other." Beah pulled her feet up onto the sofa and wrapped her legs around her shins. She sniffed, wiped her eyes on her knees and rested her cheek on the wet patch of her sweatpants. "I haven't seen you for ages. When did you get back from Florida?"

"Day before yesterday," Keely replied. "And I'm pissed you didn't call me straightaway. You know I would've come if you needed me, Bee."

Beah nodded. "I know. I just really, really needed to be alone."

Keely tipped her head to the side. "Have either of you canceled Ben and Piper's wedding with the suppliers?"

Beah shrugged. "That's Finn's problem. I'm not getting involved."

"I was just wondering because the caterer came around yesterday to look at the ballroom, to measure up for tables and a stage."

Beah's eyes widened. "Oh crap. He obviously hasn't done anything about it." Beah pulled a face. "And if I know him at all, he's somewhere isolated, hanging off a rock face by his fingertips. God, I suppose I have to do it."

Keely looked at her watch and shook her head. "It's after six. Nothing you can do about it now."

"I'll get on it in the morning. Bloody Finn." Beah drained her glass of wine and pulled Keely's glass from her hand, taking a healthy sip. Okay, she wasn't going to fight her; Beah needed it more than she did.

"I'm such a bad friend, I have no idea what's happening in your life. How's Dare?"

On hearing his name, Keely's stomach lurched. Damn, it had to stop doing that. "I don't know, we called it quits."

Beah's eyebrows arched. "Why?"

She didn't want to go into this, not when Beah wanted exactly what she didn't.

"Well?" Beah demanded, the word tart.

"He wanted more than I could give him," Keely finally admitted. Damn, she really didn't want to discuss this, not now.

"I'm sorry?" Beah asked, irritation lighting her eyes. Beah dropped her knees and her hot look suggested Keely start explaining. And quickly.

"He told me he couldn't be the only one fighting for us, that he was tired of being the only one believing in the potential of what we had. Oh, and because I wasn't willing to go there with him, he is going to find someone else. Dare is probably out there auditioning women to be the love of his life," Keely said, her tone bitter.

"And that pisses you off." Beah shook her head and abruptly stood up. "For God's sake, Keels. What gives?"

Keely took the glass of wine from Beah's hand before it could spill over the ancient, valuable Persian carpet. "I think I made the right decision for both of us because he will eventually walk away from me."

Beah stared at her and Keely started to feel uncomfortable. She wiggled in her seat and resisted the urge to drop her eyes. "It's for the best, Beah," she eventually stated.

"If Dare is anything like me, I bet he's damn sick of people thinking they are so smart and deciding the way we get to love. I love Finn and I know we could be damn good together. Dare, a smart, mature guy, seems to want the same with you but you and Finn have both decided we don't get a say? Well, on behalf of Dare, screw you. And screw Finn."

Keely's mouth dropped open. She wanted to be angry, but she couldn't. Because Beah was right, dammit.

"Arrogant, smart and scared is a freakin' deadly combination," Beah added, anger sparking in her eyes. Keely started to speak, but Beah held up her hand.

"I can't talk to you right now, Keels. I love you, but I'm mad at you. And I know at least three-quarters of that mad is directed at Finn but you're also in my firing line. Before I say something that will damage our friendship, I'm going to leave."

Beah spun on her heel and Keely stared at her back, wondering how the hell the spotlight had ended up on her and why it felt so damn uncomfortable.

* * *

Keely stood in the lobby of Dare's swanky apartment complex and waited for the doorman to contact Dare, to get permission for her to ride the elevator to his penthouse.

He might not want to see her...

Keely shook her head and looked at her screen, reminding herself why she was here. They hadn't stopped communicating, but their messages were short, to the point and always about Mounton House or Isabel's estate or the upcoming sale. He was still her and Joa's lawyer and she'd told him about Ben and Piper's wedding and that Mounton House was hosting the reception.

He needed to know that the wedding was off, so Keely sent him a quick message to tell him not to expect a check from Finn for the hiring of the ballroom.

Pity, he replied. So much work went into arranging that wedding. Is there anyone else who'd like to get married on that date instead of them?

Before Keely could decipher his message—why would he care about the cancellation?—her phone beeped again.

I was thinking you and I could. Get married, that is.

He'd been mocking her and it made her furious. Keely stepped into the elevator, still angry at Dare's comment. How could he be so incredibly flippant? It simply wasn't funny.

Nothing about this situation—or her bruised heart—was amusing.

The doors opened and Keely stormed into his hallway, dropping her tote bag to the floor. Dare stood by

the windows, looking at the amazing view of down-
town Boston.

"That was such a stupid comment to make!" Keely
shouted at him, dismayed to feel the burn of tears in
her eyes. She would not let him know marriage was her
greatest wish, her longest-held desire. A man, a wedding ring, a promise to love her forever—how dare he
make light of something so profound, so important?

"The one about us getting married?" Dare asked,
turning to face her. She hadn't seen him for weeks, but
dressed in a navy Henley and faded jeans, he looked
big and tough and scrumptious. Man, she'd missed him.

"Why is it a stupid idea?" Dare asked, sounding far
too calm.

"Because you don't love me. You don't really want
to spend the rest of your life with me!"

Dare didn't move but a small smile touched his lips.
"How do you know that, Keely? Or is that just another
of your stupid assumptions, along with the idea I'll walk
when you become too much?"

"I am too much, Dare!" Keely sat down abruptly on
the edge of his sleek, boxy settee, annoyed and frustrated by the tears sliding down her face. "I'm bossy
and demanding and opinionated and willful and—"

Keely felt his big hands on her knees, inhaled his
cologne, his Dare-ness. He didn't say anything so she
lifted her face to look at him. Love, and a touch of
amusement, blazed from his eyes.

"Why do you think I can't stop thinking about you,
Keels? I love your strong personality, I love your feisti-
ness, I love that you will jump into the ring to do what's
right. I've seen you at your best, and at your worst, and
I love everything about you."

Keely bit her bottom lip, terrified. "Dare, I'm—"

"No, enough." Dare shook his head. "I'm not a push-over, Keels, and I know exactly what I'm getting with you. I want you, *all* of you. I'm strong enough to tell you when to slow down and more than capable of stepping into the ring with you. I'm not scared of you, Keely. When are you going to accept that?"

"If you leave, as they all did, I don't know if I could go on, Dare. You mean much more than all of them put together." Keely forced out the words over the sound of her thundering heart.

"I'm more the type who digs his heels in when times get tough. Walking away is not my style. And dammit, I'm done with you pushing us apart." Dare cupped her face in his hands. "Love me, darling, let me love you and let's be happy. Because living without you sucks."

Keely briefly thought about standing up and walking away but it was more of a fleeting impression than a decision. What if she sat where she was, what if she stayed? What if she took one more chance?

Dare smiled at her, obviously sensing how close she was to capitulation. "Okay, let's do this…repeat after me. I love you, Dare."

Keely's lips twitched. "I love you, Dare."

"Thank God. Okay, now this…marry me in the ball-room at Mounton House next Saturday, Dare."

"Marry me… What?" Keely's mouth dropped open. "What? We can't—"

"Why not? Everything is arranged. I love you, you love me, we both know we are delaying the inevitable. And this way, you might finally believe I'm in it for the long haul."

Keely couldn't believe what she was hearing. "I… Jeez… Dare?"

"We'll postpone the wedding talk because I can see

your head is about to explode. But what we aren't delaying is you in my bed, naked." Dare stood up, slid his hand under her butt and thighs and scooped her against his chest.

Keely, feeling safe and secure and protected, linked her arms around his neck and kissed his shoulder through the material of his shirt. As he carried her toward his bedroom, she spoke again. "Dare?"

"Mmm?"

"I love you." There was such peace in those three words. And she intended to overuse them for the next sixty years. At least.

Dare placed a tender kiss into her hair. "I love you, too, sweetheart. So damn much."

He did, he really did. What was she waiting for?

"Dare, will you marry me next Saturday? For better or for worse? Stay with me through fights and fumbles and sickness and health and all that stuff?"

Dare's grip on her tightened and Keely felt the tension leave his body and pure happiness invade hers. "I thought you'd never ask, my darling. And hell yes."

Keely grinned and tasted his love for her on his lips.

Two days ago, he'd been in Hong Kong, watching as Ben made Piper his wife. It had been a poignant ceremony, happy and sad, and Finn, along with everyone else, had a tear in his eye as Ben held his wife in his arms to dance her around the room. They'd cut the cake, made speeches, Finn had even managed to make a toast to the happy couple without his voice breaking.

It was a happy day but underneath it all, he was conscious of Beah standing as far away as she could from him, looking remote and so beautiful it made his heart ache.

In Hong Kong, and every minute since he'd landed back in the States, he'd fought the urge to go to her, to haul her into his arms, to beg her to give him another chance. But they were impossible. They didn't fit, wouldn't work.

It was over.

Finn shook off his despondency, the heavy despair. He wasn't going to think about Beah, not today when the sun was shining, the sky clear and the powder fresh. He was going to take a couple of days here in Colorado, enjoy the snow and the solitude, push the pause button on his life and his emotions.

When he felt more settled, when his heart was a little stronger, he'd return to Boston and try to create a life without Beah in it. It was going to take some doing but he was a determined guy.

He'd succeed.

Eventually.

As a regular of the resort, he'd been told a group of expert skiers was heading out this morning, along with a couple of snowboarders to an area good for going off-piste. It was the last chance he'd have to ski for a while and Finn knew the area, called Hell's Run, remembering it was prone to avalanches. But there were no avalanche warnings and the call of fresh powder was too great to ignore. The run required total focus and concentration, exactly what he needed to dispel a certain redhead from his thoughts.

Finn placed his goggles over his eyes and pushed off, wanting to be the first to make tracks on the virgin snow. He watched as a snowboarder overtook him and his competitive spirit sprang to life. He was not going to let a teenager beat him down the run. Enjoying the silence and the fresh snow, the freedom of flying, he sped up, veering right to overtake the younger man. The color of the guy's ski jacket was exactly the same as Beah's eyes...

Finn felt the smack of one of his skis slapping the snowboard and he released a curse when he tumbled, spitting out a mouthful of snow. Finn felt his skis fly off and released a string of F-bombs, trying to think back to when last he'd taken a fall.

Ten years ago? Fifteen? God, this was embarrassing. The last way he wanted to travel down the mountain was on his butt.

Finn felt a wave of snow smack him in the face and thought one of the skiers had passed him, spraying snow into his face. But instead of slowing down, he just sped up and then the thought occurred to him that something was wrong, very damn wrong.

He was battling to breathe...

Years, months, centuries later he came to a stop, facedown in the snow. Every inch of his body felt bruised and battered and he pushed down on his hands to lift himself up but he moved maybe a half inch before hitting a solid wall. What the hell? Finn hauled in a deep breath and realized there wasn't much air. He felt like he was breathing through a heavy blanket.

A blanket made of snow, constructed by an avalanche. Yep, this wasn't good. This wasn't good in an "I think I might die here" kind of way.

Finn thought about screaming but decided it was more important to conserve air. He had a transponder on his jacket; hopefully his group would know he was missing and not think that he'd skied on ahead of them. His fault for trying to be a hotshot. The best thing he could do now was try to relax, try not to think...

But think he did.

Beah's face, pale and lovely, those red curls tumbling to her shoulders, appeared on the big screen behind his eyes and he wished…

Wished he had another chance. Wished he'd loved her like she deserved to be loved, wished he hadn't wasted the past decade trying to protect himself. He should've been braver, smarter, dammit, and accepted the love she'd offered him.

A bit late now, jackass.

Finn felt the blackness approaching, could see it at the corners of his eyes. How long had he been trapped? He didn't know but he was pretty sure he was slowly suffocating and running out of time. Eleven minutes and he'd be a corpse, how much longer did he have?

Finn moved his hand and drew a heart in the snow, managed to scrape his and Beah's initials with his finger, knowing she wouldn't see it but needing to leave something tangible on the earth he was about to leave.

Then the world turned dark…

In the hired car on the way to the hospital, Beah turned in her seat and looked at Carrick, whose hand had yet to leave her back. "Tell me again," she demanded, her voice raspy with fear.

"He was caught in an avalanche," Carrick patiently replied, giving no hint he'd told her the same story at least twenty times between picking her up to take her to his private jet and pushing her into this hired car five hours later.

"When they found him fifteen minutes later, he didn't have a pulse. They resuscitated him with CPR. He has severe hypothermia but he'll be fine."

"No brain damage from the lack of oxygen?" Beah asked, again. She'd heard this before, she knew the answer, but Carrick's and Ronan's calm voices and steady eyes reassured her.

"Today was a warm day and he wasn't wearing much gear and the hypothermia slowed his metabolism and reduced his brain's need for oxygen. It helped that Finn is super fit."

Beah looked down at her trembling hand and at her bouncing knee. "I'm going to bloody kill him!"

"You and me both, Bee." Ronan sent her a sympathetic smile. He was driving, Joa sitting in the passenger seat next to him. Sadie sat on the other side of Beah, her hand on Beah's knee.

"There won't be any recriminations, any yelling or shouting or accusations, until Finn is back to full strength," Carrick told them.

Ronan looked in the rearview mirror and caught Beah's eyes. The rolling of his eyes almost, but not quite, made her smile. Man, she'd never been so terrified, was still scared and knew she wouldn't be able to function properly until she saw Finn's face, heard him breathing, felt the thump of his heart under her hand. A part of her still thought he was dead, that she'd lost him, and a shudder racked her body.

She didn't want to live in a world without Finn.

Beah buried her face in her hands, feeling another batch of tears wetting her fingers. Then she felt the car slowing and she jerked her head upward, seeing they'd arrived at the hospital. Ronan braked, and as soon as the big SUV came to a stop, she crawled across Sadie, almost tumbling out the door.

She heard her friends yelling for her to wait but Beah started to sprint across the road, heading for the entrance. She couldn't wait anymore, not one second longer. She flew through the automatic doors and spun around in circles, looking for signs. She'd heard Carrick say he was in room 201.

Beah saw a sign and, not bothering to wait for the elevator, found the doors leading to the stairs and sprinted up one flight, then two. Bursting into the hallway, she dodged around a cleaner's cart, skidded past the nurses' station and looked around, wild with worry.

The two and one shimmered on the door and the looked through the window to Finn's room and sobbed at the sight of his closed eyes, his oh-so-pale face and his still slightly blue lips.

Beah felt hands lifting her up, felt Ronan's arms around her. "Sssh, Bee, stop crying, sweetheart."

Beah gulped, held on to his shirt with tight fists and made herself look up into those eyes so like his younger brother's. "Don't tell me he's dead, Ro. Please."

Carrick gently separated her from Ronan. Linking an arm around her waist, he pushed the door open. He pulled her over to Finn's bedside and placed her hand on his chest.

"Feel his heart, Beah. Look at this machine, it's showing his heart rate. He's fine, Beah, he's just sleeping."

Beah put her head on Finn's chest and wept.

Ten

A full week later, Finn, knowing Beah had arrived at Logan International earlier in the day, arrived at Mounton House an hour before Keely and Dare's wedding, It wasn't, he knew, the best time or place but he was done waiting…

When he'd come around in the hospital, his brothers and their partners were around his bed but he didn't see the one face he most wanted to see. His welcome-back-from-the-dead party hadn't included a curly-haired redhead.

Oh, he now knew she'd come to the hospital, heard she'd been an absolute basket case. His brothers told him that while he was asleep, Beah wept over his cold body and then grilled his doctors about his injuries, possible brain damage and his expected recovery time.

When she was satisfied he'd make a full recovery, she'd left the facility without seeing him again, without giving him a chance to speak to her.

Finn ran his hand over his beard, wishing Beah had stuck around instead of flying straight back to London. He'd spent the past week leaving voice mail messages, and not receiving any responses to his call-me-dammits, he'd sent her a barrage of text messages asking her to get in touch.

Her only reply was a brief two sentences...

Glad you're okay. Then again, God does protect the stupid.

Beah was pissed and he couldn't blame her. He *had* been stupid, but not in the way she thought. His accident had been a fluke and he planned to be back on skis as soon as he could. He wasn't going to let being caught in an avalanche kill his love for his favorite sport.

But when he went back, he wanted to go with his brothers, with his lover, hopefully with his wife.

Because in his heart, she was still his wife, still the beat of his heart.

No, he'd been stupid to let her go, then and now. That he'd admit to, on any day of the week and twice on Sundays.

Finn ran up the stone steps to the front door of Mounton House and hit the doorbell. After a minute, Dare Seymour opened the door, his untied black bow tie hanging down the front of his snow-white shirt.

"Good to see you, Finn. Glad that avalanche didn't kill you."

Yeah, so was he.

"Are you supposed to be here?" Finn asked him, shaking his hand. "You know, seeing the bride before the wedding and all that crap."

Dare grinned. "I've been told I can hang out down

here but Keely will kill me if I go up to the first floor," Dare told him. He nodded to the wide, imposing stairs. "I presume you are looking for Beah?"

Finn nodded.

"She's with Keely, up the stairs and second door on the right."

Finn nodded his thanks and ran up the steps, for once not seeing the art or the massive portrait of Isabel Mounton at the top of the landing. There was only one face he wanted to look into.

He hurried down the hallway and stood in front of the door, smoothing down the lapels to his tuxedo. This was do-or-die time, the rest of his life. He had to get the words right, tell her what she needed to hear...

Do not mess it up, Murphy.

Finn knocked on the door and without bothering to wait to be told to enter, walked inside. Four sets of eyes—makeup artist, Keely, hairdresser, her sister Joa—turned to look at him but none of them were whom he most wanted to see.

Keely jerked her head and he spun around to see Beah standing beside the wall, next to what looked to be a complicated and expensive wedding gown. She wore a soft silver-gray wraparound dress with a long skirt and a plunging neckline. Her hair was piled in a messy, natural bun and her makeup didn't, for once, cover her freckles.

She looked wonderful, gorgeous enough to take his breath away, but her eyes reflected her sadness. That had to change...immediately.

Beah looked away from Finn to Keely and back before biting down on her bottom lip. "Finn? Why are you here?"

"I've been trying to talk to you for days but you're

not taking my calls," Finn said, his eyes not leaving her face.

"If you wanted to talk to me, you could've jumped on a plane, or used the Murphy jet. I hear those planes can fly both ways."

Ouch. "My doctors, and my brothers, wouldn't release me from the hospital or I would've done exactly that."

Beah narrowed her eyes at him, as if trying to decide whether he was telling the truth or not. He was. He'd only been released from hospital the previous night, after telling the doctors he had a wedding he needed to attend, and he still felt bruised and battered and a bit wiped.

But he could see Beah was pissed. He didn't blame her. If she'd nearly died, he would be reacting the same way. "Let's talk, Bee," he said, trying to be as gentle as he knew how.

Beah sent Keely a look and Keely grinned. "Go, Bee. Just keep an eye on the time. Dare has promised to drag me downstairs if I'm even a minute late."

Finn grinned at his old friend, her blond hair in curlers and her makeup half done. "He's in the hallway, pacing. He can't wait to marry you. And you look fabulous, Keels."

"Liar." Keely's smile was bright enough to blind the sun. "But I will. Take your wife out of here, Finn."

"I'm not his wife," Beah said, throwing up her hands.

Not wanting to get into an argument in front of strangers, Finn just opened the door and waited for Beah to walk into the hallway. When she finally did, he closed the door behind him and looked at the belligerent love of his life.

She slapped her hands against his chest. "I am. Not. Your. Wife."

The urge to kiss her was nearly overwhelming, so

Finn jammed his hands into the pockets of his suit pants to keep from reaching for her. "Maybe not, according to the legal system. But in my head and in my heart, you are."

Knowing how easily he could mess up—talking wasn't what he did well—Finn kept it simple. "I love you, Beah, and I'd love to marry you again. Anywhere, anyhow."

Beah's pretty pink lips dropped open in complete shock.

"But if you don't want to get married, or even live with me, if you want to stay in London and see each other when we can, that's okay, too. I'm not proud. I'll take you any way I can get you."

It wasn't ideal, but what was his other choice? Not seeing her at all? Unacceptable.

Beah held up her hand as if trying to fend off his words. "You walked away from me, Finn. For the second time."

"And if I could kick my own ass, I would," Finn admitted. "I got scared, Beah. You scare me."

She stared down at her silver shoes, at her pretty painted toes.

"But you know what scares me more?" Finn waited for her to look at him and when she did, he took the chance to slide his thumb across her bottom lip. "Never kissing these lips again terrifies me. Not hearing your laugh, sleeping in an empty bed, not having you in my life, scares the crap out of me, sweetheart."

Beah looked like she was about to speak and Finn shook his head, needing to get it all out. "When I was trapped under the snow, not able to move, just before I blacked out, your face was all I could see. I felt such profound regret for all the time we've wasted, for the love and life we never shared, for the babies we never made. There's nothing like nearly dying to know what you most want from life."

Beah's eyes were bright with emotion. "And that is…?"

"You. It's all you. You are what the rest of my life looks like," Finn said, his voice low and cracking. He was ten seconds away from begging and he didn't care. Beah was his world…

"Let's find a way forward, Bee. I wasn't joking when I said I would take anything I could get from you."

Beah put her hands together as if in prayer and rested her linked fingers over her mouth. She stepped away from him and Finn felt his hope slipping. She was moving away; she was thinking too much, allowing her brain to rule her heart. He was about to get drop-kicked, forty-five minutes before Keely's wedding.

Crap. Dammit. Hell.

"I still want to leave Murphy's to take the partnership Michael is offering," Beah said, lifting her gorgeous but stubborn chin.

He didn't care if she chose to run for president or whether she sat at home for the rest of her life. She could do anything she damn well wanted.

"And I'd like to keep my flat in London since I'll be doing business there," Beah said, her tone thoughtful.

If she had a point, she was taking far too long to reach it. His patience was wearing thin. "Do you love me or not?" Finn demanded, his loud words bouncing off the old walls.

Beah smiled at him. "Maybe. Maybe my love for you was the reason I absolutely lost it in the hospital in Colorado, why I've cried myself stupid, why I thought my world had ended when you walked out of it."

Finn felt a wave of shame. "I'm so sorry. If you let me, I'll spend the rest of my life making it up to you."

Beah finally, finally reached out to touch him, placing her hand on his tuxedo jacket, just above his heart. "I don't need you to do that, I just want this."

"My heart?"

Beah nodded and Finn covered her hand with his. "You always had it, darling. I was just too stupid to realize it."

Beah blinked away tears. "I have a couple of stipulations, Murphy, some ironclad rules."

Here it came, Finn thought, the demand for him to stop indulging in dangerous sports. And of course, he'd agree to stop. Anything Beah wanted he'd give. She was his biggest priority. And always would be.

"I want to get married again, in a church this time, with bridesmaids and a priest, flowers and a kick-ass dress."

Easy enough to agree to since he wanted that, too. He nodded, holding her beautiful face between his hands. "What else?"

"We need to talk more, Finn. We need to connect, every day and in every way."

"I can work on that. I *will* work on that. I promise to do better, Beah. What else?"

Instead of making more demands, she smiled at him, a sweet, tender smile full of love and happiness. "I love you, Finn. I hope you know how much."

Finn brushed his lips across hers before resting his forehead against hers. "And I love you, Beah. Sorry I was an idiot."

Beah's chuckle was as sexy as hell. "You're forgiven, but if you nearly die again, I will kill you myself."

Finn pulled back, a small frown between his eyebrows. If she wasn't going to ask, he'd offer. "I'll stop the adventure sports if you want me to, Bee. If it gives you peace of mind, I won't chase those thrills anymore. You are my biggest thrill, anyway."

Beah shook her head, her eyes tender and the color of warm honey. "I'm not going to ask you to stop, Finn. I don't want to take away something you love. I can handle your passion for danger. I'm just asking you to take extra care because my heart nearly stopped when yours did. Love what you do, Finn, but love me enough to always come back."

Finn, feeling like he'd won every jackpot in the world, folded her into his arms and rested his lips in her hair, tears burning his eyes. Loving her was going to be the biggest joy and the biggest privilege of his life.

"Will you marry me again, Beah Jenkinson-Murphy?" he softly asked, his voice rough with emotion.

"Absolutely," Beah said, her eyes radiating the happiness he felt. She grinned. "But not today. Today we need to marry off our favorite bossy blonde so she can drive Dare mad for the next fifty years."

Finn kissed her again before pulling back, knowing if he started, he wouldn't be able to let her go. "Dare is looking forward to the challenge."

Beah stood on her tiptoes, kissed him and then wiped her lipstick off his bottom lip with her thumb. "As much as I want to stay with you, Keely needs me."

"I know she does, and it's fine. See you downstairs?"

Beah nodded, squeezed the hand she was holding and reluctantly stepped back. Finn watched her walk away, his heart full to overflowing. His wife was his again, and his heart was full.

In her, he had everything he'd ever need.

Epilogue

It was close to midnight on the night of the iconic Mounton-Matthews sale and Beah was exhausted. After a six-month campaign, an online sale and two days of live auctions, the disposal of Isabel's collection was complete, culminating in the sale of the lost Winslow Homer for—Beah looked at the screen above Ronan's head—was that two point five million or twenty-five million?

Beah squinted at the board: twenty-five million… taking the sale's total to more than half a billion dollars. Holy crap, that was a lot of money.

Beah ignored the giddy atmosphere in the room, the loud laughter, the buzz a result of adrenaline and relief.

They'd pulled it off.

Beah stood behind the counter with the other Murphy staff who were working the phones for telephone bids—she'd agreed to be the intermediary for Paris Cummings, who was the new owner of both Homer's painting and the Vermeer, as he'd wanted his anonymity preserved—and glanced around the room. Joa stood with Carrick and Sadie, Keely and Dare, her eyes on Ronan's face as tears slid down her face. Beah couldn't see Keely's face since Dare held her head to his chest, patting his wife's back.

Joa and Keely would make the decisions on where to spend the money they'd raised, what charities would be the ultimate recipients. Beah was pleased and thankful for their offer to make a large donation to cancer research.

Through her burning eyes, Beah noticed Carrick's pleased smile as he stood with both arms around Sadie, one hand on her rounded stomach. She'd refused to stay at home, telling Carrick she was pregnant, not an invalid, and could handle the excitement of the sale.

Beah smiled as Joa broke free from the group to run up the stairs to the lectern and fly into Ronan's arms. She swallowed down the lump in her throat as Ronan held her close, his lips in her hair.

It was a happy night, a wonderful night…

Beah watched as Carrick and Sadie joined Ronan and Joa behind the lectern, jerking his head for Keely and Dare to join them. Ronan looked around for Finn, and Beah smiled as he ran up the stairs, exchanging hugs and kisses and backslaps. He looked very happy, Beah thought. Content. At peace.

She was, as she knew, a big part of that.

Then Finn, because he didn't like to stand in the limelight, stepped off the stage and walked into the crowd. Beah watched his blond head until it disappeared and hoped he was coming to find her; she wanted to share this incredible moment with him. Her last as a Murphy employee.

She was both sad and excited. But no matter where her career took her, she'd always return to Finn. He was where she needed to be...

Carrick tapped the microphone, the room settled down, and then the noise level dropped to something close to silence.

"On behalf of my brothers, I would like to thank Joa Jones and Keely Matthew-Seymour for affording Murphy's the honor of representing Isabel Mounton-Matthews's collection. We are proud to have made many record-breaking sales tonight, but more importantly, we are thrilled to have raised an outstanding amount for charity."

Beah felt Finn's strong hands on her hips, sliding around her stomach as he pulled her back into his chest. She tipped her head back and met his green, gold, beautiful eyes. Finn kissed her nose, then dropped a quick kiss on her lips. "Hello, beautiful."

"Hi, back," Beah said, allowing him to take her weight. She was very tired and he was always happy to let her lean.

Carrick cleared his throat and Beah returned her attention to the stage. Carrick reached out his hand to pull Sadie to his side. "These past months have been hectic for the Murphy staff and I'd like to thank every one of them for their hard work."

Applause broke out and Carrick held up his hand, looking serious. "This auction will always be one of Murphy's greatest, but not only because of the range and depth of Isabel's collection and the money we raised. Isabel and her treasures brought something bigger, and more important, into many of our lives. Keely, surprising us all, married Isabel's lawyer recently. Ronan and Joa found each other, and his sons found a rock-steady and delightful second mother. I employed Sadie to authenticate the Winslow and she's not only agreed to be my wife but as you can see, we're adding to the Murphy clan. And Beah was a Murphy years ago and I know Finn is impatient to remarry her."

"Damn straight I am," Finn murmured in her ear.

"Here's to Isabel and her incredible collection," Carrick said, raising a glass of champagne a waitress brought to them on a silver tray.

Finn dropped a kiss on her hair. "Cheers, darling. Love you."

Beah turned in his arms to hold him tight. "Love you more, Finn. Shall we join the family?"

Finn nodded and smiled. "How very lucky are we, Bee?"

Finn handed her a tender smile, one so full of love and desire it heated her heart—and her body.

She was living her dream and, yes, they were damn lucky.

They'd waited a long time to find each other again and neither she, nor Finn, was going to waste a single minute of their second chance at happily-ever-after.

* * * * *

COMING SOON!

We really hope you enjoyed reading this book. If you're looking for more romance, be sure to head to the shops when new books are available on

Thursday 11th June

To see which titles are coming soon, please visit

millsandboon.co.uk/nextmonth

LET'S TALK
Romance

For exclusive extracts, competitions
and special offers, find us online:

 facebook.com/millsandboon

@MillsandBoon

@MillsandBoonUK

Get in touch on 01413 063232

For all the latest titles coming soon, visit
millsandboon.co.uk/nextmonth

MILLS & BOON

MODERN

Power and Passion

Prepare to be swept off your feet by sophisticated, sexy and seductive heroes, in some of the world's most glamourous and romantic locations, where power and passion collide.

MILLS & BOON

THE HEART OF ROMANCE

A ROMANCE FOR EVERY KIND OF READER

MODERN

Prepare to be swept off your feet by sophisticated, sexy and seductive heroes, in some of the world's most glamourous and romantic locations, where power and passion collide.
8 stories per month.

HISTORICAL

Escape with historical heroes from time gone by. Whether you passion is for wicked Regency Rakes, muscled Vikings or rugg Highlanders, awaken the romance of the past.
6 stories per month.

MEDICAL

Set your pulse racing with dedicated, delectable doctors in the high-pressure world of medicine, where emotions run high an passion, comfort and love are the best medicine.
6 stories per month.

True Love

Celebrate true love with tender stories of heartfelt romance, f the rush of falling in love to the joy a new baby can bring, and focus on the emotional heart of a relationship.
8 stories per month.

Desire

Indulge in secrets and scandal, intense drama and plenty of si hot action with powerful and passionate heroes who have it al wealth, status, good looks…everything but the right woman.
6 stories per month.

HEROES

Experience all the excitement of a gripping thriller, with an ir romance at its heart. Resourceful, true-to-life women and stro fearless men face danger and desire - a killer combination!
8 stories per month.

DARE

Sensual love stories featuring smart, sassy heroines you'd want best friend, and compelling intense heroes who are worthy of
4 stories per month.

To see which titles are coming soon, please visit

millsandboon.co.uk/nextmonth

JOIN US ON SOCIAL MEDIA!

Stay up to date with our latest releases, author
news and gossip, special offers and discounts, and
all the behind-the-scenes action
from Mills & Boon...

millsandboon

millsandboonuk

millsandboon

might just be true love...